Max Booth III

This special signed edition of

TOUCH THE NIGHT

is limited to 750 numbered copies.

This is number 261.

TOUCH THE
NIGHT

TOUCH THE NIGHT

MAX BOOTH III

CEMETERY DANCE PUBLICATIONS

Baltimore

❖ 2020 ❖

Cemetery Dance Publications
132B Industry Lane, Unit #7
Forest Hill, MD 21050
www.cemeterydance.com

First Cemetery Dance Printing

ISBN: 978-1-58767-758-8

Cover Artwork and Design © 2020 by Dyer Wilk
Interior Design © 2020 by Desert Isle Design, LLC

ALSO BY MAX BOOTH III

Toxicity
The Mind is a Razorblade
How to Successfully Kidnap Strangers
The Nightly Disease
Carnivorous Lunar Activities

THIS BOOK IS DEDICATED TO YOUR MOM.

"It doesn't matter what you think. You're not 10 feet tall and bulletproof. I used to think that…But look what happened to me. Because there's always somebody who can take you down if you don't stay aware."

—MARY VINCENT
L.A. TIMES INTERVIEW, 1997

Tell your family you ain't coming back.
Look at your home for the last time.
Tell your brother that you're gonna die,
but don't let anybody tell you that you're safe.

—ZEAL & ARDOR
"YOU AIN'T COMING BACK"

THE EMPTY
TOWN

ONE

"*L*et's get the fuck out of here."

Josh hears his friend but he doesn't respond. He can't. Alonzo's mom moaning in the next room has him fully mesmerized. He's helpless to the sound and he wouldn't want it any other way, except maybe to be the one in the room with her. To be the required sacrifice for her forbidden ritual.

It doesn't matter that it's past midnight, that Josh's parents would kill him if they found out he snuck outside, that they'd never let him stay at Alonzo's again. His dad would beat his ass and ask him if he was stupid, ask if he'd paid attention *at all* to the stories they read about other black kids his age wandering the night, minding their own business. It doesn't matter if you aren't doing nothing bad.

"Josh?" Alonzo says, raising his voice. "I know you're awake, man."

Elsewhere in the house, Alonzo's mom continues to moan. Bedsprings rattle in perpetual motion. It's the loudest noise in the world, and Josh is in love. He wants to fall asleep to the sound of Alonzo's mom like it's his own lullaby. He wants to live in this sound for the rest of his life.

So he remains corpse-still, silently begging Alonzo to give up the idea and go to sleep. If Josh doesn't say anything, then that means he didn't hear the question, and if he didn't hear the question then he isn't chicken, he's just tired.

They lie in Alonzo's room—Josh on the floor, Alonzo on his own bed—listening to the strange, wonderful, scary sounds from the other room. The blue screen on the television set atop the corner dresser showers them in its radiance. The credits of the last movie they watched stopped rolling at least ten minutes ago. Josh had read every name involved, every role required to give a movie its magic, memorizing every character, but he's already forgotten the majority of them save for the main stars. He looks at other, different stars now—pentagrams sloppily Sharpied across Alonzo's ceiling. "Isn't your mom gonna get pissed?" he'd asked a few months back, balancing the swivel desk chair with both hands as Alonzo stood on the cushion, gnawing on his tongue and drawing like the possessed. Alonzo had laughed then, didn't answer, just continued worshipping devils with his marker. Studying the pentagrams now, they don't come across scary or threatening like Alonzo intended. If anything, they're relaxing. Like those airplane mobiles parents hang over cribs. A little too easy to get lost in their hypnotism and collapse into slumber.

Movement behind him. The sound of a body fidgeting under the covers. The sound of Alonzo crawling to the end of his bed and peeking his head over the edge. He stares down at Josh and it's too late to feign sleep, he's been caught with his eyes open, his head in the pentagrams. Alonzo's puppy-dog stare is so on-point it's ridiculous. The sound of his mom in the other room only adds to the pitifulness.

"Did you hear me?"

"I was asleep."

"No you weren't. You were trying to remember the names of who played all of those goddamn cenobites."

"Well." Josh swallows, paranoid the look on his face will reveal how much he's enjoying the sound of Alonzo's mom having a good time, doing all the things him and Alonzo talk about doing with girls from school. "I was *almost* asleep."

"Let's get out of here." Alonzo jerks his head to the window. "Let's go have some fun."

Josh's instinctual response is to ask, "Isn't it kind of late?" but he can already hear Alonzo's reply: "What are you—eight?" And he can't suggest just going back to sleep, not now, not with Alonzo's mom and the man she brought home from the bar only getting louder as the night progresses. There is no falling asleep to this sound. It will only bring years of therapy for Alonzo, and years of confusing and exciting fantasies for Josh. But still. Josh tries to imagine how he'd react if they were at his house. Would it be different because Josh's parents are still married—still in love?

But are they really? When Josh is home, lying in bed, what sound does he hear more often from his parents' bedroom—the sound of sex and fun that he hears now in his friend's house, or the sound of two people who hate each other to the very core? How often has Josh woken up to his dad throwing something against a wall, or to his mom screaming loud enough to make her voice raw and worn out the following day?

Maybe there are worse noises in the world than your mom having sex.

But he doesn't tell any of this to Alonzo. It's not the kind of shit he needs to hear right now. What he needs is a distraction. What he needs are big fucking headphones.

Josh sits up, sliding the sleeping bag down. "Why don't we play a video game or listen to some music?"

Alonzo sighs and collapses the rest of his weight into the mattress. "That fucking bitch is driving me crazy."

Josh tries to imagine calling his own mom a bitch. The thought makes his stomach hurt. "Where…where do you want to go?"

"What does it matter? Why can't we just enjoy the night, breathe in that delicious moon air? Come on, bring your camera. Never know what's waiting out there for us."

Josh pauses, licks his dry lips and tries to conjure an explanation that won't reveal his cowardice. He can't say he's afraid. This isn't the first time they've snuck outside while the rest of the world is supposed to be asleep, and he still hasn't learned to not be afraid, but he *has* learned not to fight it. He's seen enough horror movies to know life is about being unsettled.

So he says, "Okay, let's go."

X

THEY SLIP OUT OF THE window and flee the back yard like seasoned convicts. Their feet slide in gravel as they run through the back alley. Josh's initial fear of abandoning the house momentarily numbs as the thrill of sudden freedom washes over him. Then, every dog in the neighborhood loses its shit at the boys' presence, and the reality of what they're doing sinks back in.

Over and over he asks himself what's the worst that can really happen, and the possibilities stretch endlessly. Most seem unlikely, and some impossible outside the realm of movie magic, but that doesn't make them any less inevitable. It's only a matter of time before every bad thing that can happen happens.

Fiction is only fiction until it isn't.

Josh warns someone's gonna hear them if they're not careful and Alonzo laughs and cups his hands around his mouth. *"Everybody wake the fuck up! It's time to have some motherfucking fun!"*

Josh's heart races faster than his feet as he shoves his friend. Alonzo stumbles and grabs a neighbor's fence post just before falling on his face. He climbs back up and glares at Josh. "What's your problem?"

"Nothing. Let's just go before one of these rednecks thinks we're trespassing and shoots us."

Alonzo smirks. "Let 'em try. I fuckin' dare 'em."

Josh considers reminding him they aren't in a Cronenberg movie, that bullets aren't gonna melt into his flesh like butter, painless and smooth. Instead Josh continues forward, pretending like he couldn't give less of a shit if Alonzo follows. When they reach the end of the alley, they pause, crouched like the petty thugs their middle school principal so often accuses them of being. Alonzo peeks over the corner of a fence and scans the suburban street in both directions, left to right, then down and up in case there's any helicopters surveilling their activities.

"Where are we going?" Josh asks, and Alonzo shrugs.

"Nowhere. Everywhere. Who cares?"

"I was just wondering."

"You scared we gonna get in trouble?"

He shakes his head, a little too desperate. "No."

The night isn't dark, not dark like Josh had imagined it being back in Alonzo's bedroom. The moon hangs over the center of town, as round and bright as an eyeball devoid of its pupil. He debates pulling out his little camcorder but doubts it'll pick up anything besides shadows. They avoid the glow of streetlights and instead sneak through front yards hidden in darkness and boobytrapped with sprinkler systems. He tries pressing one hand against his hoodie pocket holding the camcorder, adding a second layer of defense against the water.

"I didn't bring a second set of clothes." Josh grimaces at the way his feet squish in his shoes.

"Who says we're ever going back home?" Alonzo laughs, no attempt to conceal his voice. "Shit, who says we even *need* clothes?"

"I don't know about you, but I don't like walking around naked."

"What, you worried somebody might make fun of that tiny little pecker of yours?"

Josh tries to laugh, but it comes out as a weak little hiccup. He spits on the street and hopes it looks cool. "What do you want to do on Halloween?"

"I don't know. Same shit we did last year, I guess. Blow some shit up. Get candy. Steal my mom's vodka."

"This is probably our last year, huh?"

"What do you mean?"

"We're getting too old. We won't be able to get candy next year."

"Says who?"

"I don't know." He licks his lips, grimacing at the taste of dry skin. The night has a bad feel to it. The air's heavy, suffocating. He opens his mouth wide and gulps oxygen like a fish abandoned on dry land. "That's just how it works, I guess."

"Well fuck how it works," Alonzo says, voice rising in anger. "I'm gonna keep getting candy until the day I die. Even if I'm some cranky-ass old man. I'll get my little walker and wobble all up and down the neighborhood ringing doorbells." He hunches over and mimics an elderly gentleman. "*Uh, hello, yes, sonny-boy, triiiick…or…tre—oh gosh, my back! My back! Someone call an am-bu-laaaance!*"

They both bust up laughing and crash into each other. Josh trips into someone's yard and slides on wet grass, but it's no big deal, could have been worse if he landed on his frontside and crushed his camcorder. His clothes are already wet at this point so what does it matter. They're having fun. Alonzo is Josh's friend and Josh is Alonzo's friend and together they are having a good time. What time it is doesn't matter. Not really. If anything, the danger adds to the excitement, as much as he hates to admit it.

Alonzo helps him up and they keep walking.

"You gonna watch the game tomorrow?" Josh asks.

"What game?"

"C'mon, like you don't know."

Alonzo shrugs, sincere. "Baseball?"

"It's the World Series, bro."

He laughs. "You know I don't give a shit about that. And you know I know *you* don't give a shit about that, either."

"It's all my dad's been talking about."

"Man, fuck your dad."

"Hey."

He claps Josh on the back. "I'm sorry, but that guy's an asshole."

"Yeah." He sighs. "Maybe."

Josh spots a realtor sign in a lawn ahead and kicks it. It shoots up from the earth like a rocket and lands in the driveway, creating a loud *twang* aluminum echo.

Alonzo claps and tells him, "Now that's the shit, baby," and picks up the sign and Frisbees it toward the house. It bounces off the exterior and the darkness swallows it.

Josh retrieves a rock and throws it blindly. For a moment, it's as if a tear in the sky opens up and gulps the little rock down into the surreal dimensions of its stomach. But then somewhere one street over glass explodes and they both shout, "Oh shit!" as they forget about sticking to front yards and book it down the middle of the road. They don't dare look over their shoulders, knowing that not only is the Percy P.D. hot on their trail, but so is the military and national guard.

They cross Main Street without checking for passing traffic. A honk blasts to their right and tires skid on pavement. Alonzo flips them the bird and shouts, "Fuck you, car!" Josh considers joining in, but decides both of his arms are required to maintain Alonzo's pace. He is not the fastest kid in town—hell, minus Wheelchair Kid in his Social Studies class, he's probably the slowest—but he tries his best not to make it obvious. Nobody wants to wait for the fat kid.

Wheezing, Josh follows Alonzo through a deserted strip mall. All the shops are closed, the structure a series of black mirrors. Josh can't take his eyes off of them, convinced there's something standing on the opposite sides of the windows, watching them as they flee from government henchmen. Maybe they're licking their lips, the sight of two boys making their stomachs growl. If this were a horror movie, Alonzo and Josh would escape the police by breaking into one of these. They'd lay low behind a mannequin display and explore their new playground, stealing whatever fit in their pockets. But the longer they lingered, the stranger the noises they'd hear, until eventually the mannequins opened their mouths and sank their teeth into the boys' throats.

But this isn't a horror movie, and they don't know fuck-all about breaking and entering, so instead they pass the strip mall and head toward the gas station, the one they always steal chips and pops from after school.

Josh taps Alonzo on the shoulder. "Do you really think it's okay that we go in here?"

Alonzo shrugs. "I don't see why not."

"Yeah you do."

Alonzo isn't an idiot. Twelve-year-old boys can't just walk around past curfew. Not in a suburban town like this when nobody is awake. And you especially can't walk around at night when you're a black kid. You're automatically a suspect. Anything goes wrong, there's no such thing as an investigation. Your ass is getting thrown in the back of a cop car. Hell, nothing even needs to go wrong. The fact that you exist and choose to flaunt it is enough of a crime. Sure, Josh is only twelve, but that doesn't make him ignorant of reality. Maybe the white kids in town can go on with their lives surrounded by cotton candy and bubble wrap.

But Alonzo just laughs and pulls open one of the doors. Alonzo understands all of this just as well, but the difference with Alonzo is, instead of being filled with fear, he's instead consumed by rage.

Last month, the cops killed two people on a bridge in New Orleans, and it's all Josh and Alonzo have been able to talk about. *Obsessed* isn't the right word. *Terrified's* a little closer, but still not quite. Hurricane Katrina's destroyed the city and everybody is desperate to survive. Meanwhile, the cops there just seem eager to kill kill kill. This happened on the Danziger Bridge. Only a goddamn month ago. He's seen photos of the bridge. Videos. It's huge. On top of the two who were murdered, four others were shot and injured. All six black, all six unarmed. Of fucking course. As if that's a surprise. As if that's a *shock*. They'd watched the news story online at least a dozen times in Alonzo's basement, yet the repeated viewings did nothing to desensitize the acidic burn Josh feels in his stomach whenever he thinks about it. One of the deceased, a fortysomething-year-old man, was revealed to have possessed the brain of a toddler. And the other one who died? Shit, he'd only been seventeen. Probably still in high school. Older than Josh and Alonzo, but not by much, not really, not when he thought about it. The other day, Mr. Grayson in his Social Studies class brought up the encounter, and had this to say about it: "If you're going to live like a thug, you need to accept the consequences." Josh is only twelve and even he knows this shit is fucked up. Ask any white kid in his class and they'll claim the police are their friends, that they're out to protect them. Ask Josh and he doesn't know how to respond. Maybe they do protect, but they sure as hell seem awfully choosey about it.

If you're going to live like a thug, you need to accept the consequences.

"Fuck that cracker cocksucker," Alonzo had said later that day, after class. "Bitch doesn't know shit about shit."

"Yeah," he'd agreed, but that hasn't stopped him from obsessing over his words.

Josh usually doesn't have a problem with shoplifting, but you have to be smart about it. Do it in the middle of the day, when the store's busy with customers. Not at 1:00 A.M. when any customer activity is immediately suspicious.

A bell chirps as the door opens. The gas station clerk, some twentysomething-year-old, glares at Josh as he nervously waves and whispers, "Hi."

The clerk doesn't respond. He's the same guy who's typically working the shift after school. When does he get to go home? Maybe he never leaves—maybe he's not even alive. If this were a horror movie, the gas station clerk would probably end up being a ghost. Maybe some desperate criminal held the place up and, not wanting to leave behind any witnesses, stole the security tape and inserted a bullet inside the clerk's skull. Or maybe he didn't give a good goddamn about witnesses, maybe he simply enjoyed the fame—the tabloid worshipping and Nancy-Grace hysteria, and he shot down the clerk for no other reason than it felt good, like cracking your knuckles or shaking your dick a few extra times after taking a leak. Now the clerk's trapped here in this gas station, his spirit destined to remain imprisoned until justice's served, until his murderer's brought down like a rabid dog. If this were a horror movie, the spirit of the clerk would haunt Josh's every waking moment, attach itself to his aura and negotiate Josh's sanity with his willingness to carry out sweet vengeance.

"Can I help you?" the clerk asks, not a ghost after all.

Josh gulps and hurries down the chip aisle. Alonzo stands at the end, inspecting the back of a Doritos bag.

"Are you counting the calories?" Josh asks, trying to make it sound like a joke but only succeeding in reminding himself of the night two years ago his father stumbled into his bedroom, drunk, and tossed a stack of calorie charts on his bed. "Read up," he'd said, "or you're never gonna meet a girl who wants to fuck you."

Josh nudges Alonzo. "He's looking at us."

Alonzo tilts his head, acknowledging the clerk with a forced smile.

"We can't do anything."

Alonzo laughs. "We can do anything we fuckin' want." He hands him the chips and continues past the junk food and into the drink aisle. Josh stands between Alonzo staring at the frosted glass doors and the clerk staring at the both of them, just waiting for one of them to slip.

Alonzo hums. "What do you want? I'm thinking about a cream soda."

"Okay."

Alonzo takes out two glass bottles of Jones Soda from the freezer and hands them both to Josh, who has to squeeze the bag of chips in his armpit to avoid dropping the pops.

Alonzo sidesteps three doors to the left, past the juices and beer, past the Hungry Mans and Lean Cuisines, and stops at the dairy section. The eggs.

"Boom."

Alonzo places the items on the counter, still wearing that same stupid-ass grin. The clerk scans the barcodes, not sharing the same enthusiasm.

"Is that it?"

Alonzo leans on the counter, inspecting the wall of cigarettes behind him. "You know what, I think we'll also take a pack of Kools." He straightens his stance and elbows Josh in the ribs. "Some Kool cigs for some cool cats—ain't that right, Joshy?"

The clerk doesn't seem as amused. "I don't suppose you little shits have any ID on you, huh?"

"Hell, mister, we ain't even got cash."

"Then what's the plan here? Rob me?" Now it's the clerk's turn to laugh. "Because that'd be great. Seriously. You don't know how long I've been waiting for a chance to test the shotgun we keep back here."

"Bullshit."

Josh slowly steps back, figuring nobody will notice him slip out the door if he moves only an inch at a time. Alonzo shoots his hand out without looking away from the clerk and grabs Josh's arm.

"Do you really want to test me?" the clerk says, arms crossed over his chest.

Alonzo nods. "Well, yeah, kinda. But no. We're here to propose a trade."

The clerk raises his brow. "Oh, and what is it you have to trade?"

Josh is wondering the same thing. This is all a surprise to him. Which means Alonzo kept it a secret for a reason. Which means, whatever it is, Josh ain't gonna like it.

Alonzo reaches into his back pocket and pulls out a folded photograph, then places it on the counter. The clerk unfolds it and examines its contents for a moment before looking back at Alonzo, disgusted. "What the hell is *this*?"

"You know what it is."

"Why...why would I want this?"

"What, you don't like girls?"

"Kid, you got no idea how much ass I get." The clerk moves to return the photograph, then stops, holds it closer, really looking at it now. "Hey, wait. I recognize this chick."

"She comes in here all the time."

"That's right. Holy shit, yeah. She buys condoms and beer like every Friday." He glares at Alonzo, curious. "What are *you* doing with this?"

Alonzo cracks his neck. "Maybe I fucked her the other day."

The clerk laughs. "Kid, I doubt you've even hit puberty yet. She's probably like your mom or some shit."

Alonzo lowers his head and doesn't respond.

"Jesus Christ. She is, isn't she?"

The clerk inspects the photograph one last time before snickering and tossing it across the counter. It slides off and lands on a patch of dirt-stained linoleum next to Josh's feet. He looks down at Alonzo's mom situated on her hands and knees at the edge of her bed, stripped to her dark, tattooed flesh as she peers over her shoulder, seductive eyes glued on whoever was holding the camera. One sagging breast peeks out from around her large bottom. At first glance, that's all you can look at, then slowly your vision starts to travel down her crack and you discover something new, something weird and alien, and eventually it dawns on you this is what everybody's always talking about. A pussy. And not just a girl's pussy but a *woman's* pussy and not just any woman's pussy but your best friend's mom's pussy. Josh doesn't need to look at the photo to know every single detail printed on it. He's gone over the image enough times in his head to no longer require visuals. He and Alonzo had discovered the image a couple months ago on his mom's computer while downloading stupid photoshopped .jpgs from eBaum's World. An image they were never meant to see, something that'd been saved in a hidden folder. For the longest time neither of them spoke—then Alonzo eventually pressed—*punched*—the power button and told Josh to go home, to get lost, that he didn't have time to sit around all goddamn day watching stupid-ass videos, he had a life to live, so maybe Josh better go find his own. The next day Alonzo decided to talk to him again, but for a brief spell Josh had feared the worst. Although they'd never discussed the incident again, it had never left Josh's mind.

Now here it is again.

A million questions plague his mind but they go unanswered as Alonzo knocks over a Zippo display. "What, my mom's not good enough for you?"

"All right, get the fuck out of here before you get hurt."

Alonzo turns around and Josh sighs, relieved, thinking this nightmare is over, then chokes up as Alonzo retrieves the photo and waves it back at the clerk. "I'm not going anywhere until you agree to the trade."

"What are you even talking about? I ain't looking at your ugly-ass gorilla of a mother. That's fucking gross. You shouldn't even have that, you goddamn pervert."

Alonzo drops his arm down to his waist, clutching the photograph tight enough to crinkle it. "What did you just say?"

The clerk exhales loudly as he brings out his cell phone. "Kid, I wouldn't stick my dick in that STD cesspool if she were the last nigger on the planet."

Alonzo scrambles over the counter, sending the drinks and eggs flying to the floor as he swats the phone from the clerk's hands.

"Are you fucking ser—"

Alonzo bashes an awkward fist into his nose and the clerk shoots both hands to his face, moaning, "Oh, you motherfucker," and backing up against the wall of cigarettes, "you goddamn nigger piece of—"

Alonzo tackles the clerk and cigarettes rain down upon them. Then they're both out of sight, their presence evidenced by the sound of grunting and fighting. Josh struggles to move, caught in a freeze-frame of indecision, like a scratched DVD. Alonzo won't be able to take the clerk alone for much longer. A sucker punch will not grant you the upper hand forever.

He hurries around the counter and finds Alonzo sitting on the clerk's chest, shoving the photograph of his mom into his mouth.

"Eat it! Fucking eat it! She ain't good enough for you? Fuck you, you ain't good enough for *her*."

The clerk gags as the balled-up photo proceeds past his resistant tongue and down his throat.

"Alonzo," Josh says, tapping his friend's shoulder. "Stop. Please."

And he stops.

Trembling and breathing hard, he takes his hands off the clerk's bloated face and the clerk spits out the soggy ball of paper. Alonzo looks up at Josh, eyes screaming, like he just awoke from a nightmare. "*What am I doing?*"

Josh holds out his palm. "Let's get out of here."

Alonzo stretches his arm out and just as their fingertips connect, the clerk moans and shoves Alonzo to the floor. Josh catches his friend and falls back on his ass. The clerk frantically climbs to his feet and if this were a horror movie, this would be the part where the clerk mutates into some supernatural carnivore, except this ain't a horror movie, it's real life, and the clerk just scrambles away from them in search of something underneath the counter.

The shotgun.

"Shit, he's gonna shoot us," Josh says, pointing and backing up against the wall. Cigarette cartons bounce off his head but it doesn't matter, nothing is going to matter once the clerk finds what he's after.

Josh pushes Alonzo and inertia pushes Alonzo into the clerk. He grunts and trips forward and bashes his head against the register. His body goes limp and collapses to the floor, leaving behind a sticky chunk of hair and gore on the edge of the cash drawer.

They stand over the motionless body, the sound of their own hearts beating loud enough to satisfy a rock concert.

"What have we done?" Josh whispers, thinking *please be okay* and knowing that he isn't, not now, not ever—not just the clerk but also Josh and Alonzo. Their lives are ruined, there's no walking away from something like this and living a full, healthy life, not after stealing someone else's, and that's exactly what they've done—stolen a life. They're thieves. Murderers. Monsters.

Alonzo steps over the clerk's body—planting one foot on his spine— and attempts to pull open the register, but it doesn't budge, might as well be glued shut, just another prop displayed on the set of this poorly budgeted horror movie.

"Try hitting one of the buttons." Josh hardly recognizes his own voice.

Alonzo gets it open and Josh collects a bag from the counter and holds it open while Alonzo empties the cash into it, moving on autopilot, minds frozen in carbonate and bodies operating under the guidance of malignant puppeteers.

"Some beer, too," Alonzo says and Josh nods because why not? Why not take the whole goddamn store? Alonzo steps off the dead clerk and the dead clerk groans and starts sitting up and maybe he's not dead after all, maybe Satan's giving him a second chance to seek vengeance against the two cold-hearted kids who murdered him for no reason, no fucking reason at all.

"What...what happened?" the clerk asks, a deep gash on the side of his head, thick chunks of blood and gore dripping from his confused face.

But Josh and Alonzo are already fleeing the gas station, running as fast as their legs will allow, running, running, running, but no matter how fast or how long they run, Josh knows it will never be enough.

TWO

etween long gulps of beer, Josh says, "Do you think he's going to die?"

In the past, he's never enjoyed drinking, would typically only entertain a few sips to avoid being called a pussy then dump the rest out when nobody was looking—but now, tonight, here in this little league dugout, he needs this beer, he needs it more than air.

Alonzo sets down his own can beside him on the bench. "No. He'll be all right."

"How do you know?"

"Because he has to be."

"What if he ain't, though?"

"He's gonna be fine. He just bumped his head. You saw him sit up. You heard him talk. Dead men don't talk."

Josh lets that thought settle, then swallows vomit. "Are we gonna go to prison?"

Alonzo shakes his head in the darkness. "They don't throw kids in prison. It wouldn't be safe, not with all those serial killing psycho pedophiles they got in there. Nah, if they caught us—which they ain't gonna do—but if, say, somehow they did, the worst that'd happen is they'd lock us up in J.C. for a couple of months. Big fuckin' whoop. I could use the vacation, anyway." Alonzo finishes off his beer and tosses the can against the dugout wall. Leftover drops from the bottom of the can spray out and hit Josh in the face.

"J.C.?"

"Juvie. You know. Kid jail."

27

"Oh." Josh slumps over, running his shoes through gravel, trying to imagine what happens in a kid jail.

"But, like I said." Alonzo pops open a new beer. "We ain't getting caught."

"But that guy, he sees us all the time going in there. He'll tell the police."

"It's not like he knows our names or where we live. There's a lot of kids in this town. He could be talking about anybody."

"I…" He almost says he's scared, but manages to bite his tongue, reconsider his wording. "I don't know what to do."

"We don't do *nothing*. We just play it cool, right? You know how you start acting guilty, suddenly everybody knows you've done something wrong, that you're hiding something?"

"I guess."

"Well, all we gotta do is act like nothing's wrong. If we believe it, then everybody else has to, too, right?"

Josh empties the rest of his beer down his throat and drops it at his feet. He doesn't have the energy to throw it against the wall, doesn't even have the energy to stand up. Drunk, exhausted, or both? Neither of them carry a watch, so who knows what time it is. Josh leans against the brick wall and yawns, then belches. The desire to return to Alonzo's house diminishes. All he wants is to sleep here in this dugout and wake up to discover everything had been some screwed-up dream, that everything is okay and nobody is hurt, nobody is dead.

"How much money do you think we scored?" Alonzo asks, and Josh nearly vomits.

"I don't know."

"It's too dark out here, can't see shit." He rests the bag of cash in his lap. "We can count it back at my house, split it fifty-fifty."

Josh wants to tell him to get lost, that he wants nothing to do with their murder money, that it's probably forever stained with the clerk's blood, anyway. But another part of him—a much stronger, more persuasive part—thinks about all the cool shit he could potentially buy. How much money could have possibly been inside that register? Enough to purchase that collector's edition of all eleven *Friday the 13th* films? It even included the one with Freddy Krueger and came with a real hockey mask, just like what Jason wears. He's had his eyes on this thing for the better part of a year now. The sudden excitement that swoops through him makes him feel sick, makes him want to run out of the dugout and vomit up the half-frozen pizza rolls they'd eaten for dinner many, many hours ago, back when his future had seemed somewhat optimistic. Just puke the whole mess up out on first base—or is that third? He doesn't know for sure and he doesn't really give a shit. Josh couldn't care less about sports, especially baseball, as much as this has disappointed his dad, an over-enthusiastic jock, the polar opposite of his son. He'd been a pitcher back in high school, threw more than one shut-out in his time, not to mention all the ass that attracted like a magnet to athletic stardom. He liked to remind Josh of all this any time he caught him lounging around in front of the TV with a snack in his lap. Sometimes Josh purposely ate junk food out of spite. Each spoonful of Jerry Garcia was another fuck-you.

"It's probably best if we lay low in here for a while, though," Alonzo says. "If that asshole did end up surviving, I'm sure he's called the cops by now. They're probably out there this very second, with their big fuckin' flashlights."

"You think they'll search down here?" Josh stretches out on the bench, too tired to care.

"They might. You ready to fight if they do?"

"You think they got those drug-smelling dogs?"

"Shit, probably."

Josh wonders if he'd be able to outrun one of those dogs. The idea is laughable. He's seen enough episodes of *COPS* to know nobody can out-run a police dog. Once they get their scent on something, there ain't no stopping them.

He falls asleep thinking about dogs. When he wakes up, his neck is sore and his clothes are soaked in tipped-over beer.

Alonzo's out of the dugout, lightly jogging around the infield, leaping triumphantly on each base as he approaches, arms raised over his head and mimicking the roar and applause of an invisible crowd, an audience of ghosts.

Yawning, Josh climbs up the dugout steps, holding on to the arm rail just in case he loses his balance in his tired, confused state and goes tumbling back down. He digs out his camcorder and powers it on, then aims the lens at Alonzo as he sprints toward home—that much about baseball Josh at least knows—and slides through the gravel, onto the plate where he'd laid the gas station bag of stolen money. He grabs the bag and shoots to his feet, raising his arms in a V and shouting at the dark sky. "And the crowd goes wild as Jones wins the scoring run! They can't believe it! He actually fucking did it! Everybody is losing their shit down here! You should see the tits on some of these chicks taking off their shirts to congratulate the great baseball god, Alonzo Jones, number six-six-six! Not just the number of the beast but also the number of the greatest goddamn baseball player to have ever lived!"

He stops in front of Josh and hunches over, out of breath. "What do you think, coach? I got what it takes?"

Josh desperately wishes to play along, to have some fun. He doesn't understand how it comes so easily for Alonzo. How can he possibly be joking around and acting like everything is fine? How can he be so *cool* about it all?

Josh returns the camera to his pocket and nods to the street outside the little league park. "We should get going."

Alonzo slumps his shoulders and pouts. "You mean you don't even want to try striking me out?"

"I'm tired."

"We could go pick up a couple of Monsters or Redbulls from the gas station, if you want." He grins, but Josh doesn't. "All right, fine, let's go then, shit."

As they pass various houses in the neighborhood, the desire to inflict random property damage feels numb and distant. Just a few hours ago, they'd gained an immense joy in the art of vandalism. Now, after everything that's happened, Josh is convinced he'll never feel joy or excitement again.

The *Friday the 13th* boxset flashes through his mind again and he throws up a little in his mouth.

Alonzo spits in someone's front yard. "I'll tell you what I'm gonna do with my share of the money. Me, I'm getting the hell out of this shit-show of a town. Maybe get myself a train ticket heading downtown, be a Chicago street-kid. Eat dumpster food and knock off all the gas stations that cross my path. Live in alleys under forts made out of newspapers and banana peels."

Josh considers the lifestyle and grimaces. "That sounds…gross."

Alonzo nods, proud of his friend's reaction. "Gross is the best way to live."

"Girls don't like gross."

"Who gives a fuck what girls think?"

Josh shrugs, suddenly embarrassed. "Lots of people."

"Well, fuck all those people. They're stupid. Anybody who cares what anyone else thinks of them might as well go kill themselves."

"Yeah," Josh says, although he doesn't quite understand Alonzo's reasoning. They're seldom on the same page, but that has yet to stop him from following along and agreeing with whatever he says.

"So, are you gonna come with me?"

"What?"

"To Chicago. You comin' with me or what? Live together on the streets. Easier to steal when you have a partner. One person causes the distraction while the other stuffs his pockets. Just like our Dollar General heist. Right?"

"Oh. I don't know. Maybe."

Alonzo raises his brow at Josh as they walk, then snickers. "Yeah, right. That'd be the day."

"What are you talking about?"

"Like you would ever leave your precious mommy and daddy."

"I might." Of course he wouldn't, but the idea excites him all the same.

"You wouldn't last a single night alone."

"I've lasted this long, haven't I?"

"Percy is a whole lot different than Chicago, dude."

"Oh, and suddenly you know so much about Chicago. You're the Chicago expert."

"I know how to get around. When my dad was still around, he used to take me into the city, feed the ducks at the park and stuff. That's more than you can say. Have you ever even *been* to Chicago?"

Josh has never stepped foot outside Indiana—the farthest he's ever been is Hammond—but he isn't about to admit that now. Instead he spits on the sidewalk and nods at their approaching destination. "So, are we sneaking in through the window again or just walking—"

"Shut up," Alonzo whispers.

"What?"

"Do you hear that?"

Josh starts to tell him no, that he doesn't hear anything, then stops and inhales his words back into his lungs as the sound of something moving behind them suddenly makes itself present. Something loud trying to be quiet, like someone eating a bag of chips in the middle of the night, taking slow bites, praying they don't wake up sleeping fathers with quick-trigger tempers.

Josh tries to convince himself to turn around and face whatever's following them, but instead only quickens his pace toward the house.

"Oh shit," Alonzo whispers from behind him, and before Josh can say anything, red and blue lights begin flashing and illuminating the small narrow street. Josh halts and clenches his fists, squeezes his eyes shut, anticipating the loud roar of sirens, but nothing comes.

Alonzo collides into his back and tries to push him forward. "Dude, fucking run."

"Run where? This is where you live."

"Shut the fuck up. Don't you dare tell them that." He jabs his elbow into Josh's spine and Josh's camcorder falls out of his hoodie pocket. A small light illuminates next to the curb where it landed. Has it been on this whole time?

"What, that this is your—"

"I'm your brother."

"What—?"

"Just shut the fuck up and don't tell them shit."

Slowly, they cock their heads to the side, staring wide-eyed at Alonzo's lightless, silent house. A finish line within sight but impossible to reach. A safety net stripped of its safety, naked and useless. Josh wonders if Alonzo's mom is still awake.

The cop car remains parked behind them in the middle of the otherwise empty street. The lights flash strong and vibrant, nearly blinding Josh when he looks over his shoulder. Darkness fills the car's interior.

"Why is he just sitting there?"

Alonzo spits toward the car and stares it down with a well-rehearsed hardness. "Probably just trying to scare us."

"Well, he's doing a good job then."

"Don't let this asshole get to you. He ain't gonna do shit."

"In case you've forgotten, cops kind of love shooting black kids up to no good."

"Fuck them."

"You think they know about the gas station?"

"They don't know shit. There ain't shit to know."

Then a new realization hits him, and the cop car becomes ten times more frightening. "What if the gas station had cameras?"

"Shut up." Alonzo elbows him again as both the driver and passenger-side doors of the cop car open simultaneously. The doors creak loud and impossibly long, like nobody's opened them in years. Every internal warning Josh's system possesses is screaming for him to turn around and run. It doesn't matter if he's slow, he can't give up, he still has to *try*. But despite all these pleas of fright, his legs ignore all requests and remain planted in place. He is frozen. He is trapped.

The sound of heavy boots kissing concrete. Heavy sighs as two large men struggle to climb out of the car. Josh holds his breath, but he doesn't know why.

The cops take slow, deliberate steps toward them. Dark, shadowy figures in the night. Josh tries to make out their faces, but he's too blinded by the intensity of the lights.

Just run, he silently screams. *Run you fat piece of shit.*

But it's too late.

"Do not even fucking think about it," the cop on the left says, pointing at Josh. "You make one wrong move and I will not hesitate to put you down."

Josh tries to tell him he isn't doing anything, but words escape him. He remains planted next to Alonzo, who unfortunately doesn't seem to share Josh's inability to speak.

"What's the matter, guys? The doughnut shop closed early tonight?"

The two cops stop and look at each other, like they're deciding how to proceed. Then they turn back to Josh and Alonzo, heads twisting in unison, and move closer. The cop on the right laughs, but there's no humor found in the guttural rasp that emits from his raw throat.

In the darkness, Josh can't make out much. They're dressed in standard long-sleeved blue police uniforms too small for their bodies. Both are tall, tall even for adults. Taller than Josh's dad by at least a good foot. Each cop's stomach protrudes well past their belt buckles. Swollen and round like pregnant women. Their arms and legs are thick and appear on the verge of bursting through their uniforms, but less muscular and more bloated.

The one on the left says, "Say, what could two little cocksuckers like yourselves be doing out here all alone at this time of night?"

Josh digs his nails into his palms until the pain distracts him from the anger. Alonzo grinds his teeth together but it doesn't do any good. "Can we fuckin' *help* you?"

"As a matter of fact," says the cop on the left, and the other finishes the sentence, "...you can."

Alonzo starts to laugh but he's cut off as the cops move with lightning speed and each grabs a boy by the back of his neck and drags him toward the car. Despite the force, Josh still doesn't expect them to actually slam his face against the hood until a bolt of pain flashes like white light through his skull. If it made a sound, he didn't hear it. A sharp ringing that he knows only he can observe blasts through both ears. The kind of sound people in war movies hear after a grenade detonates. He wrinkles his nose, convinced blood's preparing a getaway through one or more orifices, but nothing comes. He isn't sure if he's disappointed or relieved.

He remains planted, hunched over with his cheek pressed firmly against the hood of the cop car, eyes wide open but vision blurry. All it'll take is one wrong move and he'll be on the ground, bullet holes up and down his body. Will they shoot his arm off like one of the women shot on the Danziger Bridge in New Orleans? Will he have to pick it up with his other arm and flee for his life?

"Don't fucking touch me," Alonzo says somewhere behind him, followed by the sound of something banging against the hood. The car shakes and Alonzo grunts, elbowing Josh in the ribs as he fights the cop holding him down. Josh tries to tell him to calm down, to just shut up and do whatever they're told to do, but words escape him as his face rubs against the car and he struggles to catch his breath. The engine cooks into his exposed skin. The stench of gasoline spills into his mouth with each gasp and cough.

"You think they are afraid?" asks the cop holding Josh down.

"Oh, yeah," says the cop handling Alonzo, "they are very afraid."

The cop's thick, dry fingers tighten around Josh's neck, then he leans over him close enough to whisper into his ear. "Innocent folks, they do not need to be afraid, now do they?"

"That is exactly right, brother. Only the guilty—those with something to hide—have any cause to fear authority."

Then, as abrupt as a rollercoaster turn—whiplash and all—the cop spins Josh around so they're one-on-one, and now that the cop's against the car lights, Josh finally steals a snapshot of his face. Josh immediately feels sick, an acidic ball of phlegm trickling up his throat.

This face—this yellow, bloated face—stares at Josh with sick, bloodshot eyes, and asks, "So what indecencies are you hiding tonight, boy?"

He doesn't know how to respond, knows one wrong reply or move and he could easily end up like the folks on the Danziger Bridge, knows that all he has to do is blink funny and it'll be the last thing he ever does. And he also knows that if this were a horror movie, nothing would be different, because this cop's face—this pulsating, *Hills-Have-Eyes* motherfucker of a face—it's the scariest goddamn thing he's ever seen in his life.

Instead of answering, Josh slowly redirects his vision to Alonzo squirming under the other cop. The cop holds him down like he weighs nothing, like Alonzo's constructed of straw and newspaper. This other cop looks similar to the one handling Josh—only this one's somehow more repulsive. An alien ooze drips down his chin like drool, yellow like pimple pus. An unexplainable compulsion to reach out and touch the substance overwhelms him, and he has to bite his tongue to resist the temptation.

Josh's cop snaps his fingers, recapturing his full attention. "Where do you boys live? What are you doing out here this time of night?"

"None of your fuckin'—" Alonzo begins, then yelps and coughs as the other cop punches him in the stomach.

Josh exhales. This is only going to keep escalating the longer he lets Alonzo do the talking. He tells the police his address.

"And I'm his brother," Alonzo adds. "We both live there."

The cop grins at Josh like he knows they're bullshitting him but he's going to go along with it, anyway. "That true, boy? You two kin?"

And despite knowing full-well that they're going to find out the truth here soon enough, Josh nods, goes along with the whole damn thing.

"You deaf?" the cop holding Alonzo says. "I believe you were asked a question."

Josh swallows, head hot and throbbing. "Yes, sir, he's my brother."

An extra weight collapses against his lungs. Crossing paths he can't backtrack. Already stressing how he's going to explain his lies once they're inevitably revealed.

The cop interrogating him claps his hands together, excited. "Well, that is one hell of a coincidence. You see, me and my partner here," he points to the other cop, "we are also brothers."

"Wow." Josh clears his throat. "That—that's cool."

Josh catches a glimpse of Alonzo's house in his peripherals, camouflaged in darkness. What would the cops say if they knew they were in front of Alonzo's house the whole time? Something tells Josh they wouldn't find it funny. Something tells him they're more liable to burn the house to the ground than to laugh.

The cop continues, gesturing one dirty thumb at himself. "Me, I'm Uncle. And my brother here, that's Father."

Alonzo laughs and the sound stops Josh's heart. "Your name is *Father?*"

Miraculously, they ignore Alonzo's comments and stay focused on Josh. The cop who introduced himself as Uncle says, "And what are your names?"

Josh considers lying again, but can't decide what good it'd do. Say he gives a phony name—they're just gonna figure out it's bogus once they take him home. If they even take him home. The reality sinks in that it's highly possible he might spend the night in a jail cell, depending how the rest of their encounter plays out, depending on how much control Alonzo manages to maintain, depending how quickly they're pegged for the gas station robbery. Twelve years old and already behind bars.

"I'm—I'm Josh."

"Josh what?"

"Wa-Washington."

"Joshua Washington. Mmm."

The way the cop says his name sends a sliver of disgust digging through his gut. It doesn't sound like his real name, not when it comes out of the cop's mouth. Somehow he's managed to spoil Josh's own identity.

The cop named Father grunts and grabs Alonzo by the throat. "And you, boy?"

Alonzo's eyes seem to bulge from their sockets, and it's the first time Josh has ever seen his friend so afraid. "Alonzo."

"Alonzo *what?*" The cop's bark startles an otherwise calm night, echoing down the empty street.

"Jones!" Squirming in the cop's violent grip.

Uncle laughs, attention still drawn on Josh when he speaks to Alonzo. "Funny. I would have swore you two said you was brothers. Figured you would both share the same last name."

Before Josh can fumble an excuse from his quickly deteriorating brain, Father pushes Alonzo back against the car hood and retrieves the plastic gas station bag from the pavement. He only inspects its contents briefly before dropping it at his feet. The bag spills open and loose bills drift down the street, carried by the soft October breeze and illuminated by the car's silent siren.

Uncle clicks his jaw. It sounds mechanical almost. Manufactured. "Now, what are two young children such as yourself doing with such an abundance of treats?"

"We found it," Alonzo blurts out, but the cop ignores him, keeps his attention on Josh, so Josh repeats Alonzo's answer.

Uncle sighs. "Your soul quivers when you open your mouth. Did you know that, Joshua Washington?"

Alonzo pushes himself off the hood and spins toward the cops, a fire raging in his eyes. "Hey, man, we got fuckin' rights, you can't harass us like this. We'll have your asses sued so fast you'll—"

"Oh, will you shut the fuck up already?" Father backhands him across the face and Alonzo drops like a stone.

Josh screams and bends down to help but the other cop—*Uncle*—grabs his wrist and twirls him around, squeezing Josh's stomach against the running engine. The cop's breath radiates against the back of his neck like nuclear fallout as he whispers, "We are gonna go for a little ride now, understand? And if you try fucking with us even for a second, do not think I will hesitate to slice both yours and your little cocksucker friend's throats."

The cop leans closer now, pressing his body against Josh, rubbing against his backside. "Do we understand each other?"

Uncle doesn't wait for a reply, just drags Josh around the car and shoves him into the back seat. The boy's kicks and punches prove worthless. His attempt at self-defense means nothing. Even as Alonzo's limp body is also dragged and thrown in next to him and the back door is slammed shut, Josh understands a great truth. He is but a fly caught on sticky paper. A helpless specimen awaiting its dissection.

He never even had a fucking chance.

The two cops get in the car and drive.

THREE

He pissed his pants.

As the car pulls away and his best friend leans against the window next to him in a state of unconsciousness, that's all Josh can focus on, that he pissed his pants and he's just helplessly sitting in a puddle of his own urine.

His own *piss*.

Like an infant. Like some goddamn baby.

He can only imagine what his dad would say if he could see him now—in the back of a police cruiser with the one kid his parents have always warned him to be careful with. Seeing him in the back of this car would only make them tell Josh how he should have listened to them all along, that they knew best and he didn't know shit.

Josh turns around and glares at the back window, watching Alonzo's house vanish in the darkness. Once it's out of eyesight, he settles back against the seat and grimaces at the sensation of his soaked pants refusing to properly coincide with the mobility of his legs.

The back seat smells like dirt after a heavy rain. It also smells like his own piss. The odor combo triggers his gag reflexes and he coughs, something small and slimy shooting from his throat and splattering in his wet lap.

The car drives fast and rough, sirens now off. Josh catches a glimpse of Father behind the wheel in the rearview mirror, and he's once again overcome with nausea. The cop's face, it isn't how faces are supposed to look. Like it's disassociated almost, like maybe he skinned himself one day, turned the flesh inside-out then attempted to reattach it to his skull, only he didn't quite

39

reconnect the mask perfectly even. And that's exactly what Josh is looking at—*a mask*. Has to be. Josh prays he never witnesses what's beneath this mask, but an alien confidence creeps in and assures him it'll happen sooner than he could ever anticipate.

Could their names really be Father and Uncle? *Officers* Father and Uncle? If they're brothers, at least the pattern of kooky names checks out. But still. Father and Uncle. What the fuck?

Alonzo stirs awake, groaning and grabbing the side of his head. "Where— where are we?" He figures the answer out himself after taking a moment to collect his bearings. "Where the fuck are we going?"

He looks at Josh for an explanation, but Josh only shrugs. If he still possessed the courage to speak, he'd tell Alonzo he imagines they're on their way to the police station, that they're in for a long night of interrogation conducted by the two ugliest fucking cops to have ever existed. If they're lucky, their parents will come pick them up in a couple hours. If the universe remains true and cruel, the cops will connect the awfully close dots between a dead or badly injured gas station night clerk and Alonzo's mysterious bag of cash. If Josh could remember how to talk, he'd tell his friend they're heading directly toward the end of their lives. But Alonzo isn't as dumb as most people seem to think. Josh figures Alonzo will come to the same conclusion soon enough.

Alonzo kicks the back of the cage separating them from the front seats. Kicks it again, then once more before replacing his feet with fists. The wiry window granting them a view of the car's front rattles with each punch. Surely it's strong enough to withhold the power of a twelve-year-old. Yet every strike causes Josh to wince at the anticipation of the whole cage snapping.

"*Let us go!*" Alonzo screams between punches. "*Let us go let us go let us go let us go!*"

Uncle turns halfway in his seat and studies Alonzo with amusement. "What if we let you go—right now, just pulled over and kicked your sorry ass outta the car—but only on the condition that we could keep your not-so-little friend? Would you be agreeable to such a deal, Mr. Alonzo Jones?"

Alonzo remains quiet for a moment and Josh scoots closer to his own window, the back of the police cruiser shrinking and collapsing.

Then Alonzo spits through the wires again. "Fuck you."

Uncle laughs and turns back around, not bothering to wipe the spit from his deformed face.

Josh smiles a faint smile, relieved his only real friend on this planet didn't just bargain him away, ashamed he had dared doubt their friendship.

Josh leans his head against the cold window, watching the closed fast-food restaurants and other miscellaneous shops pass as the cop car heads toward the station. This could be the last time he ever sees these buildings. The last time he's ever in this town. By the time he's released from prison, the world will be different. Changed. Hell. Who's to say he'll ever be free? Who's to say he'll even make it to prison?

Eventually Uncle turns back toward them, perhaps bored with the silence. "So, which one of you is going to admit where you found the money?"

Alonzo's response is immediate, as if practiced. "Way up in your mother's rancid, stanky-ass pussy."

The car screeches to a halt in the middle of the street. Inertia throws both Josh and Alonzo against the cage. Pain penetrates Josh's nose and vibrates through his skull. The front driver's door swings open and Father stomps around the car toward the back passenger's side. He pulls open the door and presses the dull side of a large blade against Alonzo's cheek. *A machete.*

The car is silent and still, occupied only by the heavy pounding of Alonzo breathing.

Then the cop called Father says, "Shit."

"Wh-what?"

"Shit."

"I—I *am* sitting."

"No." Father pushes the machete harder against his face. "Not sit. *Shit.*"

"Sh-shit?"

Father nods, a grim satisfaction spreading across his lips.

"I—I don't understand."

"*Shit!*" Saliva splatters across Alonzo's face and a wave of rancid, decomposition-level breath blasts Josh in the next seat. The stench is like poisonous gas threatening to snuff him. Josh fights it, although the temptation to surrender is strong and romantic.

Uncle turns around and glances at Alonzo. "I believe my brother here is requesting you promptly defecate in your pants or else he will slice through your skull."

"I—I—I—"

"Eye! Eye!" Uncle laughs loud and obnoxious, then squeals and snorts in a perfect impersonation of a pig. "No one's talkin' 'bout no eyes here, boy! Ain't not an eye in sight!" The snorting continues.

"Shit!" Father taps the machete against Alonzo's head in a steady staccato beat. "Shit! Shit! Shit!"

Uncle lets loose another squeal.

Snort. Laugh.

Squeal.

Snort. Laugh.

Squeal.

Josh can't focus on what horror requires the most energy to gaze upon. Uncle's joyous laughter. Father's unhinged demands. Alonzo's animalistic sobs.

Manic.

Lights flashing.

Lights from where—white, black, hot white. Blood red. The color you see when you're dead.

Lights in Josh's head.

On, off, on, off, on, off, on, off, on.

"*Shit,* you fucking cocksucker, you *shit* right fucking now or you're fucking dead!"

Squeal.

Snort. Laugh.

Squeal.

Snort. Laugh.

Squeal.

Squeal.

Squeal.

Why is nobody coming to save us? Why is this happening? Oh god, oh god, oh god.

Questions imploding within Josh's core and leading nowhere with a satisfying answer.

Alonzo opens his mouth and an alien, cosmic scream flees from his lungs like bats from the jaws of a cave. The scream refuses to die as a disturbing straining falls across his face. Uncle's laughter rises in volume to match the sound of the scream. Josh watches a thousand emotions drain from his friend simultaneously.

The smell is immediate and haunting.

Father eventually smiles and lowers the machete. "Now." Blade pointing back at Alonzo. "Next time you care to utter another blasphemous remark directed at Mother." Blade turning toward Josh. "I am going to make your fat friend here eat up everything you just deposited. Every delicious drop." Machete back at Alonzo. "Do we understand each other?"

"Ye-yes."

"What?"

"Yes?"

"*What?*"

"*Yes, oh god, yes, yes, yes.*"

"Good."

Father slams the back door and walks around the car and sits behinds the wheel. The new silence is a welcomed weight lifted. As the cop car continues down the street, Josh closes his eyes and tries to pretend that he's somewhere—*anywhere*—else, but the stench of his best friend's soiled pants is so strong he vomits in his mouth and swallows it back down his throat to avoid further humiliation. Josh considers reaching over and touching Alonzo's arm to comfort him, but he can't do it. He can't do anything.

So he sits and waits for what's next.

And when the cop car drives past the police station, and continues into the dying night, he begins to cry strong, violent sobs, and he does not stop until they reach the cornfield.

Then he begins to scream.

THE HOUSE THAT IS NOT A HOUSE

FOUR

*O*ttessa stares at her right hand and wonders when the red acrylic cracked on her fuck-you finger. Little bitches cost forty dollars every two weeks and they're as fragile as a drunk's whiskey dick. Probably broke it last night in bed with whatever the hell his name was. The white fella with a smiley face tattooed on his pecker. First time she ever seen a cock tat. It was strange, yeah, but also pretty damn cool. Exotic.

When she gets back home she'll look for the missing nail in her bed sheet. Maybe it's still salvageable, unlike her spawn. She's liable to crack the remaining acrylics across Zoey's cheek once they get out of here. She can't decide what she's more pissed off about, the fact that her son was once again stupid enough to find trouble with the law, or that she's the one who had to drive clear across town on barely a quarter tank of gas. After last night, she wasn't up to doing a goddamn thing except for hiding in bed with a puke bucket nearby while watching crazy white women tear each other apart on TV. Yet here she is. Bright and early with a headache straight from the darkest depths of Hell.

An officer with a gray mustache approaches her with loud, jingly boots. Who is he even trying to be, some kinda goddamn Texas Ranger? He clears his throat and extends a hand, inviting her to shake it, which she refuses to accept. "Mrs. Jones, I'm Sheriff Keene. If my memory serves me correctly, I believe we've met before."

Ottessa remains seated, motionless. "It's *Miss*. And I've never seen you before in my life."

Of course she recognizes the smug cocksucker. Just within the last month he escorted her out of Rourke's after she started breaking beer bottles with a pool stick. A month before that, he'd pulled her over on Ripley and had the balls to accuse her of being intoxicated, which she had been, but like it was any of his fuckin' business. Plus she was pretty sure he'd squeezed her ass a little too roughly during the pat down. Perverted motherfucker. Just like every other cop in this country.

Now he stands over her trying to pull some bullshit "I believe we've met" routine, like he's some important big shot, like he ain't just some redneck in a small town dumb enough to have been given a badge by some other redneck. Like any old fool couldn't pick up the same shit at Dollar General in the toy aisle.

The idiot clears his throat again—what's he got stuck in there, anyway? Mustache hairs? "Well, ma'am, the way I understand the situation is, you seem to think your son is currently in our custody—"

"Ain't no *think* about it, considerin' I damn well seen two of your fat-ass henchmen toss him and his friend in the back of their car last night."

"Right. That's what the officer who took down your story told me."

"*Story* implies I'm makin' this all up. Now, y'all better let me see my goddamn son or Hell itself is about to rain upon this entire station. It ain't right how y'all been keeping him, not even letting him make a goddamn phone call. And what about Josh? His friend? Boy, you in for a world of hurt once his folks show up. Should already be on their way, I imagine. Gave them a call before I came down."

Keene stares down at her a moment longer, clicking his tongue, then sits in the chair next to her. Ottessa's fists clench at her knees, prepared to break the man's nose if he even thinks about laying a finger on her.

"Ma'am, the only person currently being held at this station is a thirty-nine-year-old woman who keyed her twenty-year-old ex-husband's brand new BMW for falling behind on his child support payments. Your child is not here. *Nobody's* child is here."

"Maybe they were taken to another station then."

48

He makes a face like he wants to laugh but wisely swallows the urge. "Doubtful."

"Where's the next closest one?"

"Where did you say the boys got picked up?" He rubs his forehead with his knuckles. Irritated by her persistence? Fuck him. Her boy is missing. She doesn't give a shit. She tells him her address and he scrunches his face. "How old are they?"

"Twelve. As I've already done *told* you people a dozen times now. *Twelve years old*. Gone."

"Well, ma'am, the thing is, if your boy was indeed picked up by one of my officers—or, hell, any officers for that matter—anywhere near the address you just gave me, there is no other possible station they would have taken them besides the one you and I are currently sitting in. It just wouldn't make any sense. This isn't some big fancy city with a new police station on every block. This is Percy, for God's sake."

"Then who the motherfuck took my boy?" She's half-panicking, half-impatient over this redneck's clear incompetence. She fuckin' *saw* them get in that cop car, so obviously someone has failed to file the proper paperwork somewhere because where the hell else could they be if not here?

"Describe to me what this man looked like. The one you said led your boy and his friend into his car."

She sighs loud enough to attract an annoyed glare from the receptionist across the station. "There was two of 'em. Tall. White boys. Dressed like cops. Talked like cops. Slammed them against the hood of the car—not some regular car but a goddamn *cop* car, you understand? C-O-P. Cop."

"And where were you while the incident occurred?"

"Inside my house."

"Inside your house." He eyes her like she's hiding something, which of course she is, but it's not like she's concealing any facts actually relevant to the story.

"Yeah, I was inside my house. So fuckin' what?"

"Just curious, is all, why you didn't go outside to talk to these alleged officers."

49

"Maybe I figured they probably done something to deserve a night locked up."

Keene leans forward. "Something like…?"

"Something like who the fuck knows. Twelve-year-old boys do stupid shit. I figured they was probably fuckin' around with toilet paper or eggs or whatever."

Keene raises his eyebrow, amused. "As in TPing and egging houses, Mrs. Jones?"

"It's *Miss*."

"Miss Jones."

"And yeah. What else would they be doing with it all—wiping their asses and frying up omelets?"

"Mrs. Jo—*Miss* Jones, does you son frequently inflict damage on public property?"

Ottessa digs her acrylics into her knees. "I don't see what this has to do with a goddamn thing."

"Miss—"

"My child is *missing*. His friend is *missing*. Do you understand that? Missing as in not at home. As in either they were arrested or some fucking creeps dressed up like cops and snatched them. What are you going to *do* about this?"

If he asks her about Zoey's vandalism habits again, she's fully prepared to lash out with violence. In fact, she's sort of hoping he gives her a reason. Just one punch to the nose or chop to the jugular. The thought of him laid out on the ground, bleeding and gasping, almost makes her wet. No. Strike that "almost".

Instead of digging his fate closer toward a broken nose, Keene folds his hands into his lap and exhales a drawn-out breath. "Let me make some phone calls and see what I can find out. All right?"

Ottessa shoos him away. "You mean the thing y'all should've already taken care of an hour ago? Yes, please, that'd be awfully kind of you."

FIVE

It takes another two cigarettes before Mary can find the strength to stand up from the kitchen table and wake Jasper. His snores rise in volume as she nudges his shoulder, then abruptly cut off. He stares at her, not moving, first confused, then annoyed.

"What time is it?"

"A little past seven."

"Do you have any idea what time I got home from work last night?"

"I know. I'm sorry."

"Then you better have a damn good reason for waking me up right now."

"It's Josh…he…"

Jasper sits up and spills his blanket down his chest. "What about Josh?"

"I guess…" She steps back, dreading to be the messenger. "I guess him and Ottessa's boy got in trouble last night—"

"Trouble?"

"—and they're down at the station."

"The station?"

"Yeah. The, uh, police station."

"Goddammit." Jasper steps out of bed and stomps across the room toward the dresser. He kicks his legs into jeans with two violent motions. "What the fuck did he get his ass into now?"

"I'm not sure. Ottessa just said she was on her way to the station, that the boys got picked up last night."

He pauses, holding the zipper of his jeans between his fingers. "He's been there since last night and we're only just now hearing about it?"

All Mary can do is shrug, timid.

"Goddammit." Jasper continues getting dressed, repeating the word under his breath like it's a song chorus. "Goddammit, goddammit, goddammit."

"You want me to make you a cup of coffee?"

Jasper grimaces at her like he's going to say something ugly, but instead nods. "Thanks."

She flees the bedroom, relieved to have a task. The coffee's already brewed. She turned the pot on the moment she saw Ottessa's name flash on their caller ID. Only a handful of reasons she'd be calling so early in the morning and none of them were good. After her conversation with Ottessa, she'd called the office and informed them she wouldn't be making it in to work today. The manager on duty tried guilting her into coming anyway, but she reminded him of her near perfect attendance, and he quieted down. Sometimes emergencies happen. Sometimes your child gets arrested by the cops.

She fetches Jasper's travel mug from the dish drainer and fills it with coffee, then stirs some Sweet'N Low in it. She leans against the kitchen counter and lights another cigarette and takes long, strong drags as she waits for him to finish up in the bathroom.

He's warned her in the past about letting Josh play with Ottessa's boy. She's already anticipating the told-you-so remarks she'll hear on the drive to the station. The what-did-I-tell-yous won't stop for several days. Every time he gets in trouble, it will always be her fault for letting him play with his friend. Even when Josh is an adult, Jasper will still blame Mary and Alonzo. It's easier to blame someone else than to take a good hard look at your own self. Responsibility loses its weight when handed off to someone else, anyone else, as long as it ain't you.

He steps into the kitchen, snorting snot up into his brain and zipping his White Sox windbreaker. She hands him the coffee and he accepts it with a grunt. "Where are my keys?"

"Wherever you put them last night, probably." The tone of her voice adding: *You know, when you came in at three in the morning, drunk off your ass?*

"Woman. Of all the mornings, now's not the—"

"They're on the table."

"Thank you."

He scoops them up and she follows him outside, wrestling her arms into her jacket as they stomp through the front yard and get in the car parked at the curb. She tries not to notice the empty beer cans discarded in the back seat but it's like not staring at a giant mole on someone's cheek. It's right there and there's no denying its existence.

Jasper starts the car and blasts the heat. "Don't you fucking say a word."

"I didn't say anything." She buckles her seat belt and wonders if a person can still get arrested for empty alcohol containers if they're no longer drunk. If the containers are from a previous day and they've just been too lazy to throw them out. Shame fills her as she realizes she hopes they can.

"I can hear you plenty without you even having to open your mouth."

He flips on a sports station and as he drives they listen to a couple of old men talk about today's game later between the Sox and Astros. The men speculate who they think will win. If the Sox are swept, Chicago will riot, it'll burn to the ground. That's the theory, at least. The way the two men talk about it, it sounds like they're kinda hoping it happens. The idea excites them.

Jasper lowers the volume as he pulls into the police station parking lot. "I'll tell you one thing right here and now. Come seven o'clock, my ass will be in front of the TV watching the game, I don't care what's happening. This gets straightened out now or he can stay another night in a cell for all I care."

As Mary gets out of the car, she whispers, "And the Father of the Year Award goes to…"

Jasper glares at her as they walk up the front steps. She wonders what he'd do to her if they weren't about to enter a police station. He's never hit her before, not really hit her, maybe a love tap here and a shove there during fits of extreme intoxication, but it won't surprise her when he finally hauls off and slugs her. Seems like a real, honest-to-god punch has been in the making for a couple years now, slowly sautéing and discovering its flavoring.

They find Ottessa in the waiting area, sitting with one leg crossed over the other, head leaning against the brick wall behind her.

"Have a seat," she tells them.

"Nah." Jasper shakes his head and holds out an arm to prevent Mary from sitting. "Fuck that. Tell us what's going on."

"It's complicated."

"Where's Josh?" Mary asks.

"Cops say they don't have them, but I saw some of them drive off with Zoey and Josh, so obviously someone done screwed up. Sheriff is making some phone calls to see if they was taken to another station or what."

Jasper laughs, like *of course*. "What did your son get my son into now?"

"Man, you can go fuck yourself, you think you can talk to me like that."

"You think this is a joke?"

Ottessa stands and gets in his face. "I think you think I won't slap the shit out of you in a police station. Motherfucker, you ain't my goddamn husband, so back the fuck off."

Jasper looks her up and down and retreats behind Mary. He mutters something about Ottessa being a crazy-ass bitch under his breath and Ottessa nods and tells him he's goddamn right.

They sit across the room from her and wait for news. Ottessa studies her fingernails and Jasper taps his feet on the floor, legs spread wide apart. Every couple seconds he sighs loudly and checks his wristwatch with almost comical exaggeration. Mary bites her lip, fighting the urge to tell him to knock it off. She seems to bite her lip a lot these days.

A door down the hall opens and a man with a gray mustache sticks his head out. "Um…Miss Jones? A word." He waves her toward him. She remains seated, watching his hand motions, and scoffs.

Mary and Jasper follow her into the office. Mary wonders if she's the only one worried about what they're about to hear. The look on the sheriff's face did not seem promising when he called them in. His brow rises slightly at hers and Jasper's presence.

"I take it you're the other boy's folks?"

Mary nods.

Jasper cracks his neck. Trying to look hard. "That's right."

Nobody offers anybody a hand to shake.

The sheriff sits behind his desk and leans back with his hands folded behind his head. A computer monitor between them hums with electricity. He stares at the three of them without saying anything, like he's unsure of how to proceed. He stares at them as if they're the ones who invited him in here.

Ottessa throws her arm up. "Well? You got an update or what?"

The sheriff smirks. "I got something I'm gonna need you all to watch."

Silence lingers and Ottessa's impatience grows more obvious. "And that would be…?"

Without removing his feet from atop his desk, the sheriff leans forward and scoops up a small black remote next to a cluster of coffee-stained documents. He aims it at a TV set balanced on a rickety mobile cart in the corner of the room. Next to it a bulletin board hangs from the wall. Mary expects to find dozens of crime scene photos and other various clues tacked to it, but instead only sees magazine cut-outs of swimwear models and a 2005 White Sox calendar. Today and the following Sunday, Tuesday, and Wednesday are all circled in red marker. The first four games of the World Series against the Houston Astros. She's heard about it enough from her husband. Personally, she couldn't care less. The sooner the series is finished, the better. She can't think of a more boring activity in this universe than watching a televised baseball game. But hey. Maybe Jasper and the sheriff could get along, after all.

The TV on the cart blinks to life. Static dissolves and forms a collage of pixels. A black and white aerial security camera presents the interior recording of what appears to be some kind of drug store or gas station. You walk into a place enough times, you think you'd recognize it, but you don't account for perspectives other than your own. You don't consider how the employees view the place, or what the security cameras pick up in their unbiased lenses. You get wrapped up in your own point-of-view and neglect everybody else's. Mary watches the footage with a hint of recognition, but she can't quite place the location. One of the many gas stations scattered throughout Percy, surely.

But which one, and what is its significance here? And why is the sheriff showing them this? She opens her mouth to ask just that question, then freezes, jaw unhinged, as two familiar faces appear on the screen.

Josh and Alonzo, arms full of chips and drinks and what looks like egg cartons. They lay down their supplies on the front counter for the night clerk to ring up. The security footage has the date and time stamped on the bottom right corner of the screen:

01:45:57 AM

10/22/05

"So they bought some junk food." Ottessa folds one leg over the other and leans back. "So what? What's this got to do with anything?"

"Just keep watching." The sheriff speaks with humor in his tone, like he's in on a joke nobody else knows.

The longer the video plays, the smaller Mary's heart seems to shrink. A layer of dread slithers around her and constricts tight enough to cut off her air flow.

Jasper leans forward, squinting his eyes. "What is that they gave him? A...credit card? I can't tell."

"A picture." The sheriff cracks his neck and sits forward.

"A picture?"

"Ayup."

"A picture of what?"

"This." He reaches into his desk drawer, grabs a photograph contained in a Ziploc, and tosses it on the desk. He pauses the TV and waits, hands folded over his protruding gut, the smirk across his face making him look a little too pleased with himself.

Jasper turns from the TV and glances at the photograph. It's crumpled as if someone had balled it up and discarded it into the trash. His brow arches and his face sinks into a grimace. "What the fuck?" He snaps his gaze away, like the photo physically pains him.

Before Mary can bring herself to glance at it, Ottessa grabs it from the desk and holds it close to her face and studies the photograph for a near minute before speaking. Mary knows it's almost been a minute because she's counting the second hand tick on the clock in the sheriff's office.

Ottessa lowers the photograph and glares at the sheriff. "Is this supposed to be some kinda fuckin' joke?"

"'Fraid not, Miss Jones."

"This is bullshit. I don't know what's going on, but I do know it's a great big pile of bullshit."

"Maybe you should watch the rest of the video."

"I ain't watching shit."

"I'm gonna need that photograph back, Miss Jones."

"Excuse me?"

The sheriff points at the Ziploc pressed tight against Ottessa's chest. "That's evidence you're holding right there. You can't keep it."

"Like hell I can't. This don't belong to you."

"It does now."

"Bullshit."

"Watch the rest of the video."

Mary can't hold her breath any longer. "What's in the photo?"

Ottessa shakes her head. "None of your fucking business, that's what."

Jasper leans toward Mary. "It's…her." He gestures at Ottessa. "It's a… it's a nude pic."

Disgust doesn't find Mary as it had her husband. Instead, she's met with confusion. "But why did the boys have it?"

And why are they giving it to some gas station employee?

The look in Ottessa eyes mirrors the same confusion. "I don't know."

The sheriff clears his throat, enjoying himself. "Maybe we ought to finish the video before continuing this conversation."

He lifts the remote and presses PLAY.

They watch the recording unfold in silence. It presents them a story with gaping plot holes and muddled character decisions. What begins as a tale of two boys attempting to purchase snack food and eggs quickly unravels into a surreal, violent attack. Tears roll down Mary's cheeks as

Ottessa's boy leaps across the counter and tackles the front desk clerk to the floor, out of the camera's vision. There's a moment in the recording when Josh appears to be frozen with indecision, and Mary can practically hear his thoughts aloud, as if he's whispering them in her ear: *do i run away or do i help do i run away or do i help do i run away or do i help what do i do what do i do what do i do.*

Run, baby, she wants so desperately to tell him, *run as fast as you can and never look back.*

But he doesn't. He chooses to stay and help. To help Ottessa's boy carry out this seemingly spontaneous assault. It doesn't look like a planned act of violence, but what does Mary know? This all still feels like some cruel dream. Any second now she expects to wake up. She continues counting the second hand on the clock, hopeful that each click will be her ticket out of this baffling nightmareland.

The clerk manages to stand back up, but another scuffle occurs and he drops to the floor again. The camera shows Josh and Alonzo behind the counter, looking down, and Mary realizes that the guy might be dead, that her boy could be responsible for a *murder.* Alonzo steps forward and starts messing with the cash register and Josh walks off to the side for something she can't quite make out. Bags. He's collecting bags for the cash Alonzo's emptying from the register.

Before they leave, Mary's twelve-year-old son grabs a case of beer.

The TV blinks again and fills with darkness.

The three of them stare at the black screen. In the reflection, Mary can see the sheriff fooling with his ridiculous mustache. She's hit with the urge to turn around and rip it off his stupid smug face. Maybe it won't fix what they'd just witnessed, but she suspects it would still make her feel better, at least temporarily.

"So." The sheriff's chair creaks as he leans forward. They turn from the TV and give him their attention. He points at the bag still clenched in Ottessa's grip. "That photograph? Evidently they tried shovin' it down Tim Miller's throat. Tim Miller being the fella in the video."

Ottessa holds the photograph up with two trembling hands and looks at it again. For once, she doesn't know how to respond.

Mary can't stop crying and she hates herself for not being stronger. She's never felt more helpless in her life.

Jasper sits back, rubbing his chin. He's trying to appear calm but Mary recognizes the rage blossoming in his eyes, like two nukes detonating in unison. "Did they kill him?"

"Nah. He's in the hospital being treated for some serious head injuries, but I'm told he's expected to recover just fine."

Mary gasps and feels the dread slightly loosen around her. Still present, but not as suffocating as it'd been moments before.

"But with that said, your boys are in a whole heap of trouble. We're talking at the very least, robbery and assault. Once Tim Miller's conscious enough to speak, we may even push for attempted murder. I don't know yet. This is all new to me. I only just saw the recording myself a few minutes before I called you all into my office."

More tears rain down Mary's face. Jasper nods, quiet. Ottessa shakes her head, gritting her teeth. She raises her index finger at the sheriff. "Whatever the fuck they may or may not have done, that still don't explain where they are right now."

"Very good point. So why don't you go ahead and tell me where they're hiding and we can speed up this whole process?"

"What are you talking about?"

The sheriff sighs. "Cut the shit. We know you're hiding the boys, Miss Jones. Hell, maybe all three of you are in on the act." He waves his arm around the room. "But I doubt it."

Jasper taps his chest as if to say, *what, me?*

Ottessa jumps to her feet, dropping the photograph to the floor. It lands face-up, at last revealing its secrets to Mary. She looks away immediately. The content of the photo is none of her business.

Ottessa hovers over the desk and knocks down a small lamp. "You motherfucker. How fucking dare you."

"Ma'am, unless you have information about your son's whereabouts, I'm gonna have to ask you to please leave the premises."

"Go fuck yourself, you piece of shit. I told you what I saw. I fucking *told* you, and now you're trying to say I'm—what, lying? To protect Zoey? Fuck that. If he was stupid enough to do what he did in that video, then he can face the goddamn consequences. But I know what I fuckin' seen and what I seen was two of *your* motherfuckin' pig friends take them away. So you get on that goddamn phone and you make some goddamn calls right fuckin' now."

The smile on the sheriff's face fades away. He stands and stares Ottessa in the eyes. He speaks low and deep, almost in a growl. "Here are the facts. Last night, your boy and these folks' boy robbed the Shell station on Main. They also assaulted the night clerk and rendered him unconscious. They damn near killed him, is what they did. Now they can't be found. So you tell me what's more likely: that one of my officers found your boys and somehow lost them within the system, or they told you what they did and you hid them somewhere, then came here to distract us from the truth long enough to do…I don't know, I'm guessing smuggle them out of the state? What you don't understand is there is no place these boys can hide that we won't uncover. Which is why right now I have my own boys searching through both of your places, just in case you really were stupid enough to leave them at home."

"You motherfu—"

"We will find these boys, and we will punish them to the fullest extent of the law. And if I can prove you all really are in on it like I suspect, then prepare to join them. Until then, get the fuck out of my office, ma'am."

SIX

*O*ttessa swears to god if this motherfucker says another word she's gonna break his jaw.

Jasper stands between her and her car, trying to make himself as wide as possible. He refuses to move, almost seems to secretly get off each time she orders him to step aside. There's a look in his eyes that she recognizes as belonging to crazy people worldwide. Ottessa has had her fair share of dangerous lunatic encounters to know better than not to take this kind of behavior seriously. The man's son is missing. He's long past the point of rational.

And so is Ottessa.

She debates the best strategy for taking him down if push comes to shove and concludes a good knee to the balls ought to do the trick. It's never failed her before.

"Where they at?" Jasper cocks his head and glares down at her like he's the biggest player in town. "Where you got them holed up, huh? What the fuck have you done?"

Ottessa bites her lip hard enough to make her wince and glances at Mary standing off to the side, arms crossed, staring at her feet. Poor girl looks fucking terrified, and meanwhile her jackass husband hasn't done a lick to comfort her. Obviously Ottessa feels about the same as Mary right about now, if not worse, but she'll be damned if she's about to show it in front of this waste of life.

She stares down Jasper with enough coldness to freeze water. "I don't have them. I don't know where they are, and if you accuse me of lying one more time, one of us is gonna spend the rest of the day in a hospital bed, and the other in a very uncomfortable jail cell."

Jasper pauses before responding, as if contemplating the consequences of punching a woman in the face in front of a police station—even a woman as foul as Ottessa. For a moment, he looks like he's actually going to do it. Right now, right here in this parking lot, they're going to go at it—hard. She braces herself, forming her hands into claws, prepared to scratch a chunk of his cheek out the second he flinches, almost hoping it happens, practically praying for the opportunity.

The toughness in him deflates and his shoulders slump and his face sags. His voice drops to a whisper as he leans forward. "We're not finished here."

"Yeah, we are."

He pauses again, caught off guard. He shakes his head. "If I find out you're hiding something…"

"You'll what?"

Jasper grits his teeth and groans and storms off across the parking lot, leaving her and Mary alone. Key in hand, Ottessa can't bring herself to unlock the car. The air is so heavy with tension they might as well be drowning in it. She closes her eyes and sighs, too exhausted and worried to be a bitch to this woman who hasn't done a thing to her, to this woman who's in the exact same position as she finds herself in.

Missing her son.

Missing her little boy.

"Look." Ottessa turns to Mary, steps forward, feeling an awkward need to comfort her but unsure how. "I was telling the truth back there. Every word of it."

Mary nods. "I know." She wipes her eyes. "I—I believe you. I do."

Ottessa glances at the police station behind them and spits. "I know what I saw. Those motherfuckers are hiding something. If anybody knows where our boys are, it's that fat fuckin' sheriff in there."

"But why wouldn't they just tell us?" Mary's voice cracks. "Why…why hide them? I—I don't understand what's happening. Please. What…what is this?"

Neither of them speak the obvious answer, the one Ottessa can't stop thinking about.

"I don't know, but I aim to find out."

OTTESSA'S HOUSE IS A DISASTER.

She races home from the police station, not even pretending like the speed limit signs she passes mean anything. Speed restrictions go out the window the moment your little boy gets abducted. The law takes on a whole new meaning once the cops start keeping secrets from you, once they start searching your property without permission.

No one's at her house when she pulls into her driveway, but signs of their presence remain behind like distant ghosts. The front door hangs half off its hinges, like someone had kicked it open. The caved-in wound below the knob helps confirm this theory.

She slips in through the opening and braces herself for the worst and receives it. Photo frames busted. Furniture flipped over. Clothes ripped from the closet now tossed to the floor in piles. Dishes shattered throughout the kitchen, as if she'd been hiding the boys in some fucking cupboard or something. Oh, please. Give her a break. They knew damn well the boys weren't here before they even stepped foot on her property. No, this is a message. But what does it say? One of two things, the way she sees it. Either they're confirming what she already knows, that someone in the department did indeed nab the boys and now they're warning her to back off before something much worse happens to them, or the sheriff is simply playing his Macho Asshole card by teaching her a lesson on how to properly address good ol' white folks.

Or, hell, maybe they really were looking for the boys, but somehow she doubts it.

She returns to the porch, stepping over more broken glass, and sits on the swing. There's nothing for her back inside that house. Spending any time inside around that manmade disaster would only add more fuel to her rage.

But maybe that's what she needs. To get angrier. To go out and break some skulls. But she can't. Instead of getting mad, all she wants to do is curl up into a ball and cry. Maybe smoke a joint and try to calm down.

Instead, she pulls out a Virginia Slim from the pack in her shirt pocket and lights up, staring through the screen window out onto the street. The sun projects a jaundiced spotlight on the pavement where she'd last seen Zoey and his friend.

And the cops.

Jesus Christ, she's so exhausted she can barely stand it. It's amazing, she thinks, how quickly stress completely drains you. Drains you until you're nothing. Until there's not a speck of you left except for the decomposed ashes from your cigarette butt.

She leans back on the old porch swing, the one her mother bought her when she first moved into this house. She'd sat the same way last night upon noticing the cop car lights flashing through the living room window while fetching a glass of water in the kitchen. It'd been what? Two, three in the morning when she woke up covered in sweat, bed sheet glued to her flesh like it'd evolved into a new layer of skin overnight. The man's arm hung over her bare waist, which only seemed to absorb more heat and further suffocate her. She couldn't even remember his name, not then and certainly not now. Perhaps she'd never asked and he'd never offered. Does it matter? Isn't like she was planning on keeping him come morning. He certainly wasn't the most good-looking man she's brought home, and he definitely wasn't the best in bed. Not by a long stretch.

She threw his arm off of her and got up, not giving a rat's ass if he woke from the noise. She sort of hoped he did wake. It'd give her a reason to kick him out early so she could reclaim the bed all for herself. She loathed sleeping next to men. They didn't have any boundaries. Ottessa preferred to stretch out diagonally, no blanket, letting the ceiling fan sing her naked body to sleep. But throw a man into the mix and her whole sleep schedule got fucked up. She sure as hell wasn't waking up at no two in the morning when she was sleeping alone, that was for certain. Yet here she was, drowning in not just her own sweat but also the sweat from some man, and she could only hope that was the only liquid spilled upon her flesh. She couldn't quite account for the suspiciously sticky substances on her back. Nothing she could do about it now. What was done was done.

She stumbled through the house without turning on any lights and paused outside Zoey's bedroom door, pressing her head against the cold wood. She listened for heavy breathing but only heard the dull hum of his television set broadcasting the afterglow of a finished movie. She thought about sneaking inside and pressing the POWER button, but feared waking them up, especially considering all she had on was a pair of panties desperately in need of a wash. She could just imagine the phone call she'd receive from Josh's mother the next day. Bitch was the biggest prude she'd ever met, and her husband wasn't no gem either. Sometimes it astonished Ottessa that they still allowed Josh to spend the night as often as he did. It was clear they both thought her and Zoey were bad influences. Nobody in town seemed to think too highly of them, either. She knew what people thought about her and her boy, that they were trash, that they were no good. They said all she did was drink and fuck strangers while her son went around lighting things on fire and getting in fights at school. And yeah, maybe that wasn't completely false, but shit, it also wasn't like the rest of Percy were a bunch of fuckin' saints or something. If Ottessa and Alonzo were white, nobody would be saying a goddamn thing. She knew it was true even if nobody else had the balls to admit it.

She backed away from the bedroom door and tiptoed to the kitchen. Cottonmouth had its hold on her big time. She needed a glass of water pronto. Maybe a little snack, too. Her stomach felt full of booze and nothing else. She tried to remember the last time she'd eaten but all of her memories became hazy when she concentrated too hard. She opened the fridge and peered inside. Her choices consisted of expired lunchmeat and various condiments.

When she shut the fridge door, she found the kitchen illuminated by red and blue lights blinking in and out of existence. She followed the source to the living room, and through the window. A cop car was parked out front, but she couldn't see much else from inside the house, so she wrapped a throw blanket around her chest and stepped out on the porch. She sat on the swing, the one she sits on now a day later, and spied under the cover of darkness. The night was cold and she shivered as goosebumps trickled up her bare flesh. The porch swing threatened to freeze its wooden planks against her ass cheeks, but she refused to move once she realized who the cops were talking to. Once she realized this wasn't some random scene to view as an outsider and speculate about with others the next day. These weren't strangers in front of her house. Her own son, and his friend. What the fuck were they doing out of the house at this time of night? She resisted the urge to stomp out there with just the blanket around her and slap the both of them silly. Obviously they'd been up to no good. At this time of night? Dumbasses, the both of them. She decided to sit and wait, let someone else chew her son out for once.

It was difficult to fully understand what they were saying. Their voices came off low and muffled by the cop car's idle engine. Profanities slipped through the cracks. From one of the cops. One of them slammed Zoey down against the hood, and instincts told her this was enough, nobody touches her boy but her, especially no goddamn cops. But fear convinced her to remain planted on the porch. She had a problem with her mouth, and she knew she was liable just to make the situation even worse. So she stayed put and watched, and even when the cops loaded both boys in the back of their car, she still did nothing. All in all, it didn't seem that bad. She's been in her share of cop cars over the years, and she turned out moderately fine. Well, shit, she wasn't dead, she had a place to sleep at night, sometimes that was enough.

If the cops weren't coming up to her door, that meant Zoey refused to reveal his identity. No surprise there. Zoey's the most stubborn kid she's ever met. Takes after his deadbeat daddy, wherever the hell he is these days. And, to be honest, he takes after his momma as well. Eventually he'll crack, then the station will call her house. Until then, she'd just go back to bed and enjoy some more sleep. Maybe she'd get lucky and nobody would call until daybreak. Give her some time to relax. She stood off the porch and returned to her bedroom. The man from the bar stirred awake and asked about the time. She grabbed his cock and told him to make himself useful. He'd had enough of a break.

When she woke up again, the man was gone and the phone still hadn't gone off.

SEVEN

Mary cries the entire drive home.

It begins as a quiet whimpering but evolves into a messier sobbing affair the louder Jasper turns up the volume on the radio. The same two guys from this morning are still speculating on who's going to win the game later this evening. Jasper concentrates on every word they say, nodding along at the appropriate moments, looking like the opposite of a man who's just found out his son is not only missing, but also wanted for a very serious crime. The longer he goes without saying anything, the more tempting it becomes to wrap her hands around his throat and squeeze until he crashes the car. Instead she scoots closer to the passenger door, head against the window, and offers a river's worth of tears to the cold glass. It accepts them greedily.

When they pull into the driveway, Jasper leans back and closes his eyes. "Go ahead. I'll be a minute. Want to finish listening to this."

Mary's trembling now, trying so hard not to explode. "Josh…"

"I said go ahead, so *go ahead*. I don't want to talk about this right now."

"But…"

"*Go on, woman.*"

The tone in his voice is like a knife cutting her throat, preventing her from saying another word.

She gets out and stumbles up the driveway slope. The knob on the front door is loose in her hand, wiggling like it's one good tug from ripping from the frame. The door creaks as she pushes it open. She gasps at the sight of the living room. DVDs and CDs form a trail along the floor. The couch sits upside down. Flower pots lay sideways, soil spilled on the carpet. Her house has been turned into a warzone.

Excitement pushes her deeper inside, toward her son's room. "Josh? Josh, baby, is that you? Are you home?"

But he's not here. Not in his room or anywhere else in the house. She goes through each room, hope quickly fading. After she's searched it all, she heads back outside to inform Jasper of the situation, of this mess the police have created for no good reason. She needs to see him get angry at someone who isn't her for once. She needs to see him actually give a damn that their boy is in real danger. She needs to see him *care*.

Mary opens the front door and stops cold in the entrance. Jasper's still in the car, but now his face is buried in his palms and his body moves in short violent convulsions. Crying. Her husband is crying. She steps back into the house and closes the door and tries to remember the last time she saw Jasper cry, then realizes she's *never* seen him cry, not once in their thirteen years of marriage.

Seeing Jasper cry somehow seems scarier than anything else she's learned today.

She doesn't know what to think about this. Doesn't know what to say. She's relieved they're not in the same room, that he's choosing to do this in isolation. If he'd started breaking down in front of her she's afraid of how she'd react. She might cry even harder, yes, but another part of her's positive she'd start laughing. Laugh so hard and crazy someone would have to come wheel her off to a padded room and feed her liquid lunches for the rest of her days.

Her son is missing and her house is wrecked and her husband is crying and nothing is okay, nothing will ever be okay again.

She sits at the kitchen table and lights a cigarette and dials Ottessa's number on the house phone. It rings twice before she picks up.

"Yeah?" Ottessa sounds just as defeated as Mary.

"My house…"

"Mmm-hmm. Same."

"But why?"

"Girl, you know why."

"Do you know where they are? Please, if you do…"

"What I said at the station remains the truth."

"What are we going to do?"

"Either wait around for them to show up or find them ourselves, the way I see things."

"Do you think they'll come back?"

Ottessa emits a sad laugh. "Not without our help."

"Anything, I'll do anything. Just tell me. Please. They have to be okay. They have to be."

"First piece of advice is ditch that worthless husband of yours. He's just gonna slow you down. Slow us both down."

"He's outside right now. Crying."

"Exactly my point."

"He never cries."

"Well he sure picked a good fuckin' time to start acting like a pussy."

"I don't know what to do. I'm so scared."

Silence on Ottessa's end, then: "On second thought, you're just gonna slow me down, too. No one's got the time for…for *fear*." She pronounces "fear" with utter disgust. "I'll let you know when I've found the boys."

Mary tries to protest, but the line goes dead.

She continues sitting and stares at the phone wondering what the hell she's supposed to do next.

No one prepares you for the day your son goes missing. There's no possible way anybody could.

She calls her mother and tells her everything that's happening, and after nearly falling victim to a heart attack, she tells Mary she's on the way over. Her mom's never had a license before, so she'll be taking the first cab that manages to make it out to her house in a timely fashion.

The door swings open as she hangs up the phone and Jasper walks in, eyes dry, no indication of a previous crying fit.

"What the hell happened here?" He gestures at the chaos spread throughout the house, repulsed.

"The police. While we were at the station…"

He grunts, biting his lip. "I'm gonna sue those pieces of shit, I swear to God."

"Didn't they need a warrant?"

He seems to consider this, then nods at the telephone still gripped in her hand. "Who was that?"

"My mom. She's coming over."

Jasper sighs. "Great."

"What's wrong with her coming here?"

"Nothing." He grits his teeth. "Just know, come seven, if she ain't gone yet y'all better be taking your little conversations to the kitchen."

Mary can't quite bring herself to grasp what he's saying. "What are you talking about?"

"Game one, Mary. Come the fuck on. You know it's tonight."

If her jaw weren't attached to her head, it'd drop to the floor right now. "Are you serious right now?"

Jasper tosses up his hands, innocent, playing the victim card. "What?"

"Our son is missing. He might even have been…been taken. And you're worried about a baseball game?"

And he laughs. Goddamn him, he laughs. "Josh isn't missing. He's *hiding,* which is a pretty big difference, if you ask me."

"But Ottessa said—"

Jasper lifts his hand, palm out. It says *shush, you silly woman.* "Ottessa was also likely high off her ass last night, so I don't think it's in our best interests to start believing every little thing she has to say. She probably just made it up to avoid getting stuck with the blame."

"But what if she's telling the truth? What if somebody…*took* Josh?"

He pauses and looks down at his feet, like he hasn't even considered this possibility until now. Eventually he shakes his head. "They're gonna show up. Just you watch. I bet anything that drunk bitch knows where they are. If they're not at her house, then probably one of her friends'. Are they in trouble? You bet. Are they in danger? No. They're probably playing video games and eating pizza this very second. There ain't shit we can do about it until they're found, so what's the point in getting all worked up?"

Mary knows she sounds like a broken record at this point, but she doesn't know how else to sound. "But *what if...*"

But Jasper isn't hearing any of it. Refuses to listen to another word. He shakes his head again, this time harder, with more authority, and storms off into the kitchen. The refrigerator opens and closes quickly, just enough time for him to have snagged a bottle of beer from the bottom shelf. Mary listens for the sound of a cap popping off the corner of the counter and although she isn't let down, she's nonetheless disappointed.

She returns to Josh's room, the thought of laying eyes on her husband again foul enough to conjure a sickness within her. The bedroom is still empty, still a disaster. She steps over a shelf ripped from the dresser and curls into a ball on the mattress, now bare of sheets. Maybe the sheets and blankets are somewhere on the floor, mixed in with the rest of the mess, or maybe the police collected it all for evidence, she doesn't know, doesn't really care. None of this is going to bring back her boy. Crying in his bed isn't going to help find him, either, but she's too weak to get up, too scared to come up with a rational strategy. While she lies on this bed, Josh could be anywhere, doing God knows what. Is he being harmed? Is he even alive?

Mary cries long and hard, soaking Josh's pillow with her tears, and eventually grief and exhaustion drag her into a heavy sleep.

MARY WAKES TO THE SOUND of conversation. Not in Josh's bedroom, but elsewhere in the house. The kitchen or living room, perhaps. Their voices are muffled, separated by the bedroom door. Someone's closed it while she slept. Jasper? Doubtful. He'd never be so considerate. Then who? Her mother, of course. Always thoughtful, always protective.

Mary pictures them in the living room now, her mother grilling Jasper as he attempts to watch TV, gradually raising his levels of impatience and irritation. It's what her mother does best, especially when it comes to Jasper. Mary smiles and considers staying in bed, letting her mother torture him a little bit longer. Her smiles breaks into a wince as she tries to roll over and feels an intense numbing sensation spread through the arm she'd napped on. She twists her head and gasps at the newly formed knot in her neck. The pain reminds her that now isn't the best time to be smiling about anything, that while she's sleeping the day away, her little boy remains missing. At least, she *assumes* he hasn't been found. It suddenly occurs to her Josh might very well be a participant of the muffled conversation originating outside the bedroom. The likelihood is significantly low, yes, but not entirely out of the question.

Despite the dull ache in her numb limbs, she pushes herself from the mattress and runs through the house, finding Jasper and her mother sitting at the kitchen table, her hair tightened back in a ponytail, Jasper with a beer, her mother with a cup of coffee. No sign of Josh. She isn't surprised but that doesn't prevent a tidal wave of nausea from swirling around in her stomach. Her mother offers a weak, sad smile as Mary collapses onto an empty chair at the table. Her ass smacks against the wood so hard she's surprised the legs don't immediately snap and drop her to the floor.

Her mother, Agnes, looks like she's been crying since Mary got off the phone with her. Jasper looks like he's tired of talking to people, which is how he always looks, even when he hasn't said a word to anybody all day.

"Oh, baby." Her mother reaches out and curls her hand around Mary's. Her skin is cold and unsettling.

"Hi, Mom."

"How are you doing?"

"Not too good, Mom." Mary stares at the house phone hung up against the wall. "Has the station called?"

Jasper rubs his eyes. "No."

"Any updates at all?"

"No. The only calls we've gotten is that fu—is that *woman* from the PTA."

"Lois?"

He nods, frowning. "She's been hounding me about some fundraiser. I don't know."

It doesn't feel like there's ever a time when Lois *isn't* hounding her about a fundraiser. Mary doesn't regret joining the PTA, but she wishes someone had warned her about Lois first. The lady makes every meeting an absolute nightmare. "Have you called the station to make sure, at least?"

Jasper grits his teeth. "Called to make sure *what*?"

"That there aren't any updates."

"Why would I call about that?"

"Maybe they forgot to let us know something, maybe they lost our number. I don't know."

"I'm sure they'll call when they find something out."

Not for the first time today, Mary wonders why she ever said "I do". She grabs the phone and dials 9-1-1 then stops before making it official. There's no doubt in her mind that this is an emergency, but will the police see it that way? She cancels the call and dials zero for the operator, then requests a connection to the sheriff's office.

A woman who sounds like she's on her tenth coffee of the day answers. "Percy Police Department! Sheryl speaking. How may I help you?"

"I need to talk to Sheriff Keene, please."

"And who may I ask is calling?"

"Mary—Mary Washington."

"One moment." A beat passes. She gets back on the line. "Mrs. Washington? The sheriff is curious about the nature of your phone call."

Mary frowns. "The nature of my phone call? I would hope he already knows."

"Ma'am, I'm just telling you what he said."

"Well, can't I talk to him?"

"He's a very busy man. He's the sheriff, you know."

"Yeah, I know."

"So?" The woman seems annoyed, and she isn't the only one.

"So *what?*"

"What is the nature of your phone call?"

Mary holds the phone away from her ear and opens her mouth wide like she's screaming but does so silently. Neither Jasper nor Agnes seem to notice her distraught state. She returns the phone to her ear. "The goddamn nature of my phone call is my *son is missing*, so if you could *please* transfer me to the sheriff so we can talk directly, I'd be very appreciative."

Another beat. "Hold, please." Waiting music replaces her voice.

Mary's mother gasps at the language she uses, obviously full of questions but mindful enough to wait until the phone conversation comes to an end. Mary raises her pointer finger at her and mouths *oh my god*.

The muzak cuts off and Keene clears his throat. "Uh, yes, Mrs. Washington—"

"Have you found them?"

"Well, no, if we'd found them we would of course notify you immediately—"

"Is there any news at all?"

"Uh, no, not really. Unless you want to hear about Deputy Levin's lunchbox. His wife forgot to wash his last night, so today he brought in his daughter's. *Tinker Bell*, I believe. It's the talk of the whole station."

"Excuse me?"

"I'm joking, Mrs. Washington."

"My son is missing, Sheriff."

"I understand that, and—"

"—and you think humor is appropriate?"

"Now, Mrs. Washington—"

"What are you doing to find my son?"

"I have my best officers on the case."

"What about the officer Ottessa saw?"

"What?"

"Ottessa. She told you what she saw last night. Are you taking any of what she said seriously?"

"Mrs. Washington, I think it's safe to say Miss Jones was not entirely telling the truth about what she witnessed last night."

"And why is that?"

"Well, you saw the video."

"And?"

"And they've committed a very serious crime. It's a no-brainer why we can't find them. They don't want to be found."

"I still don't think you should completely disregard Ottessa's story. She wouldn't lie about something like this."

"Ma'am, no disrespect, but you don't know Miss Jones like I do."

"What does *that* mean?"

The sheriff sighs. She can picture him rubbing his forehead in his office, wishing to be done with this conversation. "It means that Miss Jones isn't exactly famous for being the most upstanding of citizens."

"She wouldn't lie about something like this."

Keene pauses. "Look, ma'am, I'm very busy today. We are considering all possibilities, okay? Now please, let us do our jobs. I'm sure your son is okay. When we find him, we'll give you a call. Until then, try to relax."

Mary wants to scream at him, wants to demand he explain to her just how exactly he expects her to *relax* when her son is gone, possibly abducted, and the people in charge of finding him won't even pretend to take the case seriously. She wants to ask him how he'd treat the situation if the boy in question had been a white kid. She wants to reach through the phone and break his nose. Instead she hangs up and buries her face into her arms and cries. Her mother leans forward and hugs her close and tells her it's going to be okay, tells her everything's going to be just fine.

Jasper stands and gets another beer from the fridge.

EIGHT

"Take off your clothes."

Josh and Alonzo stand in front of the parked car, its headlights blinding them from seeing more than a silhouette of the two cops in the darkness. Except they aren't actual cops, are they? Josh doesn't know who these people are, but he doubts they're real police. And if they are, well, maybe this is what his parents have always warned him about. Maybe this is just what cops do when the sun's down and no cameras are around. He doesn't fucking know. He just wants to go home and pretend tonight never happened. Erase it from his memory. Wipe it from existence.

A tall, ominous cornfield sways in the wind behind them. Leaves brush together and create a noise that makes Josh think of approaching snakes. In front of them, behind the cops and their car, is a large farmhouse. It sits two stories high, maintaining a multitude of darkened windows. Wide sheets of a thick material hang from the gutters and swing wildly with the wind. A porch light has been triggered since their arrival. Josh can't stop staring at it, wondering if anybody's inside the house, and if so, *who?*

Father repeats himself, now with increased anger and emphasis. "Take. Off. Your. Clothes."

Josh realizes he's crying again, or maybe he hasn't stopped since they started driving. Alonzo remains quiet, body trembling. He hasn't said anything since the back seat incident. Josh fears he will never speak again, that somehow Alonzo's mind will retreat deep within and never again reemerge into the light. There's no goddamn way Josh is going to willingly undress for these demented perverts. He's fully prepared to fight if he has to. Sure, he's only twelve, but that doesn't seem to matter in the moment. He's already possibly killed one man tonight. Fuck it. Why not add a couple more to the list?

"Relax," Uncle says, as if reading his mind. "We don't want to fuck you. You need to get over yourselves."

Josh licks his snot-smeared lips and forces the words to spill out of him. "Then why do you want us to...to get naked?"

"Because you both fuckin' smell like shit. Now go on and get to it before you make Father repeat himself a third time. It is not going to be pretty for you all if it has to come to that. Trust me."

Ahead of them, the grass crunches like someone's stepping forward. It's enough of a boost for Josh and Alonzo to quickly shed their clothing. The front of Josh's pants are soaked with piss, anyway. He can't even imagine the relief Alonzo must feel to be rid of his own pants. The cop called Uncle wasn't kidding when he mentioned the stench. The odor of feces is undeniable, especially now with Alonzo's pants kicked to the side. The cold October wind carries the smell directly into Josh's face and he has to fight away the urge to double over and vomit.

Alonzo appears fully aware of how he smells. He lowers his head, limbs limp. Ashamed. "Now what?"

Something metallic creaks in the dark, followed by a loud squeal. A stream of water gushes from one of the cops and sprays both of the boys' shivering bodies. A hose. He's hosing them down. Cleaning away the piss and shit that's come so attached to their flesh. Josh understands this perfectly, but he still can't bring himself to remove his hands from his genitals, nor can he obey the cop when he orders him to bend over. Alonzo, however, does so immediately. No smartass remark or anything. He moves on autopilot, listening to every word the cop tells him. Josh can't fucking believe how quickly reality one-eightied. Just a few hours ago Alonzo had been carrying a bag of stolen cash and fantasizing about running away to Chicago. Now here he is, behind some farmhouse, naked and covered in his own shit and following the orders of some cop. And Josh is right here with him, doing the same.

80

Yesterday Josh had looked up to Alonzo as one of the cool kids. Someone nobody would ever dream of messing with. Now, Alonzo is his equal. He might even be less than equal. Josh feels terrible for thinking like this but he can't just shut off his brain. He can't control which thoughts make it through and which ones don't. They are what they are. Just like what is happening right now is what it is.

But what is that, exactly?

Josh still can't quite figure that out.

The cop tells him to bend over again and this time he obeys and the hose washes away his filth. Father and Uncle step closer, the headlights casting away some of their shadow. Uncle holds out his hand, fist clenching something black and flimsy, like a plastic sheet. Trash bags. The wind attempts to drag them away but Uncle's grip is unbreakable.

"Put these on. Nobody wants to see your itty bitty dicks."

Josh takes the trash bags—heavy duty, made to last—and passes one to Alonzo. Head and arm holes have already been cut into them and they slip on easily enough. Josh pulls the bag down his body and wonders how long the cops have been driving around with these in their trunk, and if there are more personalized bags waiting for future victims.

Victims.

Is that what Josh and Alonzo are? *Victims?* He doesn't know how else to describe the situation they're in if they aren't victims. Victims of what, an abduction? But what comes after an abduction? *What comes next?* Josh's imagination works in overtime obsessing over the infinite possibilities and almost none of them contain a happy ending. It doesn't matter if these guys are real cops or not. They're going to do what they want. The only question is: *what do they want?*

So that's exactly what Josh asks them. "What...what...what do you want?"

And in the darkness, Uncle smiles. "Well, I suppose I want to eat some dinner. Fuckin' starvin', ain't you?" Then he laughs and pats Josh on the shoulder. "Who are we kidding? Of course you are. Look at them titties!" He squeezes Josh's nipple and twists hard enough to send him to the ground.

He kicks him in the ass and laughs harder. "Come on, get up! Y'all still gotta meet the rest of the family."

Josh remains curled up in the grass, replaying the cop's words again in his head. *The rest of the family.* Meaning there are more of them, waiting to do God knows what with Josh and Alonzo. More of them inside the house behind the cops. How many more? Josh can visualize dozens, hundreds of similarly disfigured officers lined up, each taking turns harassing Josh and Alonzo in their own unique methods of torture.

He winces as Uncle prepares to kick him again.

"Come on, fatty! Get up!"

Alonzo cries out in a surprising squeal, then spins around and books it away from the car. By the time Josh looks up, Alonzo's already disappeared into the corn field, leaving the three of them behind in the cop car's headlights.

Uncle lowers his foot, mid-kick, and sighs. "Now, where the fuck does he think he's going?"

Father points into the field. "Go get him."

Uncle hesitates. "Baby will catch him and bring him back. Nothing gets past Baby."

"Go. Get. Him."

Still in the grass, Josh watches Uncle's hands tighten into fists. He considers trying to crawl away while they're distracted with Alonzo, but as soon as the thought crosses his mind Uncle swings his leg out again and kicks Josh in the gut.

"Take good care of this one for me while I'm gone."

Uncle steps over Josh and heads into the corn field, taking his time, almost intentionally trying to agitate Father. Josh still can't get over their names. Obviously they aren't real. Probably things they made up so Josh and Alonzo couldn't snitch their identities if one of them managed to escape. But Josh can certainly believe they're brothers. For one thing, they look almost identical, and another, nobody interacts with each other the way they've been unless they're blood.

Father nudges him with his boot and tells him to get up. Josh doesn't make him repeat himself. He stands and straightens out the black garbage bag, paranoid it isn't covering all the areas on him he wishes to conceal. He strains his ears listening for Alonzo but hears nothing and wonders if that's a good or bad thing. If he was caught, surely he'd be making as much noise as possible. Maybe he'll find help.

But who helps the black kid being chased by police?

Josh looks up at Father as if to ask *now what?* and Father points to the house. He nods and moves forward, the grass wet and prickly beneath his now bare feet. He takes three steps forward, then another five, but the house doesn't seem to get any closer, as if he's walking on a treadmill, moving in stagnation. He glances over his shoulder at Father for confirmation and gasps. Both of the cops are well over six feet tall, much greater in height than either Josh or Alonzo, but looking at Father now, somehow Josh is slightly taller than him. The cop's bulk is the same, but his height has drastically shrunk. Josh backs up and studies the grass, searching for any indiction of a hill or slant he may have walked up, but the ground appears flat.

Father notices Josh's confusion and grunts, then walks past him, the cop's height increasing with each stride forward. Once he's in front of Josh, the cop's returned to his normal posture. Josh glances behind him again, heart beating fast, convinced a secret staircase or slope is hiding somewhere in the grass, but sees nothing. Maybe it's just too dark out. He's sure he'd be able to spot the source of the trick come morning. Come morning? Of course. Why wouldn't he still be here? He's not running away anytime soon and these cops sure as hell don't act like they're planning to drive them back home.

Are they even still in Percy? Josh has no idea. He could be anywhere right now. The drive here had lasted an impossible amount of time. Maybe five minutes, maybe five days. Time's been moving like a thick fog all night. Nothing makes sense. He is lost and fears nobody will notice, that in reality he's still back inside the dugout, comatose, consciousness ripped from his body and dragged to this weird purgatorial farm.

Father grunts again and grabs Josh by the ear and yanks it toward the house. "Go. Up."

Josh stops in front of the porch and cocks his head, doubting his own eyes. Hanging from the gutters are what appear to be strips of raw meat. Insects fly against it, sticking and bouncing off its delectable material. The staircase consists of half a dozen steps, each one slightly wider than the previous, but that isn't the truly breathtaking detail Josh absorbs about the staircase. Standing directly in front of the stairs, the steps no longer lead up as they'd appeared to back by the cop car. The steps now gradually slope downward into the grass yet somehow still seem to end at the top of the porch. The longer he stares at them, the more dizzy he becomes, and he has to close his eyes to prevent further vertigo from poisoning his balance. Father shoves him forward and Josh advances onto the first step, screaming at the fear of tumbling down the rest of them, but regains his composure and rushes over the remaining steps, every sense in his body convinced he's declining into the earth while his eyes tell a different story.

He stops at the top of the porch and looks back down. The staircase appears to be a normal staircase. Nothing weird about it at all. Josh backs away from it, shivering, as Father walks up the steps as if he notices nothing unusual. Josh points at the staircase and stutters nonsense, unable to articulate the confusion and horror inflicted by the staircase.

Father opens the screen door and points for him to go inside. Josh freezes in the doorway, staring at the house's interior. The inside of the structure appears to be sideways, as if a great wind had blown the house over. The walls make up the floor and ceiling and the floor and ceiling make up the walls. Framed photographs on the floor and furniture and light fixtures installed with dimming bulbs hanging from the walls. The doorway is built not on a flat surface but a corner of the interior, where the wall and floor merge. He sticks a head through the opening and studies the living room. Old discolored newspapers and various discarded trash like soggy cardboard boxes and food scrapings litter the floor that is now the wall, and the wall that is now a floor is stained with faded yellow clouds and photos too distant to decipher. The room's aroma reminds Josh of a swamp.

Father grabs him by the neck and pulls him back and slaps him across the face. Hard. If not for Father's grip around his neck, Josh would have immediately crumbled to the porch floorboards. Instead he remains standing, sniffling back tears. Father points into the doorway again.

"Inside."

Josh enters the house, stepping where the wall is now the floor, but his foot misses the wall that is now the floor and instead lands on the floor that is now the wall, only inside the house nothing feels sideways at all, but upright, normal. Maybe not normal, nothing about this night can be considered normal, but definitely more logically structured.

Is this a house or a mirage?

Dream house, nightmare house, devil house.

Josh rubs his face, thinking there's no way he can ever trust his eyes again, thinking it's unlikely he'll ever leave this house that isn't a house—at least not alive, anyway—thinking that he hopes like hell Alonzo managed to get away before Uncle found him, thinking that maybe he feels a bit betrayed that Alonzo just left him alone to deal with the two insane cops by himself, thinking that Josh wouldn't have done the same thing, he would have stayed and helped his friend, and thinking that maybe he would have done exactly what Alonzo had done, he doesn't know and it doesn't matter, none of it matters.

A light down the hallway flicks on and a door creaks open. A small, elderly tanned white man in a tank top and red checkered boxers joins them in the living room. The wooden floor of the hallway creaks loudly with each step. He isn't disfigured like Father and Uncle. If Josh saw him on the street, he wouldn't even look twice. Despite the man's age, his body is fit, more muscular than most people Josh has met.

But he still moves like exhaustion has rotted him away to nothing.

Misery fills the man's eyes as he looks down at Josh, then at Father. "A new one? *Now?*"

Father shakes his head, dragging Josh into the the next room—a kitchen. "Two. Other one ran. Uncle is after him."

The man sighs, running his hand over his balding white hair. "Two in one night." He looks at Josh again then quickly turns away, like the sight of him alone is painful enough. "That's—what? *Four* this month? You're going to draw attention to yourselves."

Father sits at the end of a table positioned in the center of the kitchen and gestures for Josh to join him in an empty chair next to him, then to the old man: "We need to eat. We missed dinner."

"Well, it's very late. I was asleep." The old man glances at his bare wrist, where a watch might be, then sighs. He turns his back on Father and leans over the sink, which is overflowing with dishes so old and dirty mold has begun to grow on them. He stares ahead, over the sink, hands gripping the edge of the basin, at a flattened cardboard box taped against the wall. Maybe a window hides behind it. Josh wonders if the man can see through the cardboard, through the glass on the other side, and if so, what does he find?

Father sighs, visibly impatient. "We need to eat."

The old man lowers his head to the repulsive contents of the sink. Like he's debating whether or not his head would fit in the garbage disposal. His body trembles. He can barely stand. When he speaks, his voice comes off weak and bitter. "And I need to sleep."

"Repeat yourself."

The old man turns, leaning his butt against the sink. "I'm not young anymore. I can't…I can't keep doing these things, not how you expect me to. You understand that, don't you?"

Father pauses, then grunts. Staring at the old man, his expression the same as it's been since he picked up Josh. The cop's face is too scarred and screwed up to move around like a normal person. It's permanent, frozen. "We need to eat."

The old man bites his lip, fighting back a scream. A wetness fills his eyes. He wipes it away with the back of his hand and glances at Josh. Josh jerks his head away, embarrassed to be caught witnessing this man's shame, and stares at the table, at the scratch marks in the wood. Scratch marks like someone trying desperately to hold on to the table. Because of what? Because they were being dragged away? Dragged where? And are they still there? Will they always be there? Will Josh soon join them?

Then it hits him, hard and fast like a bullet to the gut, that the old man might be hesitant to feed this grotesque police officer because of the kind of food the officer craves. It only now occurs to Josh that the cop could be planning to eat him. He doesn't know what a real cannibal looks like but in the movies they're always fucked-up looking. Like in *The Hills Have Eyes*. This guy's just as deformed as those weird desert mutants, and they were cannibals, too. But cannibals don't have to look like monsters. Aside from Leatherface, the family in *The Texas Chain Saw Massacre* appeared relatively normal, and they cooked people up in *chili* for Christ's sake. Anybody could be a cannibal. There's no real way to tell with these things.

Josh looks back at the old man to somehow confirm this new suspicion but the old man has turned away, heading for the refrigerator in the far corner of the kitchen. Josh tenses so tight his skin seems to stretch against bone. Any more stress and his flesh is likely to shoot across the room like a slingshot. Oh, what he wouldn't do for Alonzo's slingshot right about now. Alonzo's is real high quality, with a plastic holster to rest against your wrist and everything. Thing's so powerful it could kill a man. If this cop even is a man. Whatever he is, the slingshot would take him out, he's sure of it. But of course they left it back at Alonzo's house. The last time they took it outside, they spent an entire evening shooting rocks at passing cars. Quite a few windows ended up shattered. It was one of the best days of their lives.

Josh glares at the cop sitting next to him from the corner of his eye and fantasizes projectiling a stone directly into his stupid, repulsive face. One shot and he'd run like he'd never run before. Out of this house that isn't a house, down the street, and he wouldn't stop until he made it back to his own house, which is a house, a very real house, the only place he could truly be safe. Surely they wouldn't follow him there. Surely they'd understand his house is off-limits and retreat back to whatever hell they'd escaped from.

MAX BOOTH III

Goddammit, why didn't they bring the slingshot?

The old man opens the refrigerator and a dim light escapes. Josh manages to catch a glimpse of its interior before the man steps in front of it and blocks his view. Cans of Coke and numerous Tupperware containers rest on the two shelves. The lightbulb at the back of the fridge seemed to project a green hue, as if covered with sludge or mildew. The man takes out one of the Tupperware containers and sets it on the kitchen island, next to a pile of dirty plates, grunting and kicking the fridge door shut behind him.

Josh squints, trying to determine what's inside the container, but all he can make out is some kind of brownish substance. The man pops off the Tupperware lid and flinches away, grimacing. It takes a couple seconds for the smell to travel across the kitchen, but when it finally hits Josh he has to hold his breath to prevent vomiting, and even then a few specks of regurgitation manage to break through and splash around the inside of his mouth. He's left with the choice of forcing it back down his throat or swigging it around and spitting it out like mouthwash. And, while the kitchen is quite possibly the dirtiest room Josh has ever seen, he still fears how Father might react to him adding to the mess.

He swallows it.

The taste of his vomit is nothing compared to the smell of the brown substance on the kitchen island. Within the span of thirty seconds the odor has consumed the entire room. He gags and rubs his temple, overwhelmed with vertigo.

The old man flips theTupperware over and spills its contents onto one of the nearby plates. No one seems to care that the plate was already covered in old food crust. The brown substance makes a loud *splat* sound as it flops onto the glass. The old man doesn't seem affected by the smell. Like he's used to it. Like this is the only smell he's ever known. Or maybe he no longer even has a sense of smell. The house has effectively destroyed his soul, and now he feels nothing. He tosses the empty Tupperware container over his back and places the plate in the microwave above the stove and brings the machine to life with the press of a button. The brown substance crackles as it surrenders to radiation.

TOUCH THE NIGHT

Father sits perfectly still as the food cooks. The old man stands in front of the microwave watching the plate rotate on the saucer. Josh looks back and forth to each of them, wondering if they've forgotten he's even here, wondering what his chances of escape would be if he just stood and made a run for it. The thought of running a great distance is enough to send him into a panic, but he can't see any other way out of this. There's no way in hell he's going to fight and survive. He's barely managed going at it with guys his own age. But this cop? Josh would be killed instantly. There wouldn't even be a fight. He'd just grab Josh's head and give it one little squeeze and completely crush his skull. Squish his brain like it was a jello mold. Slurp the juices from his corpse and package up his innards in spare Tupperware containers.

Just as Josh has built up enough courage to rise from his seat and attempt an escape, the microwave shrieks its death song and his body freezes once more. Bravado deflates like a pricked balloon.

The old man pops the microwave open and takes out the plate and shambles across the kitchen and drops it on the table between Josh and the deformed cop. Brown gravy bounces off the plate and splatters on the wood. The substance appears to be a chunk of…something. Meat, maybe. Josh can't tell. It looks a bit like an egg foo yung dish he once witnessed a relative eat at a Chinese restaurant. Up close, the smell hits him harder and he has to turn away as he succumbs to his gag reflex.

Father makes a sudden guttural sound, almost like a laugh, a laugh directed at Josh's inability to handle a mere smell. Shame grasps him and the sensation weirdly reminds him of the various times he's disappointed his own dad. At his lack of enthusiasm with athleticism. At his failure to eat a proper diet. At his reluctance to make new friends, to at least try. Why is he thinking about his dad now? He has nothing to do with this. He doubts they'll ever even see each other again. Take one look at those claw marks on the kitchen table and that's all anybody needs to know. Once you're inside this house that isn't a house, there's no leaving. You're here to stay. Josh isn't sure he'll miss his dad, and he doubts his dad will even notice his absence. If anything, his disappearance will be a relief.

The cop reaches across the table and grabs a chunk of the brown substance from the plate and lifts it into his mouth, sauce dripping down his hand and chin as he takes a huge bite. His teeth aren't even teeth, not proper teeth anyway. They're crooked and spaced oddly and pointed like they've purposely been sharpened with a tool. *Vampire*, is the first word that comes to Josh's mind. *Fangs*. His chewing is loud and wet and further upsets Josh's stomach just from listening to it. Father points at the plate with his other hand, then at Josh.

"You. Eat."

Josh shakes his head no.

"You. *Eat*."

"No thank you."

The cop leans forward, staring Josh down with his lifeless eyes. "Either you eat, or"—he cocks his greasy thumb back at himself—"we eat"—he points at Josh—"you."

Cannibals! He fucking knew it.

He inspects the plate and smells it again and gags and he doesn't know if he can do it, doesn't know whether he prefers to taste this toxic waste or get eaten alive by some evil cop. The choice is too difficult. The choice is impossible.

Josh looks up at the old man, who's standing across the kitchen watching the both of them at the table. "What...what is it?"

The old man shrugs. "Nothin' you're gonna enjoy."

"Puh-please..."

"Ain't up to me, kid."

Something slimy wraps around his arm and it takes him a beat to realize it's Father's hand grabbing him. He lifts Josh's arm up and thrusts it toward the plate, squeezing tight enough to make him scream.

"Eat. It is good."

The old man sighs and shakes his head, tired. "I'm not fucking doing this tonight. I'm going back to bed."

Without loosening his grip on Josh's arm, Father turns to the old man. "Richard."

He stops halfway across the kitchen. "What?"

"Soon."

The old man—Richard—slumps his shoulders, avoiding eye contact. "Yeah. I know."

He continues out of the kitchen and back down the hall, the wooden creaking of his steps steadily declining in volume until vanishing, as if he'd never existed in the first place, leaving just Father and Josh alone at the kitchen table, Father's large hand squeezing Josh's arm hard enough to make him dizzy, hard enough that Josh is convinced he's going to rip it clean from his socket, fully believing this cop is strong enough and willing to do it at a moment's notice, that although he doesn't even need a reason you'd be a goddamn fool to give him one.

The cop tells Josh to eat.

So he eats.

NINE

lonzo is a coward.

He knows he is but that doesn't stop him, doesn't even slow him down. If anything, it makes him run faster. Josh is his friend, his *best* friend, and Alonzo just ditched him back there like he was nobody. Abandoned him with those two...what? Cops? Nah. Ain't no fuckin' way those two guys are cops. Cops are as untrustworthy and repulsive as they come, sure, no doubt about it, but this feels like something different. This feels more...*sinister*. The way they talked and acted, they weren't no police.

They're something much worse.

Alonzo doesn't want to find out what's worse than the police, not if he can help it.

He's not going to turn back—not going to slow down. He's going to run and keep on running until he's far away from this festival of deranged rednecks. Someone will find him. A boy his age couldn't just run around screaming forever without somebody eventually noticing. What happens after that depends solely on the person who happens to spot him. Indiana's full of shotgun-wielding racists eager to play vigilante. Alonzo's liable to escape the frying pan and leap right into the fire, if he isn't too careful.

But first up on the list of shit to accomplish is finding his way out of this cornfield. This *dead* cornfield. Nothing is green like how he imagines a cornfield should be. Everything is yellow and dry. Everything is dead. Expired stalks crunch loudly beneath his feet as he burrows through this seemingly endless field. The garbage bag he's wearing weighs him down, makes it difficult to run at full speed. It compresses against his flesh and suffocates him.

He considers stopping and taking it off but fears the moment he ceases movement someone will tackle him to the ground. Surely one of those ugly fucks are chasing him. No one goes through the trouble of kidnapping somebody only to let them run away without at least trying to stop them. Even Alonzo can see that, and he's never abducted anybody in his life. What a waste of time this must feel like for them. He'd be fucking pissed, if the tables were turned.

But how long can he possibly run without slowing down? How much farther can he go before stopping to catch his breath? And what will happen the moment he does? What will he see as soon as he looks over his shoulder? *Who* will he see?

He remembers the back of the cop car. Thinks of what he was forced to do. Thinks about the fear that'd consumed his body, the total surrender.

There's no goddamn way he's going back. He'd rather die. Whatever those fucks have planned is worse than death and he wants no part of it.

Poor Josh…

No. He hasn't given up on Josh. He hasn't abandoned him. Once he finds help, he'll direct a rescue party back to the farm. Josh is going to be okay. He has to be. Josh is his friend. Come to think about it, Josh might be the only real friend Alonzo has. Sure, he hangs out with other kids from time to time, but are they really his friends? In the past year, how many people have even slept over at his house, or vice versa? Not only can he count the number on one hand, he can count it on one finger.

Josh has always been there for him. Even when Alonzo was in one of his moods and acting especially assholish, Josh never once told him to get bent or anything of the sort. He stuck by him through thick and thin, because that's what friends are supposed to do. That's what makes a friend a friend.

And what does Alonzo do to his "friend" the first chance he gets? He ditches him. Leaves him to fend for himself with those two insane inbred fucks. There's no way Josh would have done the same. He would have stayed and fought, even if it most likely meant certain death. Josh wouldn't have been such a pussy. Such a goddamn *coward*.

Alonzo will find help. That's his silent pledge to Josh. He'll round up all of Percy if that's what it takes. Light up some pitchforks, stock up on extra ammo, slaughter every sick motherfucker unlucky enough to still be on this farm by the time he returns. Rescue Josh, still safe and unharmed, maybe even offer him a little smile and say, "What, did you honestly think I was just gonna leave you?"

He has to save him. He has to make things right. How else will he ever live with himself?

So Alonzo runs, and he doesn't stop, not even when his chest starts to overheat and he fears it'll explode if he pushes it a second longer, not even when the five-thousandth dead corn stalk slaps him across the face and draws blood. He's a boy—no, fuck that, he's a *man*—on a mission. He's going to escape this cornfield. He's going to save Josh. Everything is going to be okay. It has to be. He'll make sure of it.

Except Alonzo *does* stop.

And not by choice.

Something grabs his foot in mid-stride. A root in the dirt, maybe, if cornfields even have roots, how the fuck is he supposed to know? Like there's enough light out here to see anything. One second he's running with great determination, and the next gravity's dragging him with a violent, savage force to the ground.

His vision tumbles from darkness to an even deeper darkness. He face-plants into a rough patch of soil. Dirt mixes into his eyes and half-blinds him. Everything burns. His heart continues beating at the same frantic pace as it'd been going at a few moments ago, as if it's being dragged by inertia.

Inertia.

Alonzo loves that word. Even now, vision stinging, face bleeding, he can't help swishing it around his brain like how rich people test fancy wines in movies. Nobody thinks he pays attention in school. Of course he does. It's all just so fucking boring, so what's the point? Learning fancy science words like "inertia" or solving complicated word problems in math don't mean shit when you're in the middle of some scary cornfield with a bunch of lunatics on your tail.

Alonzo remains motionless in the dirt, considering not even standing back up. Exhaustion hits him with a sudden, consuming bite, and the only thing that sounds remotely appealing right about now is a deep, long nap. If someone *is* chasing him, then surely they are only mere seconds away from catching up. A second can only be stretched so far. Eventually it expires. Its demise is inevitable. Then where does that leave him?

Fucked, that's where.

It leaves him fucked.

Get up, goddamn you, get up!

He digs both hands into the soil and pushes himself from the ground. Vertigo swirls his balance and it's a struggle not to collapse straight back down. He grunts and pushes harder, screaming silently at himself, knowing all it'll take is one particularly loud sound to give his location away. Fortunately the October winds invading the dead cornfield provide a slight cover.

Alonzo reaches up for something—*anything*—to grab onto as balance support, searching blindly in the darkness, and finds a rough wooden pole sticking out of the ground. He gives it a little push to test its stability. When it doesn't immediately cave in from rot, he grasps it with both hands and pulls himself up to his knees. He looks up toward the starry sky, eyes stinging from dirt and sweat and blood.

The pole in his hands extends past the corn stalks by a good foot or two, and another pole of about half its length is tied by rope to hang horizontally across the first pole. It's the shape of a cross, but what is a cross doing out here in the middle of some redneck's cornfield?

Then it clicks, what this really is.

He climbs up to his feet then steps back from the two poles, properly inspecting its entire width and length with as much light as the stars and moon above will allow. For a small, itty bitty moment, he's forgotten about the abductors potentially chasing after him. He recognizes this kind of cross. He's seen them in countless horror movies, yes, but also other genres, basically anything featuring a farm with a large field of crops.

Except this cross that he looks at now seems to be missing something all those other things always include.

The scarecrow.

It's missing the scarecrow.

Weird, but not really too surprising. What would a scarecrow protect out here, anyway? None of this crop appears even somewhat salvageable. He starts thinking about what else a scarecrow might be equipped to protect, or what if its purpose goes beyond protection, and why would someone have one of these crosses out here without the actual scarecrow to accompany it? Religious reasons, maybe. It makes sense. It seems like God freaks are always snatching up little kids and trying to brainwash them, at least in the kinds of movies him and Josh usually rent from Hollywood Video. He doesn't understand why he's so drawn to this thing, why he can't just move past it and keep running. The longer he stays in one spot, the less likely he'll ever escape from here. There's something about it, something that goes beyond a missing scarecrow, that he can't quite place. The more time he spends staring at it, the more he feels like it's a trap, like its emptiness is an intentional trick to distract intruders.

But to distract from what?

Something crunches behind him, a corn stalk snapping under the foot of a stranger, of an unwelcome presence. All confusion and curiosity about the cross vanishes as Alonzo's heart freezes in his chest. Someone or some*thing* is behind him, and it doesn't matter whether or not he turns around and acknowledges this fact, it won't make it any less real.

Another crunch.

Followed by a third, a fourth, a fifth.

A sixth.

Coming. Faster.

Alonzo's left with two choices: run, or turn around and fight.

Or, of course, he can just stand here and not move and wait for whatever's about to happen to actually happen. Succumb to full cowardice. Embrace the kingdom of helpless crybabies.

No. Fuck that.

That's not who Alonzo is. Maybe the other fools at school would freeze up like some pussy statue but Alonzo ain't like those other kids.

Alonzo is a fighter.

His momma didn't raise no quitter.

Fists clenched, he spins around, ready to brawl with whoever the fuck is dumb enough to cross his path.

And he screams.

He stumbles back and trips and falls on his ass.

The thing in front of him moves forward, slowly, each step small and mindful of the next. If it had a mouth, Alonzo is positive it would be smiling right now.

But instead it just stares at him.

Eyes black and round like buttons.

Alonzo tries to scream again but he's forgotten how.

TEN

*L*ight does not exist in the basement.

If it has windows, they've long been boarded up. As far as Josh can tell, there's only one way out, which is how he'd entered: from the door at the top of the stairs. The door leads to a hallway on the first floor, below another staircase that rises to the house's second story. After finishing the most disgusting meal of his life, Father had forced the old, stained straitjacket over his garbage bag suit then dragged him through the kitchen and down the hall. The louder Josh cried, the harder Father squeezed. He unlocked the door below the second-floor steps with a ring of keys produced from his belt loop and before Josh could contemplate what was happening, Father pushed him into the darkness. At first, all he felt was air, then the sudden hardness of wood as he smacked against the basement stairs and tumbled to the bottom.

The experience felt both infinite and stillborn.

A part of him is convinced he's still falling, that this house is bottomless and he'll never land, he'll never age, he'll remain in this state forever, always.

And while that might be true in a more distant section of his mind, he nonetheless finds himself sprawled across a hard cement floor. His body aches like he's been run down by a car. Thanks to the straitjacket, he can't move his arms, can't do much of anything. A warm liquid flows down his cheeks and he can't decide if it's tears or blood or both. His right ankle throbs and swells as he remains motionless, too afraid to sit up, too afraid that he won't be able to even if he tries.

The basement smells like death.

A voice in the dark—a man—says, "That's the worst fall I've seen yet."

Josh gasps and wiggles on the floor, trying to determine which direction it'd come from.

This is followed by another voice, also male: "The fat ones always come down the hardest."

Both voices originate—he thinks—from the right side of the basement, so he scoots to the left, immediately distrusting their amused tones. The men laugh at his fear. Giggling together like they're watching some sitcom. Can they see him in the darkness? He goes rigid, afraid movement will surrender his location. Are they human, or are they like the cops upstairs?

The first voice stops laughing. "Hey, we're not the ones you ought to be afraid of."

The second voice finishes his thought. "You already met the real enemy. You can consider us comrades. How old are you, anyway?"

"He did seem young, didn't he?"

"Just a wee little lad. Well, maybe not so *little*..."

"I'm surprised he didn't break the stairs."

"Can you imagine if he had? I'd like to see the family try getting to us then."

"I'm sure they'd just use a ladder."

Josh pushes the heels of his feet against the floor and continues scooting farther from the voices.

"Hey, where are you going?"

"Come back here, kid. You're gonna give yourself a heart attack."

"Watch out for the bear traps."

Josh stops, not because of what the man said, but because he realizes he has no idea where he's going. If he isn't careful, he could very well smash his skull into a cement wall. He gives up on the idea of seeing and closes his eyes, concentrating on sound alone to guide him.

This is what he hears:

His own heart pounding, begging to be released.

Heavy breathing, both from himself and others. How many, he can't ascertain.

Water dripping.

Insects feasting.

A woman whispering, "Don't listen to them."

So close he can feel her breath on his face. So close he can taste it.

And it tastes old and rotten.

He screams and tries to stand but only manages to roll on his stomach, the straitjacket keeping him pinned to the floor. A hand grabs his shoulder and pushes him down. The woman shushes him.

"Calm down. You're going to hurt yourself."

In contrast to her breath, the woman's voice is sweet. Soothing. Almost motherly.

He stops thrashing and allows her to slowly caress his cheek.

"Hush now, child, it's going to be okay."

The woman's fingers are skeleton-thin and chilled as they caress his cheek. He embraces her like she's his mother, like he's only woken from a bad dream and he's back in his own bedroom where everything is safe, where everything is okay. He wants to sob against her bosom and beg her to promise him the disfigured nightmare cops are not real, that this basement does not actually exist, that he'd never gone over to Alonzo's tonight.

But this woman is not his mother.

Her touch offers no warmth. Only coldness.

Somewhere in the darkness, the two men giggle.

"She's gonna eat you, kid."

"Rip the fat from your bones."

"Gonna be eating you for days."

"Weeks."

"Months."

"Years."

"Forever."

"And ever."

The woman hugs him tighter and whispers in his ear. "Don't you pay them any mind, child. They're only trying to put a scare in you."

Her breath smells like roadkill. Josh imagines maggots spilling from her mouth when she talks. The darkness fails to convince him otherwise.

He tries to wiggle away but the woman's grip is concrete. Fear multiplies and anxiety screams for him to flee before it's too late, but it's already too late, it's been too late the moment they slipped through Alonzo's bedroom window, and to think differently is to live in delusion.

"Stop fighting." Her tone is stern, cold. "*Traps.* Everywhere. They're trying to send you into a panic, so you run blindly and trigger one. They've gotten others to do it. It's a game for them."

"Don't listen to that old crazy bitch!" one of the men shouts.

"If you don't want your fat ass eaten, you better come over here where it's safe!" the other says.

Saliva drips in Josh's ears as she leans closer. It's warm and thick, like hot liquid glue. "Bear traps, do you understand? One wrong step and you're never getting out of here."

One of the men explodes into laughter. "Shit, *none of us* are ever getting out of here, regardless of where we step. This ain't a place for hope, boy. This is a place for death."

Upstairs, metal clings together and chains rattle.

A series of locks unhinging their jaws.

The woman's grip loosens and Josh manages to break away from her embrace. He lands on his stomach, face smacking against the cement, and wiggles like a desperate worm. The woman doesn't try to grab at him. The sound has rendered him forgotten. Not like he's going anywhere, anyway, not with this straitjacket trying its damnedest to suffocate him. He stops moving when the door at the top of the stairs creaks open and presses his cheek against the cement floor, squinting at the block of light from the hallway slicing through the darkness.

Every sound in the basement dies at once.

The anticipation for what's about to come through the door is so heavy Josh can almost feel it pressing against his back, crushing his bones, splitting his flesh. He makes the conscious decision to hold his breath then realizes he already is, realizes he can't remember the last time he wasn't. He continues not breathing, not blinking, thinking *jesus christ oh jesus christ mom mom MOM PLEASE MOM PLEASE WHAT IS HAPPENING MOM MOM MOM* as a shadow appears at the top of the stairs, in the doorway.

Father.

He's holding something large over his shoulders. A body. *Alonzo's* body. Limp, unwilling to put up a fight. Almost like he's asleep.

The cop drops Alonzo on the top step and Alonzo tumbles down. The hallway light doesn't quite reach the bottom of the basement, so by the time he reaches the end of the stairs the darkness has already swallowed him. The floor vibrates slightly at the impact, then all is still, all eyes directed at the cop standing in the doorway. If he's looking at anybody in particular, there's no way to tell. The cop's body is filmed over with an abysmal silhouette. But his breathing, the heavy rasps of his drowning lungs, this cannot be disguised. If anything, it seems to echo down in this basement, bouncing against the walls like a demented game of pinball.

The door bangs shut, and the locks and chains rattle together as they're slammed back into place. Josh listens to his footsteps creak down the hallway, away from the basement, where exactly he cannot possibly know, does not ever want to find out.

He waits another couple minutes before conjuring enough courage to wiggle farther across the basement floor. By now, the two men across the room have resumed their harassment, but Josh blocks them out, doesn't even pay them any attention. Somewhere behind him, the woman whispers that it isn't safe, begs him to return to her, promises to protect him. He ignores her, too. Focuses his energy on the body Father dropped down the stairs, determined to reach him before he awakes and panics like Josh had panicked, all alone save for the strange voices fluttering around like bats in the dark.

Josh moves like a worm, blind and determined. Every push forward greets him with less confidence that he's chosen the correct direction—or, worse, that he's overshot where Alonzo landed, that somehow he's gotten closer to the two men than he ever intended.

The top of his skull collides with something cold and metal and he freezes, then slowly sways his head back and forth, attempting to make out the shape of the object before him. It seems to curve into a circle, although it's too wide for him to feel its complete structure. The shapes aren't sharp, but they aren't dull, either.

Bear traps, the woman had said. *One wrong step and you're never getting out of here.*

Josh bites his tongue and scooches back as quickly as his overloaded heart will allow. Exhaustion forces him to stop. He rests his face against the floor, creating a puddle of sweat beneath him. People take their arms for granted until they're confined within a straitjacket. The more he tries to move his arms and the longer he fails, the crazier he becomes. Panic blossoms in the season of fear. There is nowhere he can go. There is nothing he can do.

Somewhere in the darkness, his friend stirs awake.

ELEVEN

O ttessa sits on the couch looking at her phone for a good half hour before she concludes that there is nobody to call. Nobody would give a shit that Zoey's missing. They might offer some fake empathy, but nothing genuine. Ottessa doesn't have any friends, not really. A few girlfriends who like to gossip from time to time, but their relationships firmly end at shit-talking. None of them would ever give her a ride, if she needed one, and none of them sure as hell would give a damn about her son's situation. They might pump her of all the details so they can get off and immediately call someone else to spill the beans, but that's about it. She can almost hear the conversations they'd have with one another.

Did you hear what happened with 'Tesa's kid?

Always knew that boy was a thug.

Didn't I tell you he was no good?

Well, what do you expect, with a mother like that, spreading her legs all over town.

She starts fuming just thinking about it, this imaginary conversation between two women, gets so worked up that she debates calling one of them up and screaming, demanding to know where they got the nerve to judge her in this time of crisis. But that would be crazy, of course. Even she can understand that. But that doesn't mean she still doesn't want to do it. Call it cathartic, maybe.

No existing family would be bothered to drive down here, either. She burned enough bridges during Zoey's infancy to make damn sure of that. Her parents haven't been in contact in years. At this point, Ottessa isn't even

105

sure if they're still alive. Would anybody have called to let her know? She'd like to think so, but when she concentrates, no name comes to mind. Do they still talk about her? Do they wonder what ever came of their one and only grandchild?

Would they cry the way she's cried? The way she's crying now, the way she fears she will be crying for the rest of her life?

Fuck it.

She drops the phone on the coffee table and stomps outside, determined to be productive, determined to *fix this*. The cops ain't gonna do shit, that much is clear. Is it surprising? No, not in the least. Maybe if some white girl with blonde hair and blue eyes got herself abducted, she'd see some real progress. They'd make national goddamn news. You wouldn't be able to look at a newspaper without seeing her child's face, accompanied with the caption "HAVE YOU SEEN ME?".

But that isn't reality. At least not for Ottessa, not for Zoey. Not for Mary and her boy.

They gotta do this shit themselves, or nothing's ever gonna get done.

Nobody's gonna get found.

No. She's not going to let that happen, refuses to even entertain the possibility.

She will find them.

She will protect them.

She.

Will.

Fix.

This.

OTTESSA BANGS HER FIST AGAINST the door of the house across the street. Nobody answers, so she punches it harder, faster. This is the fourth house on the street she's tried. The first two never bothered to show themselves.

The last one, the guy with the pickup who lives next door, was useless, and only seemed to entertain her questions long enough to get a good look at her tits.

But this house, the one across from hers, she isn't giving up on. The car's in the driveway. The curtains are spread wide open. TV noises broadcast from inside. Someone is home, even if they don't want to admit it. She doesn't stop knocking until the door swings open. Some old fat bitch in a blue bathrobe glares down at her, nostrils flaring. Ottessa has never seen her in anything other than the bathrobe. It's stained with an assortment of unidentifiable substances. Splotches of brown, orange, white. Most days either she's inside or she's sitting on the front porch with her two thousand terrible grandkids, chain-smoking and talking loudly on the telephone.

"What."

"I got some questions for you." Ottessa has been her neighbor for years, but they've never spoken, unless annoyed stares directed from either side of the street count as conversation.

"*Wheel's* on."

"It's important."

The woman considers, grabs the door as if to slam it in her face, then hesitates. "What kind of questions?"

"My boy. He's been taken."

"Taken?"

Ottessa nods *uh-huh*.

She sighs, then waves her inside. "Out your damn mind if you think I'm missing *Wheel*, though."

Ottessa follows her through the house. Toys and discarded scraps of children's clothing litter the hallway. Framed photographs hang crookedly along the walls, white boys and even whiter girls smiling at the camera, nothing professional, all DIY shots taken at parks or outside the woman's house. The living room is a mess, as expected. One recliner, a sofa, and a love seat. Every possible cushion splotched with stains from origins Ottessa couldn't possibly speculate. She's afraid of what the bottom sides might look like if she flipped them over. The rest of the living room houses an unbelievable amount of toys. Trucks, Legos, dolls, action figures. They spread across the floor like a morgue without any vacancies. Not a child in sight, which is a surprise, given it's a Saturday afternoon. Usually her little monsters are running all over the goddamn neighborhood on the weekends.

The woman plops down on the recliner and it whips back so fast Ottessa expects it to snap and drop her to the floor, but the furniture manages to hold her weight and sling her up again into a steady rocking motion. She scoops up a bowl of Cheetos from a side table and tosses a handful in her mouth then digs a long silver remote out from under her massive ass and increases the volume on the TV just in time for the current round of commercials to come to an end and *Wheel of Fortune* to resume. The woman makes no attempt to offer her a seat. Hell, she hasn't even acknowledged Ottessa since the front door, as if she's somehow already forgotten she has company.

The woman scrunches her face, irritated, and waves Ottessa away. "You make a mighty fine window. Anybody ever tell you that?"

Ottessa looks down at where she's standing, then studies the path from the recliner to the TV. She's nowhere near in front of it. Still, she sits on the couch and folds one leg over the other, waiting for the woman to be considerate enough to turn the volume back down. They watch the gameshow in a surreal silence.

The subject is FUN & GAMES and it is two words long, first word eight letters, the second only five.

Ottessa points at the TV, excited. "Identity fraud."

The woman finally turns to her. "What?"

"The answer, it's *identity fraud*."

Without breaking her lava-temperatured glare from Ottessa, the woman points the remote at the TV and slams her thumb against the power button. The screen succumbs to the void. Static fizzes like carbonated soda.

The woman smacks her lips together. "Well, thanks for ruining my show."

She drops the remote in her lap and leans back in the recliner. She waves at Ottessa and rolls her eyes.

"Go on, then. Ask your *questions*."

Fuck her, Ottessa thinks. The whole point of watching these game shows is to guess the answers before they're revealed. Dumb bitch doesn't know anything.

She clears her throat, washing away her initial nastiness. "Last night, my son and his friend were abducted by the police in front of my house. In front of yours."

The woman nods, annoyed. "Uh huh. I saw the lights."

Ottessa's grip tightens around her knees. "You were awake?"

"Can't get more than a few hours in these days. I got…what do you call it—*sleep apnea*. Can't afford the machine, though, so I just stay up most nights. Watch my shows, drink pop." She cocks her thumb at a tall cup of black liquid on the side table next to the recliner. A small puddle of condensation surrounds the bottom of the glass.

"This morning, I went down to the police station to pick up my boy. The station says they don't have him. His friend, either. No record of them ever showing up."

"Hmm."

"Trying to say they ran away, that there wasn't no police to begin with. Saying I made them up."

The woman scratches her hair and a sheet of dandruff collapses onto her robe. "Why would you lie about something like that?"

Ottessa sighs. "They got the boys on tape, causing trouble at the gas station down the street. They think I'm covering for them so they can, hell, I don't know, make their escape or something. But it's bullshit. I saw them last night. They was two cops, both big as hell. Caught the boys right out front here." Ottessa nods out the window. "Threw them both in the back seat and drove off."

"And you told them that, back at the station?"

Ottessa nods.

"But they don't believe you, huh?"

"Nope."

"You think your skin's got somethin' to do with it?"

She shrugs. "You think it don't?"

"No, no." She balances the bowl of Cheetos in her lap and grabs the glass of old pop from the side table. Condensation drips from the bottom edges as she brings it to her mouth, creating a darkened trail of circles down her robe. "You was white, I'm sure your word might have mattered more. Keene still running things?"

Ottessa grimaces at his name.

The woman notices her disgust and smiles. "Yeah, Keene seems to have that effect on folks. Even whites."

"You know him?"

"My husband worked with him, back in the day."

"Your husband was a cop?"

The woman nods, rocking in her recliner. "Near thirty years, 'til his heart gave out. 'Course, Keene's daddy was in charge back then. Even uglier than his son, if you can believe it. Dumb sumbitch got himself drunk one night and crashed into a tree. Harry near quit the next day, when Keene was put in charge, said Keene wasn't fit to lead squat, told him that right to his face. Harry was never fired, but he might as well had been, the way folks at the station treated him after that."

Ottessa folds her hands over her lap and doesn't say anything, doesn't know how to respond. The woman doesn't sound angry or sad. More resigned, surrendered, if anything. Like it's a fact she can't change, a simple truth, like it or not. Ottessa turns to the blacked-out television screen and stares at their distorted reflection, convinced the woman's husband will be sitting next to them, a ghost or hallucination, it don't matter, but there's only the two of them, no more, no less. She turns away from the screen, quickly, afraid the screen might show her something different, something no one who values their sanity ought to ever be subjected to.

"If you told Keene you also saw the cops last night, maybe—"

The woman laughs and holds up her hand, palm out, the bowl of Cheetos nearly tumbling to the carpet. "Honey, Keene ain't the kinda man who changes his mind. And those who tell him differently? Watch out. His temper is unlike anything I've ever seen. Harry told me, back when Keene was still just on patrol, that he saw him break a kid's jaw, all because the kid smarted off to him. *Broke his jaw.* That ain't no exaggeration. Kid had to wear a cage on his face. If Keene says your boy run off, then that's what happened, and there ain't no changing it, even if you find him yourself."

"There has to be something I can do. This ain't right. Zoey—"

"Police have been crooked since they was invented, and they always will be. There's no changing it. By God, even Harry—bless his heart—wasn't always...*by the book.* Small towns like Percy, we might as well be our own countries, the sheriffs our kings. Like it or not, that's the way it is. Move to a big city if you can afford it, and if not, learn how to deal."

Ottessa springs up, standing over the woman, hands balled into fists, wanting desperately to start punching. "Learn how to deal? My boy has been taken. What kind of fucking advice is that? *Learn how to deal.* Are you fucking for real?"

The woman remains calm, unfazed by Ottessa's outrage. "If Keene's lying about your boy, then odds are somebody at the station fucked up, maybe got a little too rough with him, ended up killing him. If that was they intent, or if it was an accident, we'll never know. But I see no other reason Keene or anybody else would cover this up."

"Zoey is alive."

"Maybe." She nods, slowly, thinking. "But probably not."

"Fuck you."

"Don't be stupid. You know what happened just as much as anybody."

Ottessa slaps her across the face. The woman jerks to the side, the Cheetos and pop spilling in her lap. She cries out and holds her reddening cheek, staring at Ottessa through cracked fingers.

"You fucking bitch."

"My boy ain't dead."

"Leave, goddamn you. *Now.* Get the *fuck* out of my house."

This time, when Ottessa says it, her voice comes off weak, unconvinced. "My boy ain't dead."

Ottessa turns and stomps through the living room, hoping her weight knocks a picture frame or two off the wall. Hand around the door knob, the woman shouts for her to stop. Ottessa glances over her shoulder as the woman hurries down the hall toward her. Ottessa tenses, anticipating a fight, but the woman stops after a couple feet, out of breath.

"I'm not apologizing for hitting you, if that's what you expect."

The woman shakes her head. "Maybe I deserved it, but that still don't mean you ain't a fuckin' bitch."

"Can't argue with that."

"I was just thinking. The car."

"What car?"

"From last night."

"The cop car?"

She nods, excited. "Didn't you think it was odd?"

"Think *what* was odd?"

"The *car*. Did that look like a normal cop car to you?"

She tries to think back through a memory fogged by alcohol. "It was hard to make out."

"It was old school. Like what they used to drive when Harry first got on the force. Something from the seventies, or eighties. What the hell kinda police drive something like that nowadays?"

Ottessa waits for an answer, then shrugs. "I don't know. Who?"

The woman holds out her hands. They're empty. "No police I know."

TWELVE

"**I** don't understand why you have to go to the library right now." Mary's mother follows her through the house as Mary searches for the car keys. She sounds annoyed, inconvenienced somehow.

Mary sighs without looking over her shoulder. The keys glint on the kitchen island next to the fridge, where Jasper had dropped them probably while searching for a beer. "Because we don't have a printer."

"But why do you have to use a printer?"

Mary grabs the keys and spins around. Agnes stands across the kitchen, arms folded across her chest, perplexed. She wants Mary to spend the rest of the day with her broadcasting prayers to the Lord. Mary doesn't have the heart to tell her mother that praying isn't going to help Josh. They need to *act*. The longer they sit around doing nothing, the farther away her son gets.

"Because, Mom, I have to print signs. I told you this. Signs with Josh's photo on them."

Her mother uncrosses her arms and waves a hand, as if Mary's the confused one. "But *why* do you have to do it? Why can't you just let the police handle the situation?"

Mary shakes her head and maneuvers around her mother, grabbing her jacket from the kitchen table and throwing it on, dragging the long strap of her purse over her shoulder. "The police aren't going to help. Not the way we need them to."

Jasper looks up from the couch, although remains seated. The TV blasts at full volume. "Where are you going?"

Her mother answers for her: "She's printing stuff. *At the library.*"

Jasper squints. "Printing stuff like *what?*"

Mary considers not even bothering to respond, just walking out on the both of them. "There's some photos of Josh in my email. I'm going to make copies, post them around town."

Her husband makes a face like she's just told him a joke. "What good is that gonna do?"

She shuffles her feet, hating herself for feeling embarrassed. "To raise awareness."

"Awareness of what? That our son makes shitty decisions and is going to jail? You go right ahead and do that then, I guess. Tell the whole fuckin' world that we raised ourselves a little thug, if that's what you want to do. I don't care."

"I wasn't asking you."

"What?"

The heat builds up in her cheeks so fast there's no preventing the ensuing eruption. "*I wasn't fucking asking you!*"

She storms out the front door before Jasper can even understand what just happened.

ACCORDING TO THE STICKERED TEXT positioned on the front entrance, the library closes at 5:30PM on Saturdays, which gives Mary a little under an hour to complete what she's come here to do. She shows her library card to the person working the counter, a teenager cursed with more acne than skin, and he guides her to a desktop at the end of the computer room. He tells her how to log in, informs her that viewing pornography on public library property is strictly forbidden, then winks and reminds her of the building's closing time. "Have fun," he says, before leaving her alone and returning to the help desk.

The woman sitting next to Mary watches the librarian walk away and shakes her head, flabs of fat jiggling from her neck. "Sometimes he plays with himself behind that counter, when he thinks nobody's watching."

Mary doesn't know how to respond to that. The woman turns to her, not registering her discomfort. "But I've seen him. Oh, you bet I have, all right."

"Okay." Mary focuses on the monitor in front of her.

The woman exaggerates a grimace. "Someone ought to report him."

Mary cradles her hand around the mouse and drags the cursor along the screen, searching for the internet browser icon. The woman next to her continues ranting about the teenage librarian. Mary stops pretending like she's listening once she figures out how to access her email. It's been a while since she's logged in to her Yahoo! account. Hundreds of unread spam messages litter the inbox. She pays as much attention to them as she does to her computer neighbor, who still seems to be complaining about the librarian.

In the search bar, Mary types her son's name. The page attempts to refresh. The internet at the library loads at the pace of a snail, which is saying something if Mary notices it considering her house lacks not only internet but also a computer. Jasper's choice, not hers. Personally she feels like a computer would help Josh with his school work. Plus, sooner or later, everybody's going to have one. It's gotten to the point where she already feels embarrassed when others find out she's one of the few who still doesn't. But Jasper doesn't care. He says you can't trust a computer, that it's too easy to have your identity stolen or your bank account hacked. But really, he just doesn't understand how they work, and that terrifies him. He doesn't have to admit it for Mary to know it's the truth. Anything that he doesn't know how to build with his own two hands doesn't belong in this world. Yet, for some reason, his technology fears don't seem to include television sets. Odd how that works. If he could watch Sox games on the computer, perhaps he might feel slightly different about buying one. Although, of course, that still doesn't change the fact that they probably can't afford one, anyway. Even with the both of them working, life has never been tougher. And now Josh…

"Who's Josh?"

Mary sucks in her breath, frozen in fear.

The woman next to her scoots closer, pointing at Mary's computer monitor. A dozen or so emails have generated on the screen, all with Josh's name included somewhere in the subject lines.

"Who's Josh?" the woman asks again. She breathes like she's just finished climbing numerous staircases. Her breath expels evidence of a recent meal consisting of something pescatarian.

"My son." Mary grips the mouse tight enough to inspire a cramp in her hand. She doesn't let go. "He's my son."

"Oh, that's nice. I got two girls, myself. One's in fifth grade, the other's a whore who only calls me when she needs money."

Mary ignores her and clicks on an email dated over a year ago titled "JOSH 11TH BDAY", which she had emailed to herself after originally uploading the pictures on a friend's computer. Numerous .jpeg thumbnails attempt to load, revealing sections of her son's body in various states of celebration.

The woman tries to wiggle closer to the computer. "He sure is a cutie pie! My stars."

"Thank you." Mary leans away from her, suffocated.

"I always wished Phil and me had had a boy. Girls are such little…*bullies*, aren't they? Hey, where's your boy now?" She rises over the monitor and scans the library, butt still in seat. "Is he here? Does he like to read? Where's that little cutie hiding, anyway?"

Mary has made an effort all her life to be polite, to not cause a scene. As a result, she no longer remembers how to be anything else. If she were Ottessa, she'd smack this lady across the face and tell her to mind her own fucking business. But she isn't Ottessa. There are multiple ways to behave around other undesirable people, and they do not all consist of acting equally foul.

"No." Mary swallows. "He's not here."

"Oh." The woman sinks back in her seat. "Well, that's a shame."

Mary focuses on the .jpeg attachments in the email, scrolling up and down as if each thumbnail might piece together to form a complete puzzle. She can't bring herself to click on any of them, to see a picture in its full display. She hasn't looked at any of these since she first downloaded them, just over a year ago now, and she fears the very real possibility of bursting into tears as soon as she sees them again. She touches her face and realizes her cheeks are already wet.

Crying in the middle of a library on a Saturday evening. Not exactly how she imagined her weekend going. Ask her only yesterday and she would have had an entirely different plan laid out. She was going to cook hot wings and jalapeño poppers and cheese dip and all three of them were going to watch the World Series and have a good day. Josh had even agreed to watch it with them, although it wasn't like Jasper had given the boy much choice. Still. They were going to have a nice night. Watching the Sox. Eating tasty food. Getting *along* for once.

But instead, she's at the library, crying. Jasper's at home, getting shit-faced. And Josh?

Where is Josh?

The .jpeg thumbnails do start forming a larger puzzle the longer she stares at them. They represent an entire day in time. Not exactly the most pleasant twenty-four hours of the Washingtons' lives, despite what the photographs pretend to portray. The smile across her son's face is temporary.

The day had started out nice enough. Alonzo came over around ten-thirty and the four of them went to the movie theaters. *Dawn of the Dead.* The remake with Ving Rhames, a man Mary has had a secret crush on since seeing him in *Pulp Fiction* back in the '90s. The movie was Josh's idea, of course. He'd been talking about wanting to watch it since he first read about it in one of his horror magazines. *Fangoria,* or one of the others, it was hard to keep track of them all. None of them seemed too different from each other. Zombies or vampires or some other monster soaked in gore typically occupied the front cover. They gross Mary out, but Josh was—*is*—obsessed with them. At least he's reading something. At least he has an *interest.* Of course Jasper thinks the whole horror craze is a silly waste of time, and doesn't hesitate to speak his mind whenever he catches Josh acting "too" passionate. But Mary doesn't mind. There are worse things in this world a kid can embrace.

So they went to the theater, all four of them. Jasper driving, the whole time trying to convince Josh to go see that other movie instead, the one about the horse with that guy from *The Lord of the Rings*. But of course Josh wasn't having none of that. When Jasper requested four tickets for *Dawn of the Dead* at the front counter, he sounded not only disappointed, but embarrassed. Josh asked if they could get popcorn and candy and Jasper hesitated the way he always did before remarking about their son's weight, but Mary lightly elbowed him in the arm before he could say anything.

After the movie, they drove to a pizza buffet. One of Josh's favorites. "Mac n' cheese on a pizza? How cool is that?" he said, scanning the options behind the sneeze-proof glass like they were displayed beneath a Christmas tree. Mary took a couple photos of them in their booth as they ate and opened presents. The very photos she looks at now, a year later. Josh and Alonzo side-by-side, slices of mad-scientist pizza in their mouths. Josh unwrapping the video recorder they'd bought him. The one he's been after since forever. The one he'll proceed to use almost every day until his disappearance. Making his little videos. Practicing for his future career.

Mary wonders where that camera is now, if it's still recording, wherever Josh is. A silent witness to an unspeakable horror.

After the pizza and presents, the boys were each given ten dollars in coins and excused to the arcade section of the restaurant. Jasper had mostly managed to watch his mouth and hold off saying anything too damaging. Him and Mary walked aimlessly around the arcade, watching the various kids exchange gold tokens for streams of cardboard tickets. The tickets looked like thin, fragile snakes protruding from the games' stomachs. Always hungry, never satisfied. Jasper kept talking about how much of a waste of money the camera would turn out to be. That Josh was too young to know what to do with it, that he was probably going to break it or Alonzo would steal it when Josh wasn't paying attention. Jasper was always convinced Alonzo would steal Josh's things. But Mary didn't mind the boy. She thought he was sweet. Jasper was just a grump, plain and simple. A big darn grump.

It was on the way home that things really turned to shit. Josh asked if they could stop at Dairy Queen and get ice cream. Mary told him no, that she had already baked a cake the previous day, and they would eat that instead. Josh slumped his head in the back seat and said okay. The issue should have been finished there, but Jasper just couldn't keep his mouth shut. "How many slices of pizza did you have?" he asked, and the car went dead silent, but that didn't stop him from continuing. "Do you even know? Because I do. I counted. Every single slice. Including those desert pizzas. Do you want to know how many slices you had? I don't think you do." Mary tried to get him to shush but Jasper ignored her, raising his tone. "You ate seventeen slices of pizza today, Josh. Seventeen. That's your entire age plus six. Do you honestly think your body can even handle ice cream at this point? *Or* cake?" Josh didn't respond, just kept looking down at his hands in his lap. "Tell you what. When we get home, if you go out and run a couple laps with me, maybe throw the ball around, then we can talk about having some cake. But right now, Josh? Right now I think you've had plenty to eat today. You've had enough for an entire family, and then some." The rest of the car ride was filled with Josh softly crying and Alonzo patting his shoulder and Mary glaring at Jasper and Jasper listening to the radio. No cake was eaten that night, or the night after for that matter. Mary ended up throwing it away untouched.

Mary chooses a .jpeg containing a clear image of both Josh and Alonzo sitting together in the booth and downloads it onto the library desktop. She clicks the toolbox button at the bottom left of the screen and slowly maneuvers the mouse cursor up and down the various programs presented until locating the Microsoft Word icon. A blank document pops up on the screen and she stares at it and thinks about what needs to be typed and instead of getting it over with she minimizes the screen and resurrects Internet Explorer.

Into the AOL search engine, she types "son missing" and finds a cluster of news articles unrelated to what she's after even though she isn't sure what she's after. Maybe she's not after anything.

She searches "parents who have lost their children" and the results contain support group forums for people whose children have died. She clicks on the first link and reads three posts before pressing the back arrow. Tears drip from her cheeks to the keyboard and she continues whispering, "Josh is not dead, Josh is not dead, Josh is not dead," until she believes it, truly believes it.

She types "missing children in Indiana" into the search bar and hesitates, then adds "Percy" before "Indiana" and presses ENTER.

Of course nothing pops up about her son. As far as the sheriff is concerned, Josh is a smalltime criminal on the run, not some child who's potentially been abducted along with his best friend. A couple articles about a Percy baby who died of leukemia occupy the first five results. Mary scrolls down and discovers the link to a website dedicated to children currently missing throughout the United States. She clicks the link and waits for it to load as palpitations gather courage in her chest.

A multitude of new links generate on a white screen, each one the name of a different state. She clicks on INDIANA. The links blink away and are replaced with the faces of children. More children than she is prepared to count. Enough children to make Mary audibly gasp.

The woman next to her leans over again. "Who are they?"

Mary bites her lip and keeps looking at the screen, hoping the woman will take the hint and finally leave her alone. Text scrolls across the top of the page: MISSING CHILDREN FROM INDIANA. Below are the photos. School photos. Birthday party photos. Little League photos. Lounging-on-the-couch-without-a-care-in-the-world photos. Every one of these were taken before anybody in their family ever conceived of such a horror happening to them. When these pictures originated, neither the photographer nor the one being photographed had any idea what awaited their futures.

Everybody always thinks the same thing: *That kind of stuff happens to other people, not us.*

Until it does.

Mary feels numb and detached from her body as her index finger caresses the mouse's wheel. Slowly scrolling down the screen, looking at child after child. All of them missing. Most of them probably dead. If not dead, then what? The alternatives seem even more frightening. Of course, there's the likelihood that the majority of the older teens are simply runaways. Kids who thought they'd fare better by themselves. Maybe, in some cases, this is true. Not every parent takes care of their child. Not every guardian is a good person. Some are monsters. Read any newspaper. Parents neglect their children all the time. They torture them. Kill them. Try to hide the evidence. It happens every day, it feels like. Every day.

But Mary isn't a bad mom, at least she prays to god she isn't. She tries her best. Tries to get Josh what he wants. Tries to make sure all of his needs are met. Does everything for him. Jasper, on the other hand, maybe he hasn't always been the kindest father figure, but goddammit, it's not like he's ever hit Josh, not really, not like some fathers hit their sons. She refuses to believe that he would just run away. That he would abandon them. Josh is a good kid. Maybe Alonzo isn't always the best influence, but Josh is far too smart to do something like this.

But what about the video, the one from the gas station?

She can't explain what she saw. Can't explain her son's actions. But she also can't call Josh a criminal based off what the security camera presented. For one thing, there was no sound. For another, they only saw what happened from one angle. Anything could have really gone down in that gas station. Mary doesn't know, and neither does that ignorant sheriff.

Her son is not a criminal.

And he certainly didn't run away.

And it isn't fair for her to think any of the children on this website also ran away. She doesn't know what happened. She doesn't know anything. Every one of these pictures could be the mugshot of a ghost.

Unable to stop, she continues scrolling down the page, convinced there's no end. A bottomless well of the forever gone.

Then a face appears on the screen that sends a cramp through her hand and causes her fingers to curl off the mouse.

Josh.

No. It can't be.

It's not.

But it is.

Josh. Smiling at the camera above a plate of buffet pizza. The one from the email.

Below the photo, a box of information about the missing:

Name: Joshua Washington
DOB: Apr 4, 1993
Age: 12
Missing: Oct 22, 2005
Race: Black
Location: PERCY, IN, US

Whimpering, she reaches a shaking hand over the keyboard and tries to touch the screen to ascertain its authenticity, but stops a few inches short, too afraid to make contact. How can her son be up on this website so fast? Shouldn't she have been notified? This means the sheriff was taking the case seriously after all, that he hadn't right-out discarded Josh as some runaway thug. Mary suddenly feels terrible for all the ugly thoughts she's birthed since leaving the police station. She had assumed he wouldn't be any help. She had assumed she'd be on her own.

Yet here she is, staring at Josh's face.

Him staring back at her.

Like he's still alive, waiting, *begging* to be found. To be rescued. Saved.

Seeing his picture here, it makes the situation more real than she ever thought it could become. She looks at her beautiful son for several minutes until it occurs to her that she has no idea how the sheriff or anybody else could have come in possession of this particular photograph.

Mary's never shared it with anybody else.

She hasn't even looked at it since she emailed it to herself the day she cleaned out her camera's memory chip.

So how is it on this website?

Mary stretches her arm out and softly touches Josh's face with her index finger. In the picture, streams of red immediately begin leaking from both of his eyes. Blood. Bright and crimson. It drips down his cute, chubby cheeks, but instead of progressing onto his T-shirt, the lines of blood proceed down the rest of the computer screen, emerging from its pixelated universe into the real world, going *drip drip drip* onto the keyboard below. It sounds like raindrops falling into a puddle.

As the blood *drip drip drips,* Josh does not blink. He stares at Mary and Mary stares at him, both frozen, frozen until he opens his mouth. In the picture, as his eyes bleed, he opens his mouth.

He opens his mouth and says:

"You killed me, Mommy. You killed me, you bitch. Mommy, you fucking killed me."

Mary screams.

THIRTEEN

lonzo feels like shit.

Like he's been transported back to his bedroom and it's Monday morning on the first day of school and the bus is just down the street and his mom's yelling at him to get his ass out of bed. Every time he tries to open his eyes they don't last more than half a second before dropping again. All he wants to do is sleep, forever and ever. If he had the strength, he'd yell for his mom to leave him alone, to let him rest.

But strength fails him.

His body is wrecked. Destroyed.

And he isn't in bed, either. At least, not any bed he recognizes. This bed is cold, hard. Concrete?

He tries to move but nothing's working like it's supposed to work. He tells his legs to turn but they remain still. He tries to plant one hand against the ground to lift himself up, but his arms won't move. Something constrains them against his chest. What the fuck? Everything hurts. Everything is broken. He opens his eyes but all he sees is darkness. Are his eyes even open, or are they also broken and refuse to lift? Impossible to tell.

Somewhere close, a voice is calling his name. Above him. Next to him. His mom? No. Josh. Josh is calling his name. Of course. Who else? Alonzo has no one but Josh. Josh. Josh.

Josh nudges him, asking if he's okay, but Alonzo can't respond, can't open his mouth to tell Josh that no, he is the farthest from okay as he's ever been, that he'll never be okay again.

125

Alonzo tries to sit up but a weight remains on his chest, pushing him down. His arms remain pressed tight against him. He coughs and something wet and warm gargles in his throat, threatening to choke him.

(blood i'm choking on blood)

"Jo-Josh? Wh-what…what's happening? Where are we?"

Something brushes against his shoulder. Josh's voice travels toward him in the darkness. "The basement. The cop threw us down."

"Wh-what?" Josh helps Alonzo sit up. His throat cracks, like they're lost in some miserable desert far from civilization. So thirsty he could drain an ocean. "What basement?"

"The house. The one they took us to." Josh speaks in a panicked whisper. His breath sprays against Alonzo's face, hot and vile. "They aren't real cops. They're…they're something else."

Alonzo tries to touch his jaw, afraid it's going to lock in place, but realizes he's still paralyzed. "I can't move. What the hell did they do to me?"

"Straitjackets."

"What?"

"They put straitjackets on us."

"Like in the fucking asylums?"

"Yeah."

"Fuck. What the fuck."

"We aren't the only ones here."

"What are you talking about?"

Long pause. "There are others."

"Others?"

"Like us. Hos-*hostages*."

"Where?" Alonzo tenses, concerned they're being watched. Just because they can't see anything, doesn't mean others also can't. Night vision goggles exist. Goggles might not even be necessary. Who the fuck knows how these pseudo-pigs perceive reality, what kind of biology they inhabit. They sure as hell ain't human.

"I don't know where they are. They were just talking, before you were dropped down the steps. A woman. Two men."

"That's it?"

"I don't know."

Alonzo clears his throat and raises his tone. "Heh-hello? Is—is anybody there?"

He waits a minute, breathing heavy, not expecting to hear anything while simultaneously terrified of hearing something. Somehow the situation would feel even more horrific if others were to be added to the picture. It'd mean that Alonzo and Josh aren't the first two to be dragged down to this basement. It'd mean if others haven't managed to escape yet, then what are Alonzo's chances of pulling it off?

Alonzo exhales in the darkness and turns to where he suspects Josh is sitting, prepared to make fun of him for hallucinating, making things up, when another voice, a high-pitched male radiating lunacy, shouts, "Hi! Welcome to the basement. We're all going to die here! Isn't that swell?"

Alonzo bites his lip and resists screaming. Josh gasps and scoots next to him. "Don't listen to him. Or his friend."

Alonzo tries to pull away but nearly topples over on his side. "Who are you? What—what's going on?"

The voice responds without hesitation. "You're in hell. Isn't that obvious, little boy?"

Alonzo groans. His patience for overly ominous answers has already run dry. He attempts to stand, ignoring the ache striking every bone in his body like lightning. Josh cries out and throws himself on his lap.

"What the hell are you doing?"

"Traps!"

"What?"

"There—there are bear traps."

Paranoia sweeps in and tries to convince Alonzo of terrible things, that the person he's talking to isn't actually his friend, that there's another cop-like creature here in the darkness with him, something that's stolen Josh's voice. Stolen his voice and possibly much more.

"How do you know?"

"The woman told me. The woman in the basement."

"What woman?"

Josh hesitates, then shouts, "Ma'am? Ma'am, talk to us, please. We need help. Please say something."

Somewhere in the basement, lips smack together, then a woman speaks. "Follow my voice."

Alonzo doesn't budge. "Who are you?"

"I'll help you. I'll keep you safe. Be wary of the traps. Follow my voice."

One of the men on the opposite side of the basement bursts into laughter. "She's gonna eat you both up!"

The other one says, "She's gonna feast!"

Alonzo whips his head in their direction. "What the fuck are you guys talking about?"

"Don't listen to them," Josh says.

"Bitch is a fucking psycho cannibal. What do you think happened to the last sorry son of a bitch who got thrown down here?"

The woman interrupts. "They're lying to you, boy. I'll protect you. Both of you. But if you go with them, you'll end up bleeding into their mouths. That's what they do to the newcomers. They manipulate you until gaining your trust, then they attack. Their area is littered with bones picked clean of fat."

One of the men laughs. "We've been down here with that fuckin' loon for...well, I don't know. A long time, okay? Listen. I don't care who you trust. But if you let her near you, just know that you're gonna regret it. Bitch will eat you like a Snickers. *Crunch, crunch, crunch.* You understand?"

The other guy says, "Honestly, if you were smart, you'd trust none of us. Hell, you only just got here."

"Why are we here? What...what's going *on*?" Alonzo asks nobody, asks everybody.

"We have been chosen," the woman says, almost with pride. "We have been—"

One of the men cuts her off. Alonzo can't decipher the men's voices from one another. They all sound sick and disturbed.

"Yeah, don't listen to that nutty bitch. She thinks all this shit is destiny, or whatever the fuck. What's going on is this: you got unlucky, and the family found you. Now you're here, with us. There have been others. Many others. But right now, there is just us. Why we're here, who the fuck can say. Will you stay? Probably not. If I'm being honest, you'll probably be dead sooner than you expect. Shit goes down in this basement. Fucking horrible shit. None of us are going to escape. This is the end of the line for all of us. So if you want to get eaten by the cannibal, then fuck it, go get eaten by the cannibal. If you want to run blindly in the dark and step on a bear trap or whatever other fucking contraptions the family has set up here, be my guest. Or you can just sit and wait for what happens next. Either way, you're gonna die. There's no stopping it. The family has you now."

The other guy adds: "Hope you didn't have any plans."

Josh flops off Alonzo's lap and struggles back into a sitting position. "Don't listen to them. We're gonna get out of here." Josh smacks his lips together, breathing hard. "How far did you get before they caught you?"

Flashes of the thing in the cornfield.

Of its face, and what crawled out of it.

Of the way it laughed.

Alonzo ignores the question and focuses his vision. The basement is a void. Reality swallowed by darkness. The two men speak to each other in muffled whispers. Breathing from the other direction, a body shuffling its position. The woman. A cannibal? Alonzo doesn't know. He believes everything. He believes nothing. Upstairs—footsteps. Wood creaking.

Alonzo clears his throat, desperate for water. "Who are they?"

The woman answers, all too eager to contribute. "They're the family."

"But what...what does that *mean*? Why did they take us? What do they *want*?"

One of the men—Alonzo can't distinguish the two apart—sighs. "Boy, we been asking ourselves the same question since they stuck us down here, and we've yet to come up with a satisfying answer."

"Who are you guys? Where did you come from?"

"I'm Don," one of the men says.

"Shane," says the other.

Alonzo turns the opposite direction, as if the woman would somehow be able to see where he faced. "And you, ma'am?"

The woman remains quiet awhile before answering. "I don't remember."

Josh speaks over Alonzo. "You don't remember your own name?"

"No, child. I'm afraid I don't."

"How long have you all been down here?" Alonzo asks, and this time all three of the strangers refuse to answer. "You don't know, do you?"

"Time…moves strangely down here," Don says.

"Sometimes it feels like we've been in this basement for years," Shane says. "Other times, it feels like it's only been an hour."

"We have always been here," the nameless woman says. "Since before time existed, and we will still be here long after time expires."

"Oh my god," Shane says. "Shut the fuck up, you crazy old bitch."

"The cannibal was already down here when the family captured us," Don says. "For all we know, she really has always lived here."

Alonzo tries to make sense of what they're telling him but his brain can't catch up. Every time he starts to work out a theory, flashes of the thing in the cornfield corrupt his concentration, like a virus infiltrating a computer with pop-up ads.

"Is it just the three of you down here?"

"That's…that's a complicated question," Don says.

"What—?"

Heavy footsteps upstairs, no longer leading away from the basement but toward it. The basement falls silent, all previous conversation forgotten.

The locks on the door at the top of the stairs rattle and drop to the wooden hallway floor and the door swings open. A shadow of a large man stands in the doorway, staring down at his prisoners. No, not a man. Not a true man. Father, maybe Uncle. Maybe another member of this fucked-up family Alonzo hasn't had the pleasure to meet yet.

The only sound comes from the thing's nose. Loud, wet sniffles. Nostrils straining.

(he's smelling us oh my god he's smelling us)

"Oh fuck." Shane's voice drops significantly. "Not already."

"What's happening?" Alonzo asks, in an equal whisper. "*What's happening?*"

"Whatever happens," Don says, "just do what they say. Trust me. They'll make it so much worse if you—"

"*Silence.*"

Uncle plants a heavy boot on the top step, then stops and lifts one arm above him, fumbling for something in the darkness. A chain clinks and the basement explodes with a light so bright Alonzo's convinced his eyeballs burst, and he screams. Josh does the same next to him.

The screams last only a moment. Alonzo blinks hard and fast, getting his vision used to the new light, then scans his surroundings left and right, trying to take everything in as fast he can before the thing at the top of the stairs reaches the bottom.

This is what he sees:

In front of him, the staircase, a wooden fixture old and faded, steps thin and fragile enough to disintegrate under the slightest amount of weight. Some of the steps are already gone, presumably crumbled from previous incidents. Behind the staircase, the basement stretches farther than his eyes do not comprehend, certainly longer than the house's structure above. The space behind the stairs is occupied by a variety of objects that Alonzo has no time to properly examine. Large bags hang from the ceiling. Rows of cages pressed against the walls. And the floor, yes, the floor, composed of dirt and littered with black metal circles. *Bear traps,* Josh had told him. Fucking bear traps *everywhere.*

Strange symbols decorate the walls on either side of the basement. Images he can't recognize, doesn't even dare to speculate on. Lines and shapes and words painted in foreign languages across the bricks, left and right and up and down, hardly an inch left bare.

To his left, Alonzo spots the unnamed woman sitting against the brick wall. Pale, ghostly. Both of her legs end at the kneecaps and her right arm doesn't extend past her elbow. Nubs, but not fully fleshed over. Black and infected like cigarette butts. Dark, thick veins web down her exposed breasts, which sag down past her bellybutton.

And to his right, Don and Shane, although he has no way of knowing who's who. Both are nude like the nameless woman. Both covered in dirt and dried blood. Both malnourished, bones pressing tight against their ribcages. They're standing, not sitting, and Alonzo realizes they do not have a choice. Hooks, attached to chains sprouting from the ceiling, have penetrated all four of the men's hands, forcing their arms to hang above their heads, just low enough for their toes to touch the dirt floor. Their chests and stomachs are graffitied with cuts and bruises. Between their legs there is nothing more than infected gashes. Both of their penises have been removed.

Alonzo swallows vomit.

Behind him, Josh starts screaming again, presumably having witnessed the same sights as Alonzo. The two mutilated men and the pale nameless woman dare not utter a sound.

The thing called Uncle reaches the bottom of the stairs, still dressed in his dirty police uniform. A hammer dangles from his right hand. In the other hand he holds an empty plastic grocery bag. He drops both items in the dirt beside Alonzo's feet and Alonzo's eyes widen at the sight of the hammer, wishing like hell this straitjacket weren't preventing him from picking it up and bashing this motherfucker's head in. He steps around Alonzo and crouches. His breath blasts against the back of Alonzo's neck. Hot and rancid. The thing's hands grab at Alonzo's back. The straitjacket loosens as he unbuckles the straps, then slips off completely. His hands fall into his lap and a numbness spirals up his arms. This new freedom erases his previous fixation on retrieving the hammer. All Alonzo thinks now is, *Why am I free? What is he going to do to me?*

Uncle steps back around him and points at the hammer. "Pick it up."

"Wh-what?"

"Pick. Up. The. Hammer."

"*What?*"

132

"Say what again and I'll show you what it's like to really not have ears. Cut 'em off and make you eat 'em. Cut 'em off and make you eat 'em. Cut 'em off and—"

Alonzo grabs the hammer and studies it in his open palm. Again he fantasizes about bludgeoning the creature in the police uniform, but doubts his ability to pull it off without getting stopped.

Uncle steps around Alonzo and crouches again, so they're face-to-face. He slides a long, filthy index finger under the boy's jaw and lifts his head so he can't look away. The thing's foul breath drifts in Alonzo's mouth like a toxic gas. His eyes somehow manage to simultaneously come off both dead and full of life. Alien, unreal. He smiles and reveals teeth black with rot.

"You are scared."

Alonzo doesn't respond.

The thing called Uncle nods, satisfied. "Yes. You are scared."

"Please."

He stands and nods at the nameless woman on the floor. "Hit her."

"Wh-what?"

Uncle sighs and reaches into a back pocket and pulls out a pocket knife. "Did you just say 'what'?"

"No, no, no, please, no." Alonzo scrambles away from Uncle, toward the nameless woman. He sits against the wall, refusing to look at her, trembling from head to toe.

"Now hit her. Right in the face. Do it, boy. Hit her. Hit her."

Alonzo looks into his lap, hoping he can just ignore the situation until it goes away. Maybe the monster cop will simply lose interest after a while and return upstairs. The handle of the hammer burns his palm as if to tell him the longer he waits the worse it's going to be. The rest of the basement's prisoners remain dead silent except for Josh, who's doing a terrible job of trying not to cry. Everybody else down here, they're used to this, whatever this even is. It's not the first time one of these things have come down here. Judging by the prisoners' numerous mutilations, they've been down here many, many times.

Uncle stomps his boot against the dirt floor and a small cloud dusts up. "Hit her. Hit her. Hit her."

The tone in the thing's voice suggests extreme consequences for continuing to ignore his demands, but Alonzo still can't bring himself to move. This isn't real. This isn't real. This isn't real.

Uncle grabs the plastic bag from the ground and, without another word, brings it down over Josh's head. His friend thrashes, kicking his legs wildly, arms still confined against his chest by the straitjacket. His feet drag in the dirt as he attempts to reclaim stability. The plastic muffles his scream.

The other prisoners ignore this act of cruelty. They know the drill by now. This is what happens when you disobey. Alonzo gets it, he understands, even if he doesn't want to admit it, even if he doesn't want to embrace his new reality as this fucked-up family's plaything.

Alonzo holds up the hammer and points the claw in Uncle's direction. "No! Don't! Leave him alone!"

Uncle grins, never breaking eye contact with Alonzo as Josh suffocates. "Hit. Her."

Alonzo screams with pure rage and swings the hammer at the nameless woman's thigh. It connects against her flesh without a sound, as if striking a mound of raw meat. The nameless woman gasps and grabs at her thigh with her one arm that's still intact. Yet she does not scream. When Alonzo looks at her face, he sees she's smiling, amused at his pathetic attempt of violence.

"You can do better than that, boy," she says.

He glances back at Uncle. The bag's still over Josh's face but the fight in him has slowed down drastically. Losing the will to defend himself. Losing oxygen. Losing everything.

Uncle gives the command again. "Hit her like you mean it. Destroy her like you love it. Love it. Love it. Love it. *Hit her!*"

Alonzo hits her with everything he's got. Not in the thigh but the stomach. A mixture of various colored liquids spill from the nameless woman's mouth as she doubles over, coughing and gagging and *laughing*. Her left arm clutches her stomach, tears running down her cheeks, and laughter exploding from her lungs.

And Uncle tightens the bag against Josh's face and shouts, "Hit her! Hit her! Hit her!"

Alonzo screams, blind with rage, and brings the hammer down upon the nameless woman's face and caves in her cheek.

A gargled choking sound replaces her laughter.

Yet somehow it doesn't seem to subside the humor in her tone.

"Again!" Uncle screams. "Again! Again! *Again!*"

Alonzo does as he's told and continues swinging the hammer until the thing atop the nameless woman's shoulders no longer resembles a human skull. Chunks of bone and hair and what could only be brain matter splatter against him the deeper he digs into her memories. The hammer drops from his grasp and he falls back against the wall, staring at his hand, covered in blood, body shaking, unable to hear anything except for how the hammer sounded pounding against the woman's head, as if the horrible noise has evolved into an echo, a reverberation of death.

Eventually his vision returns as Uncle once again dresses him in the straitjacket. He rubs Alonzo's head and says, "You done good, kiddo. I'm real proud of you. See ya tomorrow." Then he walks up the stairs and turns off the basement light and closes the door and locks it from the hallway.

Next to him, he can feel the nameless woman still slouched over, motionless, and for the first time tonight he's grateful for the darkness.

He never wants to see again.

FOURTEEN

Ottessa considers picking up the shit the cops were generous enough to knock over in her house but instead decides to make a bigger mess. She smokes a cigarette while pacing from one end of the front porch to the other, not once taking her eyes off the spot in the street where she last saw her boy. Once the cigarette's been reduced to a bare stub, she flicks it off in the grass and heads back inside, determined as she stomps through the house toward Zoey's bedroom. The door's already wide open and shit's thrown all over the place but it's impossible to determine what can be blamed on the police and what's Zoey's doing. She kneels and begins shoveling piles of discarded clothing into the unhinged mouth of a black heavy-duty garbage bag. The room reeks of spoiled food and boy sweat and for once, Ottessa isn't annoyed by the odor. If anything she embraces it. She inhales it like fresh flowers blossoming in a summer garden and her ache for her boy swells. *Why can't he be here? Goddammit, why is this happening now?*

She drops the garbage bag and sits on Zoey's mattress and looks around the room and notices the window's half-open, which explains why it's so goddamn cold in here, then it dawns on her that's how they left last night, Zoey and Josh, they crawled out the window. Crawled out the window so she wouldn't notice them while she was busy getting high and fucking some random dude from Rourke's. Could they hear her from here, in Zoey's bedroom? Is that why they snuck out, to escape Ottessa's sex sounds? She gags, disgusted it's even a possibility. *They'd been asleep.* But were they? She'd only pressed her ear against the door. What does that prove? Nothing. And even if they *had* been awake, would that have changed anything? What was she going to do, tell the man—whatever the fuck his name was—sorry, but her boy and his friend were still up so he'd have to take his sorry ass home? Unlikely. Very unlikely.

But what if she opened the door when she got home and noticed the boys were already gone? What then? Would she have gone out looking for them? Maybe take the guy with her, ask him to help her out. If he said yes, hell, maybe that meant he was decent enough to keep around for a couple future lays. Drive around town shouting Zoey's name, shining headlights on any black kid resembling her boy's appearance? In a town like this, there wouldn't have been many. Would that have been enough? Just to open Zoey's door to check up on him? Open the door, see he's gone, go out and bring him home and avoid this whole fucking mess from ever happening.

But would she have gone out looking for him, or would she have still proceeded to her own bed?

Would *any* of it have mattered?

The uncertainty sits in her stomach like a rotating saw, grinding away at her innards.

Ottessa drops from the mattress and lands on her knees in the middle of Zoey's disastrous bedroom and chokes back an explosion of sobs. "Please, baby. Please. Please come back." She promises him she'll never yell again, never smack him when he's out of line, never tell him no. Whatever he wants, she vows to give it to him, no matter the cost, she doesn't care, she'll get ten jobs if that's what it takes. "Please. I promise, we'll make it work. Whatever's happened, it's going to be okay. Please come back. Please come—"

The telephone starts ringing.

Ottessa actually screams, it scares her so bad.

She scrambles up a bookshelf until she's recovered her balance and races out of the bedroom and down the hall toward the living room, where she left the phone on the coffee table.

The caller ID reads PERCY PUBLIC LIBRARY.

(it's him it's him it's him they were at the library the whole time just the library that's it that's all nothing more the library the fucking LIBRARY)

(zoey baby i'm coming baby i'm coming)

She practically punches the TALK button as she raises it to her ear. "He-hello?"

"Ottessa? It's Mary."

She almost hangs up the phone without saying another word. She bites her lip, stifling back the abysmal weight of disappointment. Then a new thought occurs to her. "Did they find them? Did they find Zoey?"

Mary hesitates, much longer than Ottessa prefers. "No. I...I made some flyers. At the library. I thought I would walk around town and hang them up."

"Oh."

"Do you want to help?"

Ottessa's first instinct is to tell her to get fucked, that hanging up flyers ain't gonna do a goddamn thing to help find their boys. But then she glances back down the hall, at Zoey's bedroom. Almost like it's begging her to return. A siren song with sinister motives. But there's nothing in there for her. All she'll end up doing is crying and breaking things, which is even less productive than hanging flyers.

And, to be honest, the thought of being alone right now terrifies her.

"Yeah," Ottessa says. "I'll be outside waiting for you."

She leaves Zoey's window open in case he decides to come crawling back inside.

PERCY IS NOT A LARGE town by any stretch. With a population just under six thousand, the residents rest in a blissful position of not knowing all of their neighbors by name but remaining comfortable enough to nod at familiar faces passing through aisles in Strack & Van Til, the local grocery store. A person can drive from one end of town to the opposite in less than fifteen minutes, assuming traffic lights play in the person's favor and a train isn't scheduled to pass through anytime soon. Yet, nearly a half hour after they get off the phone with each other, Mary still hasn't made it to Ottessa's place. The library isn't even located on what can be considered the "far side" of town, so what the hell is taking her so long?

Ottessa sits on her porch swing feeling like a goddamn idiot, a cigarette in one hand and a plastic water bottle filled with vodka in the other. She starts figuring Mary realized what a waste of time it'd be going around town with a stack of flyers and hightailed it back home, which is all fine and dandy, but the bitch could have at least let her know their plans were cancelled instead of letting her sit out here like a dumbass. The liquor warms her chest and keeps her company as she lazily sways back and forth, the tip of her shoes slithering across cement. Every second that passes without a car turning on her street is another second she debates saying fuck it and going back inside. All the vodka in the world can't rid October of all its chill. Maybe she'd finally find some hidden clue buried in Zoey's bedroom, something the police failed to locate during their hasty search of the premises. Something that'd help everything make sense. Except she knows what would happen. She'd finish off the water bottle of vodka and fill it back up and keep repeating the process until all the vodka in the house vanished then she'd vomit and pass out in the bathroom. Life is much easier to contemplate when you're unconscious, especially when your boy is missing, who-the-fuck knows where, and there ain't nothing you can do about it.

Mary pulls along the curb and Ottessa glares at her through the windshield, trying to convince the woman to keep on driving, to leave her here to cope with the situation her own damn way. Mary shows no sign of understanding the message. Foolish woman. What is she even doing here?

Ottessa flicks her cigarette butt in her front yard and plops down into the passenger seat of Mary's car. "Took you long enough."

"The printer, at the library. It ran out of ink as I was printing, so I had to wait for somebody to replace it. I'm sorry." The woman looks spooked. Pale and sweaty.

"How many flyers did you print out?"

"A hundred."

"Shit, girl."

Mary frowns. Her eyes are raw. "What? You think that wasn't enough?"

Instead of answering, Ottessa takes a swig from her water bottle. The vodka numbs her tongue and burns her throat. "What's the plan, then?"

Mary drives away from the curb, away from the last place anybody ever saw their boys alive. "I don't know. I guess I just thought we'd hang them up around town. Spread the word that they're missing. Maybe somebody's seen them."

"You think that's gonna do any good?"

Mary glances at her like she's unsure whose side Ottessa's playing on. "Why wouldn't it?"

Ottessa cradles the water bottle with both hands between her thighs and lays her head back against the seat rest. She closes her eyes before answering. "One of two things have happened here, and it's up to us to figure out which theory holds up best, us and no one else because no one else gives a good goddamn. You understand?"

"Okay..."

Ottessa glances out the window at the houses passing them by. As far as she can tell, Mary's just driving aimlessly through subdivisions until a destination makes sense. "One, what that sheriff says is the truth, and Zoey and Josh, they robbed that gas station and ran away. If that's the case, then these flyers ain't gonna do a goddamn thing, because they're long gone by now. Chicago, maybe farther, shit, who could say? Our boys, they ain't dumb, are they? Nah. If they wanted to get away, they could manage it. No doubt in my mind."

"But—"

"Or, two, what I saw last night was the real deal, and one of these motherfuckers in blue really did pick up our boys and for some reason that remains mystifying, the sheriff's trying to cover it up. Maybe our boys put up too much of a fight at the station and some trigger-happy peckerwood plugged a couple holes in each of them. I don't know."

"They're not—"

"But if that's what happened, then shit, our path ahead ain't looking too pretty, not by any stretch. If our boys are dead—"

"They're not dead." Mary says it like she's trying to convince herself of a lie.

"—*if* our boys are dead, and the cops *are* responsible, then you can sure as hell bet the sheriff's gonna do whatever it takes to make sure this shit stays buried. Don't be surprised if they come after us next, once they realize we ain't gonna just accept their little runaway fairy tale bullshit as gospel."

"I'll kill them." Mary tightens her fingers around the steering wheel as she pulls into a strip mall parking lot. Skin constricting against rubber. Ottessa swears she can smell the rage boiling from Mary's blood. "If they did something to them, I'll…I'll kill them. I'll kill them all."

Ottessa looks over at the woman behind the wheel and sees she means what she says. She nods and pats Mary on the knee. "I aim to be right there beside you, it comes to that."

Mary puts her car in PARK but keeps one hand gripping the wheel, like it's stuck there. "My husband. He doesn't understand what's happened. He doesn't care. He thinks the boys are just…I don't know. Messing around. That none of this is real. But this *is* real. Right? This is real?"

"About as real as it gets." Ottessa uncaps her drink and presses her eye against it like a pirate peeping through a spyglass. "Men are a waste. Who fuckin' needs 'em."

"But they *did* rob the gas station." Mary's voice cracks. "We saw them on the security camera."

Ottessa nods. There's no denying what they viewed. The sheriff might be an evil, scheming son of a bitch, but no way in hell is he smart enough to start editing video software. She'd be surprised if the man could tie his own necktie on the first try. "Yeah, but we don't know what happened to them afterward. Just because they did something bad, it don't mean something bad didn't happen to *them* once they left."

Mary buries her face in her hands. "Why did they attack that man? What were they even *doing* there last night? My boy isn't a criminal. He isn't."

Ottessa doesn't bother fighting back her sneer. "Meaning *my* boy is?"

Mary stops crying and lifts her head from her hands, realizing the mistake in her words. "What? No. God, no. That's not what I meant, Ottessa—"

Ottessa dismisses her with a flick of her wrist. "It's fine. I get it. I know what people in this town think about us, about me and Zoey."

"No, they don't—"

"And if you want to know the truth, I really don't give a good flying shit what they think. The opinions of a bunch of assholes ain't gonna help me find Zoey. The quicker we accept they committed a crime last night, the quicker we can start using our brains, because getting all sad and mopey and shit about your precious Josh not being the little angel you thought he was is just gonna slow me down, and if you're gonna be like this the whole time please tell me now so I can get the fuck out of this car and actually find them before some motherfucking maniac tosses their corpses on the side of the road."

Mary gasps and for a moment Ottessa fears the woman's going to vomit. "You don't think...*no*..."

Ottessa shakes her head. "I think it's possible, yeah."

"Not my boy."

"Sometimes boys get themselves killed." Ottessa despises the words leaving her mouth but she can't stop them from spilling out. A penetrated dam flooding a city. "It's an ugly truth but it's a *truth* all the same."

"Stop it. Shut up. I don't want to hear this." Mary eyes the door handle, planning her escape.

Ottessa grabs Mary's hand and squeezes until they're maintaining eye contact. "Just because it's a possibility don't for one second make it a reality. We're going to find them. You and me. Nobody else may give a shit. Fuck them then. We don't *need* them. We can do it. We *have* to do it."

"Okay."

She hands Mary the water bottle and Mary finishes it off with one quick slug, then drops the bottle and starts coughing loud and hard and cups her mouth with her palm.

"Oh my god, was that vodka?"

Ottessa slaps her a couple times on the back. "Shit, girl. Sorry about that. I thought you knew."

THEY GET OUT OF THE car and head inside a Dollar General at the end of the strip mall. Barely a dozen other vehicles occupy the parking lot. This evening Percy feels like a ghost town. The streets bare, the fast food drive-thrus vacant. It's Saturday. People should be out and about but everybody seems to be inside their homes, almost as if they're hiding from Ottessa and Mary, too afraid to show their faces. But what do they have to hide? Unless more than just the local police force are involved with the conspiracy behind Zoey and Josh's disappearance. Behind their abduction. Could it be possible? Ottessa isn't ready to rule out anybody, except maybe the woman who drove her here. She's seen enough horror movies with her son and Josh about small towns and the secret cults living in them. The kind of societies who worship dark lords and offer ritualistic sacrifices under full moons. Percy's never given her an occult vibe before, but hell, they never do, right? Not the smart ones, at least.

"Where the hell is everyone?" Ottessa asks, holding the Dollar General door open for Mary.

"The game's about to begin."

Ottessa screws up her face. "What *game*?"

"The World Series. White Sox versus that Texas team. The Astros."

"Oh." Ottessa releases her hold on the door and follows Mary inside, feeling almost disappointed. "I don't watch that dumb shit."

"Me neither." Mary stops and holds her breath, like she just muttered a blasphemy. She turns back to Ottessa and offers a slight smile. "I hate baseball. I hate it so much."

"Just a bunch of men playing with their tiny little balls."

Mary giggles, then frowns.

They walk through the aisles in search of duct tape for their flyers. Mary grabs a bottle of Diet Coke and offers to buy something for Ottessa, so she takes a cherry Jones Soda.

"That's what my husband's doing now, you know." Mary presses the Diet Coke against her forehead as they stand in front of the beverage coolers. "He's at home, watching the game. I didn't even bother calling him to see if he wanted to help us. I already knew what he'd say."

"Men like their sports." Ottessa's glad he didn't join them. The first time she ever talked to him, she knew she despised him. If she saw Mary's husband in the car when she pulled up at her house earlier, she would have likely gone back inside without uttering a single word.

"I just don't understand how he isn't worried. I've been crying all day. *All day.* Not once did he come to check on me, to reassure me everything would be okay. When he found out I was going to the library to print out flyers, he asked why. *Why.* He just doesn't care. He really doesn't—"

"Can I help you two with something?"

They turn to the sound of the voice. An old white lady with a Dollar General apron strapped to her bony-ass hip stands at the end of a check-out aisle.

Ottessa scowls at her. "Bitch, can't you see we're having a moment here?"

The cashier glares at them. Her nametag reads: GLADYS. "If you're not going to buy anything, then I'm going to have to ask you to leave."

Ottessa debates breaking her bottle of Jones Soda over the lady's face, then remembers the video she watched in the police station, the security footage of Zoey attacking the gas station clerk, and wonders if rage is hereditary. The fight in her deflates.

"Sorry." Mary approaches the register and lays her items on the conveyer belt. Ottessa sets down her Jones Soda next to them, trying to avoid eye contact with the cashier, shame and anger building up and begging for release.

The cashier named Gladys takes her time ringing up the items. Far too long for two drinks and a roll of duct tape. Eventually Ottessa looks up to see what's taking so long, and finds the cashier staring directly at her, eyes wide, mouth agape.

Ottessa cocks her eyebrow. "The fuck you staring at?"

Mary tries to play off the awkwardness with an obvious forced laugh. "Is there something the matter, ma'am?"

The cashier points one long, crooked finger at Ottessa. "I recognize you, don't I?"

If Ottessa has ever seen this old bitch in her life, it was during previous trips to Dollar General. "Nah, you don't know me, and I don't know you."

Mary continues trying to defuse a potential nuke. "Ma'am, if it's not any trouble, maybe we could just pay and be on our way?"

Gladys redirects her finger at Mary. "And you, too. I recognize both of you."

Mary touches her chest, incredulous. "Me? I hardly ever come in here. We do most of our shopping at Stracks."

The cashier sneers like she's in on a cruel joke. "And I recognize your sons, too. Oh yes. Your sons."

Mary gasps, tries to respond, and fails. Ottessa pushes her aside and grabs the bottle of Jones Soda by its neck and threatens to bash the cashier in the face. "What the fuck did you just say?"

The frail woman does not appear startled. "Yesterday, they came in here. They came in here and *stole*. Caused a great big scene, your little nigger off-spring did."

Ottessa cocks back her arm in preparation of bludgeoning the cashier, but Mary grabs her by the wrist. "*Don't.*"

"Let me go." Ottessa tries to pull away but Mary's surprisingly stronger than she looks. "I'm just going to break her skull open is all."

"*No.*" Mary wrestles the bottle from her grip and hides it behind her back.

The cashier continues talking, unfazed by Ottessa's threats of violence. "Batteries, I think they was after. The fat one pretended like he was injured while the other one pocketed a package of 'em and hightailed it out the doors. We saw it all on the camera afterward. Manager didn't think a package of batteries were worth making a fuss about, though. Consider your little niggers lucky this time. They come in here again, they're in for a whole world of hurtin'."

The Jones Soda shatters against the cashier's temple and it takes Ottessa a moment to realize she hadn't been the one to swing it.

Mary drops what remains of the glass bottle and backs away, body trembling.

Cherry-red soda drips down the cashier's face, yet she doesn't collapse, she doesn't even flinch. The impact doesn't affect her like it should. The bottle doesn't split her cheek open, it doesn't draw blood, it doesn't render her unconscious. If anything, the sudden violence only makes her smile. Wide and sinister, baring brown, jagged teeth. The cashier is amused, not injured, as if the bottle had been the punchline to a hilarious joke. She continues pointing her grotesque index finger at Mary as she speaks. Except now, something's different. Her eyes...they're milky, and her voice...like her throat's clogged with phlegm and every word she utters is agonizing.

"It's going to take much more than a bottle of pop to get your sons back. Oh *yes*. It's going to take everything you two cunts have. *Everything*."

Mary leans her ass against the next check-out aisle, body trembling, clearly useless. Whatever fight within that convinced her to swing the Jones Soda has evaporated, leaving behind a terrified mess. Ottessa side-steps between them and grabs the cashier's finger. She squeezes it, letting the bitch know how easily she could snap it in half if she chooses.

"What do you know?"

Gladys cocks her head, smile somehow stretching wider. Her pupils roll to the back of her skull, revealing white orbs in her sockets. "I see them. Don't you? Oh, I see them so clearly. They're scared. Oh yes, they're scared."

Ottessa starts to talk but chokes. She clears her throat and tries again. "Bitch, start making sense or you're losing a finger."

The cashier doesn't seem fazed by Ottessa's threats. "They're going to die, you know. Even if you save them, it's already too late. The fat nigger and his friend will open the doorway. They are her invitation. Mother will rise. Mother will rise from the blood and the earth and claim this land as her home. You will love Mother or you will love nothing. *Mother!* Mother, oh Mother. *Mother accept me Mother save me Mother love me Mother hold me Mother—*"

Ottessa twists the cashier's finger, hard and abrupt.

The snap of the bone echoes throughout the empty Dollar General.

The cashier's pupils roll back in place and stare at Ottessa. Drool spills down her jaw. Her smile remains frozen.

"*Soon.* Soon it will hit you. Soon you will know. You will know the truth, as it has always been and always will. None of you cunts ever had a chance."

Gladys collapses behind the cash register. A soft moan escapes her defeated body. A question's raised. "My head...oh, what...what happened..."

Ottessa grabs Mary and drags her toward the exit. "C'mon, girl. We gotta get the fuck out of here."

Mary follows, too terrified to respond.

Behind them, the delirious cashier continues to cry.

MARY GUNS IT OUT OF the strip mall parking lot and returns to Ottessa's house, vision in constant motion from the road ahead to the strip mall displayed in the rearview mirror. She expects to find the old lady running out of the Dollar General and chasing them down the street, hitting an impossible speed, like the cop robot in that *Terminator* movie. The store drifts out of view, swallowed by the darkness of Percy, but the nausea doesn't show any sign of deflating. They pile out of the car and flee inside Ottessa's, the flyers in the back seat long forgotten. Ottessa locks the front door and, after a moment of consideration, pushes the loveseat in front of it, as if that'll be enough to stop the police from entering.

Both of the women breathe hard and fast. Questions fly out of their mouths like machinegun fire. Questions like *What the fuck was that? What just happened? Was that real?* and *What the fuck is going on? Oh my god, what the* fuck *is going on?*

Neither offers any sort of answers to the other. At this point Mary feels like Ottessa is nothing more than a mirror reflecting her own fear. None of

this is real, but of course it is, what else could it be? A dream? No. This is no dream. Mary is awake. Ottessa is awake.

Nothing makes sense. Everything is insane.

Ottessa paces in the kitchen, attempting to light a cigarette with shaking hands and failing. Mary takes the lighter and tries to do it for her but her hands aren't any better. Ottessa grabs the lighter back and throws it on the counter and triggers the flame on her stovetop and leans over it with the cigarette hanging from her lips. She straightens back up and takes a long, intense drag before expelling smoke and saying, "That was fucking nuts."

Mary bends over the stove and lights her own cigarette in the same fashion, then stands and nods. They'd cried so much on the drive over here, there's nothing left in them. "I hit her. I could have killed her."

"Whatever that bitch was, I don't think she could have been killed."

"It was almost like she was…was…"

"Possessed."

Mary looks down at her feet. "Yeah. Like she was possessed."

"But by what?" Ottessa laughs. "*Satan?*"

"I don't know. Something…something evil."

"Holy goddamn shit." She opens a cabinet above the fridge and fumbles inside for a moment then brings out a half-empty bottle of vodka. She retrieves two glasses from the sink and sits at the table and fills them both up. Mary sits across from her and accepts one of the glasses. Ottessa downs half in one gulp and gasps, gripping the edge of the kitchen table with both hands.

Mary sips at her own glass and coughs. It burns going down her throat. She takes a longer sip. Somehow it helps. "What do we do now? Do we…do we call the police?"

Ottessa shakes her head. "Hell no. Shit. That's about the worst thing we could do."

"What then? What if that lady's hurt?"

"Does it look like I give a fuck if that crazy bitch is hurt? Good. I hope she is."

"But—"

"Listen, here's what happens if you call Sheriff Peckerwood and tell him what you did: we ain't ever gonna find our boys. Consider the search finished. Done before it even started. That what you want, girl?"

"No."

"'Cause if they got us locked up, then there ain't *nobody* out there tryin' to find our boys. You think the police give a shit about finding them? Of course not. And if you want the whole truth, I believe they'd love the chance to put us away, get us to stop asking questions, sticking our noses where they don't belong. There's a major motherfuckin' conspiracy here and Sheriff Peckerwood and the rest of his cracker comrades are right in the middle of the shit. If anybody knows where Zoey and Josh done gone off to, it's the Percy Police Department. I'm willing to stake my life on that. Are you?"

Mary doesn't respond. Ottessa refills their glasses and they both sip together. The more Mary drinks, the easier it becomes for more to go down. Gone is the struggle to keep from coughing it back up. The vodka's somehow smoother now, like water. Water with benefits.

"I don't want to go home tonight."

Ottessa shrugs. "Then don't. Who gives a shit."

"I should call Jasper, let him know. My mother might still be at the house. She'd be driving him crazy right about now."

"Fuck 'em. Call tomorrow. Let's get drunk."

"I thought that's what we were doing."

Ottessa laughs. "Girl, I said *drunk*."

FIFTEEN

Jasper stares into the fridge for a solid minute before accepting that there's no more beer. He slams the door and something inside rattles and tips over. Probably the half-empty glass bottle of ranch he'd previously spotted resting on the top shelf all by its lonesome. Hesitant, he opens the door again and the bottle of ranch immediately rolls off the shelf and cracks against the kitchen linoleum. The thick white condiment splatters against his work boots and forms a puddle beneath the shattered glass.

"Motherfucker," he whispers and stomps back into the living room, not bothering to clean up the mess. Fuck it. When Mary gets home she can tend to it. *If* she ever comes home. At this point he's beginning to wonder if she ran out on him. She left, what, *hours* ago? To print something out at the *library*? Now, Jasper isn't one to frequent such establishments often, but even he knows no library around here stays open this late on a Saturday night. Probably out wasting her time hanging up fliers around town. He can't think of a more foolish way to spend the first game of the World Series. The goddamn Sox are killing it and his wife's out buying into Josh's bullshit once again. Maybe it makes him sound like an asshole but he doesn't care. Josh wasn't kidnapped. Anybody with a single ounce of sense in them would know that, especially after watching the security video from the gas station, the one the sheriff showed them. Being abducted and being on the run are two very different things. Josh, he's on the run, him and his dumbass friend. Eventually the law will find them, probably by the end of the weekend, and then Mary will understand the real kind of trouble their son has gone and gotten himself into. But until then, Jasper isn't going to waste his time searching for a boy who wants to stay hidden. Either he'll get picked up or realize there's not a chance in hell him and his little buddy have what it takes to survive in this world alone. The first moment Josh gets hungry he'll come crawling back, rubbing his fat gut and crying for his mama. So no, Jasper isn't going to let his boy's terrible decisions ruin the game. Although it isn't just a game, is it? This is history. The Sox in the World Series, Jesus Christ, he never thought he'd see the day. The last time they won it all it'd been 1917. His own father hadn't even been born yet. This season…this season they've been killing it. And to be up against a team that only made it because of the wildcard? Oh man. Oh *man*. They're going to win it, Jasper thinks, the Sox are going to win it all, and he'll be goddamned to Hell if he's going to miss a single second of it because of Josh. No fucking way. He'd rather die.

"Is this almost over?" Agnes asks, sitting across from him on the couch.

Jasper has to bite his lip before answering. "What? No. It's not even the third inning yet."

Agnes screws up her face. "The third *what* now?" She works at some knitting project laid out across her lap and he wonders where the hell it came from.

"The *inning*. There are nine innings in a baseball game."

"And this is only the third? Goodness."

Jasper sighs and rubs his temple, salivating for another beer, hell, maybe something stronger. The longer his mother-in-law talks to him, the stronger the craving gets.

"Where's Mary?" It's probably the tenth time she's asked him this tonight, and he gives her the same answer he's given her the last nine times:

"I don't know."

"Don't you think you ought to go out and look for her?"

"She's a grown woman. She can take care of herself."

"But what about Josh?"

He sighs again. All he wants to do is just watch the goddamn game. Why is that so difficult to understand? "He'll turn up. They both will."

TOUCH THE NIGHT

The Sox are up three to one in Game One of the World Series and he doesn't feel an ounce of excitement. Just bitterness. Bitterness toward Mary for abandoning him here to deal with her nagging mother. Bitterness toward the local police for not knowing how to do their jobs. Bitterness toward Ottessa and her son, both of them a terrible influence in their own ways. And, of course, bitterness toward Josh, who Jasper's raised to know better than to do stupid shit like this. For a brief moment he wonders if he's meant to blame himself, if he's failed as a father. Jasper refuses to believe it. He's always brought home a paycheck. Never once has Josh gone without a meal, which is obvious the moment anyone takes a look at the boy. If anything, Jasper's given him too *many* meals. Never once has he missed a day of school, not even during bouts of sickness, he still made him go. An education is everything, something Jasper's father neglected to give him, and he'll be damned if he would do the same to his boy, too. Never once has Josh not had new school clothes or a decent Christmas or anything else all the privileged white boys in this country are given by their fathers. Jasper has dedicated his entire life to ascertaining Josh's future is full of promise and opportunity, and how does the boy reward him? By becoming best friends with the one kid Jasper begged him not to play with. By sneaking out. By robbing a goddamn *gas station*. By abandoning his family. By stabbing his own father in the back. So yes. Jasper feels bitterness tonight. He's fucking drowning in the stuff.

On the TV screen, Ozzie Guillen—manager of the Chicago White Sox—crouches in the dugout and cracks his neck. Stress has consumed his face as he watches his outfielder, Scott Podsednik, square off against Roger Clemens, knocking away one foul ball after another. Jasper understands that feeling Ozzie's experiencing right now, maybe not for the same reasons, but goddamn does he understand that feeling.

On the mound, Clemens blows air into his fist—his throwing hand—and readjusts his Astros ballcap. It's a cold night, not just in Chicago, but also here in Percy. These October winds begin picking up speed around this time of night, striking their hardest…well, about when Ottessa claims she saw the two boys get confronted by the police.

153

"Oh, come on already." Agnes shakes her knitting needle at the TV. "Why do they keep showing us the same thing right after it happens?"

"It's a replay."

"I know what it's called. Don't mean I get why they're doing it. What, do they think we're stupid or something, that we've already forgotten what we just saw? I mean, my goodness, come on, don't you think it's getting a little ridiculous?"

"You know, you don't have to watch this. You could go home."

"Are you kidding? With first my grandson missing, and now my daughter?"

"Mary isn't missing."

"Then where is she?"

"I don't know."

"Because she's missing."

Jasper grits his teeth, rocking harder in his recliner. Goddammit he wants a beer. Clemens throws his twelfth pitch of the at-bat and strikes out Podsednik, who responds by taking off his helmet and whipping it toward the home dugout. For a second Jasper wishes Podsednik would run after Clemens and tackle him right there on the mound and beat his stupid fucking face in, but of course it doesn't happen, and FOX cuts to a commercial break.

"Finally," Agnes says. "I was beginning to worry that would never end."

Jasper stands from the recliner and searches for his car keys. It's either that or attack his mother-in-law.

Agnes follows him around the kitchen, nosy as ever. "What are you doing? Where are you going?"

"I guess I'm gonna go find Mary. Ain't that what you wanted?"

"But what about the game?"

"Watch whatever you want."

FUCK MARY. SHE'S ONE OF the last people he needs to see right now. If she wants to spend her night wasting it on hanging up flyers, then so be it. What the hell does he care? Instead, he drives over to Rourke's, doubling the speed limit to make it before the commercial break's over. He strolls inside halfway through the next at-bat. Not bad timing at all. If anything, beer makes him a better driver.

He plops down on a stool closest to the TV hanging over the bar and orders a drink and some chicken wings. Should have just come here to begin with. Like he didn't know how impossible it would be to enjoy the game with Agnes on his ass about every little thing. How dare Mary leave him alone with her. How fucking *dare* she. She knows damn well what they think about each other. She did this on purpose. This is payback for the way he reacted to Josh's bullshit earlier. Well fuck her and fuck Josh. Of all the weekends to pull something like this. It's the goddamn *World Series* and the *Sox* are playing. How could they not understand what an amazing moment in history this is? A moment both Mary and Josh are missing. Stupid, stupid family. How did he ever get involved with such morons? Such ignorant, pathetic human beings. They did this on purpose, it's the only logical explanation. They're out to get him. They're out to destroy him.

The bartender brings him a second beer before he even realizes he's finished his first.

He tries to concentrate on the game but tonight anger consumes him. A rage of biblical proportions tightens his fists and strains the veins in his neck. He wants to hurt something. Goddamn Josh and his idiot friend. They've ruined the game. The game he's been looking forward to his entire life and he can't even fucking enjoy it. If he gets to him before the cops do, he's going to whoop his ass so hard the boy won't be able to ever sit right again, and if the cops get him first, that's fine, too, because this kind of rage, it can be patient if it needs to be. He can wait. He won't forget. In fact, it'll give him something to look forward to. Maybe get in a few practice rounds on Mary first. Dumb bitch deserves to bleed just as much as Josh. If it'd been up to him, Josh would have never even stepped foot in Ottessa's house. He's always said, that family's bad news. Stay away from them. They will only do our own family harm. But does anybody ever listen to him? No, of course not. And now look at where that's gotten them. Ungrateful, selfish fucking family. How did he get so *stuck*, so *trapped*? He never intended on being some *dad* or *husband* working a shitty job. He'd had ambitions, goddammit. He was supposed to be playing baseball. *Professionally.* He'd had what it takes. Nobody could ever deny him that. But then…but then what? Josh, that's what. He came along and he ruined everything and twelve years later the little pain in the ass is still ruining things and somehow Jasper is the only one who can see that. Mary just doesn't get it. Doesn't understand that her and Jasper could have had a great life. One lousy drunken mistake shouldn't be someone's responsibility for the rest of their life. It just *shouldn't.* Maybe it's a good thing Josh is gone. Maybe he'll do his old man a favor and stay missing. *Make me proud, boy, and never show your face around here again.*

The bartender brings him another beer and he no longer remembers how many he's had.

Going into the top of the eighth inning and the Sox lead four to three. If not for that old fuck Clemens calling it quits in the second because of his hamstring, or Crede's numerous defensive miracles over on third base, who the hell knows where they'd be right now. But still, there's plenty of time for the Astros to catch back up and steal the win from them. Steal the win from Jasper. And why *not* take it from him? The one, last thing that could potentially lift his spirits. It'd only make sense for this to end disastrous as well.

Two pitches into the inning, Contreras practically underhands the goddamn ball and Willy Taveras nearly hits it over the fence. Instead, he settles for an easy double. Taveras could have walked to second base without breaking a sweat and still wouldn't have been at risk of getting tagged out. The entire bar shouts their disapproval. Jasper considers chucking his empty glass at the TV but instead requests a refill. Ozzie lowers his head in the dugout and jogs out onto the field and the screen cuts to another commercial break. Inside Rourke's conversation rises to unbearable levels.

Someone taps his shoulder and he almost elbows whoever's sitting next to him, the tension's so tight, so eager for violence. Instead he forces himself to calm down and glances over his shoulder. Tobin grins at him from one stool over, teeth slick with tar and breath reeking of onion. Jasper offers a quick nod, friendly enough not to seem completely rude, but dismissive enough to discourage further interaction. Unfortunately, he doesn't get the hint and instead scoots closer.

"How 'bout this game, huh?" He laughs and claps Jasper on the back. Jasper winces and resists the urge to strangle him.

"It's something, all right," he manages to say through gritted teeth.

"Did you know…"—he points at the TV—"…that today is the birth of Joe Crede's second child?"

"No."

"Isn't it crazy? He hits a home run the day his little girl's born. Isn't that just wild?"

"Yeah. I suppose so."

Jasper doesn't much care for Tobin. Most of the people who frequent Rourke's have grown to dislike him, but they still attempt to tolerate him since once in a while he'll buy everybody a round. It's a hygiene issue, really. The man smells, plain and simple. He's always wearing the same red sweater every time Jasper runs into him. The front is stained with a red pasta sauce that makes Jasper doubt Tobin has ever washed it. Somehow the stain always appears *fresh*, too. Sometimes when he speaks, specks of Dorito dust spit out of his mouth, despite the fact that Rourke's does not offer Doritos.

"So how you been doin', man? Haven't seen you here the last couple days."

No way in hell is Jasper going to tell him about the bowling alley, where he's been preferring to spend his nights more and more. He'd lose his mind if he showed up one evening and found Tobin stinking up the place. "Just been cutting back, spending more time with the family. Stuff like that."

"Oh, that's cool, dude. How's your family, anyway?"

Jasper almost laughs. "They're fine. Thanks."

"You got a little boy, right?"

"Yeah."

"How old is he now?"

"Twelve."

"Oh, man." He sighs with nostalgia. "I remember when I was twelve. Oh man, oh man, oh man. Do I remember or what." He lightly jabs his elbow against Jasper's arm over and over. "Am I right, huh? Huh?"

"Yeah, sure." Jasper removes his arm from the table to discourage further jabs.

"Speaking of…" He leans in closer and his breath somehow smells even worse. "Last night, you won't believe who I hooked up with."

Jasper keeps his eyes trained on the TV. The commercial's finally over. Ozzie got chickenshit and took Contreras out of the game, replacing him with Neal Cotts. Not an unwise decision, to be fair. Cotts ain't bad at all. But still. Maybe Jasper just prefers people to finish what they started.

"I said, you won't believe who I hooked up with."

Jasper groans. "Who?"

"That black chick. Ottessa."

"*What?*"

"You know? She's always in here. The tall black lady. With all the tattoos. Last night I went over to her house and we fucked, dude. It was crazy."

"*Last night?*"

Tobin leans back, suddenly afraid. "Yeah, last night. We got to talking here, I bought her a couple drinks, she asked me if it was true, about my tattoo."

"Your tattoo?"

He hesitates, then nods. "Yeah. Uh. I have this tattoo, on, uh, my dick. It's a yellow smiley face. Sorry, I thought you knew. Everybody knows."

It takes Jasper nearly a full minute to comprehend what he just heard. He decides to ignore it and move on. "Last night, Ottessa was here? Until when?"

He shrugs. "I don't know, man. We hung out for a while. I guess we got to her house a little past midnight."

"Did you see her kid?"

"Her kid?"

"Yes. Her goddamn kid. Did you see him at the house?"

Tobin laughs. "Man, I didn't see no fuckin' kids. It was just me and her. Dude, you won't believe what she let me do."

"Did you stay the night?"

He grins, ear-to-ear. "*Did I*."

Jasper pauses, waiting. "Well, *did* you or not?"

"Oh. Yeah. I spent the night, yes."

"And you didn't see any kids?"

"No kids."

"Motherfucker."

"What's wrong, man?"

"Nothing. Fuck off."

"What?"

"I said, *fuck off*." Jasper's command comes out as a growl.

Tobin flinches. "Okay, man, okay. Sorry to offend you. Have a good night."

He jumps off the stool and flees to an empty booth in the corner of the bar. Jasper turns back to the TV and demands another refill. Rage blossoms within him and begs for him to break something, anything. Destruction as sacrifice. Obliteration as fuel.

He drinks in constant motion until the game's finished, then remains seated and drinks some more. Doesn't stop until 2:00 A.M. hits and the bartender throws him out on his ass. He stumbles through the parking lot, trying to remember what his car looks like, wondering how much money he spent tonight, deciding it doesn't matter, fuck it, why shouldn't he get to have a night of fun? Everybody else can have a good time but him? Nah. Fuck that. If Mary and Josh can have their little adventure, then there's no reason why Jasper can't also enjoy himself a little bit. Besides, it's his fucking money, anyway, so what the fuck, he'd love for Mary to try saying something. He'd break her fuckin' jaw is what he'd do. Break it and laugh laugh laugh.

The Sox won Game One of the World Series and he can't even fucking enjoy it and it's all Mary's fault.

The bitch needs to pay, it's that simple.

If there's one thing he fully understands right now, it's that this kind of shit can't go unpunished, otherwise it'll just keep happening again and again. Like letting a dog piss on the rug. You don't rub its face in the mess, how will the dog know not to repeat its mistake?

It'll just keep pissing and pissing and pissing.

Every action needs a consequence.

Otherwise the world spirals into chaos.

SIXTEEN

*O*utside a car backfires in the night. Ottessa jolts awake and the word "Zoey" trembles across her lips, but it doesn't dare make itself audible. She groans as she sits up. The living room carpet has done hell on her back. Across the living room, Mary snores on the couch. Girl's out for the count. Good for her. Last night she'd needed the booze more than Ottessa.

Last night? Hell, it still is night. One glance out the window makes a clock irrelevant, but she still searches for the blinking neon red digits located at the top of her credenza. A little after two in the morning.

Around the time the boys were confronted outside her house.

Goddamn how she wishes she could rewind the last twenty-four hours. As soon as she spotted those flashing lights, she'd stomp outside and demand answers. *Why are you stopping my boy? Has he done anything wrong? What's your badge number, asshole?*

Would those questions have altered the future? She likes to believe yes. If she had the badge numbers, then surely the pigs would have operated more carefully about their business and whatever nefarious shit went wrong last night would have been avoided. But now she knows nothing, all because she was too chickenshit to leave the porch, admit she was high and drunk. Shit, if she could go back in time, she would have never fucking gone out last night. She would have just stayed home, maybe picked up one of those $5 pizzas from Little Caesar's and watched a movie with Zoey and Josh. Maybe they wouldn't have felt the need to sneak out. Maybe she could have saved them.

Ottessa blinks and finds herself standing out in her front yard, transported from the living room, zero memory of ever standing from the floor. Sharp strands of grass poke at the soles of her feet and wiggle between her toes. The street is bare of life. Nobody waits for her in front of the house. No Zoey, no cops, no anybody.

She closes her eyes, still inebriated, and stretches out her arms, letting the breeze caress her body. *Carry me,* she silently begs, *carry me to my boy.*

Still without sight, Ottessa steps forward. The grass guides her to the unlocked gate. She pushes it open with her hips and continues onto the sidewalk, the jagged cement harsher against her feet. *Bleed if you must. Leave a trail of your blood for Zoey to find his way home.* Intuition advises her to step over a tree's swollen roots as she heads into the street. The pavement chills her body and she stops. This is where he was standing last night. This is where Zoey was arrested. Her feet are placed in the exact same spot her boy's feet had been only twenty-four hours previously. She can feel him, she swears she can feel him. She reaches forward, sure that her hand will touch his cheek, and for a second she does, she really does, holy shit, he's here, he's really here, she can feel his skin wet with tears against her palm, and she opens her eyes, trembling with relief, prepared to give him the biggest goddamn hug any mother's ever given her child, but there's nobody here, she's touching the wind, only the wind.

Ottessa chokes back a scream and starts gagging. She kneels, each hand clutching a knee, and vomits an ocean of vodka. It splatters against the street and stains her feet, ankles, legs. It sprays from her nose and mouth, invoking a burning sensation through her nostrils and throat. As she's wiping her face with the back of her hand, she spots something next to the curb glinting against the streetlight above. Something small and blue.

And her chest tightens as she realizes it's Josh's camera.

Vomit forgotten, she rushes to the curb and picks it up, desperate to hear Zoey's voice again. But no matter how many times she jabs her thumb against the power button, the screen remains black.

The batteries are dead.

TOUCH THE NIGHT

BEFORE DOING ANYTHING ELSE, OTTESSA takes a shower and washes off the vomit from her legs, the dirt from her feet, the tears from her face. After she dries off she heads into the living room, one hundred percent nude, then performs a quick U-turn at the sight of Mary passed out on the couch. In all of her excitement, Ottessa had forgotten she was even here. She throws on some sweat pants and a flannel shirt—belonging to whothefuck-knows—and hurries down to the basement. Once the power button's pressed the computer starts its long ritual of booting up. She returns upstairs and prepares a pot of coffee. Despite all the vomiting outside, there is still far too much vodka in her system. Fear tries its best to convince her there's no way in hell she's going to be able to watch whatever's on Josh's camera sober. If anything, she needs to consume more liquor.

She ignores the fear and watches the coffee slowly drip into the pot.

In her mind, each drop that splatters against the bottom of the carafe represents another scream exploding from her boy's lungs. Another second of agony added to the pile.

To the mountain.

She has to find him. She has to save him. She has to make things right again.

Couch springs in the living room adjust noisily as Mary wakes and races through the house into the bathroom. Gagging and vomit splashing into a toilet follow. Then a low moan. Ottessa smirks and thinks *amateur*, then remembers the way she'd sprayed her own feet out in the street. Goddamn, how much did they have to drink? It shouldn't be possible to even be awake so soon. Both of their bodies ought to be deep in comas, the way they'd gulped down glass after glass.

The toilet flushes and water spills from the bathroom faucet. Ottessa leans against the kitchen counter with her arms crossed over her chest and waits. Mary eventually recovers enough to exit the bathroom and stumble back toward the living room, then stops when she notices Ottessa standing there, watching her.

"What are you doing awake?"

Ottessa nods at the coffee pot. "Brewing some coffee. You?"

Mary runs her hand through her hair, as if suddenly paranoid she missed some of the vomit. "Bathroom. Why are you making—"

"I found Josh's camera."

Mary's face goes blank. "What?"

Ottessa points toward the front of the house. "Outside, by the street."

"You found his camera?"

"Yeah."

Her eyes darken and her brow lowers into a V, like she's furious. "What? When did you...? *How?*"

Ottessa steps forward, not liking this put-on-trial bullshit. "Just now. A few minutes ago, shit. I stepped out to smoke a cigarette. It was just laying there in the street."

"But...but...how..." Mary runs both hands through her hair, body trembling.

"My guess is he dropped it last night, when he got picked up."

"Where is it?"

"Have a cup of coffee with me. Sober up first."

Mary stops pacing. The furious V returns to her face. "Fuck that. Where's the goddamn camera, Ottessa?"

Ottessa retreats back against the counter. She's never heard Mary speak like that and she's surprised by how threatened she feels by it. It's sexy. She turns away from Mary and retrieves two mugs from the cupboard.

"Where's the camera, Ottessa?"

"How do you take your coffee?"

Mary hesitates, probably debating whether to continue arguing or not. "Some cream. Some sugar."

Ottessa nods as she pours the coffee. "Milk okay?"

"I guess."

She pulls out the half-empty carton of milk and sniffs the lidless rim and grimaces. "How about just sugar?"

TWO CHAIRS ARE ALREADY PULLED up to the computer desk in the basement from the last time Zoey and Josh used it. Ottessa chooses the one she remembers Zoey usually sitting in. Mary sits behind her, cradling a full cup of coffee with shaky hands.

"Have you tried turning it on?"

"Batteries are dead."

"Oh."

"I think we can still watch what's on it. Give me a second." Ottessa rests her cup on the desk and dejects the memory card from Josh's camera then inserts it into the small slot below the disk drive. A box pops up revealing a series of .avi files. The first ten are dated 10.21.05 and the last two are dated 10.22.05. "Should we start from the beginning or the end?"

Mary doesn't answer.

Ottessa double-clicks on the earliest video and forces half the cup of coffee down her throat, not giving a shit if it burns.

She hopes it does.

SEVENTEEN

0705_10.21.05.avi

Josh stands in front of a mirror, pointing the camera at his reflection. He's wearing a black T-shirt with a nearly shirtless Bruce Campbell wielding a chainsaw across the front. The words ARMY OF DARKNESS are printed above the actor, except in the mirror's image it reads as ꙄꙄƎИꓘЯА⅁ ꟻО YМЯА. One of Josh's favorite shirts. He nods along to an inaudible beat and mumbles a series of rhymes, most of them unintelligible. Somewhere else in the house, Mary shouts, "Josh! School bus!" and Josh panics as he looks down at the camera in his hand and fumbles for the power button.

0709_10.21.05.avi

The camera blinks back to life but instead of Josh's face it's now focused on the olive-green leather of what's presumably the back of a bus seat. It moves to the side and looks through the glare of a window. The town passes by as if the houses are connected to a conveyor belt in perpetual motion. A line of vermillion rips through the sky above the trees marking the outskirts of Percy. The sun hatching into another day, right on schedule as always.

Off screen, a kid shouts, "Josh! Quick! Get this on camera!" and the POV sweeps to the left, just in time to confront a boy on his knees and elbows in the seat across the aisle. His pants are pulled down, exposing his bare, pale prepubescent buttocks for all to see.

Behind the camera, Josh groans. "Oh man, when was the last time you washed your ass?"

And the boy laughs before replying, "Never!"

Somewhere much farther away, an older man shouts, "Nick! Goddammit! What did I say about that shit?"

The boy—Nick—giggles again and pulls his pants back up and sits normally on the seat.

Still filming him, Josh says, "Goddamn, man, that was disgu—"

1122_10.21.05.avi

School cafeteria. Bright fluorescent lights. The loud chit-chat of a hundred or more kids talking all at once, like rats fornicating inside a wall, an anthem of increasingly loud chaos. The camera's fragile microphone can barely handle it. Laughter. Screaming. Shouting. Sneakers squeaking against slick hard maple wood flooring.

The camera focuses on Alonzo sitting across from its operator. A long flap of what appears to be the skin of a peeled piece of fried chicken hangs over his face, like a mask. "You ready?" he asks, the chicken skin bouncing off his chin. A thumb appears in front of the screen, connected to a hand, which is connected to an arm stretching from behind the camera. Josh's thumb. Josh's arm. Josh Josh Josh.

The thumb lowers out of view and Alonzo raises both arms, extending them at unnatural levels from his chest, mimicking the composure of a zombie or perhaps Frankenstein (it's Frankenstein's monster, Mom!). He emits a raspy, drawn-out moan from behind the chicken skin mask and screams, "Leatherface comin' for ya, boy! Leatherface comin' for dat ass!"

Behind the camera, Josh explodes with laughter. "I don't think that's quite something he would say."

Alonzo points at his mask. "I don't see you with a buncha chicken shit on your face."

This comment, of course, only inspires more humor. "I'm sorry, I didn't realize you had shit on your face. That's a whole 'nother level of commitment right there, Zoey."

Alonzo rips the chicken skin mask from his face and quickly scans the cafeteria, like he's searching for potential eavesdroppers. "Man, what the fuck did I say about calling me th—"

1337_10.21.05.avi

Darkness. A man talking, not too close but still near enough to be heard.

"But that don't make any sense to me." Josh's voice. "They weren't even doing nothing. And, like, didn't they also shoot that retard in the back? On the bridge?"

The darkness dissolves as the lens pokes through an opening—the sleeve of Josh's hoodie, maybe. A classroom. Josh sits toward the back row. At the front of the room, a tall lanky old white guy stands before a blackboard, hands behind his back. The classroom's laughing at Josh's question, like he just cracked some hilarious joke, but there's not an ounce of humor to be found in his tone.

The teacher hesitates, confused, then nods. "Ah, yes. You're referring to Danziger Bridge. And regardless of what is claimed of the man's mental capacity, he was still one of the many thugs who tried to take advantage of a crisis. The police did everything they had to to maintain order."

"But that ain't what happened."

The class goes, "Ooooh."

The teacher sneers. "Oh, that ain't *what happened, huh?"*

The class laughs.

Josh doesn't respond.

Silence, then, somewhere to the right, off-screen, Alonzo speaks up: "Nobody even had any guns on them or anything. Nobody was breaking the law and they still got themselves shot."

The teacher laughs. "Son, they were responding to reports of a fellow officer who had been injured in the line of duty. Injured by the thugs you seem to think are innocent."

Alonzo again, voice getting higher: "That's fuckin' bullshit, though."

"Excuse me?"

"There wasn't no officer down or nothing like that. They made that shit up for an excuse to kill black people. Black people who weren't doin' a goddamn thing but mindin' they own business."

"Alonzo, if you want to talk like one of your 'gangsta' rappers, I think you're in the wrong building."

"Is that all you can say? Really?" A seat squeals against the floor. Alonzo standing up from his desk. "Why don't you fucking admit that the cops weren't even in uniform? Why don't you tell everybody about how they lined up with big, crazy machine guns and started shooting random black people for no good reason? Why don't you fucking—"

"That's it. Out of my class. Now."

"Yeah, fuck you too."

"You as well, Josh."

Josh: "Why?"

"I won't have this sort of disruption in my class. Get out."

"But…"

"Josh. Now."

"…Okay."

1403_10.21.05.avi

Close-up on Josh's face. Tears streaming down his cheeks. Behind him, solid brick. The walls of a bathroom stall poke into view from either side of him. He's sitting on a toilet, camera in his lap, directed up so he can stare down into the lens. His lips tremble as he whispers, "I'm not, I'm not, I'm not, I'm not I'm not I'm not I'm not I'm not I'm not I'm—"

1522_10.21.05.avi

Front of the school. Hordes of children pour from the doors like a heavy flow of water smashing through a dam. Josh stands somewhere on the lawn, filming the top of the steps. Alonzo waits behind the railing, waiting for Josh's *signal. Josh gives him the thumbs-up and Alonzo screams—no,* howls—*then sprints forward and leaps on top of the stair railing and runs down the metal bar, passing all the other kids hurrying down the steps. At the bottom of the railing he jumps once again, attempting to leap over a trash can. His foot snags the edge of the can and pulls him down to the ground, face-first. The trash can follows after him, showering his body with old, wet garbage. Behind the camera, Josh gasps and shouts, "Zo!" The camera screen goes wild as he races across the grass toward his friend. Other kids surround the fall point and laugh their asses off. Alonzo remains on the ground, rolling back and forth, holding his stomach, and he turns over on his back and looks up at the camera above him, grinning, laughing.*

"What do you think? Good enough for Jackass *or what?"*

1556_10.21.05.avi

A deafening roar threatens the camera's microphone. Josh stands in a patch of untamed grass, filming a passing train. Graffiti smothers its exterior. Mostly just penises and skulls, with the occasional gang symbol thrown in for good measure. Alonzo eventually stumbles into view, clutching a large stone with both hands. He shouts something inaudible at the camera. Josh responds with another thumbs-up and Alonzo nods and grins, then turns to the train and staggers toward the tracks. A moment of brief hesitation passes, then he lifts the rock with two shaky hands over his shoulder and throws it with everything he's got. The side of the train swats the projectile away like it's a gnat and it ricochets back the way it came, missing Alonzo's head by mere inches. Nonetheless, he turns and flees as if it hadn't already done him the generosity of avoiding contact. Judging by the shade of fear masking his face, it'll be a miracle if the boy hasn't ruined his pants. Josh remains in the same spot all this time, except now the camera's far less steady. Alonzo reaches him and they both kneel over and at first it appears like they're crying together, but no, that's not it at all. They're laughing.

1710_10.21.05.avi

Darkness again. Josh and Alonzo talking. Traffic nearby. Pants rustling together. Wind picking up momentum.

Josh: "You sure we should be recording this?"

Alonzo: "Hell yeah, man. We gotta *record it. Trust me."*

Josh: "But wouldn't this be, like, you know, evidence?"

Alonzo (laughing): "What, you plan on showing it to somebody? You got some other friend you ain't introduce me to yet?"

Josh: "No…"

Alonzo: "Who would possibly come across it besides just the two of us? We could use it as a scene in some crime movie, maybe. Something like Jackie Brown, *you know? Shit don't get more authentic than the real thing."*

Then: the unmistakable sound of an automatic door sliding open and the ensuing chirp alerting employees to their new guests. Whatever had been covering the lens disappears—the inside of Josh's hoodie pocket?—and Josh quickly props up the camera on top of something in the front corner of what appears to be the interior of Dollar General. Josh leans in close as he makes sure the camera isn't going to tip over, then backs away.

The only cashier present is the old lady—Gladys—that Mary and Ottessa would end up assaulting a little over twenty-four hours after this recording. She rings up another woman purchasing Pampers. In the background, barely visible, stands Alonzo browsing titles at a magazine rack.

Josh approaches a small Pepsi cooler and crouches, as if debating what pop to purchase. Then, quite abruptly, he shoots up and grabs at his chest and screams, "Oh no! My heart! It's having, uh, an attack! It's a…a…it's a heart attack! Yeah, that's it! A heart attack! Ow! Ow! Ow!"

Both the woman purchasing Pampers and the old lady ringing her up pause and observe the commotion, unsure of the boy's motives. Then he collapses to the floor, vanishing from the camera's view, and the women finally snap out of their daze and rush over to offer their aid.

Meanwhile, back by the magazine rack, Alonzo redirects his attention to the checkout aisle and starts rifling through the items hanging above the conveyor belt. He stuffs a couple small boxes in his pockets then quietly sneaks out of the store, leaving Josh to fend for himself.

Another ten or so seconds pass and Josh climbs to his feet with the assistance of the two women. He thanks them both and nears the front doors, stops, looks over his shoulder at the women still staring at him, then grabs the camera from its vantage point and runs out of the store. Alonzo waits for him in the parking lot, laughing and waving. "C'mon, let's get the fuck out of here before those bitches call the cops!"

2017_10.21.05.avi

Close-up on Josh's face as he struggles to prop up the camera on whatever he's trying to use to keep it from tipping over. Satisfied, he backs away and sits on the carpet next to a pile of old towels. Alonzo crouches behind him, one hand resting on Josh's shoulder to control his balance. "Should I do it?"

"Yeah," Josh says, perfectly still, eyes on the camera. "But say something cool first."

"Something cool?"

"Yeah."

"Something cool like what?*"*

"I don't know. Like something from a movie. You know, like, a cool movie line."

"Oh. Okay. Uh." He hesitates, then grins and holds up a large knife. "Leatherface comin' for dat ass, boy!"

Josh starts laughing and Alonzo wraps his arm around Josh's forehead and with his other hand brings the knife down under his jaw and slices his throat.

A geyser of blood sprays from Josh's ripped-open neck and splatters against the towels, his lap, the carpet, then it hits the camera and blinds the screen. Josh's coughing fit ceases. "Goddammit, Zoey, stop, it got on the camera, fuck, son of a—"

2039_10.21.05.avi

Alonzo sitting at the computer, Josh next to him holding the camera. Alonzo reads from the phone book and dials a number into their telephone, then clicks the speaker button. It rings four times before a man answers.

"He-hello?"

Instead of saying anything, Alonzo quickly presses a button on the computer, triggering an audio sample from Arnold Schwarzenegger: "Who is your daddy?"

"What?"

Both Josh and Alonzo struggle to muffle their laugher. Alonzo clicks the button again.

"Who is your daddy?"

"Excuse me. Who is this?"

Schwarzenegger again: "How are you?"

"I'm fine. Who's calling?" The man sounds grumpy, like they just woke him up.

"Let me talk to your mother."

"My what? Listen, I think you got the wrong number, pal, I—"

"No, it is not true."

"What?"

"I want to ask you a bunch of questions."

"Who is this?"

"First, I would just like to get to know you."

"Listen, you have the wrong number, okay? I'm gonna hang up." Now the man's voice sounds familiar. The teacher from a previous clip. The one who kicked Josh and Alonzo out of his class.

"Come on, don't bullshit me."

"Excuse me?"

"You lack discipline."

"What?"

"Get your mother, please."

"Fuck you, buddy. I'm hanging up."

"You are a fucking choir boy compared to me!"

"I was never even in the fucking choir, asshole!"

Josh can barely focus the camera, he's laughing so loud. Alonzo continues working the Schwarzenegger soundboard: "You want to fuck with me? You son of a bitch. Who the fuck are you?"

"You called me! I really ought to kick your ass."

174

"*Come on, baby, you know you're the girl of my dreams.*"

"*Oh, you think you're cute? Tell you what, pal, I would love to just break your fuckin' neck.*"

Alonzo loses control and starts laughing out loud and the man hangs up. Both boys continue laughing for a solid thirty seconds before the clip ends.

0251_10.22.05.avi

Night. A baseball field. Alonzo's running around the bases, heading toward home, and slides through the gravel. His feet smash into a plastic bag and paper flies everywhere. Money? He picks up the bag and scoops its contents back inside and holds up his arms, triumphantly. "*And the crowd goes wild as Jones wins the scoring run! They can't believe it! He actually fucking did it! Everybody is losing their shit down here! You should see the tits on some of these chicks taking off their shirts to congratulate the great baseball god, Alonzo Jones, number six-six-six! Not just the number of the beast but also the number of the greatest goddamn baseball player to have ever lived!*"

He stops in front of the camera and hunches over, out of breath. "*What do you think, coach? I got what it takes?*"

0305_10.22.05.avi

Darkness.

Alonzo's voice, a desperate whisper: "*Oh shit.*" *A beat, then:* "*Dude, fucking run.*"

Josh, just as terrified-sounding: "*Run where? This is where you live.*"

"*Shut the fuck up. Don't you dare tell them that.*"

Sudden movement. Scraping against clothing. Then the lens spins out of control, followed by a loud smash. Flashes of red and blue. The camcorder's fallen out of Josh's pocket and landed in the street. Next to the curb, where Ottessa will discover it twenty-four hours later.

"*What, that this is your—*"

"I'm your brother."

"What—?"

"Just shut the fuck up and don't tell them shit."

The camcorder faces the house across from Ottessa's. The lights from a cop car shower it red and blue. In the window, the curtain's been brushed slightly aside, revealing a woman's face as she watches the scene unfold.

Josh: "Why is he just sitting there?"

Alonzo: "Probably just trying to scare us."

"Well, he's doing a good job then."

"Don't let this asshole get to you. He ain't gonna do shit."

"In case you've forgotten, cops kind of love shooting black kids up to no good."

"Fuck them."

"You think they know about the gas station?"

"They don't know shit. There ain't shit to know."

"What if the gas station had cameras?"

"Shut up."

A loud creaking shoots through the night. Car doors opening.

"Do not even fucking think about it," someone says off camera. A new voice. Gruff, alien. "You make one wrong move and I will not hesitate to put you down."

Alonzo: "What's the matter, guys? The doughnut shop closed early tonight?"

A pause, then the man says, "Say, what could two little cocksuckers like yourselves be doing out here all alone at this time of night?"

Alonzo: "Can we fuckin' help you?"

"As a matter of fact," says the man, and another man with nearly an identical voice finishes the sentence, "...you can."

Laughter from Alonzo is short-lived as the sound of a struggle follows. Alonzo and Josh protesting, shouting to be let go. The banging of something against steel, possibly the hood of a police car. The two cops say more things to the boys, but at this point they're too far away for the camcorder to make it out. As the conversation continues, Alonzo tries saying something that sounds like, "None of your fuckin' business," but he's interrupted and instead lets out a loud yelp and begins

176

coughing. The cops are interrogating them. About what, it's impossible to say, not with the camcorder's shitty built-in microphone.

"Alonzo what?" one of the cops suddenly shouts, and Alonzo screams back his last name.

More laughter follows, then the conversation quiets down again until Alonzo starts shouting, "Hey, man, we got fuckin' rights, you can't harass us like this. We'll have your asses sued so fast you'll—"

"Oh, will you shut the fuck up already?" one of the cops says, then Josh starts screaming Alonzo's name and begging for someone to help them. Car doors open and close, open and close. Josh's screaming becomes muffled. The red and blue lights die out. In front of the camcorder, a white car speeds past, too fast for the lens to pick up any specific details, then the camcorder is left alone on the street, abandoned by its owner. It remains filming the house next door for another half hour before the battery dies.

EIGHTEEN

They sit and watch the final video run out the camera's battery, abandoned in the street during the dead of night. Stray vehicles passing the screen occasionally interrupt the neighborhood's silence, oblivious to the events that have just occurred here. At least, Ottessa assumes they're oblivious. Snapshots of that crazy Dollar General bitch flash in her mind and suddenly she isn't so sure anybody in the whole goddamn town is entirely innocent. If even a sliver of doubt had existed concerning what she'd witnessed last night, it's gone now. The video proves it. Everything she's been saying. It's all here. The motherfucking pigs are behind everything, and although Sheriff Peckerwood isn't found anywhere near these recordings, she's positive he's the bitch in charge. Who else?

Besides, it's not like the video actually showed the cops who apprehended them. One of them could have been the sheriff. She doesn't know. She doesn't know shit.

She turns back to Mary, then all excitement drains as she spots the utter devastation consuming her face. Poor girl looks like she just identified her boy's corpse in the morgue, and in a way, maybe that's exactly what she'd done. Ottessa reaches out and lightly touches her knee and Mary screams and jumps and the still-full mug of coffee tumbles to the floor, staining the carpet at her feet brown.

Mary's halfway upstairs before Ottessa can say a word.

Ottessa hangs back a moment, debating just letting her go, letting her run back home to her terrible husband where he will surely do his damnedest to prevent her from leaving the house ever again. She gets the feeling this time Mary would obey him, would stay home and give up the search—the real search, not that useless flyer-hanging bullshit—give up and watch the goddamn World Series and, aside from brief spells of longing and self-hatred sprinkled throughout the rest of her days, tonight will be the last time Josh lived in her head as someone who was still alive, as someone who could still be saved.

Ottessa swears and chases after her, sure that she's too late, that Mary will be long gone by now, but no, she never even got in her car. Instead she sits on the curb, feet spread out across the street's cool pavement. Ottessa approaches with caution, waiting for a nod of approval before sitting next to her. Immediately she regrets not grabbing a pack of smokes when she was still in the house. Could always walk down to the gas station and buy some more. Maybe have a little word with the guy working the register, ask him if he's heard any updates about his coworker's health, find out if her boy's officially a murderer yet.

"I...I just..." Mary sucks in a deep breath and takes a moment to regain her composure. "I just...they...this is where they were...in...in the..."

"Yeah." Ottessa nods, grimacing at the snot leaking from Mary's sobbing face. "This is it. This is where I saw them."

"And you did nothing."

"What?"

The crying comes to a halt. Rage blossoms. "You just sat there—where? On the porch? Watching the whole time?"

"No...not the *whole* time. I woke up toward the end."

"But you heard the way they were speaking to them. To our boys. You *heard* the language they were using."

"Baby, ain't you never heard no cop talk before?"

"It don't...it don't *matter*, Ottessa, and you *know* it. If that was me...if that was me, and I saw them being talked to by the police, I wouldn't have hesitated. I would have went out there right away, and if I heard them talking to my son like...like *that*...I would have went crazy. I would have—"

Ottessa stands, sick of hearing this shit. "It don't matter what you would've done 'cause you weren't there, and all this hypothetical bullshit ain't gonna help nobody, especially not while Zoey and Josh are still out there. Yes, I was here. Yes, I watched. Yes, I didn't do anything about it. What the fuck do you want me to say, huh? I was fuckin' *drunk*, okay? I was *high*. The way I grew up, you get in trouble with the law, then you rotted the night in a cell, give you some *perspective*, some time to think about the way you was treating your life, give you some kinda sneak peek at what was in store for you if you kept on going around actin' like some asshole. When I was sixteen—*hey*, you want to *hear* something?—when I was *sixteen*, I got caught at the mall with about a dozen tubes of lipstick in my bra. The real nice shit, too. The stuff I could never even dream of affording, like *Clinique*, none of that Wet and Wild bullshit. Barely even made it out the door before some mustached fatass grabbed my shoulder and dragged me back to his office. Apparently he'd been watching me on his security camera the moment I walked into the store. Perverted piece of shit was probably jacking off the whole time, too, come to think about it. But yeah, so they call the cops and the cops call my mama and my mama says, 'Let the little whore rot,' and if you think I'm exaggerating or making shit up, think again, 'cause they had that shit on speakerphone, couldn't believe their ears when she told them that, had to make sure I also heard it, told her to repeat it again, this time loud enough for the entire station. *Let the little whore rot.* That's what she told them, so that's exactly what they did. Threw my little sixteen-year-old ass in a cell. Nothing official, of course, shit was just makeup, fuck, they weren't gonna waste the paperwork on me, right? Kept me there all fuckin' day, then my mama comes and collects me just before nine, asks if I learned my lesson, and you know what? I never did get caught shoplifting again. I'm not saying I stopped. I just never got caught, not from that moment on. It made me smarter, made me understand my place in the world. And…I don't know, when I saw Zoey and Josh out there with those red and blue lights, I thought about my mama and what she would have done and I thought they had probably done some stupid shit and it wouldn't do anybody any good if I went out there and tried to bail them out of trouble. And, since I'm being so motherfuckin' goddamn honest right now, like

I already said, I was drunk, high on pills, goddamn *terrified*. How do you think it would have looked if I came walking out of the house, half-naked, tripping, smelling like dick, and asked them what they was doing with my son and his friend? They would have taken one good look at me and dialed the number for CPS. Do you think they would have given Josh back to you? Oh, hell no, not after *your* judgment decided it would be okay to leave your child alone with a drug-addicted alcoholic sex fiend. See, girl? I can live in hypotheticals, too, and we still ain't no closer to finding Zoey and Josh than we was ten minutes ago."

Out of breath, Ottessa returns to her seat on the curb, no longer remembering what had ignited her outburst.

After a while, Mary finally responds. "Why does it smell like puke out here?"

IT'S A LITTLE PAST SIX by the time they pull up in front of Mary's house. The sun won't be out for another hour or so. A stillness loiters about town. Sunday morning. Not a soul with a legitimate reason for being awake. Percy, taking pride in its religion, either delays the openings of most businesses until late in the afternoon or they remain closed until Monday. Not even late enough in the morning for church to begin yet.

Mary says to wait in the car and Ottessa says fuck that.

She tries to protest being followed, but she sounds more polite than genuine. Ottessa's heard Real Mary and this ain't her. As they slip in through the front door, Mary turns and gives her a librarian's finger-shush and Ottessa nods like *no shit, you think I really want to wake up your annoying-ass hubby and listen to him whine?*

Mary motions for her to stay in the living room and this time Ottessa hangs back and sits at the edge of their recliner. Judging by the ass indentation and overwhelming beer aroma, this here is Jasper's primary spot of comfort. Beer doesn't smell so good when it's coming from someone else.

Ottessa readjusts on the recliner and quietly farts into the cushion, thinking, *Take that, you fuck.*

The living room is nearly spotless compared to Ottessa's. This is the first time she's ever been inside Mary's house, despite Zoey and Josh being best friends since kindergarten. If she were someone who gave a shit about such petty matters, she might find herself offended. But it doesn't matter, not really. Hell, come to think about it, she's never invited Mary into her own home, either.

Elsewhere in the house, a door creaks open. Mary sneaking into the master bedroom, probably. Something in the living room moans and Ottessa bites her tongue. Across from the recliner a little old lady sleeps on a loveseat, wrapped in a thick quilt. Mary had mentioned something about her mother coming over to help. Obviously this is her. But still. Ottessa's a little spooked it took so long to notice her presence.

In another room, the groggy confused voice of Jasper ignites: "Mary? What—what the hell are you *doing?*"

Mary: "Nothing. Go back to bed."

Ottessa glances back at the old lady on the loveseat and hopes like hell she doesn't wake up. They're not even trying to be quiet.

Jasper: "Where have you been? You…you never came home last night."

"I'm here now."

"Yeah, at what…what time is it?—Jesus Christ, Mary, it's almost six-thirty. Are you fucking serious? Where have you been?"

"Being a parent."

"What the fuck is that supposed to mean?" His speech is interrupted by the sound of bedsprings adjusting, then heavy footsteps against a wooden floor. "You leave and don't tell me where you're going—"

"I told you where I was going."

"Oh cut the bullshit, Mary. It doesn't take all goddamn night to hang up flyers and you know it."

Someone else might have pretended to feel dirty, eavesdropping like this, but Ottessa doesn't care, she loves this kind of stuff. Other people yelling for

183

once. It's exciting and sort of scary which only seems to make it more exciting. Across the living room, the old lady stirs awake on the loveseat. She rubs her eye and groans and sits up and looks around the room, maybe trying to determine the source of the yelling—or, probably more realistically, trying to remember where she even is. The expression on her face says, *I have no idea who I am.*

Eventually her ancient eyes find Ottessa, but her demeanor does not alter. "Are you the one who murdered Joshua?"

Ottessa slowly shakes her head no.

"Do you know who did?"

"Not yet."

"Will you find those responsible?"

"Yes."

"Will you kill them?"

"Yes."

"Okay. Thank you."

She yawns and lies back down and almost immediately begins to snore again.

What the fuck, Ottessa thinks, and heads toward the sound of Mary and Jasper arguing. They both stand in the master bedroom's walk-in closet, which explains the abrupt muffled nature of their voices. Jasper leans against the closet's doorframe, dressed only in boxers, watching Mary dig through bags and boxes on top of clothing racks.

"You gonna tell me what you're looking for or not? And also, while you're at it, why you reek of cheap vodka?"

This makes Mary laugh like a lunatic. "Like you've never come home smelling like alcohol before."

"What the fuck are you trying to say? I'll fuckin' knock your lights out, bitch. You got no idea."

Ottessa clears her throat, loud and obnoxious. "Boy, you lay even a finger on her and it'll be the last thing you ever touch again."

Jasper practically leaps out of his skin. The surprise on his face when he turns around is immensely comical, and she'd laugh if she weren't so pissed off.

"What the fuck are *you* doing here?"

From the closet, Mary shouts, "Got it!"

"Got *what?*" Jasper turns back, then backpedals as Mary forces herself through the opening. The way she stomps out of the closet, it's almost like Jasper isn't even there, like he's some ghost viewing the scene in a dead world parallel to their own.

Yet, still, he thinks his protests matter.

"Is that my gun? Mary, is that my gun?"

He indicates the small blag bag slung over her shoulder. She grips on the strap and nods. "We gotta borrow it. I'll bring it back when I'm done."

"Oh, you *gotta borrow it.* Sure, why not. Go right ahead, honey, please, just show up at six in the goddamn morning after being gone all night and *borrow* my gun. Because that's real normal, right?"

He follows them out of the bedroom, back through the house, stopping in the kitchen. Mary drags a chair from the table to the side of the fridge and collects a coffee can. The floor is covered with muddy footprints and Ottessa no longer feels so bad about her own house.

Jasper's fists tighten at his sides and Ottessa promises to herself that if he takes one more step toward Mary she's gonna break his nose, and she probably won't stop there.

"Oh sure, babe, on top of my gun, please also take our emergency funds. Why not, right? Why the fuck not."

Coffee can tucked under her armpit, she climbs down and rubs her temple. An impossible headache, one that Ottessa feels just as much as Mary, a combination of too much vodka, too much crying, and too much Jasper.

When Mary talks, she can't even muster energy to look at him. "Just… just shut up. Please just shut up." Then she points at a broken bottle of some kind of white sauce on the floor in front of the fridge. "And can you clean that up? It's disgusting. This whole kitchen is a mess. You tracked in dirt all over the place."

Jasper ignores the remark and follows them out into the living room. Ottessa points at the loveseat, now empty. "Hey, where did your mom go?"

Jasper screws up his face. "She...she left last night. The hell do you care, anyway?"

Ottessa cocks her head back, giving the bare furniture a double-take. "I was just talking to her."

He stares, wide-eyed, then follows her gaze to the loveseat and shakes his head, focuses on Mary again. "Are you going to tell me what you're doing or not?"

This time Mary looks him straight-on. "I'm going to get our son back."

NINETEEN

We're fucked, Josh thinks in the dark, *we're totally fucked.* Alonzo hasn't said anything in...in too long. Josh has given up on calling out to him. He can't blame him for not talking. Not after what he was forced to do. Yet Josh remains grateful that he'd done it. Even though the bag's been removed, he can still feel the plastic pressed against his face, constricting into him like a perpetually tightening mask, his mouth wide open, trying to breathe, trying to scream, no air going in, no sound coming out.

In the darkness, Josh shudders.

Another hour, or maybe another day—who could possibly tell?—passes before anybody speaks again.

Don, or maybe Shane, says, "I'm...I'm really sorry about that. There was really no way to warn you ahead of time. Best just to...let you find out for yourself."

Shane, or maybe Don, says, "If it's any consolation, she really was a cannibal."

"Shit. Aren't we all at this point?"

"Not them. Not yet."

"It's only a matter of time."

"What—what are you talking about?" Josh asks.

"Next time one of those psycho fucks come down here," Don says, "they're most likely going to make you guys eat the old hag your pal just bludgeoned."

"No..."

"It's okay," Shane says. "They've done it to all of us. Trust me, you spend enough time down here, *any* meat is gonna start sounding good, it won't matter where it came from."

"Shit, just wait, one day—hopefully one day soon—will come when y'all will get a chance to feast upon our own flesh," Don says, "as little as there is at this point, at least it'll be something."

"They fed me some of my own ass not that long ago," Shane says. "Not as bad as you'd think."

And Josh says, "Fuck you both."

Don groans, or laughs, who can tell. "Our fuckin' days are long over, boy. In case you missed it, the family's already done collected our cocks. I'm sure they'll be down before long to take yours, too."

"They sure love cutting off the penis," Shane says.

"The cycle will repeat itself, over and over, until they finally get what they want. Whatever the hell that even is."

"Do they even want anything? I don't think so. They're just crazy, plain and simple. You don't need a reason to do something when you're fuckin' nuts. You do it just...just because you want to."

His words trail off and they sit in silence again, pondering the motives of madmen. But are they truly men? Josh has his doubts. He doesn't know what the hell they are, not really. A part of him's convinced that if he knew more about them, about where they came from, then maybe he could use the information to ultimately defeat them, like they're fucking video game bosses or something.

If this were a horror movie, maybe the bad people—*things,* bad *things*—would possess some kind of secret weakness. Vampires have the sun. Werewolves have silver bullets. But what do these fake police have? You shoot zombies in the brain, you burn the bones of a ghost, but what the hell do you do to *these* things?

And even if he *did* know, how exactly is he supposed to do anything about it? Not only are they locked down here in this basement, but they're also restrained by straitjackets. And even if, hypothetically, the straitjackets

188

loosened and they somehow managed to pick the basement locks, what then? As far as he knows, the house is still crawling with those hideous fucking mutated ghouls. Josh is only twelve, as fast as a snail, and possesses the strength of a toddler. His body is not prepared to battle monsters. If this were a horror movie, he would be a few years older, and athletic. He'd look good without a shirt on. He'd have abs other kids his age would slobber over and find enviable. He'd know how to fight. He'd be able to run fast and create cool elaborate traps for his enemies, *Home Alone*-style.

If this were a horror movie, the monsters wouldn't win at the end.

Well, okay, *maybe* they would win, but the protagonists would at least get a decent chance to fight back. They wouldn't be wearing straitjackets the whole time, that's for damn sure. No audience wants to watch a fat kid getting tortured for ninety minutes and that's it.

Jesus Christ.

What a downer.

Alonzo breaks the basement's stuffy silence with what can barely be defined as a whisper. "There's something in the cornfield."

Instinct tells Josh to reach out and touch his friend's shoulder, offer some kind of comfort, but the straitjacket prevents him from budging even an inch. "Wh-what did you say?"

Alonzo waits so long to respond, Josh starts thinking maybe he didn't say anything at all.

Then:

"It got me. When I was trying to...trying to run away. Tripped me. I fell. It came...it came at me."

"What was it, Zoey?"

"Don't..."

"What was it?"

"I...I don't know. I'm not sure. It was like a scarecrow almost, the way it was dressed, but small, smaller than us, just some kid."

"A kid?"

"It...it did things to me, Josh. It *did things*."

"Did *what?* What did it do?"

"I don't…remember. It's like I know, but when I try to think about it, I can't…it gets all fuzzy in my head. I think…I think it showed me its face."

"Its face?"

"Kid," Shane says, "I don't know what the fuck you're talking about, and I hope I never do."

"It fed into me," Alonzo says. "It…dug into my memories."

"That sure isn't terrifying at all," Don says.

"It saw the worst things I ever did. It witnessed my beginning, middle, and end."

Don laughs. "You're, like, nine years old. I doubt the worst thing you ever did was that bad."

"Dude," Shane says, "he just bashed an old lady to death with a hammer."

"Yeah," Don says, "but she was a cannibal, so fuck her."

"But so are we."

"Well, don't fucking tell them that."

"It wasn't like we had any choice in the matter. The family made us. You kids understand that, right? We never wanted to eat people. You probably don't want to eat anybody, either. But you will. You definitely will. Trust me."

"I think I already did," Josh says, body shaking and overwhelmed with anxiety.

"*What?*" Alonzo says.

"Before they took me to the basement, they made me eat something in the kitchen."

"That brown sludge shit?" Shane asks.

"Yeah."

"Well, I guess we're all cannibals then."

"They didn't make me eat anything," Alonzo says.

"Give it time."

"I'm not fucking eating somebody."

Josh takes long breaths, willing himself not to vomit. "No, no, no, no…"

"Relax, kid," Don says. "We've all done worse. Trust me."

"Like what?"

"Uhhh..."

Shane laughs. "Yeah, Don, why don't you tell them what you mean? I'm sure they'd get a real kick out of it. I know I sure do."

"I'm not going to tell them that."

"Tell us *what?*" Josh says, desperate to talk about anything other than the fact that he's consumed another human being.

"Don here ain't as innocent as he might seem, is all I'm saying."

"They don't need to know this," Don says.

"Sure they do. They'll think it's a riot." Shane clears his throat, then continues. "So, okay. Back...uh, I don't know how long ago now. Time, it don't matter much when you're down here. Let's just say, sometime pre-basement. I was working at Subway, a glorified sandwich artist is what I was, and my shift had just ended and I was walking home, a good two, three miles away, and wouldn't you know it? Rain starts pouring down like it's got a bone to pick with someone. Maybe with me, I don't know. I always seem to be pissing off someone, so I guess it wouldn't surprise me too much, is what I'm saying. But, by some stroke of luck, a passing car actually pulled over to offer me a ride. I couldn't believe someone could be so kind and generous, it about broke my heart. Anyway, guess who the driver was."

"I already told you I was sorry," Don says.

"And I've accepted your apology, so relax," Shane says. "So, yeah, it was Don behind the wheel. And it turned out he had himself some, uh, ulterior motives for picking me up."

"Ugh," Don says. "Here we go."

"What...what are you guys talking about?" Josh asks.

"So..." Shane starts laughing and struggles to control himself. "Evidently, Don here had been fascinated with the idea of murdering a complete stranger, so much so that the urge had been building up within him for years and years until finally he could no longer restrain it, so he went for a drive with the intentions of finally giving in to these desires, and it just so happened that I crossed his path first."

"What the fuck?" Alonzo asks, and Josh has to agree. What the fuck, indeed.

"Once I got into his car, Don wrapped his arm around my neck and pushed a cloth soaked in chloroform against my face. I woke up later in his trunk, but the car wasn't moving. Outside, I could hear Don talking to somebody. The trunk opened and there stood the ugliest cop I'd ever seen in my life. *Uncle.* He took one look at me, then at Don, and smiled this terrible smile. Then he claimed the both of us and here we are."

"If I had known what would happen, I would have never abducted you in the first place. I intended on killing you quickly and painlessly. Then… then that fucker pulled me over. It's not what I wanted," Don says. "You know this."

"It's cool, bro. We're good."

"How many…how big is this…family?" Josh asks. "How many are there?"

"Who the fuck knows?"

"How long does a nightmare last? How deep is a shadow?" Don says. "These aren't questions with real answers, no matter how many times you ask them. It don't matter how big the family is because we will never meet them all. We aren't going to win. We're not even going to come close."

"We can't just give up…"

"Well, kid," Don says, "in case you missed it, we don't exactly have much of a choice. And, unless you know how to escape from a straitjacket…"

Although they still sit in the darkness, Josh can feel the glare Alonzo casts his way. The boys speak in unison, both of their minds connected by a single spark:

"*Lethal Weapon Two.*"

A good thirty seconds pass before Shane says, "Wait, why did you both just say '*Lethal Weapon Two*' at the same time like that? That was weird, right?"

"Yeah," Don says. "That was definitely weird."

Ignoring them, Josh leans closer to where he thinks Alonzo's sitting. "You think you could do it?"

"I don't know. Maybe. I can't see a fucking thing down here."

"But what do you even need to see, right? Riggs didn't need to see to do it. He just did it."

"Yeah, and he also wasn't surrounded by a bunch of fuckin' bear traps."

"No, but he *was* underwater."

"What the hell are you two talking about?" Don says.

Alonzo sighs. "Jesus Christ, ain't none of you ever seen *Lethal Weapon Two*?"

JOSH'S DAD HATED HORROR MOVIES. He thought they were vile and disgusting and held zero merit. One time Mr. Washington walked in on Alonzo and Josh watching the "blood wall" scene from *Evil Dead II* and just about vomited on Josh's rug. "Oh my god," he'd said, visibly disturbed. "What in the shit are you boys watching? This is awful."

Josh didn't respond, just kept his head down, chin tucked into his chest like he hadn't heard his dad talking, but of course he did, the fuckin' dude was right there towering above them both, some kind of alcohol heavy on his breath—not the kind Alonzo's mom usually came home smelling like, this was something different—uglier, almost.

Anyway, obviously Alonzo couldn't just sit there like Josh and say nothing. Talk about rude as hell, barging in and talking shit like that. Like what he said really mattered in the grand scheme of things. Like he'd ever accomplished a goddamn thing in his whole miserable life. So Alonzo turned to him and said, "Awful?"—smiling real wide and cocky—"Nah, nigga, this shit is *awesome*," and he could hear Josh gasp next to them. The audible fear emitted from his friend was enough to spook him, too. He'd just done an unspeakable. He'd cursed in front of a parent, and not just any parent but Josh's goddamn dad of all people, a notorious asshole if there ever was one. And hell, here was Alonzo, barely eleven at this point in time, saying "shit" and "nigga" right to his face like it wasn't no thing. It was new territory. Frightening territory, yes, but equally exciting, too.

The room was quiet for an eternity. Alonzo and Mr. Washington refusing to break eye contact. Josh refusing to glance toward the same side of the room as them. Alonzo on the floor, expecting this huge argument to break out any second, a part of him not giving a shit, thinking so what if they yell it out, *so what*—yet another, more realistic part of him's suddenly petrified this will influence the end of his and Josh's friendship, that because of his big stupid mouth Mr. Washington will do everything in his power to make sure they stop hanging out together.

But that's not what happened.

Instead of getting all pissed off and acting like a predictable asshole, Mr. Washington burst out laughing, which somehow proved to be a scarier sound than anything else he could have made.

He pointed at the TV screen. "You think *this* is awesome?"

And Alonzo nodded. "Hell yeah I do."

He nudged his son with his foot. "What about you, huh? You also think this is *awesome?*"

"Well…" Josh exchanged a panicked look between his father and Alonzo then slumped his head. "Yeah. I guess so."

This only seemed to amuse him further, the smile spreading across his face dangerous, alien. "You boys, you don't even know what awesome is." He paused, licked his lips. "Tell you what. Why don't you pause…whatever this is you're watching, and come out here and let me show you what a *real* awesome movie is like."

Josh tried to protest with a "But, Dad…" but Jasper waved him off.

"C'mon, now, y'all are gonna dig this."

He led them out to the living room and gestured for them to sit on the loveseat while he dug through their collection of VHS tapes. It didn't take him long to retrieve the four films he'd had in mind. He straightened and turned, the same weirdo smile across his face, presenting the covers out for the boys. They all contained the same two men, one black, one white, both wielding handguns. Cops, not a doubt about it. Instinct forced Alonzo to grimace. The words "Man, fuck the police," almost left his lips but he managed to bite his tongue at the last second.

For the rest of the day, they marathoned all four *Lethal Weapon* films. Jasper got progressively more intoxicated. Alonzo and Josh tried their hardest to hate what they were watching but found themselves engaged almost from the get-go.

The boys became fans for life.

AND IT'S THE STRAITJACKET SCENE from *Lethal Weapon 2* they're thinking about now, here in this dark, miserable basement, imprisoned in this house that isn't a house. Two scenes, actually. One, in the beginning, when Riggs demonstrates his skills at the police station, showing off for the other cops. He makes a bet with them all, claiming he can escape from a straitjacket in a certain amount of time. Nobody believes him except his partner. As soon as the clock starts ticking, Riggs dislocates his own shoulder and wrestles out of the restraints. When asked how the hell he managed to pull that off, he comments that he dislocated it a long time ago, now he can do it whenever he wants. Then he smashes the dangling limb against a wall to knock it back in place. But that's all just foreshadowing for a scene found later in the movie, when his dislocation trick saves him from certain death. The bad guys confine him with a device similar to a straitjacket and toss him in water, where he immediately sinks. Of course, he gets out of the restraints easily enough and swims to safety.

If Riggs could do that while in the process of drowning, then surely Alonzo can figure it out in this basement.

"But that was a movie," Alonzo says, "and this…this ain't a movie."

"So pretend it is."

"What?"

"Just pretend this *is* a movie. It would make more sense if it was, right? This kind of stuff…it doesn't happen in real life. Not really."

"Josh, this is really happening."

"But it doesn't have to be."

"What?"

Josh laughs. "C'mon, Riggs, show us what you got."

"Why the fuck do I gotta play the honky?"

"Because. You're more flexible."

A pause, then: "Wait. How the hell do you expect me to even do this? That guy, he'd already broken his arm or whatever, that's how he was able to do it on command."

Josh waits for Alonzo to figure it out himself.

"Oh," he says after a while. "Oh, fuck you. Are you serious?"

"Do you have any other ideas?"

"I'm not breaking my goddamn arm, Josh."

"Then we're going to die down here."

Don, or maybe Shane, starts laughing. "You kids are crazy as shit."

Josh and Alonzo respond in unison: "Shut the fuck up."

Then, Alonzo to Josh: "*How?* What do I do?"

"I don't know. Can't you just, like, jerk it forward hard and fast?"

"If someone could break their arm by jerking it, don't you think you'd have done so by now?"

"What?"

Don laughs. "He's saying you masturbate a lot."

"I miss masturbating," Shane says.

"Wasn't it cool, when we used to have penises?"

"Yeah. It was pretty cool, all right."

"Shut up!" Josh shouts. "If you're not trying to help, then just shut up!"

"Sorry."

"Yeah, sorry."

Josh sighs, struggling for ideas that refuse to generate. "What if you just stood up and jumped as high as you could and landed on your shoulder?"

Alonzo takes his time answering. "Yeah. That could work." Long beat, then: "What if I land on one of these bear traps?"

The thought had already occurred to Josh. "Uh. Maybe just try not to do that?"

"Oh sure. Do you mind shining a flashlight over here to help me see?"

"I don't—"

"Yeah, I know you don't got a flashlight. That's my goddamn point."

"You're still by the woman, right? The one you..."

"Yeah, I think so."

"Well, I didn't see any of those traps by her when they had the lights on. Did you?"

"I wasn't paying attention."

"I think you're probably safe. Maybe lean your back against the wall to help push yourself up? You could even slam your arm against the wall. That might be enough, right?"

"Man, why the fuck are you asking me? You think I do this kinda shit all the time or something?"

"You two are so cute," Don says.

"Fighting like some married couple," Shane says.

Josh and Alonzo again: "Shut the fuck up."

More silence, followed by the sound of grunting and feet scuffling.

"What are you doing?" Josh asks.

"Trying to stand up! What the fuck do you think I'm doing, bitch?"

"Oh. Sorry. Uh. How's it going?"

"It's fuckin' going, Josh. Now will you please stop talking so I can concentrate?"

Josh keeps his mouth closed and strains his ears, trying to visualize the scene before him by sound alone. All he hears is a lot of struggling.

Then, out of breath, Alonzo shouts, "Okay! I'm up. I fucking did it."

"Where are you?"

"Against the wall, by the old lady."

"Okay, now try to—"

"I know what to fucking do, Josh."

Josh shuts up.

Alonzo lets out a long breath and says a dirty word. A soft thud follows. His shoulder bashing against the wall. Another soft thud. A grunt. A curse. Frustration.

"Shit. This isn't doing anything."

"Do it hard."

"I fucking am doing it hard."

"Harder." Josh hates sitting here and feeling useless, and he knows his advice isn't necessary, but what else is he supposed to do? He has to participate. Him and Alonzo, they're in this together. Until the end. "Do it harder, Zoey."

"Motherfucker, I told you not to call me that."

Another grunt. A thud. A yell. More thuds, fast, desperate.

"Goddammit. This isn't working."

"What about the other idea?"

"*What* other idea?"

Josh licks his lips, feeling delirious from dehydration. "Jump up and land on your shoulder, on the floor. Focus all of your weight on that one spot."

"Seems like you'd have more luck doing something like that."

"Because I'm fat?"

"Yeah."

Josh considers the idea. He has a point. "But you're already standing."

Alonzo sniggers. "Pussy."

He tries to ignore the comment, but it hurts. "Are you gonna do it or not?"

"I'm feeling around for traps. Hold on."

"This cannot end well," Don says. "I hope you boys realize that."

"I mean, it's not gonna end well for them either way," Shane says. "At least they're trying something."

"True. What did we do to escape?"

"You bit one of them in the knee."

"Oh, yeah. That didn't end well."

"No. It sure didn't."

"I think that's when they cut off my penis."

"Mine too."

"Why did they cut off yours?"

"I bit him in the other knee."

"I miss my penis."

"Me too."

Alonzo clears his throat. "All right. Screw it."

Feet sliding against the floor, then a much louder thud than before. A gasp.

"Are you okay?" Josh asks. "Did it work?"

"Goddammit, that hurt. What a stupid idea."

"*Did it work?*"

"I don't think so."

Something possesses Josh, and Alonzo no longer feels like his best friend, but something more similar to offspring. In this moment, Josh speaks to him as Josh's own father might speak. "Do it again."

"Josh, I can't."

"*Do it again. Goddammit. Again.*"

No response from Alonzo. More struggling. The sound of him attempting to stand again. Grunting. Then another thud.

"Fuck, man. All this is doing is knocking the breath out of me."

"Jump higher."

"Jump higher? Fuck you."

"You either do this or we both die. Is that what you want?"

Silence.

Then: "Goddammit."

More scuffling of feet. Grunting. A struggle as he pushes his back against the wall and crab walks into a standing position. A few more goddammits.

Josh listens to every sound, every breath exhaled from his friend.

Alonzo jumps again.

The thud this time is different.

It's met with a loud metallic *clang*.

Followed by the worst noise Josh has ever heard in his life:

Alonzo, not just screaming, but squealing.

The sound that comes out of his mouth isn't human.

It's something alien and grotesque.

Then: "*Oh fuck Josh oh fuck it got me it fucking got me oh my god Josh it got me oh my god.*"

TWENTY

ell, that was fucking stupid, Alonzo thinks, ten seconds after the bear trap bites into his arm and holds him hostage. *That was really, really fucking stupid. That was so goddamn stupid, if there was an award for doing stupid shit, you'd win first fucking prize.*

Outside of his head, the only noise he manages to make is some weird primal shriek that sounds like it's coming from someone else. Someone less human.

He tries to roll away from the device clamped against his flesh but the thing isn't willing to budge. Worse, the more he struggles, the tighter the thing seems to get. Stubborn little fuck. Both him and the trap.

Alonzo screams for help and feels like a fool. Ain't nobody coming to help his dumb ass. Somewhere, miles away, Josh asks him if he's okay, and he almost laughs at the pure stupidity of the question. *No, Josh, everything is not okay. Thanks to your brilliant plan, I'm stuck in a goddamn bear trap. Everything is the total opposite of okay right now.*

His body thrashes on the floor, out of control, the spirits of a thousand dying animals fleeing from his lungs all at once. He squeezes his eyes closed and open, closed and open, trying to blink the pain away, but it's not working, and eventually one of the times he opens his eyes, light has penetrated the basement and one of the demon cops is hustling down the wooden steps, responding to his lunatic death rattle.

Standing above him, Uncle laughs like this whole scene is the funniest thing he's ever seen. "Well, would you all get a load of this fucking idiot."

If any of the other prisoners speak, Alonzo can't hear them. Can't hardly hear anything over the intense pain spiraling throughout his body like a persistent poison. The thing nobody tells you about pain is that it's *loud* and only you can hear it. Pain hides its mating call to everybody except the one it's targeting. Pain is treacherous and elaborate and absolute. Pain is a real motherfucker.

Uncle kicks him in the ribs but the impact hardly registers. "What exactly was the plan here?" He waits for an answer and kicks him again when one isn't received. "What the hell were you trying to do?" He waits again. Nothing intelligible spills from Alonzo's mouth. Uncle sighs and kicks him once more for good measure. "You know, I ought to just let you rot in that trap. Show you the consequences of your actions." Another beat, then: "But no. Father has other plans for you and your obese acquaintance. Now, hold still." He kneels and pauses. "If you try any shit with me, I will rip your jaw off and let you bleed out on the floor. Father might not like it, but there is no such thing as an irreplaceable human being. There will be no hesitation on my part. Do you understand?"

Alonzo grunts an affirmative.

Uncle reaches down and disables the bear trap, relieving the pressure against Alonzo's shoulder. He pushes Alonzo out of the way as he begins reassembling the device. Alonzo rolls across the floor, only stopping at the wall next to the old lady he'd murdered with a hammer. The pain in his shoulder hasn't hinted at the possibility of subsiding, but at least he's free from that fucking clasp.

His eyes had gotten so accustomed to the darkness, it takes him a couple seconds to blink away the blinding dots of light brought on by the bulb hanging above the staircase. Uncle remains on his knee, back facing him, fiddling with the disabled bear trap. Beyond the demon cop sits Josh, an expression of terror permanently stamped across his face, and beyond Josh hang Don and Shane, both looking more resigned to their fates than the two boys. One look at their mutilated genitals inspires a wave of nausea in Alonzo, so he looks down at his shoulder, hoping the damage isn't too critical.

And what he sees is a tear.

Not in his arm, but in the straitjacket.

Not some tiny tear, either, but a big fucking one. From his shoulder down to his elbow.

Alonzo takes one look at this tear, then at Uncle still struggling with the bear trap, and frantically tries to wiggle his injured arm through the opening. The pain is immense. Broken? Dislocated? He's twelve. How the fuck is he supposed to know? All he's concerned about is getting his arm through the tear before the psychotic monster notices what's happening, and for this to happen, he bites his tongue hard enough to draw blood, the pain in his arm so immense it's nearly impossible not to scream about it.

The arm slips out of the straitjacket and he nearly says *holy shit*.

It doesn't take him much longer to wrestle the rest of it off, freeing him of his restraints once and for all.

He remains seated on the floor, now dressed only in the black trash bag they'd given him upon their arrival, out of breath but filled with a new kind of determination. Numerous bear traps surround him.

"There," Uncle says, "finally."

He snaps the bear trap that'd bit into Alonzo's shoulder in place and rises, clapping the dust off his palms. "I don't know how many times I've told Father that we need to invest in new equipment, but he won't hear it. Says we'll draw unwanted attention to ourselves." He says this to Josh, looking down at him like a teacher might a student. "Me, I say bring them on. There's nobody in this world or any other we can't kill. And when Mother comes? Oh, boy, you are certainly in for a treat. Of course, you probably won't be around to meet her, and that's a tragedy, but a necessary tragedy." He laughs. "But then again, name one tragedy that isn't necessary."

Josh doesn't respond. By now, his eyes are focused behind Uncle, on Alonzo, who has since risen to his feet. Uncle notices and starts turning around. "Now, the question is, what should we do with our naughty little—?"

He stops at the sight of Alonzo standing, free of the straitjacket.

Alonzo stares at him with murder in his eyes and Uncle grins, wide and proud.

"You got out! Wow. That almost never happens. Congratulations." He holds out one of his massive hands, inviting Alonzo to shake it, which he refuses. "Seriously. That's a major feat for such a dumb little boy. I'm very impressed. I'm not even going to rip your jaw off like I said I would. Well done, kid."

"Fuck you," Alonzo says, and Uncle laughs so hard he has to double over, one hand on his swollen gut. "And fuck your mother, too."

Uncle stops laughing and stands straight.

He no longer seems so amused.

But Alonzo does. Now it's his turn to laugh.

Uncle steps forward.

Alonzo grips the chain behind his back tighter and swings with everything he's got. The bear trap connected to the chain flies over him and lands directly on top of Uncle's head.

Its metal jaws snap shut.

The whole world goes quiet.

Every sound that ever existed, in this universe and all the others, is snuffed out all at once.

All eyes burn into Uncle.

Uncle, who's practically frozen where he stands, either dead or simply too shocked to comprehend what has just occurred. Slowly his large, swollen hands reach up to feel the metal contraption sunk into either side of his head. A disgusting green liquid oozes down his cheeks—*is that his blood?*—and plops to the floor.

An eternity passes, then:

A grunt.

Soft, unsure of itself.

From Uncle.

The green ooze now covers his face like a mask, hiding any emotion from his disproportionate expression. He steps forward, like he's planning on taking revenge against Alonzo, then stops, both hands still caressing the bear trap, too confused to figure out how to disable it this time. He abruptly spins in the opposite

204

direction and Josh gasps. He tries to back away and falls over on his side, making himself an even easier target. But Uncle doesn't seem to acknowledge him. The green ooze's gotten into his eyes, blinded him to his prisoners. Whatever type of brain he's hiding in that skull, it's been scrambled, reprogrammed.

Uncle grunts louder and stumbles up the stairs, nearly falling back down them several times.

The door remains wide open.

Somewhere miles away, Don says, "Holy fucking shit."

And near him, Shane says, "I can't believe that actually worked."

Alonzo's heartbeat starts going psycho. The pain in his shoulder's numbed by pure adrenaline. It won't last long. Take advantage of it now or don't even bother trying.

He hurries across the basement, careful to step around the other bear traps, and unstraps Josh's straitjacket. The restraints come off relatively easy from this angle. Josh tries to hug him and Alonzo pushes him away, tells him to knock off that gay shit, that they gotta get the fuck out of here.

Josh points at Don and Shane, still hanging against the wall with their shame exposed. "What about them?"

In all his panic, Alonzo had forgotten about the other prisoners. But now that he looks at them again, cold reality sinks in: there's simply no time for further heroism. Every second they continue to waste down here is another second closer to whoever else is upstairs to discovering what's happened and locking the door again.

Fortunately, the others realize this, too.

Don nods toward the stairs. "Go. Just make sure you send help."

"Yeah," Shane says. "And tell them to bring us new penises."

"Robot penises."

"*Big* robot penises."

Instead of answering them, Alonzo grabs Josh's arm and pulls him toward the stairs and together they scramble up to the hallway.

Somewhere back down in the basement, either Don or Shane screams, *"Don't forget! Really big robot penises! Two of 'em!"*

"And also testicles!"

Alonzo closes the basement door, thinking it'd look far more suspicious to leave it wide open. The two boys move slowly down the hallway, the only direction that doesn't lead to a dead end, which also coincidentally happens to be toward the sound of absolute chaos. Loud crashing and grunting and moaning and glass shattering. Whatever's going on in this house, Alonzo sure as fuck doesn't want anything to do with it.

They both stop cold at the kitchen entryway.

The table in the middle of the room has cracked in half. Uncle lays sprawled out between the two wooden halves, flopping violently like a fish choking on oxygen. Random junk litters the floor, but Alonzo has no way of knowing if this is atypical or not. Unlike Josh, Alonzo did not have the privilege of joining Father in here for a meal.

Cautious, they move closer toward the destroyed table. Uncle desperately claws at the bear trap biting into his face, but manages only to make it worse. The grunts escaping his bloodied mouth are less convincing now. He sounds like a bedridden hospital patient, too weak to press the red CALL button for a nurse's aid.

An old man stands in the corner of the kitchen, leaning against a counter. In one hand he cradles a bowl of cereal and in the other he grips a spoon. His skin isn't jaundiced or deformed like the rest of the family. For the most part, he looks normal. Just some old man eating breakfast and watching a creature from another world die on the floor.

His expression is blank as milk drips from his beard.

Alonzo scans the kitchen for a weapon, anything to defend himself with, but the action is more for show than anything. The old man doesn't give off a hostile vibe. He just looks…sad.

Between spoonfuls of cereal, he says, "I remember when I brought you into my house,"—eyes on Uncle only, not having once acknowledged Alonzo and Josh's presence—"oh, how it'd rained. Do you remember the storm that made us cross paths, so long ago? Do you remember making the decision to get in my car, to trust me?" He eats another dosage of cereal. It crunches in his mouth impossibly loud. "I suspect a small part of you will never forget. Some part that'll never resurface again. A part that will never forgive me for bringing you into this hell. Can you hear me even now, in your last moments?" Another spoonful. *Crunch. Crunch.* "I hope you understand, this isn't what I wanted, this is never what I intended, and I'm…I'm sorry you got caught in the crossfire."

The old man sets down the bowl in the sink and picks up a large butcher's knife, then finally glances at the two boys who stand across the kitchen, first staring at him, then at the knife.

He chuckles and waves the knife toward another doorway. "If you two are planning on getting out of here, I advise you put a rush on it. I suspect we won't be alone much longer."

He steps toward the shattered table and kneels next to Uncle, bringing the knife down toward the bear trap. *Oh fuck, he's removing it,* Alonzo thinks, and again glances around the kitchen for something to use against the old man, anything to stop him from helping the demonic piece of shit on the floor.

But that's not what the old man is doing.

Unable to stop himself, Alonzo leans forward, over the old man's shoulder, and realizes with a sick satisfaction that he's sawing the knife through Uncle's neck.

He's cutting the fucker's head off.

More green ooze spills out of Uncle's throat and Josh pulls Alonzo away. "C'mon," he says, "we gotta *go.*"

Josh leads him out of the kitchen and through a living room full of old furniture and random objects. Clocks stand upside down. Toasters hang from the ceiling. Bloody handprints trail along the walls. A small TV set sits in one of the corners of the room with a crude smiley face painted across the screen. Several mannequins hang out in various positions throughout the room, all of them staring at Alonzo.

Are they laughing?

"What the hell," he says, and Josh yanks his arm again.

"This way."

Josh pulls open the front door and all hope of escape drains at once.

Wooden boards fill up the doorframe, blocking them from continuing forward. Barricaded inside this hell house, nobody able to leave, nobody able to enter. But what about the rest of the family? What about the one who calls himself Father? Surely there's another exit. What house doesn't have more than one way out?

"Wait," Josh says, and steps forward. He raises his arms toward the wooden boards.

"What are you doing?"

"It's…it's playing a trick on us. On our minds."

"What?"

"It's the floor. From the porch."

Dubious, Alonzo tries to touch the wooden boards. His arm falls through the doorway, but fails to touch the wood, somehow still out of reach.

"What the hell."

"We just gotta walk out, like there's nothing in front of us," Josh says. "Trust me."

Alonzo sighs. "This house is fucking crazy."

Together, they walk through the front door.

Alonzo closes his eyes, expecting the wooden boards to smack him in the face, but when he opens them again he's standing out on the porch, the sun bright and alive.

Holy shit. We made it out.

TOUCH THE NIGHT

TWENTY ONE

*D*riving away from her house feels like ripping off a band-aid long rendered useless from excessive blood saturation. Why had Mary kept it on up until now? In what way had it proven beneficial to her health?

At the stop sign down the street, she risks a glimpse in the rearview mirror, expecting to see Jasper standing out on the sidewalk watching her drive away, but he's nowhere in sight, probably never even followed her out of the house. Maybe he pretends to give a shit about her, but he doesn't, not really. It just bothers him that he can't control her every second of the day, that when he tells her to stay in the house she leaves anyway. Turning right at the stop sign, she imagines Jasper back in the living room, knocking over the coffee table and screaming profanities. But he won't chase after her. Not if it risks missing the next game in the World Series. He'd never speak this horrid truth aloud, but he wouldn't need to. They'd been married how long now? She knows this man up and down, through and through, even if to him she's barely resembling more than a distant stranger.

She wonders what the office will think of her second no-show in a row. At least yesterday she had bothered to give them a heads-up. Today, she can't handle the thought of talking to anybody from her day job. It's the least important thing in the world right now. She'll just have to worry about it once Josh is safe again. Once everything is okay.

They get McDonald's for breakfast and dine in the parking lot. Neither of them feel like eating but the only substances currently floating in their stomachs are vodka and coffee. McGriddles, hash browns, and orange juices for the both of them. They eat without talking, listening to Mariah Carey's "Shake It Off" at a low hum on the car radio while staring aimlessly at the passing traffic. Workers going to work. Sinners going to church. Everybody with somewhere to go, everybody in constant motion, from point A to point B back to point A all the way around to point C. Places and places and places. And where does Mary have to go? This fast food parking lot isn't where she's meant to be, but what else is there? Every instinct in her body begs to follow the sound of Josh's voice, but it doesn't matter how hard she strains her ears: her child remains silent.

"There." Ottessa leans forward from the passenger's seat, balled-up sandwich wrapper tumbling from her lap, and points through the windshield at a passing police cruiser. "Let's follow that motherfucker, see where he takes us."

Maybe in another life, Mary might have questioned these plans, but things had changed significantly in the last twenty-four hours. At this point, she can't risk letting doubt creep into her thoughts. A single second spent caught in contemplation is another second subtracted from Josh's life. With each tick of the clock comes another moment gone forever, increasingly out of reach like a ledge for a suicide victim suddenly overcome with a fresh dosage of optimism. She cranks the gearshift into DRIVE and drifts out of the McDonald's parking lot, then lays down on the gas, attempting to catch up to the distancing cruiser.

Ottessa settles back against the head rest. "Not too fast, though. Don't want to draw any suspicion to ourselves. Try to stay a car or two behind him."

Mary smirks. "You act like you've done this before."

"I *act* like I have common sense."

"It's a good act."

"Bitch, I'll bust your fuckin' lip, go ahead and try me." Humor threatens to spill from her tone, but fails to launch once the cruiser turns left off Main Street. "Don't turn right away. Idle up to the light and wait a couple seconds first."

Mary swallows back a sigh. "I can handle this."

Ottessa tosses both her hands up and lets gravity slap them against her thighs. "Yes, *ma'am*. Sorry, *ma'am*."

Mary ignores the sarcasm and turns at the light. The cruiser's already at the end of the next street, in the process of turning right. She speeds up. Ottessa starts to protest, then stops herself. Mary slows as she nears the stop sign, and parks against the curb. She cranes over the steering wheel and glances to the right just as the cruiser pulls off the street and into the grass, behind a tall display of wild bushes.

"What is he…?"

Ottessa clicks her tongue. "He's setting up a speed-trap. What else is he supposed to do on a Sunday morning—find our kids?"

"What do we do now?"

She laughs. "I thought you said you could handle this."

"*Ottessa*—"

"Would you *go?* We stay parked like this and it's like we're just *asking* for attention."

Mary turns and drives slowly past the cruiser disguised behind bushes. The scene reflected in the rearview mirror fails to display her worst fears: instead of chasing them, the cruiser remains in its hiding spot. This does not prevent Mary from double-checking every couple seconds, eyes hopping from windshield to mirror with a speed akin to machinegun fire.

"If he was going to come after us," Ottessa says, "you'd know by now."

"Now what?" Mary's fingers tighten around the wheel, slick with sweat and nerves.

"See that church up ahead, on the hill?"

Of course she sees it. It's barely a block away from the speed-trap. The building's at the corner of another intersection. Mary drives up the slanted driveway and finds a spot in the mostly packed parking lot next to the fence facing the way they'd just come. A strange sensation hangs in the air from loitering in a place of worship. It's not the church Mary and Jasper typically attend, but that doesn't alter its significance.

They sit and watch the nefarious bushes down the street. Nobody passes from either direction. From their vantage point, the majority of the cruiser sticks out from behind the bush. It looks pathetic, like a child terrible at hide-and-go-seek. After an extended period of inactivity, Ottessa sighs. "I wish we had some binoculars or something. See what this dude's up to."

This thought is not original to Ottessa. Mary nods. "Maybe he's sleeping?"

"That or jerking off."

She grimaces. "No. You don't think so...do you?"

"Wouldn't put it past one of these slimy sons of bitches."

"This street isn't even very busy. How many speeders could possibly be passing him?"

"That's probably the whole point. More privacy to play with himself." Ottessa fiddles with the channel knob on the radio. "Or, you know what, he's probably just waiting for church to end, figures he'll catch himself one or two cars eager for whatever stupid-ass football game's on today."

Flashes of Jasper at home, glued to his recliner as the day's schedule of NFL matches roll out on the television, waiting for the next game of the World Series to begin later in the night. "I think the Colts are playing the Texans."

Ottessa guffaws, surprised Mary answered with sincerity. "Who could give a fuck."

Colts and Texans. Sox and Astros. The universe might be trying to tell them something. Maybe the boys are in Texas. Abducted by some crazed cowboy. She considers offering this theory to Ottessa but thinks better of it, fearful of ridicule.

Ottessa finally settles on a radio station. Readjusts her sitting position. "You know, I've been trying to think, trying to remember if I'd ever seen that car before. The one from the video? And I don't think I have. What about you?"

"No. Never." It's the kind of car that would stick out. She wouldn't have forgotten it.

"So the chances of us randomly coming across it...they ain't too good, huh?"

"No."

She gestures at the windshield. "And what do you think the chances are of homeboy over there knowing anything about what's going on? You think *he's* seen this car before? That he knows where Zoey and Josh are?"

"I…I don't know."

"Yeah, me neither." A long intermission of contemplation, then: "But I'm realizing one thing, though."

"What?"

"We ain't gonna accomplish shit just sitting here, watching this guy play with himself behind some bush."

THE WIND LASHES OUT LIKE an animated creature as they approach the police cruiser. Both of them on foot, arms folded across their chests. This early in the morning, the sun's barely had a chance to stretch. The cold temperature from the night before lingers, refusing to surrender its territory.

Turns out the cop is neither napping nor masturbating, but instead reading some old paperback with a retro lawman painted across the cover. Ottessa knocks on the driver's window with her knuckles and the man jumps, dropping the book in his lap. Mary winces and steps back, anticipating him drawing his service weapon and shooting the both of them dead without another word.

Pale and spooked, the cop rolls down his window. He's youngish, probably not even thirty yet. The name LINDENMUTH is written across his chest tag. "Ye-yes?"

Ottessa puts on an obviously fake layer of cheerfulness. "Oh, hi, officer, I was just hoping you could answer a couple questions we had."

The cop glances around, perhaps checking for others possibly surrounding him. Dark bags of exhaustion droop from under his eyes and Mary's positive her and Ottessa look about the same, if not worse. "Uh…questions about what?"

"Well, for starters, we were curious about your car."

"What…what about it?"

She makes a show of inspecting it, from hood to trunk, impressed. "We wanted to know if everybody…you know, on the *force,* drove the same kind? Or if anybody was allowed to have…older models?"

Lindenmuth arches his brow. "Older models?"

Ottessa nods. "Yeah. Any of you still drive cars from back in the day? Like the seventies, eighties. You know. Back then."

He pauses before answering, actually thinking about the question. "No…everybody is up to date, as far as our vehicles go. Why?"

"Oh, it's just that, my friend here,"—she gestures to Mary standing behind her—"she claims the other day she saw someone get pulled over by one of those…older cop cars. Like from the movies? Personally, I call bull-shit, but she swears by it. So we saw you parked here, figured you could settle the argument once and for all."

The cop smiles, relaxing. "Ma'am, as far as I know, none of the other officers in my department drive a car like that. I think it would go against regulations. At least while on duty. I don't know what everybody uses when they're off the clock. Frankly, it's none of my business. None of anybody's business, actually."

Meaning, none of *their* business.

The cop briefly eyes the paperback in his lap, then returns his attention to Mary and Ottessa. A visible annoyance sinks into his face. He picked this spot so nobody would bother him. These bushes offered seclusion. Isolation from the outside world while still managing to remain outside. And now Mary and Ottessa had ruined everything. His one chance for a little peace and quiet, to just sit in silence and read a book.

Well boo-fuckin'-hoo, Mary thinks, although the thought feels like something mind-scraped straight out of Ottessa. As more time has pro-gressed these past two days, it's started to feel more and more like Mary and Ottessa's spirits have aligned, merging together as one solid force to overcome the same obstacle. Their children are *missing.* They're in *danger.* Nothing else compares. Ruining some cop's plans of leisure means nothing to Mary's conscience.

Evidently, Ottessa also notices his attention dwindling. "That a good book?"

His face pales. A little boy caught in an act of sin. "Wh-what?"

She gestures her chin at the rolled-down window. "The book you're reading. Is it any good?"

Something refreshes in him and the stern authority found in most men of the law returns. "Ma'am, did you *need* something?"

Mary steps in front of Ottessa, cutting her off. "What do you know about the two boys who were kidnapped Friday night?"

"*What* boys?" He cocks his head, face all screwed up. "*What* kidnapping?"

"*Friday night.*" Annoyed that she has to repeat herself, that they're wasting time like this. "Two boys, age twelve, were abducted in this town."

Lindenmuth laughs. "In *Percy?* No way." When neither Mary nor Ottessa respond, he shifts in his seat. "Abducted by *who?*"

Ottessa balls her fists. "By the fuckin' po-*lice*, that's who. Two ugly fuckers in an old cop car. You sure that don't ring any bells?"

If anything, he looks even more amused. "I got no idea what the two of you are talking about. Are you all trying to file a missing persons report or somethin'? Is that it?"

But that's not what he wants to ask, not based off his expression. The real question clinging from the edge of his tongue is, *How much have y'all had to drink this morning?*

Before either of them can respond, the radio in his car bursts to life. A woman declaring some sort of emergency coded by a series of letters and numbers. The cop gives Mary and Ottessa one final stare-down before releasing a long, defeated sigh.

"Look. If you girls need to report a crime, I encourage you to take a trip down to the station and do things the official way. I'm sorry, but I have to go."

"Wait." Mary steps closer to the car and places a hand around the open window, preventing him from rolling it back up. "One more question? Please."

Lindenmuth glares at her like he's debating whether he should cuff her or not. "What."

"How much do you trust the sheriff?"

"Excuse me?"

"Sheriff Keene. Do you trust him?"

Long pause, then: "Ma'am, I'm gonna have to ask you to please remove your hand from my vehicle."

The cop drives away without another word, the fear plagued across his face never once fading.

As they head back to their car still parked at the church, Mary kicks a rock into the trees. "Now what are we going to do?"

And Ottessa says, with a psychotic smile contagious to all around, "Exactly what the man said. Go on down to the station and do things the official way."

TWENTY TWO

They barge into the police station not giving a single goddamn. Some receptionist at the front desk shouts that they can't just walk past the lobby without first signing in, but she's barely given a second thought. Another detour not worth the energy. Not worth Ottessa and Mary's energy, yes, but also Zoey and Josh's, too.

They find Sheriff Keene in his office, leaning back in his chair, feet across the desk, wet washcloth over his eyes. He does not seem affected by their sudden presence.

Ottessa kicks the desk. "Wake up, dickhead."

The sheriff gasps, jolted from his nap. In his panic, he knocks over a cup of writing utensils with his feet. The washcloth falls off his face and lands in his lap and his eyes widen at the sight of the office's intruders.

"You two?" He leans forward, squeezing his eyes open and closed, open and closed, trying to rid himself from this dream. "How'd you get in here?"

Ottessa ignores the question and claims one of the visitors' seats. "Any leads, *Sheriff*?"

Mary sits next to her, cradling Josh's camera against her stomach.

Keene sighs and scoops out a cigarette from the pack on his desk. It hangs in his mouth awhile, unlit, like it's a decoration. Buying time, probably. Eventually he retrieves a plastic lighter from his shirt pocket and introduces the tobacco to fire.

After further contemplation, he blows a cloud of smoke toward them and shakes his head no. "Like I already said—the moment I know something, I'll give y'all a call. Until then, there's not much else I can tell you."

"Uh-huh. Figured you might say something like that." Ottessa grabs the camera from Mary. "Which is why we went ahead and brought you some evidence proving what we've been saying all along."

He cocks his head. "And what would that be?"

"That our boys got themselves snatched up by the law."

"Well, Ms. Jones, I do admit I am curious to see what kind of evidence you've collected."

She turns on the camera, now fully charged with new batteries, fast-forwards to the end, and slides it across the desk. "Go ahead and take a gander at that, Mr. Policeman."

"What's this?"

Mary clears her throat. "It's my son's camera. We found it outside, where...where they were abducted."

The sheriff doesn't respond for a moment, just studies the device's hard plastic exterior with a slight amusement. "What about it?"

Ottessa points at the camera. "Click PLAY and find out for yourself."

He grunts and sets it down. "I don't got time for this today."

"Watch the goddamn video, Sheriff."

Long hesitation, like he's debating whether to obey or exile the both of them from his office. Wisely, he chooses the former option and clicks PLAY. The screen facing him, Ottessa and Mary can still hear the recording as it unravels. Somehow listening to it hurts more than actually viewing the thing. The sound remains the same, but now it's up to her memories and imagination to mingle together and conjure up some twisted version of the truth, and what plays out in her mind comes across far more sinister than what could possibly be reality.

Throughout the viewing, the sheriff's facial expression does not alter from its blank neutrality, yet as the video progresses his skin pales to a significant sickness. A dead giveaway, Ottessa thinks. Motherfucker knows *something*.

After it's over, the sheriff drops the camera on the desk and leans back in his chair, hands folded behind his head. His posture radiates a pseudo-confidence but nobody's buying it, not even him.

"Well?" Mary says, but Ottessa doesn't know why she's even bothering. It's obvious how the rest of this little rendezvous's going to play out.

Keene shrugs. "It's an interesting home movie you've all created, but I fail to understand what this has to do with my investigation."

Mary lets out a little cry and Ottessa laughs.

"Would you like to share with me what's so funny?" the sheriff asks.

Ottessa nods, then reaches into her purse and pulls out Jasper's pistol. She aims it at Keene and grins.

"I was just thinking about what it'd be like to put a bullet in your skull, is all."

Somehow, the sheriff gets even paler.

"What do you plan on doing with that?"

The sheriff glares at the gun from across the desk. Pointed right at him. Almost amused now that the initial shock's faded. Ottessa's arms don't shake as she tightens her grip on Jasper's weapon, index finger softly caressing the trigger. Mary's so tense her body's practically cardboard at this point. Thighs clenched together. Nails digging into kneecaps. Teeth grinding against teeth. Blood boiling. Heart jackhammering.

How did it come to this? How did things get so bad, so fast?

"What do I plan on doing with this?" Ottessa grins and leans forward. "I guess that all depends on you, don't it?"

The sheriff returns the grin. "Oh, is that so?"

Hands folded across his gut. Leaning back in his chair. Not a care in the world.

"The way I see it," Ottessa says, "either you're gonna quit with the bull-shit and tell us what you know, or I'm gonna hurt you a whole bunch."

Keene rolls his eyes. "And what is it, exactly, do you think I know, Ms. Jones?"

Another laugh from Ottessa, and Mary can hear the rage seething beneath. She can hear it because she feels the same rage. The same fire.

"Like you don't fuckin' know. Haven't we been through this shit already, man? You saw what was on the camera. You heard what we've been telling you. It's the same shit that you just watched. Right there before your eyes. And you still deny it? You act like we…what? Like we faked it somehow? Bullshit. I know we didn't fake it. Mary knows. And *you* fuckin' know. Which means you're trying to cover up something *else*. And that, dear Sheriff, is what we want you to tell us."

Long pause. Keene avoids eye contact, staring at the camera still on his desk. Josh's camera. The last thing he ever touched before disappearing from Mary's world.

World?

"Well?" Ottessa sighs, patience long run out. "What's it gonna be, Sheriff? Either you spill the truth or you spill some blood. Your choice."

Keene raises a finger, indicating *one minute,* and picks up a coffee mug from the desk. The drink that follows lasts too long. Taking his sweet ol' time. Soaking his mustache in the liquid like feet relaxing in a basin of warm water. An obnoxious sigh of pleasure follows as he sets the mug down and leans back in the chair again. He wags one extended pointer finger at the camera and nods.

"Tell you what. Let's say this video is real. Let's say y'all aren't trying to bullshit a bullshitter and proceed under the assumption that your boys really have been abducted and that they haven't run off to avoid taking responsibility for their crimes. Okay? Okay." He leans forward. The chair's bones squeak. He taps the camera hard and persistent, knocking it over on its side. "That still don't mean I know a goddamn thing about it. Yeah, I watched the video, but have *you?* Because the car shown here, for the brief second that the camera catches, it doesn't even come *close* to resembling the vehicles utilized on my force. Hell, I haven't seen an officer drive a car like that since the goddamn eighties. But you want to know something? It's not difficult to buy one. Police stations offer them up at auctions all the time. Old heaps of junk just collectin' dust behind the station. All types of whackos buy these things and, yeah, some of them even decorate the cars back up to make 'em look like official police business. We catch someone doing that, we take their ride away and issue out one mean sonofabitch of a fine." Taps the camera again, harder.

"If this is legitimate, then I'm willing to bet good money that's what we're dealing with here. A couple of lunatics who found themselves in possession of an older cop model and decided to take advantage of it in the worst possible way. But again, that's all speculation. A theory which, okay, yeah, we aren't gonna completely disregard, but it's not the *leading* theory, if you understand me. And you pointing this here firearm in my face demanding I accept one reality for another isn't gonna do much in your favor, little lady."

Ottessa starts shaking her head, probably preparing her own little speech, something that'll keep the discussion stagnant, but Mary cuts her off first:

"Sheriff, please." She folds her hands under her chin, gripping them so tight together her fingers go numb. "What we brought you is the truth. How can you watch that then accuse us of faking it? We wouldn't know the first thing about how to even do such a thing. All we want are our children back. That's it. I'm sorry for how we've acted this afternoon but we're worried and sick and so, so afraid, and all we want is your help and it seems like that's the last thing you want to give us. Don't you understand that?"

Mary takes in loud, short gulps of breaths, like any second she's going to burst out crying, and Ottessa and the sheriff just sit and watch and wait. But she manages to get herself under control and clears her throat. Not once has she broken eye contact with the sheriff. She refuses to say anything more until he offers an explanation.

And when he eventually does, there's a significant shift in his tone. Gone is the condescension, and in its place—what? *Sympathy?* As if Mary somehow broke through to him. As if he might actually care.

"Okay, I get that. But,"—he cocks a thumb at himself—"now I want you to look at things from *my* point-of-view, all right? I get a case about two teenage boys who sneak out in the *middle of the night* and decide to rob themselves a gas station. And not only do they rob the gas station, but they hospitalize the poor kid working the cash register, too. Beat him so bad, they don't know if he's dead or alive. He's alive, by the way. You oughta thank your god for that one. Oh and *then*, they up and disappear. Now what's more likely? That they ran away to escape a sure jail sentence, or—just by pure *coincidence*, mind you—a couple of crazy people pretending to be cops happened to abduct them on the way home? If you were in my position, which one would you believe? Tell me that. You tell me that right now."

Invisible hands squeeze Mary's throat as she talks. Each word a painful gasp. "But…we…have…it…on…camera."

The sheriff nods and starts fiddling with the back of the device. "You'd be amazed, what people can do with technology these days. Some of these kids, they can hack right into our database, if they got the mind for it, and delete every arrest record on file. 'Course, we keep physical archives of all that shit, so it isn't that big a deal, but still. You can't ever really trust what you see on a screen, can you?" He pulls out a small memory chip from the camera and holds it with his thumb and index finger, squinting.

Ottessa waves the gun unconvincingly. "Put that down."

Keene ignores her, hypnotized by the tiny object between his fingers. "I'll tell you girls something. Something about all this techno-witchcraft mumbo jumbo."

"Put it down, I said, goddammit." More authority in her voice this time, but it only seems to make the sheriff smirk.

"So this is a few months back, okay? Around…July, maybe? Yeah, July. It's mid-afternoon, hot as it's ever been, and one of my officers, just doing a routine patrol, he spots this real ghetto lowrider parked by the Flying J. Two guys inside, early twenties, Latino or Puerto Rican or whatever the hell. Flannels buttoned up to their throats. Shaved scalps. Tattooed knuckles. You know. Gangbangers. *Vatos.* Just…*sitting there*, staring at the gas pumps. Really concentrating on them, my officer tells me. Like they're *waiting* on something. Now, like any of my officers, this fella's been trained well. He knows what to look for. And what he's seeing here, it's hitting all the obvious warning signs. Something is not as it should be. These guys, they're up to something. So, my officer, being the good cop he is, he marches right on up to the lowrider, raps his knuckles against the window, and motions for them to roll it down. And what do they do? They *panic*. They drive away." He stretches his free hand out, palm facing the desk, and wiggles his fingers up and down, imitating a fleeing car. "Now, here's the real kicker: in the process of their speedy getaway, they happen to run over my officer's foot. Crushes it so bad, the doctors can't save it. They have to amputate it that very day. Now he's on disability and spends all day at home getting fat and watching TV. 'Course, the lowrider didn't get far. A couple other officers picked them up just a few miles onto I-90. Gave up almost immediately. And you know why? What they were doing, back at the Flying J? These sneaky sons of bitches, you wouldn't believe it. They had inserted these…these, what, *scanning* devices into the credit card readers on all the gas pumps. I don't really understand it, to be honest with you two, but basically, whenever someone inserted their credit or debit card to pay for fuel, the numbers on the card were copied and scanned to this tablet device the guys were operating back in their lowrider. Just sitting right out in the open, ripping off dozens if not *hundreds* of law-abiding citizens. Who knows how long they'd been at it before my officer caught on to their scheme. And if he hadn't? Hell. They might still be at it today. Robbing our little town blind."

Ottessa's arm's shaking at this point. No doubt tired from balancing the gun at a steady angle for so long. Her aim's evolved beyond wobbly. If she pulls the trigger, she's just as likely to plug a hole in Mary as anyone else. Mary reaches out, offering to take it for her, but Ottessa yanks it away and steadies her aim at the sheriff. "Now, what the fuck did any of that have to do with a goddamn thing?"

A genuine laugh barks from the sheriff. "What I'm trying to tell you, Ms. Jones, is that just because something looks one way, that doesn't mean it isn't something else. You understand what I mean?"

And, without waiting for an answer, the sheriff drops Josh's memory card into his cup of coffee.

TWENTY THREE

"**M**ary, I want you to go around the desk there and apprehend this motherfucker's piece. Don't worry. He even so much as blinks funny, I'ma blow his goddamn brains out and make a big ol' mess all over this office."

Mary doesn't need to be told twice. Good girl. She gets up and maneuvers around the desk, hand out. Ottessa doesn't take her eyes off Sheriff Peckerwood, not for a second. When he doesn't immediately cough up his own weapon, she sighs and waves her gun again, reminding him who has whose ass.

"Bitch, you gotta be told twice? Give her the piece."

Reluctantly, Keene points at a side-drawer below his desk. "It's in there."

"Bullshit," Ottessa says, quick as a bullet.

He shrugs. "I don't carry it on me when I'm doing office work. Never thought there was any need."

"Bet you're reconsidering that habit right about now."

"You might say so."

Mary hesitates, eyeing the sheriff with justified paranoia, then leans over his lap and opens the drawer. She pulls a pistol out, holding it by the barrel.

Ottessa sighs, but even she has to admit it's a little cute. "Wrong end, girl."

"What?" Confused, then she considers the words and nods, turns the gun around with both hands, carefully, like she's defusing a bomb, and grips the handle. Points it to the floor, arm outstretched, afraid to get too close to it. "What do we do now?"

The sheriff chuckles, throat wet and disgusting, glaring at Ottessa. "Yeah, what do we do now?"

"Shut up," Ottessa says, trying to think.

"Do you even know?"

"I said shut up."

"Do you have any *idea* what kind of shit you've gotten yourselves into?"

"Goddammit, I said—"

Mary slams the barrel of the pistol against the sheriff's head. He grunts once and slumps over, flipping his cup of coffee and spilling it across the keyboard of his computer.

They remain frozen a couple seconds, studying the man with awe, then Ottessa says, "Damn, girl, you are *vicious*."

Mary shakes her head, refusing to accept the truth of her actions. "I can't believe I just—"

Another grunt, almost a moan. The sheriff sits back up. "Did you really think that was going to knock me out? Oh, you stupid bi—"

Mary gasps and hits him again with his own pistol. Harder this time. The impact of steel against skull echoes in the office. He tumbles out of his chair and collapses to the floor. His limp body shoots the chair out from beneath him and it wheels against a wall before getting knocked to an abrupt stop.

Mary backpedals from the body. "Oh no, oh no, I killed him. Did I kill him?"

Taking her time, Ottessa rises from her own seat and leans over the desk, studying the sheriff, wondering if he's actually unconscious or if he's faking it again. The man breathes through a series of heavy, jagged snores.

"Nah. Just out cold. You got him good."

"Oh, god." Mary paces around the office. "Why did I do that? Why would I do such a thing?"

"Because he was acting like a bitch." Ottessa shrugs, not really seeing the big deal. "*Something* had to be done. If not this, then I probably would have shot his ass. Be grateful you acted first."

"What...what..." Mary steps closer so they can whisper. "What are we going to do?"

"I don't know."

"We're in a *police station.*"

"Yeah."

"He's the *sheriff.*"

"Yeah."

"Ottessa!"

"Bitch, you're the one who knocked him out."

"After you pulled a gun on him!"

"Well why else did we bring it?"

"I...I don't know."

"Yeah you do. Now's not the time to start playing innocent with me, girl. We got bigger shit to deal with." She gestures at the unconscious sheriff, in case somehow Mary's forgotten already. "Now, you think he knows more than he's saying or what?"

Mary nods. No need to consider it. "Yes."

"Good. Me too. But he ain't planning on talking, is he?"

"No."

"Not here, at least."

"What...what..."

"We gotta take him someplace else. Somewhere where it's just the three of us. And...we make him talk."

It sounds so easy, coming out of her mouth, but in truth Ottessa has no idea how they'd go about doing this. And, by the look on Mary's face, she's equally clueless. The sheriff's a big man. Tall. Meaty. Probably weighs more than Ottessa and Mary combined. They can't just drag him out of here, especially without being noticed. Who knows how many other cops are floating around the station. Plus there's that bitch secretary to worry about.

Mary points at a window in the far corner. "What about that?"

Ottessa could kiss her. How obvious. But why hadn't she thought of it?

Together, on either side of him, they lift the sheriff, hands under his armpits, warm and soaked with perspiration, and slowly drag him across the office. They try to lower him back down gently. Loud thud against the floor as the body falls. Ottessa raises the blinds and pushes the window up, then sticks her head through to make sure the coast is clear. The office faces some side road branching from Main Street. Barely a soul in sight. They can do this. The less they think and the more they act—now, no hesitation, no fear—the more likely their success. Success in *what,* she ain't even sure. Success in not getting busted, maybe. Success in finding her boy before it's too late, before…before…

No more before or after.

Only *now.*

Now they must move. *Now* they must act. *Now* they must survive.

Now.

They bend with their knees and hook arms under the sheriff's armpits, psyching themselves up to lift the body when the office door swings open and that bitch secretary strolls on in, ruining everything. One look at the scene before her inspires a banshee-like shrill. *Well, there goes that plan.* Ottessa releases the sheriff and leaps across the room toward the desk, where she'd set down Jasper's gun.

"Shut the fuck up." She shoves the barrel against the secretary's cheek and the screaming stops. Cut off so abruptly it's like the woman got unplugged. But of course it's too late. The damage is already done. Heavy footsteps sound off elsewhere in the station. Nearing the sheriff's office. Closer. Worried voices shouting out their concern, asking if everything's okay.

Mary asking what they're going to do.

Ottessa not responding, just standing there, thinking, thinking fast, off her ass, no time for fear, no time for hesitation. She spins the secretary around so they're both facing the open doorway and presses the gun against the side of her head—*"Please don't!"*—and they wait, one, two, three seconds for the first officer to arrive.

"Holy shit," he says, taking in the situation.

"Back up!" Ottessa says. "I'll kill her. I swear to fuck I'll kill her."

The cop backs up.

Behind her, Mary tries protesting. Still in denial. Still in make-believe land. "Ottessa, I don't think—"

"You don't think *what?* You don't think this is the best idea? No shit it ain't the best idea. But do you got a better one?"

No response from Mary.

"Yeah, that's what I fuckin' thought."

More cops surround the doorway. Four, maybe five. Guns drawn. Desperate and afraid. They see their sheriff on the floor and there's no telling if he's dead or alive.

"Relax," Ottessa says. "He still breathing. We just bonked him on the head is all. Knocked him out a little bit."

"What do you *want?*" one of the cops ask.

"First, set your pieces down and slide them across the office. All of you. Or, you know, I'll shoot your secretary. Then you'll have to hire a new one. Wouldn't that be just the *worst* pain in the ass? Imagine all that paperwork."

Slowly, one-by-one, the cops obey her commands. Half a dozen chunks of steel slide across the floor. Paranoia hits her and she can't help but wonder if they're hiding back-up weapons. Ankle holsters prepared to betray her the moment she lets down her guard. Would they confess if accused? Doubtful. These are po*lice*, after all. They ain't gonna admit shit.

"All right, now keep your hands up and back away—slowly. If any of y'all get out of my sight, I'm makin' it rain bullets. Don't believe me? I fuckin' dare ya to test me."

Mary kneels to collect each discarded firearm, gets about four of them hugged against her chest before giving up and laying them all back down. She studies the pile of death machines, deciding on the best way to recover them all, before shrugging and kicking them under the sheriff's desk.

Ottessa's nearly out of the office before it dawns on her how stupid of a mistake she's in the process of making. Leaving Keene in here with an entire station's worth of handguns? Jesus Christ, girl. Not using her head. Not *thinking*.

"Wait. Two of you, get back in here. *Slowly.* I mean it, goddammit."

She gestures Jasper's gun at the unconscious sheriff. "Drag him out of here."

They look at her like they don't quite comprehend English.

"Go on, get to it."

Another wave of the gun. Emphasis on how little of a fuck she gives about them. Making it clear she won't hesitate to shoot any of them if they so much as look at her funny. But do they buy it? Do they *fear* her? Impossible to say. Anyone who claims they can read the thoughts of others is liable to try selling you snake oil in the same breath.

After a lot of grunting and struggling—how much can one man possibly weight?—they get him out of the office. Followed closely by Ottessa and Mary. The expression on Mary's face asks one obvious question: *What the fuck are we doing?* Ottessa's expression gives a clear answer: *No idea.*

"Where are the cells?" she asks one of the cops.

"What?"

"The *cells*. Where do you lock up folks minding their own business?"

In the back of the station, it turns out. Not a single one's occupied, either. Slow weekend for the pigs of Percy, Indiana. Ottessa makes one of them show her how to work the locking mechanism. They don't use keys anymore, not like in the movies. It's all a bunch of buttons and switches now. Boring, anticlimactic bullshit. She corrals them into the last cell on the left like livestock into a paddock. Two of the cops drag the sheriff in with them and lay him out along the steel cot against the wall. All of the station's employees together in one cell, staring back at Ottessa and Mary wondering what comes next, Ottessa and Mary staring back at them wondering the same thing. Ottessa thinking goddamn, this was far easier than it should have been. Police stations are supposed to be difficult to overthrow. Yet... they did it. The building's theirs and it ain't even lunch time yet.

"Ma'am," one of the cops says, "what's the endgame here? Why on Earth are you *doing* any of this?"

"Isn't it obvious?" another one says, chuckling. Young, shaved scalp, uneven goatee. "They're crackwhores. Just look at them. Next they'll ask for a key to the evidence room. You after that delicious candy, ain't that right, ladies?"

Ottessa grits her teeth and paces. Motherfucker's testing her. Maybe he's suicidal, she don't know.

Thankfully, Mary speaks before Ottessa starts shooting everybody.

"I'm sorry this has happened, but we were left with no choice. Our little boys have been abducted by a police officer, and your sheriff refuses to believe us."

"What are you *talking* about?" the secretary says.

Explosive, violent coughing from the steel cot. The sheriff rubs his temple and spits on the concrete floor. "Don't listen to a goddamn word those crazy cunts say."

One of the officers rushes to his aid and helps him sit up on the cot. The sheriff leans against the wall, eyes still closed, clearly disoriented.

"They think there's some…big conspiracy. That we somehow snatched their kids and…what, I don't know. *Killed* them? Sold them to some child sex ring? Who knows." The sheriff laughs, weak and tired. "There's no getting through to the insane. They'll believe what they want to believe no matter what kinda evidence is presented."

"You want to talk about *evidence?*" Ottessa bangs the barrel of Jasper's gun against the cell bars. "Let's fuckin' talk about *evidence.* Let's talk about the video we just got done showing you. The one you fuckin' *destroyed* before anybody else could see. Let's talk about *that.*"

Another laugh from the cot. "Lady, I got no idea what the fuck you're talking about."

"Bullshit."

"Remind me, was this before or after you assaulted me and sieged our station?"

Again, Mary saves the day by opening her mouth first: "Here's how this will work. We are going to tell the truth, *our* truth, the truth as we know it. If any of it sounds familiar to you, if you know more than we do, then you're going to tell us. The quicker we have the information we need, the quicker we leave and you can all go on about your day."

The sheriff again: "Listen to them. They're goddamn nuts. They actually think there's a reality that involves them walking out of here today."

Mary ignores him and proceeds to give a quick—but thorough—

summation of everything that's happened since Friday night. The things they actually need to know, of course. There's wisely no mention of the assault that went down at Dollar General. Every time the sheriff tries to interrupt her, Ottessa bangs Jasper's gun against the bar and reminds him who has whose ass in their crosshairs.

She concludes with:

"Our little boys are missing. Both of them, just twelve years old. Sure, they've had their problems, but whatever's happened to them, they don't deserve it. They're just *children*, for God's sake. If…if you can help us, if you can help *them*, please…please do so."

Long silence. Ottessa bites her tongue and paces in front of the cell. Mary doesn't move, somehow maintaining eye contact with every cop they've imprisoned all at once. Total mom move. A couple minutes pass. Nobody has the guts to speak first. Ottessa raises Jasper's gun, thinking a blast to the ceiling might startle these fuckers out of their daydreams, but chickens out and lowers it.

"Nobody's got nothing to say, huh?"

One of the cops says, "Lady, kids go missing all the time. We do what we can to find them, but you have to understand the reality of the situation. Sometimes, no matter how hard we look, we aren't successful. Now, I'm not familiar with your case, but this is definitely not the first time Percy has had someone go missing. I'm sure whatever officer's been assigned to your kids is doing all he can do to make sure they're returned home safely, but in the meantime—"

"Hey, sheriff," Ottessa says, voice like a gunshot. "You mind telling me which *off-i-cer* you've done assigned to our boys?"

He rises from the cot, on two legs, so sure of himself. Radiating the kind of hubris only a white man without money troubles can muster. "I've decided to take on this particular case myself."

"Oh, have you now."

"Mmm-hmm."

Ottessa and Keene both refuse to be the first one who breaks eye contact. They stare each other down like dogs chained to opposite ends of a yard. She clears her throat and raises the pistol to the ceiling again, not intending to shoot it but also not entirely ruling out the idea either. "Show of mother-fuckin' hands. Who here even knew two twelve-year-old boys went missing Friday night?"

Predictably, everybody's arms remain at their sides.

"Yeah, I figured as much. What about what went down at the Shell that same night? Y'all hear about that?"

Slowly, a couple of the cops nod in recognition.

Ottessa targets in on the guy with the dumbest mustache. "Yeah? What did you hear?"

"There was a robbery. The clerk, some kids assaulted him, emptied the cash register and booked it."

"Let me guess. Your hardworkin' sheriff is workin' that case, too."

"Uhh..."

Keene laughs. "You ladies got a problem with the way I run my depart-ment, you're more than welcome to fill out a complaint card."

Ottessa can hardly believe her fucking ears. "A complaint card?"

He nods. "Uh-huh. I'll even show you where you can stick it, if it'd please ya."

A couple of the cops chuckle. The bitch secretary from earlier groans and buries her face in her palms. Bingo.

"You're the ears around this place, ain't ya?"

It takes the secretary a moment to realize Ottessa's talking to her. "How do you mean?"

"I *mean*, you sit around all day, listening to what everybody's got to say. So, what does everybody got to say? Specifically, about missing kids. Even more specifically, about *our* missing kids."

"I don't...I don't..."

Ottessa sighs, having already figured she'd play hard to get. She points Jasper's handgun in her direction, careful not to let the barrel extend too close to the bars. For all she knows, one of these devious fucks could be plan-ning to reach out and make a grab for it. Startle her just enough to initiate an accidental trigger squeeze. Get one of 'em gutshot. Cops are stupid like that. Always reacting without using their brains, what little they got to show for 'em, at least.

"Lady, I'ma make it real simple for ya," Ottessa says. "I can see by the look on your face that you know some shit. Consider the predicament we all presently find ourselves in. Do you really think it's wise to be lyin'? Spit out the truth and be done with it already. If you think I won't shoot you and every other cocksucker in here, then I guess you ain't never had no kids before."

In a near whimper, the secretary says, "They aren't the first ones to go missing."

The cop who had previously lectured them about disappearances groans. "No shit. Didn't I already say that?" He turns to the other cops for reassurance. "Didn't I already say that?"

One of the other cops nods. "Yup. You sure did."

"Will you shut the fuck up?" Ottessa asks, and nods at the secretary. "You were saying?"

The secretary hesitates, then steps closer to the bars, as if this new distance will somehow prevent her coworkers from hearing their conversation. "I been at this job nearly two years now. In that time, I couldn't even guess how many missing persons we've gotten reported. Two dozen? Three? *More?* Is that normal for a small town like this? I don't know. I hope not."

Mary steps in. "Were they all...children?"

She shakes her head. "No. Some of them. But not all. Grown men. Women. Old folks. Teens. You name it."

The sheriff chokes out a laugh. "So I guess that's proof of a conspiracy then, huh? You girls are goddamn hysterical, I swear."

"Shut your mouth. Right now." Not from Ottessa this time, but Mary. She nods at the secretary. "Go on."

"A few months back." She pauses, eyes closed, swallows. "A few months back, I took in a call from this guy, he was drunk or something, I don't know what, but he calls the station and he says his ex—they'd just broken up, apparently—he says he ditched her along the highway, off by the Flying J?

And he watched her walk for a little bit, parked out by the gas pumps, and he sees this police car stop and pick her up. He was calling us because he wanted to find out if she had been arrested or what. Maybe bail her out if so, try to make up for whatever dumb thing he did to cause the breakup in the first place."

Mary again, saying the absolute obvious. "She wasn't in the system, was she?"

The secretary shakes her head no.

One of the cops—who could possibly tell them apart?—exhales an obnoxious *can you believe this shit?* sigh. "Oh my God, somebody call up Dubya! A woman wasn't arrested for walking down the highway! What a grave injustice to our country!"

The secretary glares at him. "Why don't you just be quiet, Ron? Nobody's even talking to you."

"Yeah, Ron," Ottessa says. "Shut the fuck up."

Ron, much to their relief, shuts the fuck up.

The secretary returns her attention to Ottessa and Mary. Visibly disgusted by her superiors. "The squad car he described, the one who called us... he said it looked old. The description he gave me, it was so weird, I guess it left an impression all these months later. Nobody here drives those outdated models. It wouldn't make any sense. But the one this guy saw...it matched the one you witnessed pick up your kids."

Before Ottessa and Mary can respond, the sheriff of course feels the need to interrupt. At this point, it's become his shtick. "Correct me if I'm wrong, Miss Clementine, but I don't seem to recall you ever relaying this information on to me."

The secretary—Clementine—nods. "I wasn't sure if I should bother. He didn't ask about filling out a missing persons report. As far as I knew, the car could have been from some other precinct who just so happened to be passing by."

Another cop—a Ron lookalike—sighs. "That Flying J, I swear to god, someone ought to just burn that fuckin' place down."

"Why?" Mary asks.

The Ron lookalike shrugs, like he hadn't expected to be called out on his comment. "Ask anyone here. I can't even tell you how many calls we get about that truck stop. You want to know more about missing persons? Hell, go camp out in that lot for a week or two. Wouldn't be surprised if you find yourself the one who's missing."

Keene again, no longer so amused. "Officer, did I give you permission to discuss classified information with a civilian?"

The Ron lookalike raises his brow. "Since when are disappearances *classified?*"

"All open cases are unless I say otherwise."

"News to me."

The sheriff grins. Expression like a snake, biding its time. "Perhaps we'll have a deeper discussion about it later."

The Ron lookalike hesitates, then sinks his head. "Yessir."

The sheriff steps in front of his officers, standing tall and trying his best to reclaim his position of authority. "Look, ladies, it isn't some grand mystery. All truck stops collect themselves their share of unsolved crimes if they're open long enough. It comes with the territory. Strangers from out of town stopping for coffee, a bite to eat, a fill-up, you never know who you're serving. You got your drug addicts, your car thieves, your muggers, and, yes, your occasional abduction case. But missing kids? No. Usually, in these cases, we're talking about prostitutes or lone wanderers, and half the time, they're not even really *abducted,* they just don't want to be found. We take child abductions *very seriously.* Any respectable police station does."

Ottessa spits through the bars, hitting the sheriff's necktie. "If that's the case, then explain why we got y'all locked in here, demanding answers like a couple of goddamn vigilantes."

The sheriff grins wide, revealing a set of brownish teeth. "As I've stated multiple times, Ms. Jones, I don't for a second believe someone took your children. Here is what I believe—no, here is what I *know*—happened: on Friday night, both your and Ms. Washington's boys snuck out, thought they'd have themselves a little bit of fun, cause some chaos at the Shell. Things got out of hand awful quick. They assaulted the man working the counter and fled. Thinking they killed the clerk, they confided in you two—well, at least Ms. Jones…I haven't quite made up my mind about you, Ms. Washington. They confessed what they did, and you helped smuggle them out of town. Where? Can't say. But you better believe I'm going to find out. Knowing the Shell was equipped with cameras, you devised this…this *fantasy* that involved one of *my own officers* abducting your kids and…what? I guess losing them in the system? Accidentally killing them and hiding the evidence? I won't pretend to understand every nook and cranny of this absurd conspiracy. I doubt you two have completely figured it all out. But I do have to admit I admire the sheer commitment you've made so far. That video? It almost looked legitimate. But come the fuck on, ladies. How goddamn stupid do you think I am? Really, now. I've had enough of the two of you wasting my time. More people than just you exist in Percy, and I gotta account for each and every one of them. So if you're done here, I'd mighty appreciate you unlocking the goddamn door and fucking off once and for all. You've become one hell of an itch on my asshole that I can't quite scratch."

"Lovely imagery, Sheriff," Ottessa says.

"Thank you kindly, miss."

Down the hallway, a metal door creaks open, and a voice shouts, "Hey, where the heck is everybody? I've been radioing in for, like, the last hour…"

"Fuck," Ottessa says, just as a cop steps into view. One she recognizes almost immediately. It's the same cop they interrogated outside the church— the paperback reader. Lindenmuth.

His eyes widen with a similar recollection. "What are you…" He spots the gun in their hands, then his coworkers in the cell. "Hey, what the—?" He fumbles with his pistol holster, hands shaking.

Ottessa aims Jasper's gun at him. "Don't even fuckin' think about it, man."

Everybody in the cell's shouting now, screaming to "take those crazy bitches out." Whatever Ottessa said to him was lost in the panic. Lindenmuth pulls out his service pistol, but before he can properly focus Ottessa fires off a round into the wall behind him. He screams and leaps to the floor, but still manages to hold on to his pistol. Even a blind man can see where this situation's heading. Ottessa grabs Mary by the wrist and drags her down the hallway, toward the young cop. He's still dazed and disoriented, which comes in their favor as she kicks the pistol out of his hand and leaps over his body. Out of the hallway, through the station, both women burst through the entrance and stumble into the parking lot. A violent breeze slaps them across the face, as if greeting their return.

"Oh my God," Mary says.

"Let's get the *fuck* out of here," Ottessa says.

And Mary does not argue.

TWENTY FOUR

The land feels different removed from the disguise of darkness. Not any less threatening, but somehow more optimistic. Like walking through a cemetery, for instance: at night, anything could be waiting to jump out at you; however, even after the sun has risen, it still doesn't change the fact that you're stomping on a bunch of dead people. And it wouldn't surprise Josh in the slightest to learn the property surrounding this farm encapsulates a plethora of corpses deep within its soil. He might be more shocked to discover it doesn't.

Side-by-side, the boys race down the front porch, squinting as the rising sun tries its best to banish them back into the house. An invisible anchor manifests and weighs down upon not only Josh's legs, but also Alonzo's, given his similar lack of flight. It's like they're running through water, except the only barricade seemingly impeding their escape are the mild October winds barely strong enough to rustle the decomposing corn stalks off in the distance. The land is vacant for the most part. Grass unkempt, ranging from ankle- to knee-high. Various farming tools lay scattered. To the left and right of them, all they can see are endless rows of corn. Behind them's the house. Straight ahead, a narrow gravel driveway extending out at least a mile. Chills piano-strut along Josh's spine as he recalls what it'd been like to drive down this path from the opposite direction however many nights ago under the cover of the moon.

How impossibly infinite it had seemed then, and how impossibly infinite it still seems now.

A mirage of salvation winks at them from the endless end of the road and Josh and Alonzo stumble toward it, gasping for air, eyes still struggling against natural light, gravity slowly dragging them down to hell. They don't dare look back, don't dare risk catching one of those crazy fuckers bursting through the front door chasing after them. All eyes ahead. All thoughts of survival and nothing less—nothing less and nothing more. One foot after the other. No negativity allowed. Don't slow down. Don't *stop*. Move move move.

Move.

Chest on fire. Mouth wide open and throat raw, not asking but *begging* for air, fucking *crying* for just a little air, just a little oxygen, anything to make this hurt go away, anything to soften this excruciating punch to the lungs, this strange and terrible nightmare cursed upon their bodies, their minds, their souls.

The harder he pushes forward, the heavier his legs weigh, until progression proves impossible, until he can no longer remember the point of movement, and they both collapse into the tall grass. The impact of their defeated bodies signal tremors throughout the haunted earth. A heavy flow of blood pours down Alonzo's arm and chest, originating from the bear trap bite in his shoulder. When Josh sees the severity of the injury, he discharges another cry, not having realized what kind of damage the device would inflict, not having realized what kind of sacrifice his friend had made to ensure their survival. Tries to tell himself, if he had known, he would have never suggested the idea. Tries to tell himself that he would have done the same, but if that were true, why didn't he? *Why didn't he?*

"What the fuck is going *on?*" Alonzo says, struggling to sit up.

"Maybe we've been drugged." The words leave Josh's mouth without any real thought, but now that they've been uttered, it suddenly feels like a very real possibility.

"Drugged from *what?* We haven't eaten shit in…fuck, how long were we down there?"

"I don't know. A couple weeks?" But of course that can't be true. No way would they have survived for such a long stretch of time without food or water. Yet, even a couple weeks sounds like an underestimate. Months. *Years.*

A lifetime. "Maybe it's *because* we haven't eaten. Like…this could be what happens when someone is starving to death. Their bodies stop functioning."

Alonzo shakes his head no. "It's that fucking house. It won't let us leave." He glances over his shoulder, indicating what direction he meant, and a horrible wet sound emits from his lungs. "Oh fuck."

Josh follows his gaze. The house—this house that is not a house—it's only five or ten feet away from them, as if they've barely made any distance at all, but that can't be true—it *can't*. Unless the house has been following them all this time. Creeping up on their pathetic attempt of escape, silently laughing, unhinging its jaws and preparing to swallow them back down into the basement. This house with its raw meat hanging from its gutters. This terrible place. This unholy den.

But even in this new world of monsters, this idea sounds insane. What's more likely is their minds fooled them into thinking they'd gotten closer to the driveway than they'd actually had. The house has found a way to infiltrate their skulls and scramble their brains. It's the same kind of geographical hoodoo Josh experienced when first brought here. Life is different on this land. The universe flows abnormally.

Up ahead, the low rumble of an engine nears.

They don't need to wait around to know what kind of car it is.

Josh forces himself to his feet and helps Alonzo up. "We gotta go into the corn."

Alonzo's face breaks down like he's about to start sobbing. "No. We can't."

"Don't you hear them?"

He shakes his head, hard and fast. "There's something…there's something in…"

"*We gotta go, Zoey. Now.*"

Josh leads him across the yard, and this time gravity loosens its resistance. Because the corn is where the house wants them to go? Josh can't bear to entertain the thought. There is simply no other choice.

They can already see the cop car at the end of the driveway.

But can it see them?

Closer to the end of the yard, they come across a rotten tree stump with some kind of pickaxe stabbed into the surface. The side penetrating the wood is axe-shaped, while the opposite end of the tool's head resembles more of a gardening hoe. *A mattock,* Josh thinks, although he has no idea how he knows that—some old horror movie, probably. He releases his grip on Alonzo's good arm and pries the object from the stump. The wood relinquishes it without much of a fight, almost like it's relieved to finally be rid of it. Quite the opposite of an Excalibur.

He risks one last glance at the approaching cop car before they enter the corn field.

Josh has to carry the mattock with both hands, surprised at its weight. The majority of it balances against his right shoulder. Each step forward forces the handle to bounce against him, invoking a new jolt of pain upon every strike. Considering the condition of Alonzo's shoulder, Josh doesn't bother to complain.

Wrinkled corn stalks slap them in the face as they hurry toward whatever lies ahead. Neither of them saying a word. All of their energy focused on lifting their legs up and down, up and down, not looking back, just getting as far away from that fucking house as possible. Alonzo grunts loudly as he limps alongside him, one hand over his injured shoulder as if that'll somehow stop the pain, as if it'll erase the damage already inflicted. The sun only seems to shine brighter the farther they run. Its beam attracts to their black garbage bag suits like ants writhing under a child's magnifying glass. Sweat generates from every pore drilled into their bodies. The garbage bags constrict like snakes suffocating new kills. Slowly at first, then it's as if the bags cease being a secondary entity altogether and instead merge into their flesh.

Their frantic pace can only continue another couple minutes before exhaustion kicks in again. Limping now, they still refuse to stop. Panting and coughing and groaning. They will not give up. They will not surrender. They've done too much. They've gone too far.

Josh readjusts the mattock to his opposite shoulder. "How big do you think these things usually are?"

A sound comes out of Alonzo that can be interpreted as either a laugh or a cry. "The hell do I look like? Jonathan Davis?"

"*Who?*"

This time the sound's definitely a laugh. "You know. The guy from KoRn?"

"How's your shoulder?"

"How do you think?"

An awkward silence as Josh figures out how to tell him what he really means to say. "That was really...cool of you, you know. How you saved us."

"What?"

"Just...thank you. For what you did back there."

"Man, don't be gay. Let's go." Alonzo's own way of saying, *Anytime, friend. You know I love you.*

Josh stops and doubles over, too weak to continue. The mattock drops to the ground. "But...what if there's no end?"

Alonzo stops and turns around. "What?"

"The field." He points ahead. "What if it just keeps going and going? And we're stuck out here forever, until we die?"

"There has to be an end."

"Why?"

"Because everything has one."

"An end?"

"Yeah."

"But what if it doesn't?"

"Josh, goddammit, shut up." Alonzo continues through another wall of corn.

Josh tries to find the strength to follow, but a searing fire in his chest refuses to comply. He lingers back a moment, eyes closed, nails digging into his palms. How long can the human body even survive under these kind of conditions? No food. No water. No *sleep*. It's been days, at the very least. If he were to collapse right now and cease living, nobody would be surprised. Surrender is expected. Anything else, that's what's out of the ordinary. To die, that would only be following nature's plan. To live would be going against it.

He retrieves the mattock from the ground and straightens his back just as Alonzo reemerges from the corn ahead. The confidence previously displayed across his face is no longer present, now replaced by another familiar expression: dread.

"What's wrong?"

Alonzo hasn't blinked since his return. "Kids. Two of them. Up ahead."

"Kids?"

He nods.

"How old?"

"Young. I don't know."

"What are they doing?"

"Just…standing there."

"Did they see you?"

"Yeah."

"What are they doing out here?"

"I don't know."

"Did you talk to them?"

"No."

"Why not?"

"They're…uh…stuck together."

"They're *what?*"

Alonzo sighs. "They're *stuck together*. Like, twins."

"Wait, what? They're conjoined?"

"Yeah."

"What the fuck."

"Yeah."

"What were they *doing?*"

"Nothing. Standing there. Looking at me."

"Well." Josh tries to process this new information but has no idea what to do with it. "That's weird."

Alonzo nods. "Yeah."

"I guess you should show me."

His lips quiver. "What? Why?"

"Maybe they need our help."

"I don't think so."

"Why do you say that? They could be like us. They could have escaped from that…that house. And now they're lost."

Alonzo pauses, thinking about it, then slowly shakes his head. "Nah."

Josh pushes past him, half-convinced Alonzo's screwing around. Through another wall of dried-out corn stalks and he steps into a small rounded clearing in the field where the agriculture's been flattened against the ground. A crop circle. And standing, side-by-side, in the *(dead)* center of the circle are two small children of identical physique. A comically wide set of overalls expands across both of their chests. If they're not actually conjoined at the hip, then they're awfully dedicated to pretending. Blonde spaghetti strands of hair hang down either side of their heads. Clearly children, yes, but their faces look aged by a severe illness, making their sexes indeterminable upon a first impression.

Both of them stare directly at Josh, as if expecting his arrival.

"Oh," he says, and returns to where he'd left Alonzo, hidden safely behind the wall of corn. Alonzo hasn't moved. "Well, you were right. There's something definitely wrong with them."

"Creepy as shit, right?"

"Yeah."

"You think they're like…the cops?"

"They're kids."

Alonzo bites his lip. "Maybe."

"Maybe?"

"All I'm saying is, we can't trust anything we see out here. Shit's…different. Don't you think?"

Josh nods, wishing he didn't agree. "Yeah. Okay."

"So I say we walk past them, and if they try anything, we just…we just knock them right the fuck out."

"What do you think they're going to try?"

"Hopefully nothing. Hopefully they just keep staring at us all creepy without saying anything and let us go on about our way."

They break apart and return to the crop circle. The twins remain in the same spot, seemingly not having budged. Their expressions appear neither amused nor bored. Blank, maybe. Emotionless. It occurs to Josh halfway across the circle that these two kids might not even be real, that instead they could be some bizarre set of scarecrows. Scarekids. Propped up by their kidnappers to scare off something a bit different than birds.

But then they talk, both of them, each mouth lifting and dropping in perfect unison:

"You friends? You friends?"

Josh and Alonzo, deer in headlights. Josh doesn't need to be a mind reader to hear the thoughts rushing through his friend's head. They're the same as Josh's:

Oh shit oh shit oh shit—

"No go away, friends. No go away." Again, the words spill from both of their mouths. Their heads cock to the side at the same time, but opposite angles. Like they're one entity. One being. Their voices are high, childish, almost innocent, but not quite. No, there's something distrustful and malignant in their tone.

Slowly, Josh points ahead, the direction they've been traveling all this time. "We're going home."

"Home?" The twins giggle. Nails on a chalkboard. "Home! Home!" They clap their hands together and dance around on their shared two legs, laughing harder. "Home! Home!"

Alonzo whispers, "Fuck this," and continues toward the edge of the crop circle, which prompts both of the twins to cease dancing.

"Where goin', friends? Don't wanna play? Friends. Don't wanna play?"

Josh shakes his head, too afraid to look away from them. "Not right now. Sorry. Maybe later?"

The twins step forward, no longer smiling. "Why not right now? Friends, why not right now?"

"We have to go." Josh finally breaks eye contact and starts turning away, then an insane, high-pitched squeal escapes from the twins, a noise so loud both Josh and Alonzo drop to their knees and plant their hands against their ears and grit their teeth and pray pray pray for it to end. The mattock dropped and forgotten. Time pauses and throws the boys into a loop of torture where their bodies age and rot and get ground up into compost all with this noise, this sound, this lunatic squeal accompanying their every second, their every breath and unbreath, into life and death, the squeal lives eternal through all realms, all realities.

PLEASE GOD MAKE IT STOP OH PLEASE GOD I CAN'T TAKE IT OH FUCK IT HURTS IT FUCKING HURTS GOD MAKE IT STOP STOP STOP—

And, eventually, their prayers are answered.

When Josh opens his eyes again, the twins are standing in front of them.

"You okay, friends? You okay?"

He just stares, at a loss for words, not believing such a cosmic sound could originate from such small creatures.

"Friends, you want play now? You want play?"

Nodding, slowly, feeling like he's in a dream, Josh realizes with great horror that if they do not obey their requests, then the twins will make that noise again. Less of a noise and more of a weapon. A bullet straight to the nerves. He'll do anything to avoid it. *Anything.*

At the sight of Josh's surrender, the twins grin wide, but keeping their lips closed, revealing not a single tooth.

"Ring-a?" they say. "Ring-a-ring-o'-rosie? Friend? Ring-a? Ring-a-ring-o'-rosie?"

"What the fuck are they saying?" Alonzo says, kneeling next to Josh.

"Ring…around the rosie?" Josh says, and the twins nod enthusiastically.

"Ring-a! Ring-a-ring-o'-rosie!"

"That's what you want to play?"

More nodding, their hands extending out. A trance hits them. Josh and Alonzo each accept one of the hands and the twins drag them up with unexpected strength. When they try to pull away from them, the twins' grips tighten and only pull the boys closer.

"Ring-a! Ring-a-ring-o'-rosie!"

"What the fuck is happening?" Alonzo says, but Josh can't answer. A sudden dryness has consumed his mouth and rendered his speech impotent. The twins maneuver their shared feet into a wider gap, forcing Josh and Alonzo to mimic their stance until they've all formed a decent-sized circle, connected by hands and hips.

Connected by flesh.

"Ready play, friend? Ready play?"

They don't wait for an answer. When their feet move, so do Josh and Alonzo's, almost like by forming this circle, by sharing this bond, the boys' bodies have merged into the twins, like they've conjoined. Conjoined into the conjoined. Their rotation increases speed. No longer in control of their own legs. The world spins. Together, along with the twins, Josh and Alonzo recite the nursery rhyme.

"Ring-a-ring-o'-rosies!" all four of them scream, so loud, so violent. "A pocket full of posies!" Their throats raw. Sand in their lungs. "Mother! Mother!" Vision distorting. Reality melting. "Rise from the ground!"

They collapse to their knees, both the boys and the twins, *laughing*, Josh has no idea what's so goddamn funny but he can't control himself. He can't remember the last time he's ever had so much *fun*. So much pure, uncontaminated joy. How did he know the words to the song? Who cares! Maybe he's always known them, somewhere buried deep inside him, and the twins found a way to unearth such knowledge, to tap into the secret truths of the universe.

"You like game, friends? You like game?"

"We like games," Josh and Alonzo say, now also in sync. "We like to play games with friends."

Whose words are these?

Josh's right hand remains connected to one of the twins, his left wrapped around Alonzo's sweaty fingers, Alonzo's other hand embracing the opposite twin, keeping the circle complete, maintaining the embrace no matter the cost. Josh's brain feels like an ocean flowing in every possible and impossible direction. Up, down, left, right, inside, out, forever, never. His skull no longer encompasses only his own thoughts but also the thoughts belonging to everybody else in the circle. Alonzo, the twins, an onslaught of myriad unidentifiable voices eager to join the party—hidden passengers pervaded with impatience and vehemence.

Ring-a-ring-o'-roses!
A pocket full of posies!
Mother! Mother!
Rise from the ground!
Mother! Mother!
Rise! From! The! Ground!

No longer on their knees, no, but standing again, keeping the circle flowing, fast, faster, never stopping, the nursery rhyme loud enough to shatter worlds.

Mother! Mother!
RISE. FROM. THE. GROUND.
MOTHER. MOTHER.
RISE.
MOTHER.
RISE.
FROM.
THE.
GROUND.

The crunch of a corn stalk cuts off their train of thought—thought as in *singular*, thought as in *one*. The circle pauses. All attention snaps to the edge of the clearing, to their new intruder.

A child half the height of the twins, dressed in dirty rags and wearing a brown sack over its head. Black buttons are sewn to the front of the bag.

Two little lifeless eyes. The rags on its body hang like loose strips of flesh, and in the intensity of their spinning Josh realizes the thing isn't wearing rags at all but actual flesh—or, at the very least, a material made to resemble flesh.

The twins break their hold from Josh and Alonzo and rush across the clearing, toward the…*thing* watching them.

A blockage in Josh's brain clears and he doubles over, gasping for breath, Alonzo next to him doing the same. Now that the friendship circle's no longer complete, rational thought's found a way to return. What the hell are they *doing?* Playing ring around the rosie? Jesus Christ. They don't have *time* for this. They have to leave. And what the *hell* is *that* thing? He doesn't want to find out. No way. They've wasted enough time here…here, wherever *here* is.

"Zoey, we gotta—"

Alonzo's staring at the crop circle intruder wide-eyed, lips trembling, trying to say something, trying to say…what?

"What is it? Zoey?"

"Don't…don't…let it…show you…"

"What?"

"Don't let it show you its face."

"*What?*"

Up ahead, the twins point their shared fingers at the intruder. "No! *Our* friends, Baby! You no have them. They want play with *us*. Not you, Baby. Not you!"

The thing—*Baby?*—doesn't respond, just continues staring at Josh and Alonzo with its black, button eyes.

The twins keep going, unable to subdue their rising temper tantrum. "We found first, Baby! We found first. No fair. They our friends. *Our* friends! We play ring-a-ring-o'-rosie, Baby. We play *ring-a-ring-o'-rosie!*"

Alonzo taps Josh's arm and motions for them to sneak away. Josh nods and they head toward the opposite edge of the clearing, stopping briefly to retrieve the abandoned mattock.

The twins notice their escape just as they divide the first layer of corn stalks. "Friends! Where goin', friends? Don't want play, friends?"

"Fuck! Run!" Alonzo screams, and makes a break for it. Josh follows. Behind them, the twins screech that terrible, ungodly sound again, and nausea threatens to send him tumbling down, but he fights through it, not giving a shit if it permanently scrambles his brains, as long as he gets away from them, as long as he makes it back home, back to his bed, back to his mom.

(Mother! Mother! Rise from the ground!)

Something grabs his ankles and flings him face-down. Consciousness blinks in and out, in and out. *Where's the mattock?* His body may have stopped, but inertia hasn't quite given up on his heartbeat. *Where's Zoey?*

Where's Zoey? He knows where Zoey is. He's long gone. Ditched Josh once again. Can't slow down to help the fat kid. It's everybody for themselves. And if you fall, you're on your own. Them's the rules of life. First thing any beast in the animal kingdom learns.

You. Are. On. Your. Own.

Palms against dirt. Nails into earth. Push. *Push.* He tries to turn on his back. Can't. Something's still caught around his ankles. No, not something. *Hands.* Tiny *hands.* Fuck fuck fuck. He looks over his shoulder. The twins lay on their stomach behind him, gripping his ankles. Grinning.

This time they're showing their teeth.

Oh shit oh shit oh shit—

He screams and kicks one of the twins in the face and they both gasp and let go of his ankles. He scrambles to his feet. Dizzy. Don't fall. Alonzo in front of him. The mattock in his right hand, his left arm bloody and hanging lifelessly at his side.

"Move," he says, and Josh falls back down, too tired to stand. Alonzo continues forward, raising the mattock over his head. Approaching the twins as they too push themselves into a stance, still dazed from Josh's face-stomp.

Genuine worry, confusion. "Friend? What doin', friend? What doin'?"

Alonzo swings the mattock.

Axe-end first.

It lands between the two heads and buries into the patch of flabby flesh where their shoulders connect.

Their mouths unhinge.

The noise again.

The *scream*.

Josh covers his ears and convulses, begging for it to stop.

Alonzo, seemingly unaffected, pulls the mattock out from the twins' shoulder and swings it down once more, striking the same area. The blade digs deeper this time, stopping at their conjoined hip. A wide, gruesome valley of gore splits between the twins, crudely resembling the liquid metal terminator at the end of *Judgement Day*. Their scream evolves. Josh leans on his side to prevent choking on vomit. Alonzo struggles to pull the mattock out a third time, but manages to get it free. The twins raise their shared hands, palms-out, fingers stretched, one final surrender that's ignored as Alonzo swings the mattock down again. A clean cut through their hip. The mattock stabs into the dirt beneath their groin.

The twins stop screaming and just sort of stand in place for a moment, as if they haven't realized they've just been split in half.

The absence of their screech makes the cornfield disturbingly quiet.

A thick, green ooze spills from either half of them. Chunks of diseased organs and rotted bones follow.

"What wrong, friend?" the twin on the left says, no longer in sync with its counterpart.

"What wrong, friend?" echoes the twin on the right, a moment later.

"No want play with us?"

"No want play with us?"

Alonzo shakes his head, panting. "I'm sorry."

"Later? Friend? You play later?"

"Later? Friend? You play later?"

The green ooze trickles out of their mouths.

"Friend? Friend? Friend?"

"Friend? Friend? Fr—"

The twins collapse, first the one on the left, then the other. Their impact makes a repulsive wet sound and Josh vomits again.

"Jesus fucking Christ," Alonzo says, and turns around. Blood streams from both of his nostrils.

"You're bleeding," Josh says, trying to stand.

And Alonzo laughs. "Shit—who ain't?"

TWENTY FIVE

*O*utlaws. That's what they are now. Wanted by the police with no place to hide. They can't go home, that's for sure. It'd be the first place Sheriff Keene would send his officers to check. And even without the threat of police apprehension, the thought of Jasper confronting her back at the house provides plenty enough disgust to avoid the area altogether.

Mary races down random backroads, focus juggling between the rear-view mirror and the path ahead. So far, nobody's following them—or, if they are, they're doing a terrible job at it. She still doesn't ease up on the gas, though. Surely any second one of their cars will pop up behind them—a fleck of dirt on the mirror getting progressively larger until it eventually plows into her bumper and knocks them off the road.

"I can't believe you shot at that police officer," Mary says, gripping the steering wheel so tight it's a miracle it doesn't pop off. "What were you *thinking*? How are we supposed to take care of our children if we're in prison for the rest of our lives on *murder* charges?"

Ottessa cradles Jasper's gun with both hands in her lap, eyes droopy, jaw loose. "It was an accident. I'm sorry."

"You almost hit him."

"I wasn't trying to. I was aiming away."

"I thought you just said it was an accident."

"What?"

"Was it an accident, or were you aiming away?"

"Both."

"Either you meant to pull the trigger or you didn't mean to pull the trigger."

Ottessa groans and slaps the gun off her lap. It bounces around at her feet and slides under the passenger seat. "What does it matter? It got pulled regardless, didn't it?"

"I don't know where I'm going."

"I also don't know where you're going."

"We can't go home."

"Fuck no we can't."

"A part of me thinks I should call Jasper from a payphone and warn him. But I don't want to talk to him right now."

"Fuck that guy, anyway. He sucks."

Mary glares at her before returning to the road. "That's my husband you're talking about, you know."

"Yeah, well, your *husband* sucks, okay?"

Mary pauses, considering it, and nods. "Yeah. He really does suck."

"He's the fuckin' worst, is what he is."

"Okay, now."

"Can you think of somebody worse than him?"

Pause. "Maybe that sheriff."

"Okay. Your husband's the second fuckin' worst, then."

"I think we need to go to the media."

"What?"

"Like, a news station. The paper or something. Tell them what we know."

"They ain't gonna give two goddamn shits about what we tell them."

"You don't know that."

"Look in the mirror, girl. Tell me I'm wrong."

Mary squeezes the steering wheel. "You're wrong."

"When was the last time you ever saw someone like us on that bitch Nancy Grace's show? The quicker you understand that, the quicker you'll understand that we are officially on our own. Besides, after the shit that just went down, I don't exactly feel comfortable announcing my location to the public. There's a better chance they'd just call the police instead of sticking a microphone in our faces. Nobody's gonna help us, and nobody's gonna help Zoey and Josh except for you and I and nobody else. You dig?"

Mary nods again, slowly, not sure what she thinks about the matter. "I think I know somewhere we can go. Just to rest a moment and think about what to do."

"Where?"

"There's this woman on the PTA who's always inviting me over for coffee."

Ottessa coughs. "Did you just say the *PTA*?"

"What's so wrong with the PTA?"

"Jesus fucking Christ."

Lois's house isn't too far away. Mary's only been over there once, after Lois insisted every mom on the committee join her for coffee and pie one evening. Her daughter's in the same class as Josh. Clementine or Gwendolyn or something equally lengthy and obnoxious. She hadn't stayed long but just from her brief time there, it'd been clear the woman lives a lonely existence and craves constant company. Hence the constant coffee invitations. As far as Mary can tell, there's no man in the picture. She has no idea what she does for a living, but it has to be something that allows for copious free time otherwise there's no way the woman would accomplish as many PTA-related tasks in a given week. She's always volunteering to run errands during the day when all the other moms are at work. Others have speculated exactly how she can afford such a nice house (a two-story along one of the few cul-de-sacs in Percy). Some have suggested she's secretly a drug dealer, like the woman in that new Showtime program. Others are convinced she murdered her husband and cashed in on the life insurance. Mary isn't sure she cares one way or the other, but it's definitely questionable. At this point, she's sort of hoping the woman's a criminal. It'll be easier to convince her to let them hide out at her house.

"If ever there was a street that said, 'We Shoot Black Folks on Sight,' I do believe we just found it," Ottessa says.

"Oh, stop. Nobody's going to shoot us." Mary stops in front of Lois's house and cuts the engine.

"I feel like we gotta hold up a sign that promises we ain't gonna rob anybody just to get out of the car."

"Come on."

"Wait, hold on a minute, I think I spot a sniper held up in that window down yonder."

"*Yonder?*"

"What, you think I don't know the word 'yonder' now?"

She hesitates, then shakes her head. "There's no sniper."

"All right." Ottessa shrugs. "Don't you go whining to me when you got some crazy cracker's bullet lodged into your cranium."

As they walk up the driveway, Ottessa scans their surroundings, clearly disturbed. "Girl, where the hell have you brought me?"

"Just...don't say anything, okay? Let me handle this."

"Mmm."

Mary rings the doorbell and a dog immediately starts barking somewhere inside the house. Seconds pass and the curtain on the front window brushes aside. At the bottom stands a small dog balancing on its hind legs, screeching at its intruders. A wild patch of hair hangs from the top of its head, while the rest of its body is completely shaven.

Ottessa explodes with laughter. "What in the good holy fuck is that thing?"

"It's her dog."

"That is no dog."

Lois opens the door grinning wide enough to reveal every one of her teeth in all their shiny whiteness. She's wearing a purple cocktail dress that looks like it cost more than what Mary makes in an entire month at the office. The dog yaps in a continuous circle around high heels of a matching color. Mary remembers how irritating the dog had been last time she visited and regrets ever driving over here.

"Mary! To what do I owe the pleasure?"

"Oh, I'm sorry. Are you heading out?"

Lois scrunches up her brow, confused by the question. "No...? Just been lounging around the house all day like some lazy cow! How are you?" She offers Ottessa one of her notoriously obnoxious smiles. "And... Mary's friend?"

Ottessa points at the screeching animal near her feet. "What kind of dog is that?"

"Oh." The smile widens, excited to talk about her stupid pet. "That's a Chinese Crested."

"A Chinese Crested *what?*"

She blinks, trying to comprehend the question. "Just a Chinese Crested."

"Just seems like there should be another word afterward."

"There is not."

"Oh." Ottessa examines the dog again, grimacing with pure disgust. "Looks like a Chihuahua with a mullet."

Lois gasps, like she's just been slapped across the face. Mary coughs back a laugh. Lois's dog, Mona Lisa, has served as ridicule fuel for years now, but always behind her back at PTA meetings whenever she left the room. "A Chihuahua with a mullet" couldn't have been a more perfect description. She silently reminds herself to bring it up at the next PTA get-together, then realizes there will never be another one—not for her, at least. Her days of being a member of the PTA are long over.

Mary clears her throat, tries to recompose herself. "Lois, I was hoping to have a word with you. Mind if we come in?"

"I guess that depends if you're planning to insult Mona Lisa any further."

Ottessa laughs. "Your dog's name is Mona Lisa?"

"What's wrong with Mona Lisa? It's a perfectly reasonable name."

Ottessa pats Mary on the back. "Mary, I just wanted to thank you for bringing me here. It's not even my birthday yet and you're already spoiling me." Then she steps past Lois and enters the house, disregarding her noticeable lack of permission to do so.

Lois stares at Mary, slack-jawed, and Mary just shrugs and says, "Thank you," then follows after Ottessa who's already halfway through the house gaping at items neither one of them will ever be able to afford, not even after combining both their salaries.

Ottessa points at a series of silverware hanging in a glass frame and spits laughter. "This bitch's got spoons on her wall! Spoons!"

"Those spoons are worth several thousand dollars," Lois says, closing the door and meeting them in the living room, arms folded across her chest.

Ottessa waits, as if expecting a punchline, then shakes her head. "Bullshit."

"I collect them whenever I travel to another country."

"How many countries have you been to?"

Lois rolls her eyes up to the base of her skull, configuring some unseen data. "Twelve."

"Twelve! Nobody's been to twelve different countries." Ottessa glances at Mary and motions to Lois. "You hear this? She's saying she's been to twelve different countries. Twelve!"

Mary shrugs. "So what?"

"I've barely been to three different *states*."

Mary squints. "Barely?"

"It don't count completely if you was too fucked up to remember it."

Mary turns away and focuses on Lois. "I'm sorry to just barge in like this, but we're in a little bit of trouble, and I couldn't think of anyone else likely to offer us a place to sit and talk."

"Well, I haven't offered—"

"Yeah," Ottessa says, cutting in, "this is real cool of you, seriously. Most women like you, they take one look at a couple of black gals like us and start calling for help. But not you. You're a real goddamn hero, ma'am."

Mary gestures at the living room furniture surrounding them. "Do you mind...?"

Lois hesitates, going over the pros and cons of each potential answer, then sighs. "I'll make some coffee."

TOUCH THE NIGHT

THEY END UP TELLING HER a very condensed version of the last two days. Just the bare facts: their children are missing, possibly abducted; the police refuse to cooperate; while investigating the crime by themselves, they stirred up trouble with the law, and now it's wise they lay low for a couple hours.

"It's not like we're *wanted* or anything," Mary says, suddenly terrified Lois will call the cops on them immediately after this conversation. "It's just best if we don't show our faces for a little while. They think we're trying to do their jobs for them. You know how men can get."

"Why can't you *lay low* at your own home, though?" Lois eventually asks.

"My husband and I are going through a disagreement."

"About your kid?"

Mary nods. "That would be the root of the trouble, yes."

She gives Ottessa a dirty glance. "And I suppose you're also going through a disagreement with your husband?"

Ottessa sniggers. "I ain't chained to no dick."

Mary cuts in: "To be honest with you, Lois, Ottessa's house is very dirty, and it's difficult to concentrate with so much clutter all over the place."

Ottessa feigns offense. "Bitch."

"That's another reason we came here. I knew your home would be nice and tidy. A perfect place to think."

Lois smirks. Finally something she can understand, something they can see eye-to-eye on. "Well, I guess you two can stay here for a little while. I planned on staying in this evening, anyway."

"Now, let me ask you a very important question," Ottessa says, stepping closer.

"Yes?" Lois asks, refusing to back away.

"What's the booze situation here?"

"I'll have you know I am the president of the PTA."

"I don't know what that means."

"That means the booze situation here is very satisfactory."

Ottessa grins. "Shit, girl, maybe we can be friends after all."

TWENTY SIX

"What *was* that thing, anyway?" Josh asks, readjusting the black trash bag constricting against his chest. Panting, desperate for air.

"What does it matter?" Alonzo long gave up trying to mess with his own bag. He's ten minutes away from shredding it from his body altogether and doing the rest of the journey in the nude. Ain't like there's anybody out here who's gonna see him besides Josh and those goddamn monsters.

"I was just thinking, maybe if we knew more about it, we'd know how to stop it. How to kill it."

"You sayin' we need to prepare ourselves for some...*what?* Boss fight? Let me tell you something, man. When you die in a video game, you get to respawn to your last saved point. In real life you don't get none of that shit. You just stay dead."

"Aren't you even interested to know what's going to kill us?"

"I just think it's a waste of energy, thinking about it."

"What else is there to do?"

Alonzo points ahead. "Walk."

"We been walkin'."

"And we gonna keep doin' it."

"What did you mean when you said it showed you its face?"

Alonzo doesn't respond. Maybe if enough time passes, Josh will forget he asked the question. But of course that's not going to happen. This isn't the first time Josh has asked it.

"I know you heard me."

265

"I don't remember, okay?" Alonzo finally says, because a lie is better than the truth. "I was in this...this goddamn field. Somewhere. And I tripped. It came from out of nowhere. Something happened, something that paralyzed me. I couldn't move. Could only watch as it slowly walked up to me, then...then...then..." He stops walking. No longer avoiding eye contact with Josh. "It's like waking up from a dream, you know? The more time that passes, the easier it gets to forget. I know something happened. Something bad. But the harder I think about it, the more nauseated I feel, like I'm gonna fuckin' puke or something. I know it showed me its face, but I don't know what that means."

Josh takes his sweet time before responding. "Your shoulder looks like shit."

"It feels like it looks." Alonzo risks rubbing it and winces.

"Do you think you're going to lose it?"

"Lose what? My *arm*?"

Josh nods.

"Why the fuck would you ask me that? What the hell?" He paces in a circle, trying not to touch his wound. "Do *you* think I'm going to lose it? Fucking hell. *Why* would you even *ask* that?"

"I think it's very funny when you freak out."

"Oh, you think it's funny?"

Josh smiles. "It's a little funny."

Alonzo smiles, too, betrayed by his own lips. "Well, then I'm glad to be of service. Maybe you'll get lucky and the goddamn thing will just fall off while we're walking."

"That would truly be hilarious."

Alonzo contemplates the imagery. "Honestly, yeah, you're kind of right."

"I'm sorry your arm got all messed up."

"Next time, you get to jump on the bear trap."

"Deal."

They try to shake hands, but they're too exhausted to lift their arms. Instead they return to their regularly scheduled program of walking, followed by even more walking.

"Tell you what, though," Alonzo says, suddenly afraid of silence, "bet you never had so much exercise in your life."

Josh laughs and coughs. "My dad would shit bricks if he saw me now."

"Wait. Like, *whole* bricks?"

"What other kind of bricks are there?"

"I don't know. Like, shredded bricks or whatever."

"Shredded bricks?"

"Yeah."

"Ain't no such thing as shredded bricks, Zoey."

Alonzo stops again. "Goddammit. How many times do I have to tell—"

Josh points ahead, wide-eyed. "Fuck! The thing!"

"The thing…?" He follows Josh's direction and finds the scarecrow creature standing a couple feet away, just watching them argue. Like it's *entertained*. "Oh! That thing." He gulps. "Shit."

Stupid fucking idiot, Alonzo thinks, wishing like hell he hadn't left the mattock back with those creepy twins. Those creepy *dead* twins, he reminds himself, trying to instill some kind of confidence.

It doesn't work.

Urine trickles down his thigh.

The thing in front of them cocks its head, as if detecting the scent of his piss.

"What do we do?" Josh asks.

"We can't let it take off its mask."

"Why not?"

Alonzo bites his lip. "We just can't."

"Is it listening to us talk right now? Why isn't it doing anything?"

"Fuck. Let's just charge it."

"*Charge* it?" Josh's voice squeaks like a little petrified mouse.

"Yeah. On the count of three. Ready?"

"No! I'm not *ready*."

"Okay, good. One two three go!"

"Wait!"

Alonzo lowers his head and sprints with everything he's got left in him, and Josh follows a moment later. Both of them releasing their best warrior cries, which mostly resemble tired grunts. The thing—*Baby*—doesn't react at first, like it's coexisting on some delayed plane of existence, but when they're within five feet of each other it suddenly raises both of its arms, palms out, a thick honey-like texture dripping from its ashy skeletal fingers, spread wide in surrender.

Fuck your surrender, Alonzo thinks, and tackles Baby against a wall of dead cornstalks. Josh lands on top of him, crushing all the air from his body. It occurs to Alonzo then that he did not plan this strategy out too well, as he has no idea what to do now that he's gotten Baby on the ground.

"I'll kill you!" he screams, trying to buy time. "I'll kill your whole crazy fuckin' family!"

Then: the sound of a million insects flapping their wings in unison. Coming from beneath Baby's brown bag. Coming from its lungs. Deep down from its grotesque belly protected by strips of unidentified flesh.

This is how monsters laugh.

"Get the fuck off me!" Alonzo shouts at Josh. "This was a terrible idea!"

Josh scrambles off to the side, wheezing and crying about hurting his knee or some shit. Alonzo tries to get up by pushing against Baby's body but as soon as he applies the slightest bit of pressure, the creature's chest caves in and devours both of his hands and now he's *inside* its body oh god oh holy shit his hands are *inside the fucking thing's body.*

Alonzo expects to feel something wet and slimy but instead is greeted with the opposite sensation. Dry. Rustling. Like leaves. Or cornstalks. And...dirt? Balls of *dirt.* He tries to pull his hands out of its body but they're stuck. Something inside its chest has a fierce suction around his wrists and refuses to release him. Baby's body convulses beneath him like it's having a seizure. The insect-laughter increases in volume. Gets so loud he isn't even sure if the noise is real or exists solely inside his head, bouncing around his skull like lightning bugs imprisoned in a mason jar. He pulls and pulls but the creature's chest has somehow melted around his wrists, making Alonzo and Baby become one. They're no longer separate beings but a single entity, sharing a conscience, sharing a soul, sharing every-goddamn-thing. Inside its chest his fingers scratch at anything within reach. Nothing wet. Not like how the inside of a body should feel. Nothing here is correct yet nothing is wrong, either. Everything is in its right place. The neutral coarseness of plant life and grainy absolution of soil. A piñata reanimated.

"Let me go!" Alonzo screams, face inches from Baby's bag mask. "Let me go! Let me go! Let me go!"

Baby's convulsions do not stop.

Josh wraps his arms around Alonzo's waist and tries to drag him off but it's no use. Whatever Baby is, it's stronger than both of them combined. Josh says something behind him but his voice is drowned out by the insect-laughter. He lets go of Alonzo's waist and crawls around, sobbing, tears pouring from his eyes like he's got a leak, and pounds his fists into Baby's head. One, two. One, two. Its skull bounces off the earth. One, two. One, two. The insect-laughter somehow gets louder, taunting Josh's pathetic attempts of violence. Pain is for weaker creations.

With each strike, Baby's bag loosens. Another couple punches and it's bound to fall off altogether. Alonzo opens his mouth to warn Josh, but words from an unrecognizable source spill out instead of the ones he intended: "Take off the bag! Take off the bag!"

Josh stops hitting the creature and looks up, puzzled. "But I thought—"

"Take off the bag! Take off the bag!"

Alonzo means to tell him to leave it on, no matter what you do you leave that fucking bag on, but his body doesn't belong only to him now. The creature. *Baby.* It's feeding its own language through him. Its own demands. Turning Alonzo into some kind of vessel. A messenger.

"Take off the bag!" he screams again, nearly choking now. "Take off the bag!"

Josh grabs the bag with trembling hands at the base of Baby's neck and pulls it off with one desperate motion.

And Alonzo cries out at what's revealed beneath him. Staring down at the face Baby presents as true. Staring down at…himself. Alonzo's own face, yes, but *changed*. Distorted. Like looking at yourself in one of those haunted house mirrors. A nightmare face. As if Baby's face is made of the same materials used on Alonzo's, only arranged differently. More hazardously. Flipped inside-out and lit on fire. A toothless mouth grins up at him. Cheeks sunken. Eyes black as cancer, not a splotch of white within sight. It grins wide and humorlessly, and every ounce of fear and hate Alonzo may have once held for this being vanishes. In its place arrives love. The kind of love with which a parent might behold their child. The kind of love his own father might have once shared for Alonzo before passing away or running off or whatever bullshit excuse his mom last fed him. A sweet warmness swirls through Alonzo and he leans closer, welcoming Baby's embrace, hands still merged into its collapsed chest.

Then: a scream from above.

Alonzo jerks his head up just as Josh stomps his bare foot down into Baby's face—into *Alonzo's* face. His *other* face.

Alonzo screams, "No!" but it's too late.

It is always too late.

Josh's foot smashes through Baby's face like a decayed pumpkin. He lifts it up again and strikes down once more. Then again. And again. And Alonzo is helpless. All he can do is watch his friend destroy the only thing he's ever truly loved. Watch and mourn and bathe in the grief raining down like nuclear fallout. The pitch of its insect-laughter is significantly altered with each round of destruction. Josh's kicks muffle it to a grating static until it eventually extinguishes into a godawful beautiful nothing.

Out of breath, Josh falls on his ass, crushing a cluster of cornstalks. Alonzo remains on top of Baby, hands still inserted into its chest although no longer caged there against his will. Slowly he removes them from Baby's bizarre innards and considers peeking inside, then thinks better of it and rolls off. Whatever's inside Baby is Baby's business and nobody else's. Some things aren't meant to be seen.

"How?" Josh says, writhing on the ground, hugging his chest. "How how *how?*"

"I think it's dead." He forces himself up and vertigo threatens to knock him right back down. "We gotta get going. Come on."

Josh shakes his head violently side-to-side, eyes closed, snot bubbling up. "My face. My face. My face. How? How did it get my face?"

Alonzo blinks long and hard. "Wait. What?"

"How did it get my face, Zoey? *How did it get my face?*"

TWENTY SEVEN

Then the cornfield ends, and they stumble out onto a dark, empty highway. Mere seconds ago, back in the cornfield, the sun had practically been blistering their flesh. Yet now—again, only *seconds later*—any sign of day has been thoroughly erased from the night sky. A terrible blackness now blankets the clouds. A cold stillness that makes Josh oddly miss the suffocating warmth provided by the cornfield. Somewhere nearby crickets taunt their presence.

Alonzo sighs, annoyed, exhausted. "I'm not even going to question this. What about you?"

"Do you think if we go back in…it'll still be day out?"

He licks his lips, staring at the wall of decomposed stalks. "I'm thinking if we go back in there, we ain't ever gonna find ourselves out again. That's what I think."

"Yeah. Me too."

"Then let's just keep going."

They start walking down the middle of the road, the pavement rough and cold against their bare feet. A new fear hits Josh and he can't contain it. "Do you know where we are?"

"No clue," Alonzo says.

"What if we're walking right back to that house?"

"Then I guess we'll turn around and go the other way."

"What if it's too late by then?"

"Then I guess we'll fucking die, Josh. What do you want me to say?"

"I don't know."

273

"The hard part's over," Alonzo says. "Now we gotta—"

"Truck."

Alonzo pauses, confused. "Now we gotta…fuck?"

"Truck!" Josh points ahead at a pair of approaching headlights. Yes, a truck. A big ol' semi, heading directly their way. He grabs Alonzo's arm and ushers him to the side of the road.

"Well, I guess this is our ride," Alonzo says.

"What if one of those…those *guys* is driving it? What if he's looking for us?"

"Did you see a truck back at the farm?"

"No, but—"

"I'm tired, Josh. I'm so fucking tired."

"Okay."

As the semi nears, Josh and Alonzo wave their arms back and forth and shout for it to stop, and sure enough, the semi slows and pulls over shortly after passing them. They run toward the truck, Josh lingering slightly behind, terrified they're heading into a trap. Damn near positive of it.

The door pops open and a heavy boot steps out, followed by its partner, both of them attached to an overweight man dressed in dirty jeans and a white T-shirt. He squints at them as they near, then hops off the final footrest attached to the truck, landing on the road with a soft *thud*.

"You boys all right?" the truck driver asks, cautiously meeting them near the back of his vehicle.

"These crazy motherfuckers are after us," Alonzo says, panting. "Please. You gotta help us."

The driver cocks his head and scans the area. Of course there's nothing out here. Nothing visible, at least. "*Who* is after you?"

"These…these…these…"

Josh catches up to them, each step forward like walking through wet concrete. "We were kidnapped."

"*Kidnapped?*"

"They held us hostage, in their basement. Did things to us." Josh resists the urge to vomit. "But we escaped. Ran through the cornfield." He gestures to the treacherous agriculture behind them. "Can you help us?"

The truck driver looks them over again, skepticism fading. "What on earth are you boys wearing? Are those...*garbage* bags?"

THE DRIVER INTRODUCES HIMSELF ONCE they're all squeezed into the truck and back in motion. Says his name is Victor, or Vic, or Uncle Vic if they prefer, and when nobody laughs at what's apparently a joke, he nervously scratches his head and says it might be wise to just stick with Vic after all. Alonzo's seated shotgun and Josh sags down on the small mattress set up behind them. The whole interior reeks of coffee and Funyuns, or maybe that's the smell of feet, Josh has always had a difficult time telling the difference. The odor's unpleasant, is the point.

"Ayup. Been driving for ten straight hours now." The truck driver sighs and wipes sweat from his brow. "Regulations say I ain't supposed to exceed eight, but I got deadlines to meet, and besides, I don't sleep much these days anyway. It'd just be a waste of time, pulling over like that. Ayup. A complete waste of resources, is what it'd be." He switches off the radio, which had been broadcasting some sports announcer. "Was just listening to the World Series recap. Those Astros can't catch a break, huh?"

"Are we in Percy?" Josh asks from the back of the truck. The last thing he wants to talk about right now is baseball.

The driver chews on the question. "Now that you mention it, I seem to recall a sign for Percy a ways back. That where you boys live?"

Alonzo adjusts himself in the passenger's seat. "We need to get back there. Can you take us?"

"Tell you what I'm gonna do." Vic points ahead at the seemingly endless highway. The truck's headlights pierce the darkness only slightly. It is clear who the real winner is here. "I'm gonna keep driving, and the next time we happen across a town, I'm pulling off and stopping at the nearest police station or hospital, whichever I see first. Maybe the next town will be this Percy of yours, maybe it'll be someplace else, I don't know, but that's the best I can offer right now, and I think it's a pretty fine offer, if we're being honest here. It sure beats where you were just a couple minutes ago, wouldn't you say?"

No argument comes from either boy. At this point they're grateful just to be off their feet, to be under someone else's care for a little while. The fear remains, and will perhaps never leave them again, but for the moment it is at least subdued.

"I don't suppose any of you feel up to clueing me in on what exactly happened, huh?" When neither of them respond, he nods. "Ayup. Figured as much. Is okay, no problem. None of my business, anyway, is it? Me, all I do is drive, not exactly an occupation rich on conversation, you know what I mean? So I see you two, and I know you got your own traumas to deal with, and the last thing y'all want right now is to relive it all just for my...uh, what would you call it? My benefit? My *voyeuristic* convenience? Ayup. That's hitting the nail di-*rectly* on the head right there. Forget I even asked, how about that?"

"Thanks. We appreciate all your help, mister," Josh says, quick and urgent, afraid Alonzo's on the verge of responding with something a little less kind, something that'll convince the driver to kick them out of his truck and bid them good riddance. "We really appreciate you stopping."

Vic shrugs, radiating modesty. "What kind of soul could I call mine were I to ignore two abandoned children in distress out in the middle of nowhere? Could you believe it? Could you look yourself in the mirror? God almighty. My conscience would grow so heavy, I swear, gravity would snatch it up and plant it right on into the earth and out would grow little devils to do the work of Satan and all of his fellow comrades of evil. And we can't have that, now can we? Ayup. Can't have that at all."

Alonzo turns toward the driver, face all screwed up. "What the fuck?"

Vic chuckles softly. "Sorry there, kid, been listening to some weird audiobooks lately. They got my language all funny. I don't tend to notice it until someone looks at me exactly the way you're looking now."

"When's the next town?" Alonzo faces forward, finally catching on to what Josh's already figured out: this guy's a weirdo.

Vic gestures lazily at the windshield and all that awaits beyond it. "You boys ever think about just how *dark* darkness truly is?"

Alonzo sighs and rubs his eyes. "Man. No."

The driver glances in the rearview at Josh. "What about you, son? You ever contemplate the depths of night?"

"I don't know."

"Well, I sure have. Ayup. It's difficult *not* to think about such things, with a job like mine, you know? All I ever seem to do is dive deeper into the muck of it all. Darkness...people like to think of it as this...this...this in-*tangible* substance. But they don't seem to realize, nah, they don't get it, they don't understand that at a certain point, the dark of a night becomes so thick, it's no longer just some trick of the eyes, some de-*ception* of reality, you understand? You can reach out and touch it. Twist it and reconfigure it at your will. Sometimes darkness, it evolves. Evolves into this...what? This *canvas*. This *putty*. The right kind of people—the right kind of *things* get a hold of it? Lord have mercy. You don't want to see what kind of abhorrent nightmares escape their imaginations. Ayup."

Josh clears his throat and tries not to sound terrified out of his mind as he says, "You know, we can probably walk the rest of the way, if you want to let us out."

Alonzo nods. "Yeah. I'm starting to get a cramp in my leg, anyway. Some walking would do us good."

Again Vic laughs. Not *menacingly* or anything. More like an uncle realizing he's had a bit too much to drink. "I'm spooking you again, huh? Geez. I'm sorry about that."

"We're not spooked," Alonzo says, clearly spooked.

"You boys don't want to find yourselves caught out in a darkness like tonight. Trust me. There's all types of wicked hiding out there, ayup, just waiting for their chance to scoop up something as delicious as you two."

"We'll take our chances."

"Can I tell you boys a story?" Vic glances at Alonzo, then over his shoulder at Josh. Nearly ten seconds pass and he still hasn't broken eye contact with him and Josh realizes with horror that he's not going to return his eyes to the road until he receives an answer.

"Okay."

The driver grins and turns back around. "On nights like this, all I can think about is this woman, you see. Not a woman I ever knew, mind you, but she tends to find herself the subject of conversation between fellow truckers nationwide. Ayup. At this point, her story's become more of a fairy tale. Who knows how much of it's even true, right? Personally, I believe every single detail. Something about it just feels...*right,* although that's an awful word given the context of the story I'm about to tell you."

"Man." Alonzo buries his face in his palms, beyond exhausted. "We don't care about some fuckin' story, dude. We got our own shit to deal with, okay?"

The humor drains from the truck driver's tone. "I do believe this particular story pertains to the both of you, so why don't you just shut the fuck up and pay attention, how about that?"

Alonzo drops his hands back in his lap and stares at the stranger behind the wheel. "Yeah. Okay."

"Thank you." Vic grunts and cracks his neck. It pops in multiple stages, sounding more like a sputtering engine than bone. "Now, I take it you boys probably aren't too familiar with the name Mary Vincent, are you?"

No one offers an answer, neither positive nor negative, and eventually he nods as if their silence is enough.

"Now, that's all right. Most folks, they're clueless about the makings of the world. They don't understand the true com-*plexities* of darkness. Not like how I do, and *certainly* not like how Mary Vincent does."

"Who's Mary Vincent?" Josh asks, voice like a mouse in the back of the truck.

"Mary Vincent is a woman who reached out and touched the night."

Alonzo sighs again. "And what does that mean?"

"Back in the seventies, the late seventies, Mary Vincent was just a teenager. Older than you boys, I imagine, but not by much. Fifteen, sixteen, ayup, just a little girl. In Las Vegas, she was. She'd run away from home, the story goes, and was living in her car with some boy. They were together until they weren't. The boy, he got arrested or some such thing, ayup, and then it was just Mary Vincent all by her lonesome. I don't know what the situation was with her family. Why she felt the need to live in a car rather than with them. Maybe they were monsters or maybe they were just assholes. Kids got themselves plenty of reasons for leaving home. Some of them are justified and some are just spoiled. It's not the storyteller's business to play judge and jury, is it?"

"I guess not," Josh says, weak and hungry.

"Now that her fella found himself inca-*pacitated*, Mary Vincent decided to leave Las Vegas once and for all, so she began the long, strenuous journey to California. Los Angeles, specifically. If I had to guess, she held aspirations for becoming a famous movie star of some sort, much like every teenage girl in America. Ayup. Everybody wants to live eternally through a camera lens, don't they?"

"I guess," Josh says.

"Anyway. There's a good three hundred miles or so between Vegas and L.A., and Mary Vincent was hitchhiking her way there, an activity that is fortunately falling by the wayside these days."

"Wasn't she living in a car?" Alonzo asks.

"Ayup."

"Then why didn't she just drive that instead?"

The driver pauses, as if he's never contemplated this before. "I don't know the answer to that, I'm afraid." He falls silent again, thinking things over. "Maybe it wasn't operational, or she couldn't afford to refuel. Some kind of barricade was involved that prevented her from using it, I'm sure. It doesn't matter. For whatever reason, the car was no longer an option. So she hitched. And, for the most part, her journey was uneventful. Now I won't pretend to know everything that happened to Mary Vincent during her adventure from Vegas to California. Only Mary Vincent knows that. But for this story, the details don't really pick up steam until she arrives in Berkley early one morning, before the sun's even had a chance to rise, when a man by the name of Lawrence Singleton stops his van and offers her a lift. Says he can take her the rest of the way, that it's no problem at all. Well, eventually Mary Vincent nods off in the passenger's seat, and when she wakes back up she realizes they aren't heading toward Los Angeles like they'd originally agreed upon. The road signs instead indicate a retreat to Nevada. Ayup."

"Man. Why are you telling us this shit?" Alonzo says.

"Because I am your host, and you are my guests, and this is the least I could do." He coughs and cranks the A/C on. Sweat pastes his shaggy hair against the back of his neck. Something inside the truck housing reluctantly rattles to life, then cold air blows through the vents. "So, it's at this point in our story that Mary Vincent begins suspecting this van operator's hiding himself some ne-*farious* intentions. She locates some sort of sharp object in the truck, a knife or stick, I can never remember exactly *what*, and points it at Lawrence Singleton demanding an explanation. He sees this stick, or knife, or what*ever* it is, and he realizes that he screwed up, that he'd been careless. He apologizes to Mary Vincent and somehow convinces our teenaged protagonist that he doesn't mean her any harm—never has, never will."

Alonzo groans. "What a bunch of bullshit."

Vic nods. "Couldn't have said it better myself. Ayup. What a bunch of bullshit, in-*deed*."

"What happened?" Josh asks, leaning forward on the old mattress, hating himself for getting invested in this lunatic's tale.

The truck driver pauses before responding, a seasoned storyteller reeling in his audience. "I'll tell you what happened, ayup. What happened was, shortly after this con-fron-*tation*, Lawrence Singleton all of sudden says he has to excuse himself, that Mother Nature's calling, and pulls his van over on the side of the road. Much like how I picked you two boys up not too long ago, if you really think about it, huh?"

Josh squeezes his thighs, thinking this guy raises a valid point, thinking they have no way of knowing if he's involved with the family or not and even if he isn't with them, that doesn't mean he doesn't belong to some other organization of psycho-killers, of inbred monsters. Fortunately, the truck driver doesn't torture them too long with the silence of their own paranoia.

"While this Lawrence Singleton fellow's outside, doing his business—Mary Vincent, she decides to step out of the van, too, and...well, I'm not sure. Stretch, smoke a cigarette, whatever. Either way, they're both outside at this point, and this is when Lawrence Singleton sneaks up on Mary Vincent and, surprise surprise, begins to punch her repeatedly in the back of the head. After that, well, look. You two boys are young, but judging by the looks of ya, neither one of you's ignorant. You might not understand the true *tur*-pitude of your fellow man—who does, really? Who on this Earth is brazen enough to admit to such for-*bidden* knowledge?—but there's certainly an inkling there, resting, ready to hatch. You already know what happened next without me having to spell it out. Lawrence Singleton was a man and Mary Vincent was a woman, and sometimes, when these two beings collide, bad things happen. Ayup. Very bad things in-*deed*."

"He raped her?" Alonzo asks, a crack in his voice.

Vic nods. "After it was over, after Lawrence Singleton was *sa*-tis-*fied*, he went over to the back of his van, grabbed a hatchet, then proceeded to chop both of Mary Vincent's arms off, right there on the side of the road. Not another car in sight. Nobody to help. Just Lawrence Singleton and Mary Vincent, alone together in the impossible, forever-expanding night."

"What the fuck," Alonzo says.

Josh closes his eyes, terrified vomit will spray from his mouth if he dares open his lips. He doesn't want to hear this doesn't want to hear this doesn't want to hear this—

"Once both arms were severed, Lawrence Singleton then picked up Mary Vincent and tossed her body off a nearby cliff. We're talkin' about a good thirty-, fifty-foot drop here, boys. Not a *straight* drop, of course. A lot of rolling and tumbling was in play, ayup, but still—we're talking major business here. Now remember this is a woman who had just been severely beaten and raped, not to mention losing both of her arms in rapid succession. Can hardly blame Lawrence Singleton for figuring Mary Vincent was as good as dead. He got back in his van and drove away, sure he'd never see her again."

"But he did?" Alonzo says, staring at the truck driver with unblinking eyes.

"Ayup, you betcha. But not for quite some time, of course. Because, let me remind you, she was still at the bottom of a cliff, no arms, naked, bleeding pro-*fusely*. She woke up hours after her fall and instead of just giving up, instead of surrendering to a victim's destiny, Mary Vincent decided to choose a different path. She decided to be a survivor. She climbed herself back up that cliff, right on up to the highway, and she marched herself down the pavement screaming for someone to help her. Blood pouring from both severed arms. Wounded and beaten and nearly dead, she still refused to give up."

"Did someone help her?" Alonzo asks.

The truck driver nods. "Eventually, yes, sir. If memory serves me correctly, I think one car took one look at the state of her and kept on driving, probably figuring they was being set up for some sort of prank or mugging. But the second or third car? Yes. Someone finally had the common *de*-cency to pull over."

"What happened to the guy?"

"Lawrence Singleton? Well, he was arrested. Mary Vincent lived to testify and get him sentenced to prison. Of course, he only served eight years, but that's a story for another day, boys. The point of what I'm saying here is, look at everything that happened to this woman. Look at everything she *went through*. Do you think you could survive that? Do you think you could withstand such ex-*tremities?* I doubt, if you'd asked Mary Vincent prior to her incident, she would have said yes. But put under pressure, there's no telling what a human being's capable of doing to ensure their survival. Now, I don't know what's happened to you boys, but surely something within the realms of ol' Lawrence Singleton and Mary Vincent. I'd bet my entire paycheck on it. Tell me I'm wrong."

Crickets from Josh and Alonzo.

"Ayup. I'm never wrong, not when it comes to things like this. So let me say one more thing: even when you think you've reached your breaking point, there's always more that can break. You boys have been through a lot. I can't even imagine what and I don't want to. The tale of Mary Vincent haunts me enough on these dark highways. But I do know this: if she could survive her horrors, then I know for a fact so can you. All you got to do is decide you want to live. Only you can make that decision, nobody else. But once you give up—well, that's all she wrote."

"That's all *who* wrote?" Alonzo asks, and Josh sighs.

The truck driver wisely ignores Alonzo's question and points ahead. "I take it that's the Percy you boys have been so keen on."

Josh springs from the dirty old mattress and grips the passenger seat's headrest as he peers through the windshield just in time to spot the blue rusted PERCY 1 MILE sign pass them by, followed by an advertisement for their local Flying J truck stop. A cold excitement jolts through him. They're almost there, and then what? How the fuck could him and Alonzo ever be expected to live a normal life after everything they've been through? How did that woman with no arms ever properly function again? Maybe people can survive, yes, but Josh doesn't know if they always *should*.

He wonders what Alonzo would say if he asked the driver to keep on going, to take them wherever he's heading. Start their lives over. Just like how Alonzo wanted him to do, before Father and Uncle forced themselves into their lives. Go to Chicago or wherever and try to make it on their own, forget their pasts, rewrite their histories and redirect their futures.

If they could survive the basement then they could survive anything.

Then Vic the truck driver groans and punches the steering wheel. "Goddammit."

"What?" Alonzo asks.

"Just my luck."

"*What?*"

Josh, still crouched between the two front seats, spots the problem instantly. Red and blue lights dance in Vic's side mirror. The sight's enough to knock him back down on the mattress. "Don't," he tries to say, but the word comes out too weak and soft to be audible.

"What the hell is going on?" Alonzo says, still not understanding, not even as Vic begins to slow his truck and drift into the breakdown lane. "Why are you stopping?"

"I'm being pulled over," the truck driver says.

TWENTY EIGHT

"**N**o," Alonzo says, arms shaking, unable to resist comparing himself to the girl from the driver's story, plagued with the thought of losing both limbs, one minute they're there, then *poof*, the next they're not, abrafuckincadabra, "do not fucking stop, oh my god, *do not stop*."

He reaches for the steering wheel, not sure what the plan is exactly, just knowing that he has to do *something*. The truck driver slaps his hand away, clearly irritated.

"What are you doing? It's fine. I was just driving a little fast, is all. Sometimes it happens."

"No, you don't—"

"Hell, this honestly might not be such a bad thing. We was heading to the police station, anyway, weren't we? I can just save time and unload you boys off right here. Ayup. Won't even have to get off the highway."

Alonzo shakes his head so hard his neck cracks. "No, no, no—"

The mattress spring readjusts behind them as Josh stands back up and rushes toward the front of the truck, breath heavy and frantic as he whispers, "What if Lawrence Singleton was a cop?"

A mixture of emotions wash over the truck driver's face. "Wh-what?"

"The people in the dark...the ones who took us..."

His jaw drops as recognition hits him. "They're the police?"

"You can't let them find us."

A moment of internal debate passes, then Vic nods. "I can't just drive away. I wouldn't get very far. Both of you, hide under the mattress. After they're gone, you boys are gonna answer a couple questions. Deal?"

Josh nods, and leads Alonzo from the passenger seat. Together they squeeze under the mattress. Alonzo grimaces, the smell hitting him for the first time since they entered the semi. He plugs his nose and tries to only breathe out of his mouth. Next to him Josh struggles to fit under the mattress, but manages to work his way inside just as Vic rolls down the driver-side window. With this glass barricade absent, the sound of the engine rises to deafening volumes and Alonzo has to strain his ears to eavesdrop.

"What!" Vic shouts. "Oh! Oh. Yeah, you betcha!"

The truck's engine dies.

"Sorry about that, officer." Vic releases a nervous laugh. "You spend enough time listening to this baby purr, you end up forgetting just how loud she really is."

Outside the truck, someone speaks, but Alonzo can barely hear them. A man, he thinks. A man with a thick voice. A *wet* voice.

Of course he recognizes it.

How couldn't he?

"Step outside?" Vic says. "Did I do something wrong, officer? Not to be a dick or anything, I'm just on a tight deadline here. You understand."

The familiar raspy voice utters something else, and Vic sighs, says, "Well, okay," and opens the door. A second later it slams closed. Alonzo worms his way from out of the mattress, convinced his heart's going to give out, it's beating so goddamn fast, there's no way an organ can withstand this kind of intensity, any moment it's going to finally explode and everything will be done, everything will be over, he'll no longer have to be afraid, he'll no longer have to be *anything*.

Something tugs at his ankle and he nearly screams, then realizes it's Josh trying to pull him back under the mattress.

"*What are you doing?*" Josh says in a half-whisper, half-scream.

Alonzo jerks his head back to the front of the truck. "It's him. *Father.*"

"You don't know that."

"*It's him.*" He kicks Josh's hand away and continues crawling forward. He climbs just high enough to sneak a peek at the driver's side mirror. There, in the cop's headlights. Father standing in the road, lifting Vic up by his face and pressing his body against the side of the truck. Vic's legs kicking out wildly, hands slapping at Father's face without much effect. Father's thumbs digging into Vic's eyeballs, trying to penetrate his skull.

"Fuck," Alonzo says, "oh fuck, oh fuck fuck oh fuck," and grabs the keys previously abandoned on the passenger seat by the truck driver, perhaps conscious of this possible outcome. He's seated behind the wheel and inserting a random key into the ignition before Josh even manages to remove himself from beneath the mattress.

"What's happening?"

"He killed him." Alonzo tries another key, prays to whoever the hell's listening, and twists. The truck's engine roars to mighty life. A lion disturbed from its slumber. In the side mirror, Father drops Vic's body and starts marching back to them. Taking his time, like he knows they're not going anywhere. Like he planned this whole night out years ahead of time.

Myriad profanities swish around Alonzo's mouth like a washing machine running its last rinse cycle. Desperation forces him to grab the gearshift and pull it up. No idea what he's doing but doing it anyway. Foot slamming on what he guesses to be the gas pedal. Assuming correctly. The truck kicks forward, throwing his neck back against the seat headrest. Josh somewhere behind him falling back down, screaming sounds that technically should be words but Alonzo doesn't have time to fully process them.

The truck launches away from the breakdown lane and he straightens out the wheel, sweating and panting and watching the demon cop turn around and calmly return to his vehicle. Something rumbles beneath the semi, bouncing each wheel, and he realizes it's the noise a body makes while being run over, that he's running over the truck driver's corpse, the truck driver who picked them up and offered temporary shelter, the truck driver who gave his own life trying to save theirs. Running him over and obliterating the empty shell that had once made him a human being. Dead and gone and forgotten within seconds. Goodbye, Vic. Goodbye, Lawrence Singleton. Goodbye, Mary Vincent. It was nice knowing you all—well, two of you, at least.

Alonzo scoots forward on the seat, not just pushing on the gas pedal but stomping it, screaming for it to *go go go* and desperately glancing in the side mirrors over and over again. Sure enough, the cop car's already chasing after them, sirens blaring, cutting the night wide open with its red and blue screams.

Josh collapses next to him into the passenger seat, gasping for breath and desperately fumbling for the seatbelt. *What a genius idea,* Alonzo thinks, and risks taking one hand off the steering wheel to do the same. The truck drifts to the right as he attempts to buckle so he lets go of the strap and returns both hands to the wheel. Ain't worth it.

"Where are you going?" Josh says, tears and snot leaking down his face.

Alonzo nods at the windshield. The answer seems clear enough. "Away from the thing chasing us."

"We can't get away." He wraps both arms around his knees and rocks as he talks, less to Alonzo and more to some unknown third passenger only he can see. "Can't get away, can't get away, can't get away..."

Up ahead, the road twists dramatically to the left. Alonzo notices far too late. No time to react, although he tries. He jerks the wheel to the side and kicks the brake pedal like it owes him money. The truck smashes into a guardrail and bursts through a wall of corn. They continue to make a slight turn while progressing deeper and deeper into the field, both of them screaming loud enough to drown out the engine as it strains to make sense of its new surroundings. A mythical creature plucked from familiarity and dropped in this new world of maize and leaves. It was not designed for this kind of land and it will not last long. In fact, the truck only manages to stay on all eighteen tires for another five seconds before the sudden environmental change and Alonzo's ignorant persistence in turning the wheel force it to take a sudden, inevitable tumble onto its side. For just a moment, as the entire left side of the semi's lifted off the ground, the whole world freezes like they're in some movie or cartoon, and Alonzo is gifted with an ocean's worth of time to obsess over every single choice he's made in his life up until this point, leaving him to conclude that maybe he hasn't always made the best decisions, then the freeze frame erupts and slams the right side of the semi truck to the ground with a force strong enough to make him briefly believe in God.

When Alonzo regains consciousness again, it takes him a minute or two to realize he's being dragged. Mounds of soil and rough stalks of corn rub against his bare back and ass like sandpaper. Considering everything he's endured over the last couple nights, the pain registers as the equivalent of a gnat buzzing in his face. He tries to push the nearly shredded garbage bag down his body to prevent further friction between him and the ground but something's wrong, he can't move his arms. Broken? No. The person or thing dragging him, they're pulling him by his wrists. Pulling him deeper into the cornfield. Back to the house.

Back to the basement.

Alonzo thrashes away but it's no use. Every bone in his body aches and begs for rest. *"Let me go, you bastard!"* he tries to scream, but the words come out like a drunken slur. *"Let me gooooo."*

"Zoey, knock it off, I'm trying to help you."

Josh's voice. Above.

Alonzo concentrates. His friend's face manifests between him and the cancer that is the sky. *"What's going on?"*

"Can you walk?" Josh releases his grip on Alonzo's wrists. His arms drop like they're made of concrete.

"What…what happened?"

"You wrecked. Can you get up or not? He's out here somewhere. Searching."

"Who?"

Josh groans softly. "You know who."

"This is never going to end, is it?"

"Can you walk? Yes or no."

"I don't know."

"You have to try. We aren't going to get much farther with me having to drag you."

"Let's be grateful it wasn't the other way around."

"I should have just left you in that truck."

"I mean, yeah, probably."

Alonzo tries to sit up but an invisible weight pushes against his chest, keeping him pinned to the ground. Crushed. He rolls over on his stomach and digs his fingernails in the dirt. Slowly he rises to his knees, then his feet, Josh hooking a forearm under his armpit and providing an extra boost. Behind them, a light penetrates the field. Headlights from the tipped-over semi. Holy shit, how are they even still alive at this point?

"Come on," Josh whispers, pulling him away from the light. "*We gotta go.*"

Limping, Alonzo follows Josh through the cornfield, brushing past stalks that are green and stable, unlike the yellow and withered agricultural found on the family's property. He hates that he thinks of them as *the family*. The word "family" implies something more homey. Something *welcoming*. There's nothing welcoming about those fuckers' house. If they are a family then they are a family of monsters. They are a family of evil.

And none of this is going to be over until Alonzo and Josh have killed every last one of them.

Or until the family's killed *them*.

Somewhere back by the truck, a creature breathes in loud, obnoxious rasps. Father on the prowl.

TWENTY NINE

Most criminals will agree that fleeing to the one location you discussed with a police station shortly after holding them all hostage is probably not the best of ideas. Ottessa knows this, and she's only *barely* a criminal. Judging by the way Mary keeps saying, "This is a bad idea," she too shares this opinion. But that doesn't stop them from doing exactly that. At this point, what other choice do they possibly have? After everything they went through today, the only solid clue they've managed to scavenge is the Flying J. The number one hotspot for abductions, the secretary told them. A haven for crime. Going any other place would be a mistake, a waste of time. Time they don't got. Time their boys don't got. It doesn't matter that the cops will almost definitely be keeping an eye out for them there. It's a necessary risk. Either they take the gamble or they what? They go back home, they turn themselves in, they drive around this goddamn town the rest of the night, circling the same streets they done already circled a thousand times before.

Zoey and Josh ain't gonna just pop up in the middle of the street. Someone has them somewhere, hopefully still in Percy, otherwise Ottessa has no idea what they're gonna do. The odds of finding their boys while they're still local sounds a lot more promising than the alternative. How the hell are they gonna manage to track them down if they've crossed the state lines? Shit, they could be out of the country by now. Indiana to Mexico isn't a short drive by any stretch, but surely manageable with the time that's passed since Friday night. If they're in Mexico, then this whole thing was over before it even began. But something tells Ottessa this isn't the case. Zoey and Josh are still in Percy, and goddammit, she's going to find them. She's going to find them and she's going to make whoever's responsible scream until their lungs stop working.

But with that said, Ottessa isn't a fool. Obviously they can't just stroll into the Flying J and assume a gaggle of cops won't immediately tackle them to the floor—or, more realistically, shoot them in the back. There's a McDonald's located on the other side of the highway. A perfect vantage point for someone with aspirations of spying on truckers and lot lizards. Ottessa parks Lois's minivan behind the restaurant, paranoid the vehicle's owner will somehow get loose of her restraints and rat them out. As they exit the van and move cautiously across the parking lot to the back entrance, Ottessa wonders who will have to return to the house and untie her once this is all over. What will that conversation be like? Fucking *cringe*. Mary can handle that. She's *her* friend, after all. Ottessa barely even knows the bitch. Assuming they get out of this alive. Otherwise Lois better get herself real comfortable. Her and that ugly rat she tried to pass off as a dog.

Everybody in Percy made such a big deal when they built this McDonald's. Two whole stories. In a *McDonald's*. Nobody had ever heard of such a thing. Of course, people eventually realized they aren't *that* rare, but still, they aren't exactly common either. But for one to be built in Percy of all places? It's bizarre. Nothing special ever happens in Percy. The buildings are standard, nondescript. Some of their windows are boarded up, out of business. Here and there graffiti comes into play, but graffiti's everywhere these days. Inescapable. Percy is perfectly average, except for its two-story McDonald's. People sometimes travel from neighboring towns to visit the restaurant, like it's a goddamn tourist attraction or something.

At this time of night, it's not too busy, but it also isn't entirely vacant, either. Drunks booted from bars with nowhere else to go. Stoned teenagers craving cheeseburgers and milkshakes. Night owls succumbing to the only food place still open besides Denny's. Ottessa's stumbled in here before at later hours, too wasted to go home, not wanting to risk Zoey still being awake and having to listen to his shit about what a terrible mom she is.

Of course, right now she'd do anything to hear his voice, no matter what he has to say. Just as long as he's talking. As long as he's *alive.*

A red-eyed, sleep-deprived kid meets them at the register. He's wearing a uniform one or two sizes too small, the buttons threatening to shoot off his stomach at the first sign of trouble. A name tag with the word "GARRETT" printed on it hangs upside down from his clearly erect nipple. When he speaks, there is zero enthusiasm in his tone. Out of everybody in this building, he wants to be here the least.

"Welcome to McDonald's. What do you want."

Just the thought of eating something makes her stomach turn acidic. But there's no way they'll last more than ten minutes here unless they place an order. McDonald's is a corporation, after all, and if corporations hate one thing above all else, it's freeloaders. Hidden in the basement of every rich white man's house are the corpses of a thousand homeless black folks.

So they both order some food. It doesn't matter what. Balls of greasy meat guaranteed to make her stomach feel worse than it already does. Less substance and more of a distraction than anything. They find a booth on the second floor against a window overlooking Interstate 94. If she presses her face against the glass and shapes her hand into binoculars to shield her vision from the restaurant's fluorescent light reflection, she can manage a decent view of the Flying J. And what she sees ain't much. Semis take up most of her perception. A few regular cars are idling at gas pumps or parked in front of the diner connected to the truck stop. Nothing in the slightest resembles a cop car, especially the type of model they're after. Ottessa sighs and sinks back in her seat.

"You think we're wasting our time here?" she asks Mary, who's nibbling the edge of her cheeseburger.

Mary takes her time answering, thoughtfully considering the question as she chews and swallows, then says, "I don't know."

Ottessa shrugs, not sure what kind of answer she was expecting. "Fuck it. Better than nothing."

"You think we're going to prison?"

"Yeah. Without a doubt."

"Who do you think will end up looking after Alonzo?"

"You trying to make me feel guilty or some shit?"

Mary shakes her head, alarmed. "No, no. I just keep thinking about Jasper taking care of Josh, and…it's a difficult thing to imagine. Then I think about you, and Alonzo's dad isn't in the picture. At least, not that I know of. Josh has never told me much about him."

"That's because there ain't much to tell, except that yes, he *is* out of the picture, and there is presently zero chance of him stepping *back* into the picture."

Mary hesitates, like she's trying not to appear eager for gossip and failing hilariously, and leans forward. In a whisper: "Is he dead?"

"I sure fuckin' hope so." Ottessa swigs from her pop. It's flat and watered down. She drinks some more.

"You don't know where he is?"

"Let's just say even speaking of him now is a waste of both our breaths, and leave it at that."

They pick at the food neither of them really wanted and stare at the truck stop across the highway. The same old same old. A cop car here and there, but all newer models, clearly following a routine patrol, nothing worth investigating further. She wishes they had binoculars. Something to enhance their vision. Right now they're both relying on dry, tired eyes. Plus, the light from inside the restaurant is doing them no favors. The reflection against the glass proves to be a greater pain in the ass than anticipated and Ottessa wonders if they'd just be better off moving their stakeout to the Flying J parking lot. And if anyone notices their presence, well, they *do* still have a gun. Not that she has to *use* it, but just bringing it out and waving it around like a lunatic seems like it'd do the trick. It worked last time, at least.

The second story of the McDonald's is mostly deserted compared to the bottom floor. Too many drunks below wisely skeptical of their ability to handle steps in their current states. Upstairs, besides Ottessa and Mary, a white man and woman dine with their child, no older than four or five. Travelers stopping for a late-night dinner. All of their clothing heavily advertises the

Disney brand. The child has a Mickey Mouse hat clasped tightly to her skull, curly locks of blonde hair poking out from the rim. Returning from Florida, no doubt. Not a trouble in the world. Laughing together and experiencing *joy*. No issues with the police, that's for goddamn certain. Ottessa wonders what they would do if someone were to come along and snatch their precious princess out from under their grasp. Take her far away, where they'd never see her again. But of course, if Ottessa and them switched positions, things would be a whole lot different. Someone reports a little white girl missing, and the whole world loses their minds. John Walsh from *America's Most Wanted* personally flies to your house and jerks you off in your bathroom. The same thing happens to two black boys, and you can't even fucking convince people they were abducted.

Several booths behind the Disney family, a black man in a dirty trench coat snores loudly. Cheek flat against the table's formica, arms sprawled out around his head. An empty fountain drink cup rests on its side at the edge of the table, one light breeze away from tumbling to the floor. Even from across the room, Ottessa can smell the booze off of him and she's envious. Enough with this pop bullshit. There's no way she's going to make it through the night without hard liquor. She briefly considers sneaking over there and going through the man's pockets, but figures Mary might have something to say about that. And, while she doesn't give a shit what this woman thinks, they're still stuck together for the time being, and she'd prefer to avoid getting bitched at. Or who knows? Mary isn't the same woman Ottessa knew a few days ago. Things have changed. They've done things they can't reverse. At this point, Mary's just as liable to steal booze from an unconscious drunk as Ottessa.

"Josh used to love playing here when he was younger," Mary says, apparently oblivious of Ottessa's current state of mind. Her attention's focused entirely on the jungle gym display set up in the center of the second floor. The Mickey Mouse kid has abandoned her parents to attempt climbing up the tunnel slide. She manages a couple feet of progress before slipping and rolling back down, cackling with laughter. The mother snaps a photo with her digital camera while the father eggs her on to try again, both of them still on duty as tourists.

Ottessa wants to tell her no shit, there ain't a child in this town who hasn't at one point enjoyed playing here. What else is there even to do in this town? You want to show your kid a good time, you bring him here, buy him a happy meal, then set him loose with the rest of the rugrats thrashing wildly in the ball pit. Percy has never been a town flooded with fun attractions. Yeah, there's a Chuck E. Cheese, but only rich white families can afford the luxury of eating cardboard pizza more than once a year. Those game tokens can drive most single moms into bankruptcy if they aren't too careful.

Mary's saying other things, but Ottessa is only half-listening. Exhaustion has snuck up on her and suddenly she can barely keep her eyes open. She raises her hand and cuts Mary off mid-sentence. "Tell you what."

Mary gives her a look that says *bitch did you really just interrupt me?* but of course she's far too polite to actually say it. "Huh?"

"Neither one of us is going to make it much longer without some rest. I'm thinking we should take turns keeping watch while the other one naps. An hour on, an hour off. How does that sound?"

"Uh. Okay. Yeah. That makes sense. Do you want to sleep first?"

Ottessa nods. "I'll go down in the van, otherwise one of these assholes might try kicking us out. If anyone starts looking at you funny, get a drink refill or something. You'll have to come wake me up when it's my turn. Obviously get me sooner if you see a car that might be the one we're after."

She starts getting up and Mary reaches out, stops her. "What…what are we going to do, if the car *does* show up?"

"Follow him. Then kill him."

THIRTY

Eventually they reach the end of the field, bursting through the corn with a mixture of surprise and paranoia. Past experience has taught them to suspect a trap when something's too good to be true. The last field they tried escaping took an entire day to locate its exit. This time barely thirty minutes passed, if not less, but Josh can't be sure, can't begin to guess the time or even the *day*, for that matter. Maybe they've been in this field for a fucking year. He's no expert. All he can do is move his legs forward until something happens, and now something has happened.

They both freeze at the sight of the farmhouse up ahead, terrified it's the house that will haunt their days and nights for the rest of their lives—however long that may be—but upon further study determine the house is nothing like the other one. Someone else's house. Someone who might be willing to help them. To *save* them.

"What do we do?" Josh asks, already knowing the answer.

Alonzo limps past him. "Come on."

Darkness covers the farmhouse. Not a single light forgotten. If anybody's home, they're not going to enjoy being woken up. But then again, it's not like Josh fucking asked for any of this, either. Sometimes shit just happens, then you either deal with it or lie down like a dog.

And Josh ain't no dog.

Together they approach the farmhouse, tall and looming like a great shadow. Josh goes over possible dialogue in his head as they near the structure. *Uh, sorry for waking y'all up, but there's a demonic cop trying to kill us. Can we use your phone?* Maybe leave out the "demonic" and "cop" part. Just tell them it's a crazy guy. Change the "police car" to a "featureless white van". When it comes to creeps abducting children, featureless white vans are always the way to go. Leave the real details for later, once they're somewhere safe, wherever *safe* is. It doesn't seem possible such a place could ever exist, not while Father continues to chase them. Wherever they hide, he will find them. Josh understands this fact more than anything else. They will never be safe. There is nowhere far enough they could ever hide. Father will find them. Father will kill them. *Father Father Father…*

The porch explodes with light and Josh shields his face, blinded by the obtrusion. Next to him Alonzo gasps. Josh scans the porch quickly, tightening his fists, fully prepared to spot Father standing there, waiting for them all this time, yet another trap, another dead end. But the porch is empty. A couple of rocking chairs on one side and a long swing on the other, all of them motionless and absent of hosts.

"It's a motion sensor," Alonzo says. "One of those security lights rich people have."

They barely make it to the top of the porch before the front door swings open and an old white guy comes bursting outside aiming a shotgun at them. Josh backpedals, forgetting they're on stairs, and falls on his ass at the bottom. Alonzo remains standing, both hands in the air, telling the guy not to shoot, telling him it's not what he thinks.

"On your knees, thug!" he screams.

Alonzo drops to his knees.

Now he points the shotgun down at Josh. "Both of you!"

Josh obeys. Pain instantly skyrockets at his kneecaps. He ignores the discomfort and folds his fingers around the back of his head.

"What are you doing on my property? Just what do you think you're *doing?*"

Josh tries to talk and he just ends up crying. Jesus Christ. What an embarrassment. What a waste of human life. His dad (*father*) was right. What a fucking crybaby.

Thankfully, Alonzo takes over. "We need help. Please."

The guy grimaces, tightening his grip on the shotgun. "You need *help?*"

"Something bad happened to us and we need to call…we need to call…"

He trails off, and Josh understands why. Who exactly are they supposed to call? The cops? How can they be sure Father and the rest of his devil family aren't really connected with the police? Who's to say every cop in Percy ain't one of them? So who, then? Their moms? No use in getting them involved, although they must be worried sick at this point. They're just their *moms.* There's nothing neither one of them will be able to do. If anything, Josh would just be putting their lives in danger. Best to just leave them alone, until…until when? Until this is all over. Until something *changes.* So who, then?

"We need to call the FBI," Alonzo says.

The farmer's eyebrows nearly touch his hairline. "The *FBI?*"

He nods. "We can't trust the cops. We gotta go higher up. We gotta call the FBI. Please."

The farmer lowers his shotgun. "But why…?"

"Man, ain't you listening? Some *major fuckin' shit* has gone down. Shit you ain't ever gonna believe so there's no point getting into it all. The last person we told about it ended up dead. You wanna end up dead? No. So just let us use your phone. And also your *Yellow Pages.* Or your computer, if you have one. I don't know the FBI's phone number. Unless you do?"

Josh realized halfway through Alonzo's speech that the old man wasn't listening. He'd made up his mind the moment he grabbed his shotgun.

"You must think I'm just some dumb hick, huh?" He shakes his head and steadies the aim of his weapon, the barrel inches from Alonzo's skull. "You think you can sneak up on my property, break in, have yourselves a little fun, right? Figured, if I got the upper hand, you'd just make up some ridiculous story about needing to call the FBI, because us hillbillies, we'll believe any little old thing, is that it?"

"No, man, that's not—"

"Shut up!" The man raises the shotgun like he's going to smash the stock against Alonzo's face, then thinks better of it and aims the barrel back at him instead. "Do you two even realize I'm completely within my rights to shoot the both of you? You're on *my* property. You are *intruding*. I could blow both of your heads off and get awarded a medal. So tell me the truth. What was the plan? Were you just going to rob us or go a little further?" He leans close to Alonzo, lips quivering with rage. "Be honest with me now. You came here for a lot more than our money, didn't you?"

"No, we—"

"You thought you could have yourselves a taste of my wife, isn't that right? You wanted to try out a white woman for a change. Thought you'd come right in and take her while she was in bed. But what about me, huh? What were you going to do, slit my throat while I slept next to her? You tell me the truth and maybe I'll take it easy on you. Maybe I'll only rough you up a little bit before calling the cops. But only if you're honest."

"Holy shit," Alonzo says, "why can't we catch one motherfucking break."

Then the old man swings the shotgun against his skull and he rolls down the stairs, knocking Josh over like a solitary bowling pin. Before Josh can recover, the old man's already standing over him, screaming something about raping his wife. He can barely understand the lunatic. Slobber drips from his mouth and splatters against his face. Reminds Josh of a rabid dog. Some humanoid Cujo. Is this guy demonic or just racist? The look in his eyes promises something more diseased than your average Klan member. There's no use trying to talk him out of this. He's crazy. A fucking maniac.

He makes Josh stand then pushes him up the porch and into the house. A weary Alonzo follows. The man points the shotgun at a couch and orders them to sit, so they sit. He pulls the chain on a lamp and light blesses the living room. Josh steals a glance at Alonzo's head and nearly screams. Both of them are already pretty messed up at this point, considering everything they've gone through, but the fresh gash split along the right side of Alonzo's skull is certainly nothing to ignore. Blood oozes out of his head in thick waves. His eye has already swollen so severely Josh wonders if his friend can even see out of it. How much pain can two twelve-year-old boys withstand before surrendering, before withering like the decomposing cornstalks outside the family's farm? He thinks about

Mary Vincent and all the shit she went through and realizes with a spooky certainty that neither one of them could ever be so strong. It's a miracle they've lasted this long.

The farmer paces back and forth in the living room, shotgun never straying too far from its intended targets. "Just a couple of *thugs,* that's what you are. A couple of thugs looking for trouble. Well, I'll tell you what. You went and *found* it."

He raises the shotgun, this time preparing to bring it down upon Josh's head, then stops at the sound of footsteps on the floor above them.

"Gary?" a woman says, the word coming out like a croak. "Gary, what's going on down there?"

The farmer goes bug-eyed as a nearby staircase creaks. Someone—the farmer's wife, presumably—heading down to investigate the ruckus. His voice drops to a whisper, glaring at Josh and Alonzo on the couch:

"If any of you even *move* funny, I'll do it. Go ahead and test me. I hope like god you do."

A woman around the same age as the farmer enters the living room, wearing an ash-colored housedress that extends to her ankles. She gasps at the scene laid out before her, taking a step back and holding an open palm to her mouth. Almost like she rehearsed the act before coming downstairs.

"G-G-Gary, wh-what—what is this?"

"Now, Marge, calm down, it's okay." The farmer, Gary, lowers the shotgun and joins his wife at the doorway. "I caught these two boys trying to break in. And you thought I was a fool for spending money on those security lights. *Now* who's the fool?"

The woman, Marge, still hasn't closed her mouth since entering the living room. A drawn-out *what* stretches from her throat like an ancient attic door slowly opening. Gary ignores the weird noise emitting from his wife and continues.

"I was just about to call the authorities. Get these two hoodlums straightened out. There's really no reason to be down here, honey. Everything's okay now. I have it all under control."

The woman steps around her husband, pointing one long crooked finger at Josh and Alonzo. "You broke into our home? You're…you're *children*."

"They're not children, Marge. They're *thugs*."

Josh tries to answer, tries to set her straight, but the threat of her husband's shotgun is too great and silences him before anything manages to come out. Alonzo, on the other hand, doesn't seem to have any trouble doing what he does best.

"Ma'am, that ain't even true at all. We just want to use the phone. Something happened to—"

The farmer stomps his bare foot against the living room's hard wood. He refocuses the shotgun at the couch. "Shut up! You shut up! Didn't I tell you what I would do? Didn't I tell you?"

"Gary, they look like they're in trouble…"

He stomps his foot again, this time making his wife wince. "What would you have preferred, Marge? That I let them come in and violate you in bed? You getting sick of me, honey? You want some of that nigger dick now?"

The woman's face ages decades within seconds. "Gary, what…what on Earth has come over you?"

Josh and Alonzo exchange glances. Alonzo redirects his gaze at the still-open front door. Asking him, *Should we make a break for it?* Josh shakes his head. *No way. We wouldn't make it five feet.*

Although a part of him wonders what would happen if they leapt at the old man. Surprise him while he's arguing with his wife and take him down. Get that shotgun out of his hands before he goes and does something stupid. There's no way he's fast enough to get both of them. Maybe one. But, then again, maybe none.

"I'm going to call the cops," the woman says, and storms off to the kitchen.

"Isn't that what I've been telling you to do this whole time?" the farmer shouts after her, then spins around, aiming the shotgun back at the couch and looking disappointed when he doesn't catch either of the boys attempting to escape. Josh doesn't understand what's stopping the man from shooting them if he wants to so badly, but he isn't about to raise the question. "Just wait.

Just you two wait. The law will be here soon enough, and there will be hell to pay. You ever spend the night behind bars? Of course you have. Just *look* at you. That's probably where you came from, isn't it? Get out of jail and immediately search for some hard-workin' American to steal from. Well maybe that's how things have worked for you in the past, but *not tonight*. Tonight the *white man* won for a change. Mark it up in the history books, folks. Ring *Guinness* because we got ourselves here a new world record! Dubya himself will praise my achievements. I'll be the talk of the goddamn country, I tell you what!"

Marge's voice drifts from the kitchen as she recites her address. Obviously talking to the cops. Telling them about the fictional home invasion. Whatever. At this point Josh would be grateful to actually get arrested. There's something wrong with the farmer, something that's evolved past everyday bigotry. The image of a parasite drilling into the farmer's brain won't leave his thoughts and he doesn't know why but of course he knows why. Maybe the farmer isn't technically a member of the family—his physical attributes appear far too normal to share blood with one of those deformed freaks—but somehow, somewhere, they've still managed to sink their teeth into him. *Possessed* is another word he can't stop thinking about. Whatever disease has found itself inside of him, it hasn't been there long judging by his wife's confusion. Something tells Josh she's just as scared of him as they are right now. This isn't how he normally acts. Something's *off*. Something's scrambled his mind and mutated his behavior. Blended his soul into some kind of abhorrent milkshake for the damned.

Marge returns to the living room wiping away fresh tears with trembling hands.

When she doesn't say anything, the farmer sighs and lowers the shotgun to his feet. "*Well?*"

"Someone's on the way. They said not to do anything and just wait for them to get here."

Gary cocks his head, eyebrow raised. "What do you mean, *not to do anything?*"

"Wh-what?"

"Why would they think I was going to *do something*?" He steps closer to his wife. "What did you *tell them*, Marge? What do they think I'm going to *do*?"

"N-no-nothing. All I said was we had them trapped. That's it."

The farmer pauses, letting her words digest, then shakes his head. "You told them I was acting nuts. I can smell the betrayal from your *cunt.*"

She gasps. "Gary! That is enough! I don't know what has gotten into you but I do not—"

Sparks explode from the end of the shotgun. A patch of blood generates along the front of Marge's housedress. Her feet leave the floor as she flies across the living room and smacks her back against the wall and slides down, leaving a trail of her innards in the paint, ass slamming on the hard wood and head slumping to the side. A river of red spills from her gut. Her left leg kicks out with a rogue tremor then goes still. The farmer remains planted, shotgun aimed at the spot his wife had been standing mere seconds ago. Josh doesn't hesitate. He springs off the couch and slams his shoulder into the farmer's back, knocking him to the floor with one clean strike. The shotgun slides across the room and Josh doesn't realize he should have picked it up until he's halfway down the front porch and by then it's far too late to turn around. The only reason he looks back over his shoulder is to make sure Alonzo isn't still on the couch, frozen in fear.

But no, his friend is right behind him, limping as fast as he can.

Together they flee down the driveway. The gravel stabs into their bare feet but the pain is hardly noticeable. It's not like they have much of a choice, anyway. There's no goddamn way Josh is stepping foot in another cornfield, tonight or ever again, and he has a feeling Alonzo's opinion about the matter is mutual.

Up ahead, lights flash from a lone police car.

THIRTY ONE

Mary has to pee almost as soon as Ottessa leaves.

She considers leaning over the staircase and shouting for her to wait a minute, but decides that would only draw more unwanted attention in their direction. Best to play it cool and just leave their booth unattended for a couple minutes. Nothing's happened in the last hour and she's starting to seriously doubt anything's going to happen at all tonight. Surely these abductors don't stalk victims every single night at the Flying J. The government would have shut the place down years ago if that were the case. The odds of her randomly catching these mysterious cops in the act are not great. In fact, when she really breaks down the numbers, they're near nonexistent.

So, yeah. One pee break isn't going to make much of a difference.

The only public bathroom in this restaurant is located downstairs, which means not only abandoning her post but leaving the second floor altogether. Somehow she doubts every booth facing the Flying J will be occupied by the time she returns. For a brief, idiotic moment she considers leaving her purse on the seat to save her place, then laughs the way a skeleton might laugh as the final stages of decomposition take effect, and heads down the steps.

She has not entered many public bathrooms between the hours of midnight and five A.M., but on those few occasions she's been left without a choice, her experience has always been somewhere south of pleasant. Tonight marks no exception. The odor emphasizes its presence the moment she pushes open the heavy wooden door. Whether or not something's died in here finds itself becoming less of an exaggeration and more of a real concern. She debates turning around and squatting somewhere outside, then holds her breath and pushes forward.

Flies orbit her head, excited for their new visitor. She picks the only stall with a door still attached to its hinges. An unidentifiable liquid puddles around the toilet. It's been on this linoleum so long, strange fungi has sprouted in it and claimed squatters' rights. She wipes the same substance off the seat cover with a triple-layered strip of toilet paper.

Graffiti covers the interior of the stall door. Random phone numbers promising a good time. Cartoonish genitalia. Swastikas. Enclosed-As. Every profanity in the book.

FUCK DA POLICE

KILL ALL JEWS!!!

BURGER KING IS SUPREME

So on and so on.

Then, toward the bottom of the door, in what looks like fresh ink: YOU WILL NEVER FIND HIM.

She stares at the sentence far too long, then finishes up and washes her hands with scalding hot water. Out in the lobby, she approaches the front counter and orders a coffee from a young girl more sleep-deprived than the last kid who took their order. The plastic cup burns her palm as she carries it back upstairs. It's a sensation she welcomes. Anything to distract her mind from returning to the same depressing downslope.

As it turns out, someone *has* taken her booth in her absence. The overweight cashier from when they first arrived. *Garrett*, his upside-down name tag announced. He's slumped over in the seat Ottessa had previously sat in. Face buried in his palms. McDonald's ball cap flipped over on the Formica, the bottom of the bill tainted with old sweat stains.

He is sobbing.

An aroma similar to the downstairs bathroom attaches itself to his aura and she stands above him, wondering if she should interrupt or leave him alone. To hell with it. What else does she have to do? She sits across from him, setting the coffee down and wrapping both hands around the plastic, its heat absorbing into her fingers. She takes a sip and winces. Waits awhile, watches his whole body convulse, then glances to the side, pressing her face against the glass. The Flying J appears exactly the same as before she left. This is a terrible idea. Even if something happens over there, they probably aren't going to notice it from across the highway. They'll be sitting here all night, wasting their time while whoever does whatever to Josh and Alonzo.

She turns away from the window and the cashier has stopped crying. He's staring right at her, eyes red and swollen, face drenched in tears and snot.

"Are you okay?" she asks after a while, when it becomes clear he isn't going to be the one to initiate conversation.

When he speaks, his voice is cracked. Exercised raw from excessive crying. "You ever get so tired, you start wishing you weren't alive?"

"Wh-what?"

"Too tired to exist." The kid smirks. His lips are filthy with snot and burger grease. Pimples surround his mouth like an approaching plague. "Every night of my life is spent in this place. It will never end. I am going to be here forever and there is nothing I can do about it, there is nothing anybody can do about it."

Mary's suddenly regretting sitting back down. "Uh. Can't you quit?"

This inspires a full laugh from the kid. A gust of sewer breath sprays from his tongue and slaps her in the face. "Quit? You should know better than anyone that I can't just *quit*. Quit and rot on the streets, maybe. Quit and feed myself to the strays that roam Percy when all the lights go off. Is that what you're suggesting?"

"You're...you're young. I don't—"

The cashier, Garrett, leans forward. Drool drips down his chin. "Are you going to quit?"

"What?"

"If it's so easy to quit, then why don't you do it?"

"Quit what?" Asking a question she already knows the answer to.

The kid settles back against the seat and cracks his neck. His gaze wavers out the window, toward the Flying J. His expression displays zero emotion. "Every night I look out these windows and I pray for the sky to fall and it never happens and I'm beginning to think it never will."

"Oh," Mary says, because what the hell else *can* she say?

"There is something wrong with this town." He turns back to Mary. "There's something living here that isn't right. Something...contagious. I can feel it. It's getting stronger and stronger and soon something's going to happen and I don't know what it is. I don't know what it is but I know it's here. It's everywhere. It's all around us and soon wherever it's hiding won't be able to contain it anymore and then what? Then what happens?"

"I...I don't know."

The cashier's gotten so worked up his whole body is shaking with anger. He clenches the end of the table with both hands and grits his teeth. "It used to be, when I slept I would dream of violence, I would dream of death, I would dream of blood and blood and blood. But now things are starting to change. Now I don't need to sleep to dream. Now all I need to do is blink. Soon I won't even need to do that. What do you dream about? Do you dream about your son? Do you dream about how he's going to die?"

"*What?*"

Now the kid is grinning, wide and unafraid, revealing teeth coated with braces. "Everything is eventual, ma'am. There is no preventing what has already happened and what will happen again and again. It is done."

"What...what are you talking about?" Mary scans the restaurant for Ottessa but of course she's still outside, napping in the van. The Disney family and sleeping drunk have also vanished. It is just her and the McDonald's cashier. She doesn't even have Jasper's gun.

The kid leans closer with his red, lunatic eyes. Tears begin pouring down his cheeks yet he still does not blink. "*He will die and so will you and so will I he will die and so will you and so will I he will die and so will you and so will I he will—*"

"*STOP IT!*"

Mary flings her cup of coffee forward.

The liquid splashes against his face and he stops talking. Doesn't scream or jerk away, doesn't even acknowledge the burning sensation. He just sits across from her, still refusing to blink, lips twitching, while the flesh masking his skull slowly starts bubbling and blistering and oozing blood and pus. He maintains eye contact, as if he hasn't realized she already discontinued his deranged rambling. Slowly she rises from the booth and backs away from the scene. The cashier's pupils follow her movement but otherwise he remains immobile. She's almost afraid to look away. Like a monster in a nightmare that only attacks when left unsupervised. Halfway across the room she sucks in a breath and sprints down the stairs. She doesn't glance back over her shoulder, not once.

Outside in the parking lot she frantically bangs her fists against the minivan until Ottessa opens the door.

"Goddamn, bitch," Ottessa says, squinting in the darkness, "I haven't even had a chance to sleep yet. Are you serious right now?"

"We gotta go." Mary pushes her aside and climbs into the van.

Ottessa's tone changes. "Wait. Did you see something? What happened?"

"No. I didn't—something happened inside. We can't stay here. Where are the keys?"

Ottessa pulls the key ring out of her pocket and Mary snags them without another word, then climbs behind the steering wheel and starts the engine. Ottessa remains in the back seat, demanding an explanation. Mary ignores her. No way is she prepared to try explaining just what the hell happened inside the McDonald's. Instead she reverses the minivan from their spot next to the dumpster and drives around to the front of the parking lot, toward the exit leading onto the access road.

And slams on the brakes upon discovering the path blocked off by a shiny white car flashing its red and blues.

Before Mary can even think about putting the minivan back into reverse, Lindenmuth's sprinting out of his own vehicle, both arms raised over his head, fingers spread, no weapons in sight.

"Wait!" he screams. "Don't go! It's only me. I just want to talk."

"This motherfucker," Ottessa says, and the interior light pops on as she slides the minivan's back door open and hops out onto the pavement, waving Jasper's handgun around in the cop's general direction. Lindenmuth emphasizes that he's unarmed and Ottessa emphasizes that she doesn't give a shit. "What did you think would happen, you try to stop us? What did we already done tell you peckerwoods? We got motherfuckin' *business* to attend to, and right now you're conflicting with that."

"I'm not trying to stop you! I want to help!"

"Shut the fuck up and get back in your car and forget you ever saw us. How about that?"

Now it's Mary turn to get out of the minivan. "Wait. Why don't we hear what he has to say?"

Ottessa gives Mary an *are you fucking serious right now?* look and says, "Are you fucking serious right now?"

Mary nods. "What else do we have to go on?"

"I don't know, Mary, why don't you tell me about what just happened inside the McDonald's?"

She hesitates. "Not right now."

"Uh huh." Ottessa directs her attention back to Lindenmuth, who hasn't dared move during their conversation. "Sounds like you just want to distract us long enough for backup to arrive. Why the hell would you possibly want to help us?"

"I—I believe you. Kind of. Something's...wrong. I know that. Something weird's been going on for a while now. This town, these people, you feel it, right? I don't know if the sheriff is responsible but I also don't know if he *isn't*, and that there is plenty enough to make me question what's going on here."

"Our children were taken," Mary says, voice weak.

"I want to help you find them."

THEY END UP RETURNING TO the back of the McDonald's, out of sight from traffic passing through Interstate 94. Lindenmuth admits to not knowing who else might be patrolling the area, or who they can even trust at this point. Maybe the entire station's somehow involved, and they've all been keeping secrets from him. It wouldn't surprise him, he says. As far as the Percy Police Department goes, Lindenmuth's never exactly fit in with everybody else. Most of his fellow officers tend to view him as somewhat of an outcast. They consider his college degree a joke, something to ridicule rather than congratulate. When Lindenmuth enters a room, conversation suddenly quiets down or changes topic. Nobody at the station thinks of him as an equal. He's more of a rodent, a pest they haven't figured out how to exterminate yet. Lindenmuth's fully aware of the way things are, but there's not much he can do about it besides resign or request a transfer. And transferring would require either a lengthy commute or moving to wherever they stick him, meaning he'd have less time to visit his mother who has recently been diagnosed with dementia. His mother, who has nobody else in her life but him. His dad passed years ago, also a cop, heart attack at the age of sixty-five, just a few years after retirement. Barely even got to enjoy his new free time. No way is that an option. So either he quits or...or what? Just sticks it out, hopes something eventually changes? Fat chance. Cops like the ones found in Percy, they were born ignorant and they will die ignorant.

But that doesn't mean he has to be just like them. That doesn't mean he can't try to make *some kind* of a difference.

"How'd you know we were here, anyway?" Ottessa has since returned Jasper's gun to her purse, but she looks like she's one nervous twitch away from whipping it back out. They're all standing around the cop car, now wisely snuffed of its siren. Mary keeps glancing back at the restaurant, expecting any second now for the injured cashier to come stumbling through the door, flesh melting from his face.

"We received a call from this woman."

"Do women usually not call you?" Ottessa asks. Trying for a joke, but not quite succeeding.

Lindenmuth smirks. "She's claiming you two tied her up, locked her in a closet, then stole her vehicle." He nods at the minivan behind them. "*That* vehicle."

Ottessa sighs, but remains quiet.

"She, uh, she also said you tied up her dog." He clears his throat and shuffles his position. Behind them, various voices recite codes and locations in his car radio. The volume's low, but still present, like a mosquito gambling in someone's ear. "Anyway, my best word of advice? Don't discuss plans in front of hostages. They love to snitch. Uh. Unless you kill them, I guess. But I would also advise not to kill hostages. Heck, I'd advise not to take any hostages in the first place. All it ends up doing is making you look bad."

"We'll take that into consideration, thanks." Ottessa kicks a pile of gravel and exhales.

Mary hugs her arms close to her chest, shivering, wondering why nobody else seems to be reacting to the weather. The wind hasn't let up for a second since departing the McDonald's. Just this constant assault against her clothing and flesh. Her teeth chatter together. What are they even doing out here? This all feels so…pointless. If this cop knew anything, if he possessed any information that would help them track down Josh and Alonzo, then he would have already come clean. Maybe Ottessa's right. Maybe he's only stalling for more time. She glances around the parking lot, paranoia level increased, certain she's going to spot more cop cars slowly creeping up on them with their lights turned off. But no. The parking lot remains empty, save for a McDonald's employee leaning against the back of the building, taking a smoke break and pretending like she isn't trying to eavesdrop on their conversation. Mary wonders if she's the same cashier who handled her coffee order. Has she received word yet of her coworker's fate? If so, does she realize Mary's the one responsible for her new disfigurement?

She turns away from the building, body haunted with chills.

"So," Ottessa says, using the silence as punctuation, "what's the plan here, then? You came all this way. Tell us why."

Lindenmuth hesitates for only the briefest of seconds. "If *anybody* at the station has something to do with…what's going on here, then it has to be Keene. I don't trust anybody who works there, but that doesn't mean I think they're all capable of masterminding some kind of…what, child abduction ring? Our sheriff, on the other hand, there's something off about him. You talk to him and you get the sense there's a whole other person hiding somewhere in him, like being sheriff's just this…this…this tactic, I guess. Does that make sense?"

Ottessa nods. "Yeah. We all think he's a shady motherfucker, too."

"We had a recording, of someone taking our sons," Mary says, realizing Lindenmuth hadn't been around for the majority of their interrogation at the police station. "It showed this old car, like the kind cops drove in the seventies or eighties. Whoever owns this car, they're the ones. They're the ones who…who…who did it. We showed the video to the sheriff and he destroyed it. He accused us of making a fake video, but…but…"

Lindenmuth pales. "Jesus."

"What are you suggesting we do?"

"Well," he says, leaning closer and speaking in a hushed tone, "I know where he lives. Tomorrow, when he's at the station, we go over to his house and look through his stuff. He isn't, you know, the smartest guy out there. If he's involved in what's going on, we're bound to find some kind of evidence. I doubt your kids are there, but maybe there's a clue leading to where they are. I'm not even saying he's the one who took the kids, but still, he knows more than he's letting on. That much is obvious, at least. You said the abductors were driving an old squad car?"

"It was hard to make out all of the details in the recording," Mary says, "but yes. It was dark out, and the angle was bad, but I'm positive if I saw it again I would recognize it right away." She gestures to Ottessa. "You'd be able to do the same, right?"

Except Ottessa's no longer paying attention to the conversation. She points at the cop car behind Lindenmuth. "Tell her to repeat that."

Lindenmuth slowly follows the aim of her finger, then turns back her way, brow raised. "What?"

"On the radio!" She's practically shrieking now. "Tell the woman to repeat what she just said. Right now, goddammit!"

The tone of her voice kicks him awake, like a whip lashing across a horse's ass. He dives behind the wheel and frantically fumbles for the mic.

"Yeah, dispatch, this is car seventeen. I'd like to request a ten-nine, please."

The dispatcher on the other end responds, and Mary realizes it's the same woman they'd held hostage back at the station. "That's a four-fifty-nine at Twenty-Seven Oak, car seventeen. I repeat, that's a four-fifty-nine at Twenty-Seven Oak, car seventeen. Two juveniles, African American. Homeowner currently has suspects confined in his living room."

"What's a four-fifty-nine?" Mary asks, trembling, terrified she's about to hear *homicide*.

"Burglary," Lindenmuth says. Then presses the mic again. "Yeah, dispatch, I'm gonna go ahead and take this one. I'm pretty close to the location already."

"Roger that. Update me when you arrive."

"Will do."

He returns the mic to its cradle, then faces Mary. "It might not be them."

"I know," Mary says, although every part of her's screaming that it is, that they've found them, finally they've found their boys. "But it could be."

"Bullshit," Ottessa says. "It's them."

Lindenmuth pauses, maybe weighing the possibilities, then finally nods. "Well, let's go then."

THIRTY TWO

The cop car's getting closer and neither Alonzo nor Josh have moved. They stand in the center of the gravel driveway, blinded by its headlights. No doubt they've been spotted at this point. The lights on its roof flash but no sound emits. Whoever's in the car doesn't want to alert anybody of its approaching presence. They should have already started running by now. Back into the cornfield. Back into their home. Yet they still haven't, and Alonzo realizes they're not going to. Both of them are too exhausted and injured to keep performing these goddamn marathons. Whatever's about to happen, they'll stick their ground, they'll fight, they'll do whatever it takes to defend themselves, but they're fucking done running.

Alonzo squints into the lights and tries to make out who's behind the steering wheel, but it's no use. The car, however, it's not the same one that Father's been using to chase them down. This car looks less like it was stolen from a junkyard. It looks…*authentic*. Which of course doesn't mean anything. Just because they've seen Father driving one kind of car doesn't mean there aren't other models back at the farm. The family could own dozens of vehicles for every occasion. Taxi cabs, ambulances, ice cream trucks, whatever.

"What are we going to do?" Josh whispers next to him.

"Wait and see what happens." Alonzo tightens his fists, which only seems to stretch the bear trap bite in his shoulder. He chews on his tongue to prevent screaming.

The cop car slows to a stop a good ten, twenty feet away from them. The roof lights and headlights remain engaged. Nobody moves. A standoff. The cop car surrenders first and the front passenger's door creaks open. A head sticks out, but the headlights prevent them from making out any features. Then, a voice. A woman's voice.

"*Josh!*"

And then the head forms a body, and the body comes running at them, and suddenly the body's no longer just any body but the body belonging to Josh's mom. Alonzo blinks hard and fast, certain of trickery, but the woman remains as she appears.

"M-M-Mom?" Josh croaks out, and abandons Alonzo to embrace his mom halfway between him and the car. He watches her hug him tight, sobbing and kissing his cheek, and confusion turns to jealousy. He glares at the cop car, waiting for his own mom to walk out, and sure enough the driver's door pops open, except instead of his mom out steps an actual police officer. A regular cop. Not deformed or fucked-up like one of the monsters from the family. He maneuvers to the back of the car and opens one of the rear doors, and his heart sinks as yes, there she is, his mom, his *mother* finally emerges from the vehicle's interior and pushes the cop out of the way as she sprints toward him, and before he can so much as utter a word she's wrapped her arms around him and squeezed. Pain immediately erases joy as his shoulder injury stretches.

"Let go!" he screams, and to his relief she obeys.

"Zoey," his mom cries. "Baby, I'm here. We're here. We found you. Are you okay?"

Alonzo wants to say yes, wants to say they're fine, but the truth's stronger than the lie. "My shoulder. Be careful."

His mom leans forward, inspecting the injury, and gasps. "Holy shit, Zoey, what the fuck happened?"

"How'd you find us?" he asks, glancing around her at the cop still lingering around his car. The cop witnesses their reunion with his arms crossed over his chest, smiling. What the fuck is he smiling at? Who the hell does he think he is, and what was he doing with their moms?

"I'm so sorry," she says, spreading her arms to hug him again then remembering his shoulder. "I'm so sorry I let this happen."

"You let *what* happen?"

"I should have saved you sooner. I should have…"

"Mom, stop." He points at the cop. "Who is that?"

"Oh, honey, that's just our ride."

"Okay," he says, then points at the other cop car driving toward them from the end of the driveway. "And who's that?"

The cop who had driven their moms here follows Alonzo's finger and lets out a heavy sigh. "That'll be the sheriff," he says, and unbuckles the strap of his sidearm.

At first Alonzo thinks the cop's about to draw his gun on them, then realizes it's for the other car. The sheriff. Surely not Father, right? No way in hell Father's been the sheriff of Percy all this time and nobody's at the very least filed a hygiene complaint. No, this is someone else. Someone else also worthy of caution, apparently. His mom squeezes his hand hard enough to crack his knuckles and even if she breaks his fingers, he will never complain. There's no way this is real. Where did they even *come* from? And why can't he stop crying?

The second cop car parks in the center of the driveway, successfully blocking them from escaping. Maybe that's not his intent, but it sure feels that way. The cop who brought their moms here stands his ground, not drawing his weapon just yet, but his fingers keep wiggling at his side like they're preparing for a showdown. Athletes warming up before the main event. Earthworms pleading for their lives as a much larger predator turns their innards into a buffet.

The sheriff gets out of his car, grinning and readjusting his hat.

His boots jangle as he walks.

Alonzo's mom wraps her arm around him, careful not to touch his shoulder, and squeezes him close against her warmth.

"Not another step closer, sheriff," the cop says, a roughness in his voice.

"Well, well, well," the sheriff says, on the verge of laughter as he nears them. "Looks like you ended up finding your little rugrats after all, huh?"

The other cop straightens out his spine, making himself tall but still not taller than the sheriff. "I thought I told you on the radio that I already had this under control."

The sheriff nods, agreeing. "And *I* thought I told *you* that I would take over from here. So, Officer Lindenmuth, I thank you for handling the situation until my arrival, but as you can see," he extends his hands and performs a slight twirl, "I have indeed arrived, which no longer renders your presence here required. You can be on your way now."

"Now, I don't think—"

The sheriff holds up his hand, palm out. "In fact, I'm a little confused as to why you were on duty in the first place. Correct me if I'm wrong, Officer Lindenmuth, but shouldn't you have punched out…well, *hours* ago?"

"I was off-duty when I received the call."

"Yet you still felt the need to answer it, even after I informed you there was no need."

The cop, Lindenmuth, shrugs, fingers still wiggling at his side, almost like they're spasming now, out of control. "It just so happened to be that I was near the location."

"It just so happened, huh?" The sheriff's grin widens, then he acknowledges Alonzo and Josh's moms. "And what about you two? Let me guess: my officer here discovered you with the suspects when he arrived, caught you redhanded trying to smuggle them away from yet *another* active crime scene."

"Actually." Lindenmuth clears his throat. "The parents were with me when the call came through."

"They were *with* you?"

"Yes, sir."

The sheriff grimaces, then laughs and winks. "Why, Officer Lindenmuth, you little horndog. I had no idea you had it in you." He leans forward and whispers loudly, "Although, if you were me, I'd definitely schedule a checkup in the immediate future. I'm not too worried about Miss PTA over there, but the other one," he nods at Alonzo's mom, "well, golly, Officer Lindenmuth, I don't think you need me to tell you that she's had just about every cock in Percy in her mouth at one point or another."

Alonzo pushes away from his mom. She tells him to stop and he ignores her and charges forward. Lindenmuth drops his guard and grabs him before

318

he can make contact with the sheriff. Alonzo tries wrestling away from the cop's grip but he's too weak and hungry to make much progress. He surrenders and lets the cop hold him for a moment as he tries to catch his breath. Once he regains his composure, he realizes the sheriff has drawn his own sidearm and is pointing it directly at him.

"Son, you so much as move another inch and you're finished. You understand me, *homie?*"

Alonzo debates charging him again just for the way he said homie, but the cop still has his arms around him.

The sheriff's grin still hasn't faded. "Good. That's wise. The less you move and talk, the better this will be for everybody involved. I'm sure we can all agree on that, can't we?"

Nobody responds, and he shrugs. "Anyway. As I was saying, your attendance is no longer needed, Officer Lindenmuth. You may return to your vehicle and go home. Hell, you even have my permission to take a personal day tomorrow. Judging by the way you've been behaving, seems to me you might need it."

The cop shakes his head, loosening his grip on Alonzo. "I'm taking them with me."

The sheriff cocks his head. "I'm sorry, Officer Lindenmuth, you'll have to excuse my ears. I'm getting awfully hard of hearing these days. Care to repeat that?"

"They're coming with me. Not you."

"Ah." He nods. "That's what I thought you might have said. Care to explain why?"

"I think you already know."

"Mmm." The sheriff licks his lips, narrowing his eyes. "Okay then." He raises his sidearm and a flash explodes from the barrel. Thunder cracks in the night.

Behind Alonzo, someone screams but he can't decide if it's his mom or Josh's mom or Josh or, hell, even Alonzo. Maybe they're all screaming. Slowly he looks up at the cop. His jaw's missing. Blood and slime drip down from the roof of his mouth as he attempts to say something. Alonzo can't quite make out the words. Then the cop's legs collapse beneath him and his body slams against the gravel. Alonzo allows exactly two seconds to pass before screaming, "*Run!*" and hurrying back behind Lindenmuth's car and grabbing his mom's arm and dragging her into the cornfield.

The sheriff fires his weapon again and the sound only makes them run faster.

Alonzo tightens his grip on his mom's hand and refuses to let go no matter what.

MOTHERS

THIRTY THREE

Everything happens so fast, Ottessa barely has time to process it all before it's already over. Time moves at a surreal pace that simultaneously acts as slow-motion and hyper speed. First they're stopping in the driveway, headlights revealing the two boys they've spent the last couple days searching for, the two boys Ottessa was beginning to convince herself they'd never see again, no matter where they looked, no matter who they threatened. Then Lindenmuth's letting her out from the back seat and she's racing over to Zoey, hugging him and apologizing for being such a shitty mom. Noticing the gash on his shoulder, the blood and dirt stained on his face, the bizarre trash bag clinging to his body in lieu of actual clothing. Trying to make sense of whatever fucked-up shit has happened to her son. Not having enough time to. even talk to Zoey before the sheriff showed up. Started talking shit. Zoey running after him, only for Lindenmuth to catch him. The sheriff shooting Lindenmuth. Everybody screaming. Zoey grabbing her arm and screaming that they had to go, that they had to *move*. Everybody running. More gunshots behind them. Terrified one of the bullets would catch Zoey in the back.

Eventually they pause for a breather, doubling over and panting. She can't remember the last time she ran so hard. Zoey's next to her, on his knees, dry heaving. Even in the moonlight he looks like shit. She has a thousand questions she wants—no, *needs*—to ask him, but she knows it's not the time, doesn't know if it will *ever* be the time. When's a good moment to question your son about his recent abduction? How is she supposed to ask those kind of questions? Worse, how the fuck is she supposed to sit there and listen to the answers?

Behind them, Mary paces in a circle, hands digging through her hair, not bothering to push aside the corn stalks smacking her in the face. "Josh!" she screams. "*Josh!*"

"Shhh!" Ottessa whispers, hating herself for it. "That motherfucker's still out there."

Mary looks at her like they're strangers. "I don't care *who's* out there. Josh isn't here. *Josh isn't here.*"

Somewhere out in the corn, back in the direction of the driveway, a boy screams.

"*Josh!*" Mary spins toward the voice and disappears in the corn.

"Ah, fuck," Ottessa says, wishing she hadn't left her purse in the back of Lindenmuth's car. Her purse, which had been used to stash Jasper's gun. She taps Zoey on the back. "Stay here, okay? We'll be right back."

Zoey shakes his head hard enough to give himself whiplash. "Nobody should be in this corn alone."

"What?"

"*Never be in the corn alone.*"

He grabs her hand again and takes off. Together they follow Mary and the sound of Josh's screams.

Then, as quick as a knife slices through flesh, the night once again falls silent.

And they run even faster.

There's no way to tell how close they are to the driveway until they burst through the cornfield edge and stumble out onto the gravel. Ottessa skids against the rough ground, hating to be caught so off-guard, convinced the sheriff's waiting there with his gun still aimed, ready to blow a hole in both her and Zoey.

She finds Mary collapsed on her knees where Keene's car used to be parked, sobbing and screaming Josh's name. She punches the jagged pebbles surrounding her, spraying clouds of dust in random directions. A couple feet behind her lies the corpse of Lindenmuth. Half of his face is missing. A distant part of Ottessa orders her to shield Zoey's eyes from the scene, but it's only barely present and in no way strong enough to achieve any progress. Instead she remains frozen with her arms dangling at her sides, watching Mary cry, watching the dead cop collect flies. The sheriff is gone, and if not for the rough tire marks leading away from them, she wonders if she would believe he had ever been here in the first place. Everything about this weekend feels so much like a nightmare. Surreal and nonlinear. Like they're all floating from scene to scene. Every blink of the eyes generating a new grotesque set piece.

In the end, it's Zoey who acts. Brave Zoey, who's been through who-the-hell-knows what. Zoey, stronger than Ottessa could ever aspire of becoming. He lets go of her hand and moves in on Mary, kneeling so they're eye-level, one hand resting on her shoulder. He whispers something Ottessa can't quite make out and Mary starts shaking her head hard and fast, sobbing louder, screaming, *"He's gone! He was here and now he's gone! He's gone!"*

And Zoey nods and says, "Then let's go get him back."

IN THE END THEY LEAVE Lindenmuth where he died. What else are they supposed to do with him? Drag him off into the corn and give him a proper burial? Stuff him in the trunk of his own car and drive to the local morgue? They can't go back to the police station, that's for certain. There's no telling who else Keene's managed to corrupt. Returning to the station would be walking into an ambush. Same thing with a hospital. They can't just show up with a dead cop and a kid looking the way Zoey looks and not expect them to snitch. So yes, as far as Lindenmuth goes, they don't do a damn thing about him. They're grateful for the help he provided but his services are no longer required. Someone else will eventually stumble upon him and know the appropriate measures to take. Or maybe he'll remain here in the middle of this driveway forever unnoticed, slowly decomposing and disintegrating into the gravel. Birds and other stray animals pecking away at his delicious meats until there is nothing left worthy of salvaging. There are worse fates.

They do, however, take his car. It's not like he's going to be needing it any time soon, anyway. Ottessa drives, Zoey rides shotgun, and Mary continues crying in the back seat, routinely slamming herself against the door and screaming Josh's name. The woman from the police station spits out codes over the radio and it takes Ottessa a minute to realize dispatch is talking to Lindenmuth's car, that's she's requesting some sort of status update. She ignores the noise and pats Zoey on the thigh, who immediately flinches and starts crying.

"It's just me, baby," she says.

"I know. I'm sorry."

"You gotta tell me where we're going."

"Where we're going?"

"Where did that shithead sheriff keep you two? There has to be some place you were locked up, right? And you escaped?"

His voice downgrades to a weak whisper. "The basement."

"He had you in a basement? At his house?"

Zoey shakes his head. "I've never seen that guy before in my life. It wasn't him."

"What? Then who?"

"The family."

"What?"

"They have a farm…somewhere."

"Zoey? Where's the farm, baby?"

"I don't know."

"You have to remember. Please."

"I don't remember!"

"Okay. That's fine. That's okay." She pats him on the thigh again, not knowing what else to do. Does he really not remember, or is he faking amnesia to avoid having to return? No. Zoey wouldn't do that. Josh is his best friend. He'd do anything to help him. Zoey's just been through a lot, that's all. He needs some time to rest. He needs a long bath and a hot meal. It suddenly occurs to her that the last time Zoey may have eaten was Friday

326

evening, and she can't even be sure of that since she hadn't gotten home until after Josh and he went to bed.

Goddammit. She doesn't deserve to be a mom. She never did. Zoey belongs somewhere else, under the roof of someone with their shit together. She grips the steering wheel tight enough to hurt her hands and grits her teeth and resists the urge to put a bullet in her skull. What matters now is that she found him and that he's alive. Yes, Josh is still out there, somewhere, but saving him is not her top priority. Josh is not her son. His health comes secondary at best. It's a terrible thing to think and something she'll never admit aloud, but it's the truth.

Zoey is alive and right now nothing else matters.

THERE'S A SUPER 8 THE next town over. She's visited this place on more than one occasion, but she's never actually stayed the night. They can't go back to either of their homes. Not right now. Possibly never again. The sheriff undoubtedly has eyes on both residences, waiting for one of them to make a mistake. Just because she has Zoey again, it doesn't mean he's safe. That motherfucker's still out there somewhere. He's not going to just *give up* and leave them alone. Life doesn't work that way.

Ottessa parks Lindenmuth's car behind the Super 8, away from the eye of the interstate. Neither Zoey nor Mary haven't made a sound in several minutes. Their eyes remain half-open, mouths ajar, as if caught in a daze, rendered catatonic by their own internal horrors. She collects her purse from the back seat next to Mary's feet and leaves them both in the car as she walks around the building and nearly smashes into the glass of the front entrance. Every time she's come here—which, admittedly, hasn't been a *ton* of times, but at least in the double digits—she's forgotten that the doors lock at eleven for security reasons. She rings a bell next to the sign warning of the present blockade. Nearly a minute passes before the doors spread apart. A young woman waits behind the front desk in the lobby, a look on her face making it clear she's just been disturbed from a nap. Ottessa recognizes her but she doesn't seem to recognize Ottessa. It's understandable. Who knows how many lunatics she runs into every day, especially at this time of night. She wonders if the woman's afraid Ottessa's about to shove a gun in her face and demand to have whatever's in the register. Has she ever been robbed before? Is she afraid of death? Does she have kids at home? Is someone trustworthy looking after them?

When Ottessa doesn't immediately say something, the woman behind the front desk rolls her eyes. "Yeah? Did you need something?"

Ottessa snaps out of her trance, realizing she has one hand in her purse, softly caressing the steel of Jasper's gun. Was she about to pull it out? What the fuck is wrong with her? Instead of a firearm, she collects her wallet and tells the woman she needs a room with two beds. The woman quotes her a rate and starts copying down the information on her driver's license. Then an idea occurs to her and she nearly reaches across the front desk and knocks the card out of the clerk's hand.

Instead she says, "I'm gonna need you to use a different last name, if possible."

And the front desk woman looks up from her computer, drool dripping down her bottom lip. "Huh?"

The lie spills out, natural and smooth. "My husband—my *soon-to-be-ex-*husband, he's trying to track me down. We had ourselves a disagreement and he thinks the only way to come to any compromise involves beating me half to death. So…I would highly appreciate it if you could enter a different last name, in case he starts calling up all the hotels around asking if I'm a guest."

The front desk woman slowly nods. Drool continues smearing across her chin. "Oh, we aren't allowed to give away private information like that. If someone asks if someone else is staying here, we can't tell them."

"But what if someone called asking to be connected to their room? Would you connect them?"

"Well. Yeah. I guess so."

"Don't you think that's kind of the same thing?"

328

The woman pauses entirely too long for Ottessa's patience.

"Look, all I'm asking you to do is enter a fake last name. Make a copy of my license for all I care. I just don't want anybody knowing I'm a guest. If my husband tracks me down, he'll fucking kill me. Get it?"

Something in her snaps awake. "Okay, yeah, no problem. What name would you like?"

Ottessa tells her some bullshit name and pays up, then collects a key packet and returns outside through the back exit. She feels somewhat dirty, playing the abusive housewife on the lam card. The last man who found interest in bruising her flesh fled her house with two broken fingers and a crushed scrotum.

She collects Zoey and Mary and leads them back in through the back door, hoping to avoid being spotted by the sleepy front desk clerk. Fortunately, their room isn't too far from the exit and they manage to slip in undetected. The room reeks of Lysol and cat piss but at least it has four walls and a roof. A box to hide in is all they really need right now. An intermission from nonstop violence and anarchy.

She guides Zoey into the bathroom and turns the shower knob to the H, then helps him shed the black garbage bag from his torso. He doesn't say a word as she inspects his naked body, as she gasps at his many injuries. Injuries no boy his age should ever have to experience, under any circumstances. Injuries no *man* should ever know as reality. Dried blood and dirt provide an extra layer of protection over his flesh. An open wound in his shoulder shaped like a jester's smile has turned black from infection. Mercifully, the water spraying from the shower head against the tub floor drowns out the soft whimpers escaping her lips. Every instinct in her screams to rush him to a hospital before it's too late, but she resists. Not yet. Not until she's personally slit the throats of every motherfucker responsible for what's been done to her boy. Only then will it be safe. Only then can life move on.

"C'mon, Zoey, you gotta wash this shit off."

He moans as the water slaps against his flesh but otherwise remains quiet. Some of it ricochets off him and hits her and only then does she realize just how hot the temperature is. She adjusts the knob only slightly. For filth this complex, the water must be scalding. She helps him with the soap and forces a washcloth in his hand and pushes it where it needs to go. Something inside him shut down. Damaged beyond repair? No. Hell no. She can fix him. She *must* fix him. Her job as a mother is to protect him and up until now, she has failed horribly. But no longer. She'll make him better or god-dammit she'll die trying.

A half hour of intense scrubbing passes and they've only barely made a dent, but all the hot water's expired so she dries him off and wraps his mid-section with a towel and leads him out of the bathroom. Mary's still sitting at the edge of one of the queen-sized beds, gripping the comforter and burning holes in the wall with her eyes. Ottessa lays Zoey down on the other bed and tucks him in and kisses him on the forehead.

"I'm gonna go get us some supplies, okay? I'll be right back."

He shoots his hand out from beneath the comforter and grabs her wrist. His eyes widen. "No," he whispers. "No, don't go."

"You need to eat, Zoey. Plus you need clothes. And medicine."

"No."

"I'm just going down the street. I want you to close your eyes and rest. Josh's mom will look after you while I'm gone. You're safe here. I promise."

A single tear runs down his cheek and stains the pillow under his head. "We will never be safe again."

WALKING OUT OF THE MOTEL, it occurs to Ottessa that it probably isn't a wise idea to leave a stolen cop car next to where they're sleeping. Plus, don't these kinds of cars usually have built-in GPS systems? Ways other cops can track their location in case something happens to them. Maybe, maybe not. She's pretty sure she's at least seen something similar on a TV show or movie before. Better safe than sorry, right? She drives the car a mile down the interstate then pulls off into a dirt path leading through the woods. Drives another half mile and ditches it next to a tree with branches resembling the overgrown fingernails of a witch. Let the sheriff chase his dick all the way out here and get it bitten off by some curious raccoon. Oh, that mother*fucker*, that cock*sucker*. Should have trusted her gut all this time. He was crooked from Jump Street. Knew where Zoey and Josh were all this time. Did who-knows-what to them. Goddamn, she can't wait to find him again. Can't wait to blow his fucking brains out. Can't wait to make him feel every ounce of pain Zoey's felt since Friday, and double it, triple it, make it last eternally. It's all she can think about as she hikes back down the interstate, periodically squeezing her fists, making sure they still work. Yeah, Keene might got a gun, but so does Ottessa, and next time there won't be any fuckin' talking, it'll be gun against gun, bullet against bullet, and she ain't gonna be the one on the receiving end.

She stops at a twenty-four-seven Walmart located across the interstate from the Super 8. A dead-eyed cashier drools at her as she heads toward the boys' clothing section. For a minute she just stares at the choices, brain frozen, unable to remember what size Zoey wears, prepared to smash a brick into her face if the information doesn't come to her, what kind of mother doesn't know her own boy's clothes size, what kind of mother isn't home to take care of him, isn't home to make sure he's safe, to make sure he's alive, what kind of mother doesn't protect her son, her only child on this earth, her precious goddamn joy—

The size comes back to her, and she grabs a pair of pants, a shirt, some socks, underwear, and a box of new shoes. Hugs it all against her chest since she was too stupid to remember a basket at the front entrance. Hugs it tighter because it's like hugging Zoey. Zoey who's back at the motel, Zoey who she can hug all day every day now, Zoey who will never be the same ever again, no matter how tight and how often she hugs him. The Zoey she knew last week is dead. In the Super 8 rests a new version of her son. Something alien and fragile. Dissect too hard and he'll break beyond repair.

She bumps into an empty shopping cart at the divider between boys' and men's clothing. Nobody else stands near it so she dumps her items in the basket and pushes the cart to the grocery section. After scavenging a few snacks and drinks, she maneuvers around the store toward the medicine aisle. Loads up on gauze and tape, alcohol wipes, peroxide, and Neosporin. Aspirin. Anything that looks like it might make her son feel better. She has no fucking idea what she's doing. Not really. She never researched any of this shit before. Zoey's almost thirteen and despite all the injuries he's gained over the years, she's never once bothered to *try*. But on the other hand, he's always turned out okay. Cuts heal. Broken bones don't stay broken. Blood dries. Kids are supposed to fall down. They're supposed to get hurt. Pain is how they evolve.

But not the kind of pain Zoey is experiencing now.

This is something different, something no human being on the planet should ever have to feel.

This is the kind of pain reserved for devils.

The drooling cashier rings up her items without uttering a single word. Ottessa pays with the coffee can cash she swiped from Mary's purse, collects her bags, and walks across the street to the motel. Mary and Zoey are curled up in bed next to each other when she enters the room. Both look like they've gone through a deep crying session during her absence. If Zoey was asleep, he's awake now. At the sound of Ottessa setting down the Walmart bags on the sink, he sits up and reaches out for her. Looking like a lost toddler. She takes his hand, so desperate for her touch, and leads him into the bathroom, careful not to disturb Mary. Let the woman sleep while she can. In the morning, she'll need her energy. They all will.

"Everything hurts," Zoey whispers, lips trembling, and Ottessa nods, tells him she knows, tells him she's gonna make it all better. Lying right to his face and both of them know it. Playing a game of good parent charades. Meaningless words, empty, lacking substance.

She unloads the medicine bag along the edge of the sink and applies ointments and wipes to the areas of his body with open wounds. He winces and bites his tongue to prevent himself from screaming out. She apologizes for hurting him, whispers *I'm sorry* over and over but it doesn't do either of them a bit of good. Only the pain is real. She wraps gauze around his shoulder and secures it with tape. Easily the worst of the injuries on her son.

"What did this?" she asks, no longer able to stand the mystery.

"Bear trap," he says, matter-of-factly.

"*What?*"

"The basement. There were bear traps. I jumped in one."

"You fell?"

"No." He shakes his head, rubbing the multiple layers of gauze around his shoulder. "They put straitjackets on us. The bear trap ripped it open." He pauses. "Ripped me open, too."

It takes her half a minute to comprehend what he just said. "Straitjackets?"

Instead of responding, he goes through the other Walmart bags. "Are these clothes for me?"

"Yeah. Put them on. I brought some food, too. Not much. But some."

"I'm so hungry."

"When was the last time you ate?"

"I don't remember."

"Get dressed, then eat."

She looks away as he puts on the clothes. Even wrapped in bandages, her son's body resembles a roadmap of torture. Their conversation isn't close to over, but a part of her wishes they could just avoid ever finishing it. They don't need to talk about it. All she needs to do is hug him and never let go again.

He practically destroys a bag of chips attempting to open it, then the contents are gone within two minutes. He goes through the rest of the snacks like a wild animal feasting upon a trash can missing its lid. He eats like he's starving, and that's because he is.

"Zoey." She pauses, takes her time catching her breath. "Zoey, I need to know what happened. Everything. I need you to tell me. Okay?"

He ignores her question and continues eating, avoiding eye contact.

She reaches out and touches his jaw, moves his head so they're looking at each other again. "If we're going to find Josh, then you have to talk. You have to tell me."

"It's bad," he says.

"I know," she says. "I know, baby, I know."

And Zoey laughs then, only it doesn't sound like his normal laugh. It sounds...*raw*. Animalistic.

"No, Mom, you don't."

HE WAS RIGHT.

She really didn't know.

Had no fucking idea, in fact.

Could never have possibly anticipated the story he told her there in the bathroom.

Early on, she started crying, and she didn't stop until after he finished and they were holding each other in bed, whispering how sorry she was, him saying it was okay, her saying no it wasn't, it wasn't okay, and him saying they had to get Josh back, saying they had to save him, and her hugging him even tighter, promising they would, promising him anything he could ever want for the rest of his life, just as long as she could hold him a little longer.

THIRTY FOUR

osh doesn't even make it into the cornfield before his feet betray him. His feet, bare and bloody from the rough gravel, no longer ache. Instead, a dull numbness swallows them from toes to ankles. Moving them with any punctuality beckons comparisons of walking through water. An unstoppable force laughs at his pathetic attempt of escape. One foot gives out, then the other. He reaches for his mom's hand but only grasps air. Had she ever really been here, or had her appearance amounted to nothing more than some screwed-up mirage—a hallucination brought on from severe exhaustion and hunger? Either reality doesn't matter because she's not here *now*. Not even Alonzo is here anymore. It is just him and the dead cop and the other cop who killed him. The sheriff with the big gun, standing over him now and grabbing his wrist and dragging him facedown through the driveway. He tries to scream his mom's name and a load of gravel empties into his mouth. Friction sets his face on fire.

Thunder cracks the sky again.

No, not thunder. A gunshot.

At him?

He stops resisting and goes limp, waits for death to gobble him up, but he keeps breathing, keeps thinking, keeps living. If he's shot, the pain hasn't registered yet. A piercing ringing overcomes his senses. He's either already dead or on the verge of being dead and at this point he's no longer sure which one he prefers.

Where is his mom?

A door swings open. The sheriff releases his ankle and tells him to get in, but the words are faint, far away, drowned out by the ringing in his ears. When he doesn't immediately obey, the sheriff gets frustrated and kicks him in the stomach, then points the gun first down at him, then toward the open door. Josh gets the picture. Groaning, he pulls himself up and crawls into the back seat. The door bangs against his mangled feet as it slams shut behind him. He lifts his head and watches the sheriff through the windshield as he stands in front of the car, gun pointed toward the wall of corn where everybody else managed to escape. Waiting…waiting for what? Waiting for Josh's mom to realize he's missing, waiting for her to turn back around and try to save him. As soon as she emerges from the corn, the sheriff's going to shoot her. He'll shoot his mom, he'll shoot Alonzo's mom, he'll shoot Alonzo, then he'll shoot Josh, and that will be the end. The inevitable is unpreventable. Everything that is going to happen will happen. It can only be fought for so long. Fought, yes, but never conquered.

Josh wants to scream, wants to warn his mom not to return for him, to keep running and never, under any circumstances, turn back, but he can't move, can't talk, can't do a damn thing but wait and watch. Fear has its grip on him, like sharp unforgiving teeth sinking into his throat.

The sheriff waits another couple minutes, then slides his gun back in its holster and stomps over to the car. He collapses behind the wheel, shaking his head, clearly pissed off.

"Looks like you've done been forgotten, boy." He cranks the gearshift and reverses against the corn, then shifts to DRIVE and starts rolling down the driveway. "One of you's better than none of you, I suppose."

"Wh-what are you going to do?" Josh says, wishing he had the courage and strength to bust through the mesh wall separating the back seat from the front and strangle the sheriff as he drives.

"Don't ask questions you already know the answers to, boy," the sheriff says. "Please, don't."

"You got any idea what a pain in the ass your mother's been to me? I ought to put you down right here and now off of general principle." He sighs as they near the end of the driveway and pull out onto the road. "Will you quit that goddamn crying? I said I *ought to*. I didn't say I was *gonna*. Not yet, at least. We got other shit to attend to first."

IT DOESN'T TAKE LONG TO figure out where they're going. Like Josh couldn't have guessed from the moment he was thrown in the back seat. They pull up to the farm and maybe Josh is screaming, he isn't sure if he's actually making any noise or if it's only in his head. The driver's door opens up front and an overhead light flashes on and an irritating alarm ding goes off inside the car. The sheriff opens the back door and grabs at Josh and Josh kicks out at him. He gets one foot against his face but the attack doesn't seem to affect him much. The sheriff grabs both of his legs and drags him out of the car. His head slams against the grass and nausea forces him to keep his eyes closed for a moment. The ground is wet against his cheek but he can't remember the last time it rained. The sheriff doesn't give him time to recover, a chance to fight back. He drags his defeated body across the lawn, back to the house that isn't a house. But if it's not a house, then it's…what?

> *What is a house if it isn't a house?*
> *What is a shadow if it isn't a shadow?*
> *What is a memory if it isn't a memory?*

Josh keeps his eyes shut as his head bounces against the porch steps. When he finally opens them again, he's inside the living room. The stench of decay doesn't make a show of being shy. It hits him fast and it hits him hard. A rabid maniac half-submerged in his subconscious screams, *Honey, I'm home!* He tries clawing away but the act is pointless. His fingernails are ground up and bloody. He goes limp again as the sheriff continues dragging him through the house, toward a familiar door down the hallway. He manages to catch a glimpse of the kitchen and wishes he could take a photo. The room's a fucking disaster. Uncle's corpse remains amongst the chaos, now sans a head. All that's left is a rotting stump at the base of his neck. If this is the last sight Josh beholds before he dies, then he will leave this Earth content.

The sheriff slams Josh's legs against the floor, grunting and sweating. "You know, you're making this more difficult than necessary."

If Josh had more strength, he might have laughed at that. Instead, he coughs and refuses to make eye contact with the man.

The sheriff pauses, noticing Uncle's headless corpse. "What the fuck." Long beat, then: "Did you do this?" Talking to Josh. "What the fuck did you do?"

Josh doesn't say a word.

The door leading into the basement is wide open, making it easy for the sheriff to drag Josh down the steps, each one smacking him against the skull and reminding him of his place in the universe. It takes Josh a moment to register what's awaiting him at the bottom of the stairs. The old man, Richard, is hanging upside down in the center of the basement. His feet are hooked to chains attached to hooks in the ceiling. His hands are tied behind his back and his body lightly swings back and forth. Beneath him a puddle of blood spreads like cancer. Father stands next to him holding a machete. The blade's unsurprisingly stained with the same liquid currently spilling out of the old man.

Josh snaps his attention where Don and Shane had been chained to the wall, but they're no longer there. It only takes him a second to guess their relocation thanks to the shovel sticking out of the dirt. Directly below the old man, where his blood has spilled the most, the earth is loose and chaotic, as if someone's recently been digging in the spot. As if someone's been burying something there.

Burying something like bodies.

Maybe last week his mind wouldn't have immediately gone to this conclusion, but after everything that's happened over the weekend, there's not a doubt in his mind.

Don and Shane are buried under the hanging man. His blood is soaking into whatever remains of their corpses.

"Oh, God," he says, practically croaks out.

Father glares at him, brows scrunched and furious. He points the machete forward, fresh blood dripping from the tip. "This is your fault. This is all your doing."

"I'm sorry," he says, relieved Alonzo isn't nearby to hear him apologize, happy that he made it out safely with their moms, that it'll just be him to accept their punishment for escaping, "I'm sorry, I'm sorry, I'm sorry…"

Realization dawns over Father's disfigured face. He redirects the machete's tip at the sheriff. "Where are the others?"

The sheriff shrugs and sighs in the same way Josh has witnessed Alonzo shrug and sigh before lying to a teacher about why he couldn't turn in a homework assignment. "Look, it's dark out there, there was too many of them. I'm lucky to have even caught the fat one, if we're being honest here."

"I need them all."

"I know, and you will, but—"

"*Now!*" Father raises the machete and the sheriff cowers. "*I need them now!*"

"Okay! Okay! I'm on my way, all right? I'm gonna go get them right now. I was just dropping the fat one off to clear room in my car, okay? I'm *going.*"

Father lowers the machete, but only slightly. "The mothers, too. You cannot forget the mothers."

"Do you really need *both* of them, or is just one fine?"

"*You cannot forget the mothers.*"

The sheriff nods and backs away, clearly terrified. "I saw Uncle upstairs. What ha—I was just wondering. You know. If a new spot's now available, if maybe you might consider—"

"First, the mothers. Then we will see."

The sheriff grins, suddenly excited. "You won't regret this, Father. I promise."

Josh lunges at the sheriff, fists tightened. "Leave my mom alone, you fu—"

Father grabs the back of his neck and flings him across the basement.

"Don't worry, kid," the sheriff shouts as he climbs the stairs. "You'll be seeing your mom real soon. I'll make sure of it."

UNFAZED BY JOSH'S DEFENSIVE STRIKES, Father binds his arms to the same chains that held either Don or Shane. Then he's hanging from the ceiling, both arms stretched out, feet nowhere near the ground. If every inch of his body weren't already consumed by pain, it definitely would be now. The chains are too tight. They're going to tear the skin from his palms off. *Deglove* him, it's called. Remove his flesh gloves and render him an honest skeleton.

Josh doesn't bother screaming for help. He's spent enough time in this basement to already know help doesn't exist down here. Instead he watches Father return to the old man hanging upside down.

The man is nude and tattooed with cuts and gashes, both old and new. He breathes in short, harsh rasps and takes his time between blinks. When Father starts sawing the machete against his thigh, he grimaces but otherwise doesn't show emotion.

"You don't want to watch this, boy," the old man says, and it takes Josh a moment to realize he's talking to him.

"Why is this happening?" Josh asks, arms feeling like they're about to pop out of their sockets. If anyone might be able to offer an explanation, he figures it's the old man. *Richard.* That's what they called him earlier. Richard.

"Stopped asking that question long ago." Blood from his thigh spills into his mouth and he spits it out. "Used to think it was my fault. Maybe still is. Don't matter now, I guess."

Father finishes removing a chunk of flesh from the old man's thigh and tosses it over his shoulder, then begins sawing at the opposite leg. Josh doesn't understand how the old man isn't shrieking right now. *His flesh is being removed* and somehow he's still engaging in a conversation. Has this happened before? What kind of other tortures has this old man endured over the years to make something like this seem like child's play?

"You should know, if you don't already, that this is gonna happen to you, too." The old man spits out more blood. "You can't run away from it. Once… once they like you. They always find you."

"But *why?*" Josh screams it louder than he meant. Even Father pauses with the machete and casts him a stern look of disapproval.

"Nothing I could offer you would…be…satis…fact…ory." He closes his eyes for half a minute before opening them again. "They're a family, and they got separated." Another long pause. He spits out more blood. "Isn't that what you want? To reunite with your family?"

"Y-y-yes, but—"

"Would you do whatever it took to see your mother again?"

"I-I-I-I—"

"Well, that's what they're doing. Whatever it takes."

Father finishes up on the second thigh then moves the machete down to the old man's stomach. Slowly he cuts away at the flesh and unravels it like a fine layer of clothing.

"I'm sorry this is happening," Richard says.

"What do I do?" Josh screams. "*What do I do what do I do what do I do?*"

Richard attempts to say something else, but bubbles of blood pop out of his mouth instead of words. Then his eyes close again and this time they don't reopen.

Father continues skinning the old man without acknowledging Josh's increased distress. And, as he nears closer to completing his goal, he begins to mutter something. Josh has to will himself to quiet down before he can make out what's being said, and he almost wishes he hadn't. The words come out in a steady, hushed tone to form a bizarre chant. Josh tries to make sense of what he's hearing but the language is alien and incomprehensible. Josh has seen enough horror movies to know what this is. A chant, yes, a spell, *a ritual.* But a ritual for *what?* He doesn't want to know, doesn't want anything to do with whatever's about to happen.

What can he do, though? Not a damn thing but continue hanging from the ceiling. Wait and watch.

The audience does not get to interact.

The audience does not get to change the channel.

The audience shuts the fuck up and prays they don't also get called up on stage.

Father increases the volume of his chant but the words don't make any more sense. Josh can't even pinpoint the language. But when did he become a linguist? This could be Latin for all he knows. Kid is only twelve. But he doesn't think it's Latin. In fact, he doesn't think it's any language known on Earth. This is a language from another world. The language spoken from whatever crevasse Father and the rest of his grotesque family crawled out from. He knows this because of the way his skin tingles when he hears it. He knows this because it's the truth. He knows this because he's in the basement and in the basement there is no room for falsehoods. This is the basement beneath the house that is not a house. This is the basement where reality takes off its mask. This is the basement where Josh and everybody he's ever loved is going to die.

The chant gets louder. So loud, Father's screaming it. His dead eyes are focused on the earth under the old man. On the puddle of blood and gore and discarded flesh. He points the machete at the mess and keeps his arm still like stone. The chant continues. At first Josh thought it might be a language of the insane but now he recognizes it's the complete opposite. It is a language of clarity. It is a language of absolute truth. It is the only language that's ever mattered.

The earth beneath the old man moves.

Trembles.

Shakes.

Rumbles.

It's alive, Josh thinks, wide-eyed, but no, not the earth, whatever is *underneath* the earth, that's what's alive. And he already knows what's underneath, doesn't he? He's known it since the sheriff dragged him down here.

Without blinking, Josh watches as the corpses of Don and Shane claw out of the dirt. As their mangled limbs take on a new life. As they crawl from their graves and scan their new environment. Their heads move in unison, first left, then right.

The twins from the cornfield.

They're back.

Slowly, they turn to Father and ask, again in unison, "Where is Mother?"

And Father drops the machete, exhausted, and tells them, "Soon, my children. Soon."

THIRTY FIVE

J asper's slumped over on the couch, can of beer nestled between his thighs, sound asleep when a car door outside slams shut. He jolts awake, terrified that he'll find Agnes standing over him, one stern finger pointed and waving in front of his face, prepared to bitch at him for any number of goddamn things. He's snoring too loud. The kitchen is dirty. The TV isn't playing her favorite program. Even in Heaven she could find a reason to complain.

But no. Agnes isn't standing above him. She's not even in the living room. She's still out in the back yard where he left her. Buried in the dirt next to Josh's old gerbil. And it is there she will remain.

A car door. That's what woke him up. Out in his driveway. Mary's finally decided to return home. He tightens his fists, fingers sore and calloused from handling the shovel. All he wants to do is make Mary bleed. Make her scream and beg for his forgiveness. Oh, that stupid fucking bitch. He still can't believe how much she disrespected him. For Christ's sake, she took *his gun*. What the fuck was she thinking? He ought to dig up a companion hole out next to her mother, let the both of them spend eternity together. Would serve the bitch right.

Sunlight streams in through the half-closed curtains on the picture window. How long has he been asleep? He still feels drunk from the night before. Soon enough the hangover will outweigh the intoxication and the ensuing migraine will knock him back on his ass. Might as well just drink more beer before any serious repercussions can take effect. Wait, what *day* is it? Shit, is it already *Monday*?

One glance at the clock over the TV is enough to send him into panic mode. Should have already been out the door at this point. God*dammit,* where the hell is Mary? Why wasn't she here to make sure he woke up on time? Now he's gonna be late for work and it's all her goddamn fault. Add another item to the list of reasons why she desperately needs her face caved in by the sole of his boot.

He climbs off the couch, lightheaded and on the verge of puking, and the can of beer that'd been resting between his thighs spills to the floor. Who gives a shit. The house is a wreck anyway. What's one more can? He heads for the bedroom then stops cold as the front door swings open. Mary really has come back after all. He spins around, itching for a fight, then loosens his fists at the sight of the goddamn sheriff standing in the doorway. *Keene*, he'd called himself. Sheriff Keene.

And boy does he look like shit.

"What are you doing here?" Jasper asks. "Did you find my son?"

The sheriff shakes his head and gestures toward the kitchen. "We got a lot to discuss, Mr. Washington, and I'm dying for a cup of coffee. It's been one hell of a night. Care to oblige?"

"Do you have Josh?"

Again he shakes his head. "You seen your wife lately, Mr. Washington?"

Jasper pauses, feeling the anger boil up again. "Wait, what does Mary have to do with this?"

"Yes or no. Have you seen her?"

"Not since yesterday."

The sheriff nods, thinking, then gestures to the kitchen again. "How about that coffee?"

"I'm late for work."

"I'll write you an excuse." Sheriff Keene grins.

"I don't think it works like that."

"It'll work however I say it works. Now—coffee. How 'bout it?"

"Okay. Sure." Jasper wants to fight the issue more but gets the feeling the sheriff isn't really asking him. He leads him into the kitchen and offers him a seat at the table while he goes through the motions of brewing a pot. "So, sheriff, what'd you want to talk to me about?"

"Difficult to know where to begin," Keene says, sounding distracted. Jasper glances over his shoulder and nearly drops the can of coffee in his hands. The sheriff's eyeing a path of muddy footprints trailing through the kitchen and to the back door. Footprints that match the soles of Jasper's boots perfectly. His brow arches with curiosity.

"Well, well, well," he says, almost gleefully, "someone sure did cause a ruckus in here, didn't they?"

Jasper shrugs, trying to play innocent, and in the process nearly spills the coffee grounds. "Oh, you know how it is. Get home late from work, forget to wipe your boots off, come in for that beer you've been thinking about all day…"

"And then go out to the back yard?"

"Sure. What kind of man doesn't enjoy a beer in his back yard?"

The sheriff grins again. "No man at all, that's who."

Jasper turns back around and continues preparing the coffee. The sheriff couldn't find a corpse if he woke up next to one in bed. He has nothing to worry about. The law isn't here for him. The only reason he's here is because of his goddamn son. No, scratch that. The only reason a law enforcement officer is in his house right now is because of his son's goddamn good-for-nothing friend. If it weren't for Ottessa's dumbass kid, then Josh would be perfectly fine. He would have been home with Jasper all weekend, not just enjoying the World Series but *appreciating it.* For fuck's sake. Didn't he realize how rare this was? The Sox are killing it! And he's where? On the lam with his little faggot boyfriend. Some days Jasper's ashamed to admit he even has a son.

He finishes preparing the pot and clicks BREW, then turns back to the table and finds Keene absent from his seat. A taunting wind slips in from the back door, which now seems to be wide open.

Fuck.

He sprints through the kitchen, smacking his knee against the table edge and shouting a curse. No time to stop and mourn bruised flesh. Outside, Keene's studying what is obviously a recently buried gravesite. It's not like

Jasper did the greatest job covering his tracks. The earth is sloppy and cracked, like a tremor recently erupted his back yard. Plus, he'd discarded the shovel not even two feet from where he'd dug the hole. The sheriff retrieves it from the grass and examines the mud caked against the spade, then glances back at Jasper with amusement.

"Mr. Washington! Did…did you kill your wife?"

The way he's smiling, it's almost like he's hoping the answer is yes.

Jasper doesn't respond. He *can't* respond. Refuses to acknowledge what's in the ground. This is not a conversation he's the slightest bit prepared to have. Goddammit, none of this is his fault. Why isn't Mary here? She would have stopped him. She would have fixed everything. That dumb fucking bitch. Now there's a sheriff in their back yard, and there's something even worse buried beneath his feet.

"Mr. Washington, I'm gonna have to advise you answer the goddamn question. Did you kill your wife? Yes or no."

"I have to go to work. I'm already late."

Keene laughs and tosses the shovel at him, then draws his pistol from its side holster. "I don't think you're gonna make it to work today." He points the pistol at the buried gravesite. "Now, you're gonna dig this up and show me what you're hiding in there."

"No, I—"

The sheriff raises the pistol and points it at Jasper. "Listen, Mr. Washington, you got no fucking idea just how much my patience is already run thin. Now pick up the shovel and start digging or I'm going to kill you in your own back yard. Do you understand me?"

AFTER THE HOLE'S BEEN DUG up again, the sheriff takes one look at what's waiting inside and says, "Who the fuck is this?"

Jasper shuffles in front of him awkwardly, not sure what to do with the shovel now. "Uh, it's my mother-in-law."

"Oh." Keene pauses, staring at the corpse with fascination, then snaps back up at Jasper. "Wait—what?"

"I don't want to talk about this."

"We're gonna talk about it."

Jasper lowers his head, tucking his jaw against his chest, head hot, sweat soaking through his clothes. Gripping the shovel tighter and contemplating swinging it against the sheriff's skull. Is there enough room in the hole for both him and Agnes? If not, hell, he's already late for work at this point, might as well take the rest of the day off to expand the grave. Maybe even widen it enough for three people once Mary decides to bring her happy ass home.

And the sheriff laughs again, reading his thoughts. "Fella, you lift that shovel an inch more and it'll be the last thing you ever do. Drop it. Good boy. Now, let's mosey ourselves back into the kitchen and have ourselves a little pow wow, what do you say? I'm even willing to bet the coffee is done by now."

Keene guides Jasper back into the house and over to his own kitchen table then goes about the business of preparing two cups. "How do you take your coffee, Mr. Washington?" he asks without looking back, and when Jasper doesn't respond he shrugs and says, "Black on black. I can dig it." He sets one mug on the table in front of Jasper then sits across from him cradling a second mug. He sips it and grimaces. "So, I think to start with, you should probably fill me in a little about what's going on out there." He nods toward the back yard.

Jasper keeps his eyes glued on the full cup of coffee in front of him. "I don't want to talk about it."

Keene chuckles, tapping his finger against the brim of his own mug. "Now, I thought it was already done established that we *were* going to talk about it."

"I have nothing to say to you."

"Mr. Washington, do we really have to once again go through the motions of me threatening you or can we just cut the bullshit already? Why did you kill your mother-in-law?"

"I didn't—"

"*Mr. Washington—*"

"I thought it was Mary."

Another pause. "You thought you were…killing your wife?"

No response from Jasper.

"Now, Mr. Washington, why would you want to kill your wife?"

"I don't know."

"You don't know or you don't want to say?"

Jasper lifts his head, at last looking up from the coffee mug. "*I don't know.*"

"Why don't you just walk me through what happened?"

"I can't."

"What do you mean, *you can't*?"

"I can't *remember.*"

"Bullshit. What happened?"

"I was drunk. I was mad."

"And?"

"And…" Jasper sighs. Feels his eyes watering, his cheeks getting wet. "And I can't *fucking remember.*"

Keene nods, evidently satisfied. "Why don't we take a break from your mother-in-law for a little bit? Aren't you curious why I came to pay you a visit this morning?"

"I thought you found Josh."

"Mmm-hmm. I did."

He chokes on his next breath. "Where? Is—is he okay?"

The sheriff lets out a long, practiced sigh. "Turns out my suspicions were correct. Your son and his pal weren't abducted in the slightest. Instead, as I had previously suggested, they were merely hiding from the law."

"Uh-huh." Jasper shakes his head, disgusted. "That's exactly what I told Mary."

"Well, I'm not too surprised she didn't believe you, considering her and Ms. Jones were themselves involved in the scheme. They were indeed harboring your son and his friend. Late last night—or, early this morning, if you prefer—I discovered their whereabouts at an abandoned farm just a little ways off 94. Both boys and their mommas. You should have seen the looks on their faces once they realized who I was." Keene laughs, leaning forward, like he's hoping for Jasper to join in with him, but when Jasper doesn't show any emotion the sheriff wises up and continues, sans humor. "Your boy committed a serious crime, and your wife helped. Maybe she didn't help him commit the actual crime, but she certainly helped him escape, and in the eyes of the law that's just as serious."

Jasper caresses the top of his mouth with his tongue. Everything suddenly tastes like cotton. "Where are they now?"

"Well, that's the million-dollar question, now isn't it?"

"You don't know?"

The sheriff shakes his head, fooling with his now-empty coffee mug on the table. "I was hoping you could maybe help me out a bit with that."

"No." Jasper stands, nearing knocking over his own coffee, still full. "I don't got any idea where they are. I haven't seen Josh since last week and I haven't even heard from Mary since…"

"Since…?"

Jasper sits back down and takes his time replying. Finally sips from his coffee. It's no longer hot like he likes it but the act of drinking is enough of a distraction from going insane. He gulps half of it down then squeezes the glass with both hands, hoping it shatters and stabs his palms and floods the kitchen with his blood. Anything to make this conversation stop. Anything to get this man out of his house. He needs to go to work. He needs to find Mary. He needs to hide Agnes. He needs to go back to sleep.

"Yesterday, her and Ottessa barged in bright and early and stole my gun."

"Your gun?"

His shirt collar tightens against his throat. "I'm licensed. It's my right."

"Why'd they take it?"

"I don't know."

"You didn't ask?"

"They didn't answer."

The sheriff seems amused by this. "And you just…what? Let them have it?"

"What would you have supposed I did? Hit her? Rough her up a little?"

This provokes another chuckle. Keene points at the back door. Not just the back door, but everything beyond it, too. "Seems to me you aren't opposed to acts of violence against women."

After a while Jasper sighs, all the thoughts in his head scrambling and reconfiguring. "I don't know what I am."

"Say your wife were to walk in the house right now, and I weren't here but you knew what you know now. What would you do?"

"I don't know," Jasper says, and it's the truth.

"Bullshit. What would you do?"

"I don't know."

"Would you do the same as you did her momma?"

"No."

"Why not?"

"Why are you here?" Jasper bangs his fist against the table and coffee splashes out of his mug. "What do you *want* from me?"

"I want you to give me your wife."

"I don't *got her.*"

"You're gonna help me find her."

"How?"

The sheriff eyes the house phone hanging on the wall across from the fridge. "If she hasn't called yet, then she will soon enough. I'd bet my life on it."

"So…so what?" He tightens his fists, prepared to punch the table again, not giving a shit if he breaks it in half, kinda hoping he does. "We just gonna sit around here and wait all goddamn day?"

Keene grins, finishing off his coffee. "Now you're getting it."

"But I got *work.*"

"And so do I."

THIRTY SIX

The way they're talking in the bathroom, they must think Mary's asleep, but she couldn't be more awake. Yet she remains still, keeps her eyes closed, and listens. Listens and tries her hardest not to break down in tears. Listens to every word Alonzo says to Ottessa. Every little detail starting from the night of their abduction to their reunion in the cornfield.

She hears it all, especially the things she doesn't want to, things she would pay all of her life savings to never have to hear again.

And even as they climb into the bed next to her and cry each other to sleep, Mary does not dare break the illusion that she's asleep. She remains statue-still, terrified of having to look one of them in the eyes. How could she possibly talk to Ottessa's boy again? After everything that's happened… what is there even to say? "I'm sorry" wouldn't even begin to do it justice. Not that she has anything to apologize for. She wasn't the one watching the boys that night. She wasn't the one who let them sneak out. That was his own momma. But thoughts like this aren't going to help anybody. What's done is done. Ottessa messed up, yes. She messed up *big time*. But she's gone above and beyond since then. People make mistakes. It's what makes someone a person. How they recover from these mistakes is what divides a person between decency and wickedness.

She lays in bed for hours unable to move. Too afraid of what might happen once she decides to finally get up. As long as she continues pretending to sleep, then she won't have to take action. The longer she stays here, the longer she can put off the inevitable. But what *is* the inevitable? Facing this family

Alonzo fabled. This group of maniacs who kept them prisoner in a basement. Because that's where Josh is right now. Back in the basement. Alonzo was sure of it when he talked to Ottessa in the bathroom. Said there was some kind of force, a power that existed down those steps. There was a reason they had kept them in the basement, but he didn't know what, except that it was meant to be. If the family has Josh again, then they've returned him to where they escaped. The question is—if he is even still alive, how much longer could he possibly have? Why hadn't the family just killed them outright to begin with? Why keep them as prisoners if they possessed no intentions of asking for a ransom? They kept them for the thrill. For the love of torturing helpless children. Deep down Mary knows her boy is still alive, because he'd be no good to them dead. As disturbing as that sounds, she firmly believes it to be true. But how long until they get bored with him? *How long?* And she's just wasting valuable time pretending to be asleep when she knows damn well there's no way—*no way*—she's going to sleep again until Josh is home and safe where he belongs.

Home.

God, she'd like to be home right now. Away from this motel. Away from this whole nightmare. She misses waking up Josh for school. Making him breakfast, dinner. Playing board games and watching TV together. She misses everything. She even misses Jasper, as impossible as it sounds. Misses his voice. Misses his touch. Misses his warmth. As much as she hates him sometimes, she still loves him, and right now all she wants in this little ol' world is for Jasper to wrap his arms around her and Josh and tell them everything's going to be okay, everything's going to be all right.

She stays in bed until she can't any longer, and by then Ottessa and Alonzo have actually succeeded where she has failed. They're both asleep, wrapped around each other like they're one entity. One look at them shoots a spike of jealousy through her. Why does Ottessa get to have her boy and Mary doesn't? What makes Alonzo so special? Why not Josh? *Why not Josh?*

She slips on her shoes and creeps out of the motel room, careful to leave the latch pulled out so the door can't close all the way. *Where is she going?* No idea. Just moving, moving, moving. Needing more space than a tiny motel room provides. Feeling claustrophobic. The desire to scream until her lungs rip is so overwhelming she feels like she'll die if it doesn't happen soon. Rushes down to the lobby, vision narrowing, the inside of her stomach twisting and turning. She charges into the lobby restroom and barely manages to kneel in front of the toilet before spraying a stream of vomit. Some of it hits the bowl, but a good chunk sprays against the tank and wall. Brown sludge. Turning her throat to acid. Watering her eyes until she can't keep them open any longer and the vomit's coming out of her nose now, sticking to her hair, running down her chin, it's everywhere, and it won't stop coming out. Consciousness blinks in and out. One moment her face is buried in the toilet, then she's sprawled sideways along the linoleum, left arm wrapped around the toilet's porcelain base, other arm hanging lifelessly over her waist. Face smeared with vomit and sweat and tears and snot. A woman hovers over her asking if she's okay. She tries to nod but her head's too heavy to lift. Everything is so heavy. Gravity has her pinned to the floor. Trapped. Imprisoned. *Is this how Josh feels right now?* Do they have him confined in another straitjacket, locked up in their terrible basement? *Oh, Josh, where is Josh, where is Josh?*

The woman helps her off the floor and wets a handful of paper towels under the sink. Mary's limbs are useless as she leans against the wall and lets the strange woman wipe vomit from her face. Her legs shake like they belong to somebody else and it's a miracle she doesn't collapse back to the floor. Somehow she manages to remain upright, squeezing her eyes shut, too embarrassed to look at the woman cleaning her like she's some helpless infant. She guides Mary closer to the sink and pushes her head down into the bowl as she washes her hair. Who is this woman, and why is she being so kind? An angel. She is an angel.

"Are you an angel?" she asks, voice raw and worn out.

"I'm the night auditor," the angel responds. "I heard you from the front desk. C'mon, let's get you something to eat."

Mary follows the night auditor from the public restroom into the lounge area of the lobby. She sits at a table and watches as the woman prepares two slices of toast and pours a glass of orange juice. She brings Mary the items and tells her to eat and drink and Mary obeys without any resistance. At this point her body is simply too weak to do otherwise. If the night auditor believes Mary needs this toast and juice then who is she to argue? Who is Mary, anyway, except for a helpless sentient bag of meat? She can't save her son. She can't save her marriage. She can't even save herself. She's useless. Why did she even bother embarking on this journey with Ottessa? She knew from the very beginning that she wouldn't be able to contribute anything. At the most, she'd just get in the way. Maybe if she hadn't been back at the cornfield, Josh might have actually managed to escape. And besides, what kind of mother flees from gunshots without ascertaining her son's right next to her? No mother worthy of even having a son, that's who. A failure. A pathetic waste of space.

"How's your toast?" the night auditor asks, still standing in front of her, arms behind her back.

"Huh?" Mary says, then discovers the plate empty and the juice cup drained. She possesses zero memory of eating the toast. It's almost as if multiple versions of herself are sitting at the table, one on top of the other, layers of a human being fighting for the spotlight, and they're each thinking and breathing and acting as separate entities. "Oh, it was good, thank you."

"Would you like any more?"

"No thank you. I think I need to be going now."

"Are you sick?"

"What?"

The woman nods back toward the restroom. "That was…quite a lot of vomit. You got the flu or something?"

"No, not the flu. I just…" She pauses and rubs her stomach, no longer sure what exactly is wrong with her. "It's been a stressful weekend, that's all."

"Mmm. I feel ya. Just let me know if you need anything else. I'll be around 'til eight. Or nine. Depending on how late my relief ends up being."

"A phone."

"Excuse me?"

"Is there a phone I can use?"

"Mmm-hmm, in your room."

"Is there one down here?" She pauses, mouth hot and numb. "My friend is asleep and I don't want to wake her up."

"Don't you think you might wake her up if you call her?"

"What? Oh. No. I mean, my friend who is in our room. She's the one who's asleep."

"And you want to call the room?"

"I…no. I want to call someone else."

"Someone who isn't asleep."

"My husband. He should be at work right now."

"You want to call his work?"

"No, I want to call our home."

"Oh. Who's there?"

"Nobody."

"You want to call an empty house?"

Mary swallows back another wave of vomit. "Can I please use the phone?"

The woman laughs but Mary isn't sure what's so funny. "Yeah, sure, come on."

She guides Mary to the front desk and scoops up a mobile phone cradled in a charger. "Have fun." She gives her the phone then disappears in an office behind the front desk. A beat passes and loud heavy metal music begins blaring somewhere back there, muffled by the wall between them. Mary lingers at the front, unsure if the night auditor's going to return. She gives up and steps outside with the mobile phone and calls her house. Nobody's going to pick up, not now, Jasper should have already left for work at this point, but it'll be nice to leave a message for him that he can listen to after he gets home. Just an apology for the way everything went down over the weekend. An apology, yes, but also a vow that things will change once she gets Josh back, that if they want their marriage to work, then he sure as hell better learn how to become a better father and husband. Somewhere inside him exists the man she originally married. The man she fell in love with all those years ago.

"Hello?"

Mary almost screams. Jasper, of course. Who else?

"I thought you'd be at work." She gulps, palms sweaty, almost too slick to maintain a grip on the phone.

"Mary?" He sounds more shocked to hear her than she is to hear him. "I called off today. I've been worried sick about you."

"About me?"

"Yeah. You and Josh. Where are you?"

"I don't have Josh."

Long pause on the other end, then: "Mary, I took a sick day today. You got me all concerned. Can I come see you? Please. I want to apologize."

"Apologize?"

"Yeah, baby. Apologize. I've been such a dick to you about this whole thing, and it isn't right. I don't know what was wrong with me but I'm better now, and I want to see you and Josh again, I want to help you find him, I want us to be together. Where are you? Tell me and I'm there."

Jasper's words sound like they've been ripped straight out of a fairy tale and she can barely believe them, but there they are, coming out of his mouth, going into her ear, fictions evolving into fact, and all she wants right now is for him to hold her, for them both to hold Josh, for everything to be right and perfect.

So she tells him where they're staying. The name of the hotel. The room. Everything. She begs him to come, begs him to help. Exhaustion and hunger and desperation take over and she tells him that she needs him, needs him now more than she's ever needed him before. So please, honey, please come.

And Jasper says, "I'm on my way."

THIRTY SEVEN

fter she hangs up, Jasper stares at the dead telephone a long time before returning it to the wall mount. Convinced that he just imagined the phone call. Behind him, the sheriff's chuckling. "Well," he says, "I guess we didn't have to wait too long after all."

It's almost like they manifested the phone to ring. Keene hadn't even been sitting at the table an hour. Jasper had convinced himself they'd be spending the entire day in his kitchen, jerking each other off. But now… god. He wishes that she hadn't called. Wishes he never heard from her again. Wishes it more than anything. But it's too late. She *called*. She told him where she's staying. Told him everything he needs to know, and now there's no stopping what happens next. If the inevitable were preventable, then it wouldn't be inevitable. Of course, he could lie to the sheriff. Tell him she's somewhere else, buy her some time to escape. Except, as much as Jasper wants to lie, he wants to tell the truth even more. His brain feels cracked and confused. He wants to save her. He wants to kill her. He doesn't know what he wants. Hatred and love blend together into one fucked-up concoction and he gulps it down like a man dying from dehydration.

"She's at the Super 8," he says, the words tasting bitter and rotten.

And behind him, the sheriff claps his hands, all giddy. "Not bad, Mr. Washington, not bad at all."

Jasper faces him, prepared to strike him, prepared to bow at his feet and surrender. "What do we do now?"

"Now?" He stands from the table, finishing off an old cup of coffee. "Now we go say hi to Mrs. Washington."

357

"WHAT ARE YOU GONNA DO to my wife?" Jasper asks, sitting in the back seat of the sheriff's car, feeling like a jackass with his hands folded in his lap. Up front, a woman reads various codes and messages on the radio.

Keene eyes him in the rearview mirror, chewing on the butt of a mangled cigar. "What would you like me to do to her?"

He thinks the answer should be obvious but nothing clear comes to mind. Like he possesses two mouths, one begging for the sheriff to spare her, the other pleading for her execution. "Are you going to hurt her?"

"If she resists, sure. But if she does what I say, then everything will be peachy."

"Are you taking her to jail?"

"Somewhere even better."

"What are you talking about?"

The sheriff cuts the volume on the radio and waits a long while before responding. "Suppose I tell you a story."

"A story?"

He nods. "Suppose I tell you about a man I once knew. Back when I first joined the force."

"What man?"

"Man by the name of Daniel."

"What about him?"

"Well, Daniel and I, we were good friends. Went fishing together and all that shit. I didn't even mind that he was queer. A lot of people did, but it didn't bother me much. Way I see it, it's no one else's business what a man sticks his dick in. Unless, of course, the man's fucking something crazy like a cow or a horse." Keene howls with laughter and punches the steering wheel. "Well, would ya look at that? I just came up with a little rhyme, didn't I?"

"Sheriff, why are you telling me this?"

Keene sighs and glares hard in the rearview. "Will you shut the fuck up? I'm telling you a story here for Christ's sake." He cracks his neck before continuing. "Now, Daniel had himself a long-term boyfriend. Man by the name of Richard. Real cowardly piece of shit. Always thought he was a bit of a dickhead. We didn't get along too well, but it wasn't that surprising. Think about your male friends. Do you always get along with their wives? Practically the same thing. Anyway, Richard and I, we avoided each other most of the time, mostly for our own sanity, so imagine my surprise the day he comes knocking on my door. All it took was one look at him to know something was seriously wrong. He said Daniel was sick. Not like, oh-no-I-got-the-flu sick. Something…different. You understand?"

"No," Jasper whispers.

"Yeah, neither did I, at least not back then. But I went back to the house with Richard, being the good friend that I am, and he…he showed me what he meant. Did it make any more sense? No. But did I under*stand*? You betcha."

If they weren't in a cop car right now, Jasper would open the back door and leap out into incoming traffic. He doesn't like the sheriff's tone. Something about it hints of a dark future.

"I struggle now to describe what I saw in their bedroom that night, so many years ago. Memories are funny like that, I guess." He falls silent for a minute, then: "Richard had him tied up in their bed. Arms spread out against the bedposts. You have to understand, Daniel is a big man. No way were those bedposts keeping him there for very long. If he had any ounce of strength left, he could have easily cracked the wood in half and went off on his merry way. But no. The man I saw in that bed was not a strong man. He was barely a man at all at that point. He was pale…so, so pale. And he had these veins along his face, like they were fixin' to burst. Never seen anything like it before, and I wish like hell I could add 'or since' to that sentence."

Is the sheriff about to cry?

Jasper leans forward, afraid of his own voice. "What was wrong with him?"

"What was *wrong* with him? Well, it wasn't *him* no more, is what was *wrong* with him."

"Wh-what?"

"Something had got inside him. Some…some parasite, I guess. Although that still don't do it justice. Somehow it crawled into him and spread its infection from head to toe, throughout his entire soul. Made him someone new. Like you know how caterpillars cocoon themselves then hatch into little butterflies? Best way I can describe it. The friend I had once known had evolved into something else. Something from another world. Something with a whole goddamn family. That's why they needed me, you see. Why Richard came and got me that night."

"A family?"

"That's what he called it, at least. The new Daniel. Except he doesn't use that name no more. Says to call him 'Father' now. Which is, yeah, okay, pretty fuckin' hokey if you ask me. But if you were in the same room as him, you'd call him whatever the fuck he told you to call him, trust me." The sheriff pauses and tosses his chewed cigar out the window, grimacing. "So, he had this family, back where he came from originally. This…other world. Whatever the fuck. I don't know. It's never exactly been explained to me, at least not in a way I've ever understood. But his family, he needed help getting them to join him. He needed…bodies."

"Bodies?"

Long sigh up front, then: "Yeah. Bodies."

"What did you do?"

"I did what they asked."

"What did they ask?"

"Listen. It's been a long time, a long, long fucking time, but it's finally almost done. The family is almost complete."

"What does that *mean*?"

The sheriff laughs. "Who the fuck knows?"

"What are you going to do?"

"Every family needs a mother, Mr. Washington. Wouldn't you say so?"

Jasper says what they're both thinking. "You're going to give them Mary."

"Don't think of it as a negative. Once Mother is here, you have no idea what is going to happen. The changes they will make…the improvements…

honestly, Mr. Washington, it's not going to be as bad as you think. In fact, it's gonna be paradise. Doesn't that sound nice? And, considering it'll be *your* wife we've selected, goddamn, you're in for a treat, no doubt about it. They'll make you a fucking king. A ruler of men."

"You're insane," Jasper says. "This is crazy."

"Yeah, maybe." The sheriff licks his lips and grins in the rearview mirror like a goddamn lunatic. "That don't make it untrue, though, does it?"

THIRTY EIGHT

Ottessa's sitting at the desk, taking long concentrated drags from a cigarette and blowing the smoke out the open window facing the back of the motel, wondering where the hell Mary could have gone. She woke up a half hour ago to the sound of the door closing against the latch and found Mary's bed empty. Gave some thought of chasing after her, but couldn't bear the thought of leaving Zoey unaccompanied. Not even for a minute. Not even for half a breath. Instead she's just been sitting at this goddamn desk, smoking cigarette after cigarette, *waiting*. A thousand possibilities running through her mind. The cops got her. Keene got her. The family. She went rogue and tried saving Josh by herself. Everything became too much to handle and she just…ran away. Time to start a new life.

Except if Mary meant to leave for good, then why bother propping the latch between the door? Why not just close it all the way and be done with it? But if she's coming back, then where the hell is she?

As if reading her mind, the door creaks open. Ottessa's body tenses, anticipating the devil himself walking into the room. But no. Just Mary. Wet hair, exhausted eyes. She looks like she's been sobbing but what else is fuckin' new.

Mary spots Ottessa at the desk and pauses, a deer caught in headlights, then recovers and says, "Good morning."

"Where did you go?"

She points a thumb over her shoulder. "I was eating some toast in the lobby."

"Oh." All the fight deflates out of her and she flicks the rest of her cigarette through the window and slides it closed. "They got coffee ready?"

"Yeah."

"Can you keep an eye on Zoey for a couple minutes?"

She nods, but refuses to make eye contact.

"Something you gotta say?" Ottessa asks.

"I called Jasper."

"Okay." She swallows, trying to control her anger. So what if she called her husband. It's her goddamn right. "What did you tell him?"

Mary shakes her head, shuffling her feet. "Not much. He's gonna meet us here later."

"*Why?*"

"Because, Ottessa…" Mary bites her lip as she paces around the room, keeping her voice hushed. "We can't handle this by ourselves. We tried and we can't. Not if we're going to save Josh. We need all the help we can get."

"And you think *he* is going to be much help?"

"You didn't hear the way he sounded."

"I've heard him plenty."

"It's different this time."

"You keep telling yourself that, girl."

"You haven't even given him a chance."

"I think you've already given him plenty."

"He's coming, either way. We need help and you know it. You're just… you're just being *stubborn* because you don't like him."

There's no point in arguing. What's done is done. Ottessa slips out into the hallway, barefoot, and heads into the lobby, shaking her head and mumbling about how stupid Mary's acting. The girl who checked them in last night is still behind the front desk, now talking to another woman who looks like she just arrived, probably her shift relief. Besides them, the lobby's miraculously empty. She narrows in on the coffee pot and fills a styrofoam cup. Gets another cup for orange juice and loads up a plate with donuts, then juggles the items back to their room. The idea of eating right now is enough to make her sick, but Zoey will need something and donuts are better than nothing. Hell, he'd probably agree donuts are better than most things.

He's awake when she gets back, but barely. Groggy, tossing and turning. Probably would have slept all day and then some if not for Ottessa and Mary making so much goddamn racket. She sets the cups and plate down on the desk and rushes over to him, asking if he's okay, trying to gauge his pain levels.

"Everything hurts," he whispers.

She retrieves the orange juice and makes him sit up a little and take some ibuprofen. "I got some donuts, too. You should eat something."

He shakes his head and points at Mary over by the window, who hasn't said a word since Ottessa returned. "She was going through your purse."

"What?"

Mary steps forward. "It's not what it sounds like." She lifts her shirt, revealing the handle of her husband's gun tucked into the front of her pants. "I was just afraid of how you'd react when Jasper shows up. I didn't want things to get out of hand."

Ottessa snorts out a legitimate laugh. "*Girrrl*, look at you. You motherfuckin' *gangster*."

Mary blushes. "I'm sorry."

She shrugs. "Hey, it wasn't mine to begin with." She pauses, hating the way they left things, hating that she suddenly gives a shit about her relationship with Mary. "Listen. I don't like your husband. I think he's a piece of shit and that he's going to do more harm than good, but if you feel like he needs to be involved, then you won't hear nothing more about it from me."

"Okay."

"We cool?"

"We're cool."

"Peachy." She returns to Zoey, wincing at how swollen his face is. Shouldn't it have gone down by now? Shouldn't he be *better*? "Hey, Mary, could you please go get us some ice? For Zoey's jaw."

"Mom, I'm okay."

"Aww, honey, you look like shit."

"Thank you."

"Yeah," Mary says, laughing with them, "I can get some ice. No problem."

She grabs the empty ice bucket from the sink and leaves the room. Ottessa brings Zoey the plate of donuts and sets it in his lap as he sits up against the bedrest. Half a donut disappears in his mouth before she can sit down next to him.

"Are we going to get Josh?"

"That's the plan."

"We have to go back to the farm."

"Yeah."

Zoey runs his thumb along the half-eaten donut on his plate. "I hate that fucking place."

"I know, baby."

"We gotta kill them. We gotta kill them all."

"Yes."

He nods, satisfied, and continues his breakfast.

Except, Ottessa isn't satisfied. There's one question left that's been nagging at her since Saturday morning. "Zoey…I have to ask you something."

"Okay."

"What…why did you have a photo of me?"

"What are you talking about?" he says, staring straight ahead at the wall.

"I saw a recording from the gas station. What…what you did to the cashier. You had a picture of me. You know which one I'm talking about."

"I found it on the computer."

"And you…printed it out?"

"I guess."

"But *why?*"

Zoey shrugs and lowers his head. "I'm sorry."

"It's okay. I ain't mad. I just…was confused."

"I don't know why I had it. I just did."

"Zoey, what happened at that gas station?" She touches his chin and he yanks away.

"You just said you saw the video."

"The video didn't explain *why*."

"I don't know, Mom, okay? I don't know."

"You attacked that man."

"He said things about you. Bad things."

"About *me*?" She leans forward on the bed. "What are you talking about?"

Zoey closes his eyes, struggling not to cry again and failing. "I don't want to talk about this, Mom."

"Zoey, please."

"He was saying you were a...a...he was calling you names. I got so angry and I just...I just..."

"Hey, it's okay, baby, it's okay." Ottessa wraps an arm around his shoulder and squeezes. "Whatever happened is in the past now, okay? It's done."

"Mom?"

"Yes?"

"I—"

Sound explodes down the hallway.

A gunshot.

Followed by a scream.

Followed by more gunshots.

More screams.

Ottessa pulls Zoey tight against her, spilling his plate of donuts to the floor. Neither one of them say a word, both of them trembling on the bed, straining to listen.

"They found us," Zoey whispers, rocking back and forth, "they found us they found us they found us they found—"

"Zoey, hush, be quiet now."

"—us they found us they found us they found us they found us—"

"Just stay here, okay? Just...just stay here." She scrambles out of bed and sprints to the front door, then stops and turns around, pacing around the room. She can't leave Zoey here alone. But Mary's in trouble. No goddamn doubt about it. Yes, this is a motel and other guests are staying here, but

Ottessa's no fool. Whatever's happening down the hall isn't some random unrelated incident.

Fuck fuck fuck.

She kneels next to Zoey and grabs his head and makes him look at her. "Listen to me, Zoey. You listen to me right now. I have to go make sure she's okay. You see that clock?" She points at the alarm clock on the nightstand between the two beds. "If I am not back in five minutes—*five minutes*—you climb out of that window and you don't stop running. You understand? You start running and you *don't stop.* Not until you're far away from this town. *Are you listening to me?*"

Crying, Zoey says, "Yes."

"I love you, baby."

"I love you too, Momma."

She kisses him on the forehead and, once again, leaves her son alone.

OUTSIDE THE ROOM, TERRIFIED GUESTS poke their heads through their doors, curious eyes wide and unable to look away. Something very bad has happened, is *still* happening. Vicarious pleasures await them all. She ignores their gawking and moves onward down the hallway, body tense, preparing for the worst despite not knowing what the worst could even be. The two hotel clerks from earlier now hide behind the front desk, whimpering and holding each other, shaking, crying. One look at them should be enough of a sign to turn around and flee the opposite direction, but of course it has the opposite effect with Ottessa. She forces herself forward, pushing against an invisible wave fighting her back.

She finds Jasper of all fucking people sprawled in the middle of the lobby, on his stomach. Part of his face is missing, like someone shot him from behind and the bullet exited through his nose. Behind him, Sheriff Peckerwood's thrown sideways on the floor, half in the lobby and half in the foyer, surrounded by broken glass and blood, the automatic doors opening and closing against his gut. It's almost funny-looking.

But then.

But then she comes across who else has joined this crime scene.

Mary.

Mary on her back, staring up at the ceiling with unblinking eyes.

Mary, body full of holes.

Mary, a puddle of blood beneath her lifting spilled ice and carrying the cubes like wreckage from a plane crash.

Mary, who had just stepped out of the room to help Zoey.

Mary, who had never done a goddamn thing wrong in her life except trust Ottessa.

Mary.

Mary Mary Mary.

Mary.

THIRTY NINE

Alonzo doesn't have to wait long for his mom to come back. Barely half a minute passes before she barges inside and locks the door behind her. One look at her face tells him everything he needs to know.

"She's dead, isn't she?"

She doesn't answer, but she doesn't have to. "We have to leave. Come on."

"Was it the sheriff?"

She pauses, exhaling a drawn-out breath. "Yeah."

"Okay."

He forces his feet into the new shoes his mom bought him. They're half a size too small but it's not like he has the pleasure of nitpicking right now. They climb out of the window and run around the parking lot. He follows his mom to a cop car idling out front. Not the one they used last night. But he still recognizes it all the same. It's the car the sheriff had been driving.

"What are you doing?" he scream-whispers.

"Trust me," she says as she climbs behind the wheel. The key's in the ignition already, the engine warm and ready. He runs around and dives in the passenger seat and steals a glance at the motel entrance, spotting the sheriff's body on the floor. He isn't moving.

"Did you kill him?"

"No," his mom says.

"Then what happened?"

"I don't know."

She shifts into DRIVE and they haul ass out onto the interstate and away from the motel. Neither of them talk for a while. She just drives, Percy long gone behind them. He doubts she knows where they're going. Maybe she'll never stop and they'll just driving, away from Indiana, away from the whole Midwest. Where then? California, maybe. The ocean. Would the family still chase them? He tells himself the answer's unknowable but of course he knows the truth. They're not going to stop chasing them. Not until they find him.

Or he finds them first.

Plus, they still have Josh. No goddamn way is he going to leave him in that basement. They escaped together once already, and they'll do it again, too.

Josh's mom died helping Alonzo. That has to mean something.

It means everything.

"We have to go back," he says after a while.

"I know," his mom whispers.

"Then why aren't you?"

"I don't know."

"Okay."

They keep driving the opposite direction of Percy for another half hour, then his mom gets off the interstate and stops in a Kmart parking lot. She closes her eyes, still squeezing the steering wheel.

"I don't know what to do, Zoey."

"We have to save Josh."

"What if we can't?"

He rests a hand on her arm and squeezes softly, wincing at the pain caused from bending his own shoulder. "We have to try."

"Do you—do you even know how to find this farm again?"

"No. Maybe. I don't know."

He doesn't know how to explain what he's really thinking, that it doesn't matter if he can't get them back to the farm, that the farm will somehow guide them, that the farm will lure them back to its fucked up nightmareland no matter where they try to hide.

"Okay. I guess we can just drive around," his mom says, "see if anything looks familiar to you, then continue from there. First, though, we gotta ditch this asshole's car. I'm surprised we haven't already gotten picked up. They probably know exactly where we are, thanks to the GPS." She goes to turn the engine off then stops and leans forward, inspecting the glowing screen near the dashboard.

"What's wrong?"

"I just had an idea." She starts pressing buttons on the screen, eventually bringing up a list of addresses. "Oh shit."

"What?"

"The GPS, it keeps a recorded history of past stops. Look at this, Zoey. Do you think this might be the place they took you?"

Alonzo reads the address, but it doesn't mean anything to him. The time, however, is a pretty big indication. Where else could this shithead have possibly gone at three in the morning? His mom must also notice the time, because she doesn't wait for an answer before reversing the car and reentering the opposite side of the interstate.

Leading back to Percy.

"ZOEY, I KNOW WE'VE ALREADY talked about this, but we need to go over it again."

"I already—"

"Tell me about the family. What they look like. How many there are. Everything you can remember."

"Mom, I don't...it's hard...everything's fuzzy, like a dream."

"Please, just try, okay? You have to try."

"The two who were dressed like cops. They call themselves Father and Uncle. Uncle's dead, though. I hurt him real bad, then the old man cut his head off."

"The old man?"

"Yeah."

"What old man?"

"I told you, Mom."

"What old man, Zoey?"

"He was just this…guy, I don't know. He was at the house, but he wasn't all crazy-looking like everybody else. He looked normal. He looked sad."

"Sad?"

"Like he didn't want to be there. Like he was a prisoner."

"Was he chained up?"

"No. The family let him walk around the house by himself."

"And he…he cut…?"

"He cut Uncle's head off, in the kitchen. He saw us trying to escape and told us to hurry. He isn't one of them. I don't know what he is but he's not bad."

"This is fucking crazy."

"I know, Mom."

"Who else?"

"The twins. They were conjoined. We killed them."

"You cut them in half."

"Yeah."

"Jesus Christ."

"And…Baby."

"The one with the mask."

"Yeah."

"Tell me about him."

"Mom, please don't make me talk about that one."

"Okay."

"The only one I know who's still alive is the one called Father, but who knows how many others there were? Maybe we didn't see them all. Maybe there are hundreds more."

"And they're all on this farm."

"It's not…it's not like a normal farm, though, Mom."

"You said the ground was all weird."

"Kind of. Yeah. It's hard to describe."

"Maybe give it a shot."

"It was like…like…like the house was haunted."

"Haunted?"

"None of it made any sense. The gravity…the way things looked, far things were close, close things were far. It was like we were hallucinating."

"Did they drug you?"

"I don't know."

"Think, Zoey. Did they give you anything at all?"

"Mom, *I don't know*."

"Okay, baby, calm down, you're fine, you're doing good."

"I'm scared, Mom."

"Me too, Zoey."

"What are we going to do?"

"…"

"Mom, what are we going to do?"

"I don't know, baby. I don't know."

THEY CAN'T JUST SHOW BACK up to the farm empty-handed. That much is obvious. Father would take one look at them and crush their skulls together. Pop their eyeballs with his thumbs like he did the truck driver kind enough to offer them a lift. "We need weapons," he tells his mom, and she agrees, but the question remains: How? They can't just stroll into a gun shop. Not like either one of them knows how to operate a gun, anyway. They'd be more likely to shoot themselves than anyone else. So then what? A hardware store, maybe. Except there's still the issue of every cop in the county looking for them, especially now that the sheriff just got discovered at the motel full of bullets. They hear all about it on the car radio. Dispatchers are freaking the fuck out. Anyone sees them out in public and they're screwed. Nobody else is coming to help Josh but them. They get caught, then Josh is all by himself, forever and ever. They cannot get caught. They must save Josh.

"Wait," Alonzo says, feeling like an idiot, "what do you think is in the trunk?"

And his mom pulls off along the highway and pops the trunk and they look inside and sure enough, there's a whole goddamn arsenal waiting for them. A shotgun, extra pistols, ammunition, a baton, tasers, all types of shit. Most of it neither one of them understands how to operate, but it all looks very cool and threatening. Maybe if they wave some of it around, Father will surrender and hand over Josh and everything will be okay again. Since Josh's parents are dead now, Alonzo wonders if this means Josh will be able to live with them. The thought makes him happy and the thought makes him sad and he wants to smile and he wants to cry.

Josh, we're coming for you.

"STOP!" ALONZO SCREAMS AND HIS mom slams on the brakes. The car skids through the long, gravel driveway, nearly losing control and crashing into a wall of dead corn.

Ahead of them waits the house, flaps of raw meat hanging from the gutters, swaying with the wind. It looks weird in daylight. Almost innocent.

"Is that it?" his mom asks. "Is that the house?"

"Yes."

She continues down the driveway and stops at the end, both of them paranoid, scanning the yard through the windows. The place is empty, at least the outside. When him and Josh escaped this fucking place, he promised himself he'd never return. Now look at him. Barely a day has passed and he's already back, here at the mouth of Hell ready to be swallowed up all over again.

They open their doors at the same time and his mom grabs his arms, pulling him back inside the car. *"What are you doing?"* she says, almost hissing.

"What are you talking about?"

"You're not going in there." She shakes her head, already deaf to any possible arguments he might throw her way. "No goddamn way. Not again, Zoey. You've already been through enough."

"Mom, you can't go in there alone…"

"That doesn't mean you get to come with me."

He tries yanking his arm free from her grasp but she only tightens her grip. "You don't know what's in there. *Mom, you don't know.*"

"I know Josh is in there, and I know there ain't nobody else coming to save him, so the sooner you stop throwing a fit and stay in the car, the sooner we can all leave."

"You don't even know where the basement is. How are you going to find him?"

"Zoey, it's a basement. How dumb do you think I am?"

"Mom, you don't fucking *get it.*"

"Hey, now—"

He pulls again, this time ridding himself of her ninja fingers, and scrambles out of the car before she has a chance to grab him again. She shouts his name and curses, then climbs out through her own side and chases him around the front of the car.

"Zoey, we don't have time for these games, goddammit."

"Exactly!" He throws his arms up, trying to emphasize his bewildered agreement, but only succeeds in reminding his shoulder that it's currently not in the best shape.

She points at him, that *ah-ha!* look on her face, then freezes before any words can leave her mouth. No longer looking at Alonzo but *past* him. He follows her gaze and spots two pale, lanky nude men shuffling toward them from the edge of the cornfield. Their bodies are covered in gashes and purple bruises. Both of their genitals are missing; in their place, infected scabs from a previous failed attempt at healing.

Alonzo knows these men.

How could he not, after the precious time they spent together in the basement?

His mom, on the other hand, has no fucking idea what to make of them. She raises one of the pistols taken from the trunk, screaming, "Get back, motherfuckers! Get the fuck back!"

Shane and Don keep moving toward them, unaffected by her threats.

"Mom, it's okay," he whispers, "these guys are cool."

"*What?*"

"They're not bad. They were…like us. In the basement."

She takes another look at the approaching duo and lowers the pistol. "Oh my god," she says. "Oh my god."

Alonzo waves at them. "How the hell did you two manage to escape?"

"We are free," they say, getting closer, and something odd sticks out about their voice, but it isn't clear. Probably just hearing them out in the open like this instead of confined in a basement.

They say something else, but they're too quiet, he can't make it out over the wind, so he hurries over to meet them at the midway point in the front yard, his mom following closely behind. "What did you say?"

"You want play?" they ask. "You want play with us?"

Both of them asking the question in unison, their jaws dropping and lifting together, their tones stuck on the same grating monotone. They walk together, side by side, matching each other's pace. Arms reaching out for Alonzo the closer they get. Shambling like the undead, which maybe isn't too far off of a comparison.

"Zoey," his mom says behind him, "what the fuck is wrong with them? What's going on?"

"We gotta go, Mom. We gotta go *right now*."

Just as Shane and Don or whoever the hell they are now swipe at him, he spins from their grasp and attempts to flee back to the car, grabbing his mom's wrist for guidance. Only something's blocking their path now. Something Alonzo knows he'll be seeing in his nightmares for the rest of his life, however short that might end up being.

Father, still in his disgusting police uniform, towering over them. Brown sludge leaks from his ears, his nose, his mouth. A sewage stench assaults them like a punch to the face.

He raises his machete, blade stained with old blood, and tells them, "It is time."

Then he takes them to the basement to finish what he started.

FORTY

To prevent Josh from attempting another escape, Father devised a solution.

After reanimating Josh's former cellmates, Father unhooked him from the chains suspending him in the air and stripped him of his tarnished garbage bag suit.

Then he tied his hands behind his back with rope. Knotted it tight enough to tear flesh and draw blood.

With his hands confined, Josh was led into the shadows of the basement, careful not to step on any of the bear traps. They came upon an empty wooden tub. Father pushed him into it and helped him sit down Indianstyle. Josh tried asking what he was doing but received no response. He left him there in the tub and walked upstairs. Josh sat and thought about rolling out of the tub, but figured he'd just end up landing on a bear trap. Probably face-first, too. There was no point in trying. Especially not when the stairs began creaking again barely five minutes later, and Father returned with more supplies.

The smell arrived before he did.

He popped open the lids of Tupperware containers and emptied their contents into the tub. Rotten meat plopped into Josh's lap. The brown sludge Father had forced him to eat in the kitchen. Surely other substances Josh would have preferred not to identify. Father tossed the containers to the floor and lifted a gallon of milk, which he proceeded to pour over Josh's head. Long expired, by the smell of it. It slapped against his face with brutal strikes, like waves from an unforgiving ocean. Next came a jar of something sticky and warm. He stuck the tip of his machete into it and lathered it across Josh's cheeks, his mouth, his ears, his eyes, all over him.

Honey.

"Please stop," Josh begged, and a slab of rotten meat fell into his mouth, which triggered a spray of vomit down his chest, into his lap, into the tub.

After that he didn't dare utter another word.

The honey coated his eyes shut. It dripped into his ears and made the world sound muffled and distant, like he was underwater. Father wrapped something made of rough leather around his neck. A collar of some sort. Then he wiggled a long, cold steel object through the front of the collar and tilted Josh's head back at a hair-washing angle. Sharp points dug against his chest and Adam's apple.

"If you lower your head, even an inch," Father told him, "your chest and throat will be penetrated simultaneously. Your death is in your hands."

Then he shuffled away and the stairs creaked as he returned upstairs, followed by the closing and locking of the door.

Well, shit, Josh thought.

And it is in this tub he still sits, hands confined behind his back, rope grinding into his wrists, blades pressed against his throat and chest, face and body covered in honey, milk, and rotten meat, soaking in its hellish broth and waiting, waiting, waiting for what? Waiting for whatever happens next. That's all he can do now. There is no escaping from this. If he moves, he's dead. Of course, if he waits, he's going to die anyway. Father is not going to let him live and nobody is going to rescue him. He is alone, forever alone.

Except for the flies.

At least they're keeping him company.

The flies…

It didn't take long for them to catch the scent of Josh's unorthodox bath. First came the buzzing, so close to his ears he wondered if they were wiggling their way inside of him. Then on his face. On his lips. Over his eyes. His neck. His stomach. His dick. Everywhere. Feasting on the honey layering his flesh. Every instinct begs him to twitch and jerk away but somehow he resists. The flies cover him whole. There have to be hundreds of them. Thousands. Where have they been hiding? Have they been waiting this entire time, watching, hungry, desperate? Every inch of him itches. There's no goddamn way he can last. Not even the strongest willed man in the world could survive this.

Survive survive survive.

He can't. He won't.

Might as well just give up, slam his head forward, be done with this bullshit life once and for all.

The flies are so loud oh god won't they shut up, won't they shut the fuck up?

Mary Vincent was a survivor. Josh? Josh ain't shit. Mary Vincent crawled up a cliff *without any arms* and somehow still lived. Josh is going to die in a bath tub covered with flies. Mary Vincent is a survivor and Josh is a coward. He is a worthless piece of shit who should have never even made it this far. Blind goddamn luck, that's all it was. If it hadn't been for Alonzo, he would have never escaped the first time. Now Alonzo isn't here and there is no one to save him. There is no one. *No one no one no one.*

The flies continue their feast and everything itches and he wants to die, he wants to die more than anything, but if that's true then why can't he do it, why can't he just lower his head, that's all it'll take, so simple, so quick, pretend you're sneezing, *achoo*, god bless you, god bless you, *god bless—*

Hours pass.

Then more hours.

Possibly days.

It is impossible to judge time like this, when every passing second feels like another eternity. He never gets used to the flies, but the flies get used to him.

But he also doesn't lower his head. He can't make himself do it, despite how much he wants to. So he sits and he waits and he waits and he waits until—

—until the door unlocks and opens again, and the stairs creak, creak, creak.

Father, maybe. But not just him. Multiple voices. *Screaming?* He can't tell, can't fucking hear anything with the honey in his ears, with the flies in his brain, all the buzz buzz buzzing driving him insane, *shut up shut up shut up*, then the blade wedged inside of his collar is pried loose and Josh slumps his head forward, so relieved for a moment he no longer minds the flies, feasting and sucking and fucking upon his flesh, no longer minds the scent of shit and rotten meat, no longer minds anything, because this is a rescue, Alonzo came back and saved him once again, the best friend he's ever had, he knew he could count on him, he knew he could—

"Stand up," Father says. "Mother is near."

The flies swarm in enraged clouds around Josh's head as Father leads him through the basement. His legs shake and wobble like he hasn't used them in years. He can open his eyes but only barely, still half-blinded by the honey. Father unties his hands but they're so weak it's not like he can do anything with them. There's no fighting what cannot be stopped.

He walks until he sees where they're going, then screams and tries to run in the opposite direction. Father grabs him by the neck and drags him onward to the destination. Where the old man named Richard had once hung upside down now hangs someone else.

Zoey…

Nude, body a mess of blood and gashes, feet tied by rope connected to the ceiling rafters, hanging over the mound of dirt the reanimated Shane and Don emerged from. Hands cuffed behind his back. His eyes are open wide as he screams something at Josh, but the words come out unintelligible through the duct tape wrapped generously around his mouth.

"No!" Josh cries out, swatting at Father's chest. "Leave him alone! Please leave him alone!"

"Mother is near," he says again, and Josh stops hitting him, realization clicking into place.

"No. Not my mom. Not my mom. Please. Anything."

"Do you love?"

"What?"

"*Do you love?*" He points at Alonzo.

"Yes. I love him. Please. I love him."

"*Do you love Mother?*"

"*Yes.*"

Father nods. "Who do you love most?"

"What?"

"You can have one, but not both."

Suddenly Josh misses the tub. He tries to back away but Father tightens his grip on his neck, keeping him still. He knows what Father's asking of him but he refuses to accept the question. He can't choose. He *can't*.

And, as if reading Josh's mind: "Choose one or choose none. Who do you love?"

With his free hand, he raises his machete, holding it by the blade, the handle out.

An offering.

Do you love?

Josh loves.

Yes.

He looks at Alonzo, then the machete, then Alonzo.

Fuck fuck fuck.

"I want my mom," he says, whimpering. "I just want my mom. Please."

"Then choose."

"I *did.*"

"No." Father shakes his head. Pushing the machete into Josh's hand. "*Choose.*"

Alonzo's scream increases as he thrashes around, wiggling like a worm caught on a hook.

"Oh, no, no, please, I can't, I can't." He holds the machete up and it weighs a ton. He can't do this. He should have lowered his head against the knife when he had the chance.

Do you love do you love do you love?

Josh steps forward.

Alonzo won't stop screaming and it's the worst sound he's ever heard, worse than the flies inside of his brain, worse than anything imaginable only he doesn't have to imagine it because the sound is real, the fear is real, the horror is real. Alonzo hangs in front of him and Josh approaches, machete in hand, and he can't rewind, he can't stop, inertia thrusts him forward, raises his arms and brings them down and (*I'm so sorry Zoey oh god I'm so sorry please god I'm sorry please*) the machete slices into the side of Alonzo's hip. The blade buries itself into his flesh and he tries to pull it out but it's stuck, like his friend's body is made of wood, made of stone, and he yanks harder and finally it's free and there is so much blood and Zoey's no longer screaming but squealing and he didn't mean to hit him like that, the swing was so awkward and fucked up and he's still alive, still alive, oh god, he's still alive.

"*Again,*" Father hisses.

And Josh screams and starts swinging the machete at Alonzo and he doesn't stop until the handle slips out of his hands from all the blood.

All the blood spilling into the mound of dirt beneath him.

The mound of dirt that, Josh discovers, is surrounded by white carnations. *Have they always been there?* No, they're new, he would have noticed them before. *How long has he been killing his best friend?* Jesus Christ. Oh god. *Why did he do that what is wrong with him what is wrong with him—*

A song, then.

Sang in unison by Shane and Don, somehow in the basement with them now, hands linked, laughing, dancing around Alonzo's death site, around his murderer, singing singing singing—

—singing:

> **Ring-a-ring-o'-roses!**
> **A pocket full of posies!**
> **Mother! Mother!**
> **Rise from the ground!**
> **Mother! Mother!**
> **Rise! From! The! Ground!**

Meanwhile Father kneels before the dirt and bows and Josh screams, *"Where is my mom? Where is my mom?"* and he raises his hand to strike Father with the machete but the machete is gone and all he can do is stand there and watch and listen as Father chants in the strange alien language he had used before, as the ritual's mantra repeats over and over louder and louder so loud the flies in his head are finally drowned out and oh god he misses the flies he misses everything this can't be happening this can't be—

Mother! Mother!

—Father raises both his arms, hands tightened into fists, and kisses the dirt, kisses the blood—

RISE. FROM. THE. GROUND.

—the ground begins to tremble—

MOTHER. MOTHER.

—no it's not just the ground it's the house too—

RISE.

—the house that is not a house is shaking is screaming is laughing—

MOTHER.

—it's going to kill them all please kill them all—

RISE.

—the world is collapsing—

MAX BOOTH III

FROM.

—the moon the stars the universe everything is death everything is beautiful—

THE.

—do you love—

GROUND.

A hand bursts from the dirt.

Slowly, its inhabitant claws out of the grave.

Emerges from its subterranean womb.

And into the world.

Into life.

Zoey's mom, gasping for breath.

Ms. Jones.

Ottessa.

Shane and Don kneel next to Father, burying their faces into the dirt. Bowing. Only Josh remains standing. Watching as his dead best friend's mom crawls out of the ground.

Mother.

Oh, god. Oh fuck.

What has he done?

Where is his *mom?*

Oh god what the fuck has he done?

He turns around and frantically scrambles up the stairs on all fours like a child. He leaves the house, naked and covered in honey and rotten meat and fly corpses and shame. He must find his mom, he must find his mom, *he must find his mom.*

TOUCH THE NIGHT

Outside the sun is a perfect crimson orb and black birds circle above the house that is not a house waiting to meet their new queen and Josh runs into the cornfield and he does not look back.